Why hadn't she guessed who he was?

It was now obvious to Davina that Saul liked playing games.

Davina held on to her temper...just. "You should have made your purpose known, Mr. Jardine. I would have been pleased to discuss your proposals. But they're not really *your* proposals, are they?"

"That's correct." Saul was surprised. Davina was shrewder than he'd expected, different, as well. He wondered why she'd worn such an unsuitable outfit. It was something a sophisticated woman might wear to meet her lover; the kind of woman with the sexuality to wear it over a body that was otherwise naked, and who was able to find some subtle way of allowing her lover to know it.

Davina James simply wasn't that kind of woman. Or was she?

Lingering Shadows

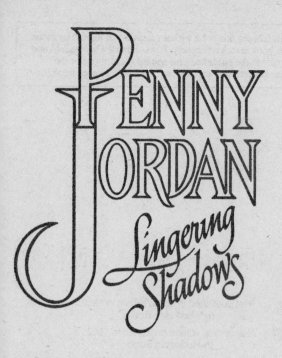

PENNY JORDAN
Lingering Shadows

HARLEQUIN

TORONTO • NEW YORK • LONDON
AMSTERDAM • PARIS • SYDNEY • HAMBURG
STOCKHOLM • ATHENS • TOKYO • MILAN
MADRID • WARSAW • BUDAPEST • AUCKLAND

First published in Great Britain in 1992
by Worldwide Books

Hardcover edition published in 1992
by Harlequin Books

This edition published in 1993

ISBN 0-373-97122-2

© Penny Jordan 1992

CHAPTER ONE

'SO, MY clever little brother has succeeded where our late father could not and has persuaded the Americans to cede manufacturing control of our medicines to us. And how did you manage that? By employing the same means you used to persuade our father to change his will in your favour?'

Beneath Wilhelm's sneering contempt, Leo could hear the bitterness in his elder brother's voice.

There was no point in reminding Wilhelm that he himself had been just as stunned, if not more so, to learn that their father had left outright control of the Hessler pharmaceutical corporation to him and not, as everyone had expected, to Wilhelm.

Leo relaxed his grip on the telephone receiver. He had flown in to Hamburg from New York earlier this morning and had gone straight to the Hessler Chemie offices from the airport, to report briefly to the board meeting he had had his assistant convene.

Wilhelm had not attended that meeting, but he had obviously heard what had happened.

Leo knew he had every right to be pleased with what he had achieved in New York, and every right to be annoyed with Wilhelm. Before he left his office to come home he had informed his assistant that he was not to be disturbed—by anyone.

So Wilhelm's call was not welcome.

'Father must have been out of his mind when he made that will,' he heard Wilhelm claiming furiously now. '*I* was the one he wanted to take over from him. He always said so...I was always his favourite.'

5

Leo gritted his teeth, letting his brother's vitriol pour viciously out of him.

His favourite. How many times when he was growing up had he heard those words from his brother? Leo wondered, when Wilhelm had finally hung up. How many times had he suffered the pain of paternal criticism and rejection, until he had finally realised that he had a right to define his own view of life; that there were other worlds, other values than those to which his father had laid claim?

He glanced tiredly at the telephone. He and Wilhelm had never really got on. There had always been rivalry and resentment between them; divisions which it had sometimes seemed to Leo their father had deliberately fostered. Wilhelm was obsessively, compulsively possessive. Perhaps it came from being the eldest child and from believing that he would always be an only child.

After all, with fourteen years between them, he had for the majority of his formative years been an only child. And certainly while he was growing up Leo had never been in any doubt as to who was their father's favourite.

A weakling, his father had once called him as a child, although now, with his six-foot frame, Leo could hardly be regarded as weak. With his amber-gold eyes that matched the thick texture of his gold-brown hair, one of his lovers had once likened him to a lion. He possessed the same powerful fluidity of muscle and tone, she had said, the same sleek goldness, but, as she had also laughingly noted, without the lion's desire to hunt and maim.

Certainly physically he took after his mother's family, Leo acknowledged. Physically and, he sincerely hoped, mentally and emotionally as well. He wanted no part of any genetic heritage from his father. And no part of any material inheritance either?

He moved uncomfortably to the window, staring out towards the river. This was a quiet, affluent part of

Hamburg, his tall, narrow and relatively small house squashed in between its much grander neighbours. It was an old house with creaking timbers and awkwardly shaped rooms.

Wilhelm had tried to get their father's will overset on the grounds that he could only have made it if he had either gone insane or somehow Leo had blackmailed him into doing so.

The corporation's lawyers had warned Wilhelm that it was a court case he could only lose, reminding him that right up until he had had his fatal heart attack their father had remained omnipotently in control of Hessler's and his sanity.

Of course, it hadn't helped that Leo had been the one to find him, collapsed on the floor of his study, but still alive... just. None of them had known he had a heart condition. He had kept it a secret. Leo had rung for an ambulance immediately, but seconds after he had replaced the receiver his father had suffered a second and fatal attack.

In those few seconds his father had spoken to him.

'My son...' he had said thickly. '*My* son.'

But there had been no love in the words. No love, only the same furious, bitter rejection Leo remembered so well from his childhood.

On the floor beside his father had been a small, battered locked deed box. The safe in the wall was unlocked, and the doctor had suggested that maybe the effort of removing the box from the safe had been what had triggered the first attack.

Leo wasn't so sure. The box wasn't heavy.

He turned round abruptly now. The box was still on his desk, where he had deposited it six weeks ago, intending to open it but somehow never being able to find the time.

Well, he had that time now, he reminded himself.

He looked at the box. This should have been Wilhelm's task and not his.

Just as Hessler's should have been Wilhelm's ... Just as their father's love had always been Wilhelm's. Or, rather, their father's approval. He doubted if his father had ever loved anyone. He was simply not that kind of man. Why had he left control of Hessler Chemie to him, when for years he had been grooming Wilhelm to take his place? His new will had been dated shortly after their mother's death.

Tiredly Leo reminded himself that there was no point in constantly asking himself questions he knew he could not answer.

He glanced at the deed box and frowned, his brain, freed briefly from the inevitable strain imposed upon it by his responsibility for Hessler's, suddenly prodding him into a sharp awareness of the incongruity of the box's shabbiness, of the fact that it had been on the floor alongside his father at the moment of his death.

Curiosity stirred inside him, curiosity and something else.

He walked over to his desk and touched the box reluctantly.

He had the keys. They had been in his father's hand. He opened his desk drawer and removed them, looking at them with a frown. Like the box itself, they were worn and shabby and of poor workmanship, and hard to equate with the kind of man his father had been.

Still frowning, he reached for the box, and then hesitated, unwilling to touch it, to unlock it.

Grimly he reminded himself that he was exhibiting the very qualities his father had most detested in him: emotion, imagination, fear. Fear of what? Not of his father. He had lost that fear at the same time as he had forced himself to accept that, no matter what he did, no matter how hard he tried, nothing he did would ever earn his father's love and praise.

There was nothing to be gained by going over the past, he reminded himself firmly. He was thirty-eight years old, an adult now, not a child.

He inserted the key into the box's lock and turned it firmly, pushing back the lid.

The only thing the box contained was an envelope. Leo picked it up, tensing a little as he felt the old, worn, and somehow unpleasant texture of the paper.

He reached inside the unsealed envelope and removed its contents, placing them on the desk in front of him.

There was a notebook, and several newspaper cuttings printed in English. As he picked up the notebook he glanced at the headline of the top one. It was an article describing the work of some British servicemen in a German hospital. Glancing at the date, Leo saw that it had been written shortly after the Allies had entered Germany.

There was a photograph: a gaunt, emaciated man lying in bed, arms outstretched in supplication to the man leaning over him.

Leo felt his stomach muscles contract at the sight of the gaunt figure. A victim of one of the death camps, quite obviously; beside him in the next bed lay another man, who, according to the writer, had not been so fortunate. He was dead.

The dead man, the article continued, had confided to Private Carey before he died the names of certain German SS officers and undercover agents who had sanctioned the use of prisoners as guinea-pigs for medical experiments. Acting on this information, the Allies had then rounded up a number of these men and arrested them.

Grimly Leo looked away and then forced himself to look back again. When he picked up the small bundle of clippings his hand was trembling. He flicked back the first one and read through the others quickly.

They were all in English and they all related to a small British pharmaceutical company—Carey Chemicals. The name of the private in the first yellowing article, Leo noted absently.

They charted Carey Chemicals' meteoric rise just after the war when it had patented the formula of a heart drug which had revolutionised the treatment available for people with heart problems, and they also charted the company's decline.

Carey Chemicals... These clippings. What did *they* have to do with his father? *Why* had he collected them... kept them?

Leo frowned and picked up the notebook. His father had started Hessler Chemie after the war. The Allies had been keen to re-establish order in the chaos of post-war Germany, and because his father had had no part in the war or its atrocities—he had left Germany shortly after war had originally broken out, to live in neutral Switzerland—he had been allowed to return and establish his company. That company had produced a new drug, a tranquilliser which had helped to ease the suffering of many victims in the aftermath of the horrors of war.

Leo picked up the notebook and opened it. He had studied chemistry at university—his father's choice and not his. He was, after all, a von Hessler, even if he did not look or behave like one, his father had told him sneeringly, and as such he must play his part in the corporation's continued success.

Now, as he stared at the faded handwritten chemical equations and notes, Leo recognised immediately what they were.

What he was reading were the original notes for the tranquillising drug on which Hessler's had been founded.

Leo looked closely at them. There were a variety of stories about how the notes had come into his father's possession. The official version was that his father had

been given them by a dying man whom he had visited
at the request of the allied soldiers to whom he had been
attached as a translator.

From time to time, far less flattering stories had surfaced, but by then Hessler's had been too powerful for
anyone really to challenge them or their founder.

As a teenager Leo had heard rumours that his father
had secretly been employed as a spy for the SS, based
in Switzerland but travelling throughout Germany and
the Continent, and that because of this he had had access
to the information produced by the laboratories of the
notorious death camps.

Foolishly he had dared to challenge his father with
what he had heard. His father had said nothing to him,
neither denying nor verifying his challenge, but the next
day Leo had discovered his mother in bed, her body so
badly beaten that Leo had insisted, against her frantic
pleas not to do so, on sending for their doctor.

He had never raised the subject of the rumours with
his father again.

He turned the pages of the notebook and then tensed.

There was a second set of equations here, together
with notes in the margins and a doctor's signature—a
doctor who, Leo was sure, had been tried for his part
in a certain camp's medical atrocities.

He read through them once quickly, and then a second
time slowly and carefully while his heart turned over
inside his chest and his body became heavy and cold
with the weight of the knowledge descending on him.

These further pages showed detailed study and a
formula proposed for a heart drug—a heart drug like
the one that the British company Carey Chemicals had
produced.

Like a dealer with a pack of cards, Leo slowly and
carefully fanned out in front of him the separate newspaper clippings, and then above them he placed the
notebook, his eyes bleak.

Had his father died trying to carry the deed box, or had he tried to reach it only after he had had his first attack, knowing what it contained and what it betrayed, knowing that it must be destroyed? Leo looked at the newspaper cuttings and the references to Private Carey. Was the young man's rise in the field of pharmacy after the war linked at all to his father's notes? Why had his father kept them in the first place? Were they a form of insurance against Carey, the medical-orderly-turned-blackmailer who knew the truth about the German's secret SS dealings and had been paid off with that second formula?

But the man Carey had died several years before his father. The relevant newspaper notice was here. *Why* had his father not destroyed the contents of the box then, if they were as incriminating as Leo suspected?

Had Carey confided what he knew to someone else before he died: passed on the secret? It stated that the business was now being run by his son-in-law. Had he handed on to him more than just control of the business?

Perhaps he was wrong. Perhaps it was all merely co-incidence. Every instinct he possessed howled in derision at the thought.

He knew, he thought, knew in his bones, in his soul that what he had in front of him was evidence of the man his father had actually been; that he was now closer to the essence of him, the true nature of him, than he had ever been during his lifetime.

No need now to question the animosity that had always existed between them, nor his own awareness of and aversion to that darkness he had always sensed within his father.

As a child he had feared that darkness; as an adult he had been shudderingly grateful that it was a genetic inheritance which had passed him by, just as his father had always despised him for his lack of it.

And yet his father had left him control of the corporation.

'My son... *My* son...'

Those had been his last words to him and they had been full of bitterness and hatred.

Surely he could not deliberately have left this grim evidence for him to find; a final act of cruelty, a final reminder of the blood he carried in his veins?

No... Because how could he have known that Leo would be the one to find him? No, he had been trying to destroy the evidence, Leo was sure of it.

The evidence...

He looked down at the papers on the desk. Odd to think that they had the power, the potential to damage the mightiness of Hessler Chemie; that they could potentially be more powerful than ever his father had been.

Was he right? Were his father, working as a translator, and Carey, the medical orderly, linked by mutual greed in a tangled skein of murder, theft and blackmail—and worse?

The man who had died, the man who had confided to Carey the names of those men secretly working for the SS...had *one* of those names been his father's? Had Carey recognised it...approached his father, threatening to expose him? Had his father bought him off with that second formula?

The links were tenuous; frail and perhaps unprovable, but they were still strong enough to rock Hessler's, and still strong enough to fill Leo with such revulsion, such anguished pain and reflected guilt that he knew somehow he had to at least try to discover the truth.

Had things been different...had Wilhelm been different, this was a burden he could have shared with him.

Another thought struck him. Had his *mother* known the truth? Was *that* why she had stayed with his father, despite his physical and emotional abuse of her—because she had been too afraid to leave? Because she knew she could never reveal the truth knowing what it would do to her sons . . . to him?

Wilhelm had never been as close to her as he had. Like their father, Wilhelm had treated her with contempt and cruelty.

Slowly Leo picked up the newspaper cuttings. He glanced towards the fire and then looked at the papers in his hand.

His mouth grim, he replaced them in the envelope along with the notebook. Perhaps he should destroy them, but he knew that he would not do so, could not do so until he had discovered the truth. Or as much of it as there was left to discover. And somehow he must find a way of discovering it without implicating Hessler's, not for his own sake and certainly not for his father's, but for the sake of all those who worked for the corporation, all those who depended on it for their livelihood.

No, this was a problem he must deal with himself. Quietly . . . discreetly . . . secretly. He grimaced over that last word. It reminded him too much of his father.

Secretly.

It left an acrid, sour taste in his mouth and shadowed his soul with bleakness.

CHAPTER TWO

'I MUST say I'm a little surprised by your attitude, Saul.'

The voice, the smile were benign, almost avuncular. They were also, as Saul knew quite well, a complete deceit.

He said nothing, simply waiting.

'Of course I realise that Dan Harper is a friend of yours,' Sir Alex Davidson commented kindly, and then when Saul remained silent he added less kindly and very smoothly, 'After all, weren't you sleeping with his wife at one time?'

Saul hadn't been, but he let the comment pass. He knew enough of his boss's tactics by now to know how much Sir Alex enjoyed the feeling that he had touched a raw nerve; that he had succeeded in slipping his knife into an unprotected and vulnerable organ.

'However, business is business, and it was your responsibility to me to see that the take-over of Harper and Sons went through smoothly and discreetly, and not instead to warn Harper that we intended to buy him out and then to strip his company of its assets, and to close it down after dismissing its entire staff. Which, unless I am mistaken, is exactly what you did do.'

Now Saul did speak, simply saying calmly, 'A rather dramatic interpretation of events.'

His eyes were cold. He was a very formidable-looking man despite the fact that he was twenty-five years his boss's junior, despite the fact that he was merely an employee in the company Sir Alex headed and owned. An employee whom Sir Alex had been grooming to take his place.

'But you did warn Harper what was in the wind.'

'I didn't *warn* him about anything,' Saul responded in a clipped voice. 'I simply pointed out to him what *might* possibly happen if he sold out.'

'Semantics,' Sir Alex accused. He wasn't smiling now and his voice most certainly wasn't kind. 'Absolute loyalty, that's what I demand from my employees, Saul, and most especially from you. *You* are my most trusted employee... I pay you extremely well.'

Under his breath Saul murmured cynically to himself, '*Caveat emptor*,' but there was self-contempt in the words as well as cynicism.

Sir Alex was still talking and hadn't heard him.

'As I said, I was very disappointed. However, something more important has cropped up now. I want you to go to Cheshire. There's a company there called Carey Chemicals. I want it.'

'Carey Chemicals?'

'Mm.' Sir Alex picked some papers off his desk. 'A small one-man-band company... or at least it was. The man in charge died fairly recently. The company is in trouble, sinking fast, and all too likely to go under. We are going to perform a rescue operation.'

'Really? Why?' Saul asked him sardonically.

Sir Alex looked at him and then asked acidly, 'Before I tell you, can I take it that you *don't* have a close friend or a mistress working for them?'

Saul gave him a cold close-mouthed stare, which for some reason made Sir Alex's own gaze waver slightly.

'All right,' he said testily, even though Saul hadn't said anything. 'Carey's is a drug-producing company; not that they have produced anything remotely profitable for the last few decades. The widow who has inherited the business is bound to want to sell out.'

'And you want to buy.'

'At the right price.'

'Why?' Saul asked him.

'Because a little bird has told me that the government is making plans to offer very generous, and I mean *very* generous incentives to British-owned drug companies that are prepared to invest in drug research. In turn, if those companies succeed in producing a marketable drug they will repay the government's generosity by providing the National Health Service with their drugs at a lower than market price.'

'Thus wiping out the benefit to the company of the government's financial incentives,' Saul said drily.

'Well, there would always be the profit from overseas sales,' Sir Alex pointed out, 'but, in essence, yes.'

'So why are *you* interested?' Saul asked him.

'Because if the research does not produce a marketable drug, the government cannot claw back any of its investment.'

'Ah, yes, I think I begin to understand,' Saul said. 'You buy the company, fund what on the surface looks like a genuine research department, with very generous assistance from the government, of course, but, as we know, with the complexities of modern company finance, a good accountant can quite easily lose large, if not *vast* sums of money by moving it from one company to the other, and, if ultimately the research fails to produce any marketable results, well . . .'

Sir Alex smiled at him.

'I'm relieved to see that your recent attack of conscience and friendship hasn't totally atrophied your brain, Saul. There are several other companies worth investigating, but none quite as perfect as Carey's. It is a very shorn little lamb, so to speak, and I'm very much afraid that without our protection it could all too easily fall prey to the ravages of some hungry wolf.'

'And you want me to find out as much as I can about how vulnerable this lamb is and how cheaply we can acquire it.'

'Yes. You can be our wolf in sheep's clothing. A role for which you're admirably equipped.'

A wolf; was that how the other man saw him, a predator who enjoyed the terror, the mindless blind panic his appearance created in others? Saul wondered acidly.

As he took the executive lift down to the ground floor, a line from one of Byron's poems came into his mind.

The Assyrian came down like the wolf on the fold.

The words, like the visual images it conjured up, disturbed him. He had been suffering far too many of these disturbances recently, of these unfamiliar attacks of conscience.

Of conscience or of rebellion—which? The thought flitted across his mind and was quickly dismissed. He had work to do.

The receptionist watched him as he walked past her desk. She sighed faintly to herself. He was one of the sexiest men she had ever seen. All the girls who worked for the Davidson Corporation thought so, and yet he never exhibited any interest in any of them. There was an austerity about him, a remoteness, that challenged her.

He would be a good lover, too, you could see that from the way he moved. She wondered if his body hair was as thick and black as that on his head.

His eyes were the most extraordinary shade of pale blue, his face hard-boned, like his body. There was a hunger about him, an energy, an anger almost, that stirred a *frisson* of sexual anticipation in her body.

Saul walked out of the building into the early summer sunshine. Cheshire. His sister, Christie, lived there.

Perhaps it was time that he visited her.

He would ring her this evening. He would have to ring Karen as well. It was over five weeks since he had last seen his children. He had had to cancel his last access visit. He frowned, his body tensing. He doubted that either his daughter or his son minded not seeing him. But *he* minded like hell. They *were* his children, for God's sake. He remembered his own father, how close they had been.

Too close, Christie had once told him. He had accused her of being jealous and she had laughed at him. Theirs had been a turbulent relationship. They were alike in so many ways and yet so very different in their outlooks on life, so very, very different.

Again he felt the shadow of the malaise which seemed to be clouding his life, confusing and disturbing him. He, who had always seen his life's objectives so clearly. And he had achieved them, hadn't he? He had succeeded, fulfilled his promises to his father. So *why* did he feel this emptiness, this fear that somehow he had omitted something, neglected something, this hesitancy about reaching out for the trophy that was now so nearly within his grasp?

In another few years Sir Alex would retire and Saul would take his place. It was what he had worked for... what he had planned for... what he had promised his father.

But was it what *he* wanted? He cursed under his breath. Why the hell did he have to have this attack of mid-life crisis now?

Saul strode out into the street, joining the crowds, joining them but not becoming a part of them, nor being absorbed by them. He wasn't that kind of man. His contemporaries, his peers, envied him, he knew that, and why shouldn't they? The financial Press praised him, acclaiming his astuteness, his shrewdness. In the years he had been with it he had taken the company Sir Alex had founded to the very top of its league.

If Sir Alex was the old-fashioned type of entrepreneur, a buccaneer almost, then Saul was the financial diplomat, the man who had turned the raw materials of Sir Alex's company into the sleekly powerful thing it was today.

Through Saul its growth had been planned, controlled. When the recession came, Saul had been prepared, Saul had looked ahead, and where Saul went, others followed.

He was a pioneer, admired and envied, and now he was virtually throwing it all away, breaking his own rules, the rules laid down for him by his father.

Even he wasn't sure why he had warned Dan Harper that Sir Alex wanted to take over his company. They were friends, it was true, but not close friends. Saul did not allow anyone to get close to him. Not any more.

Not men, nor women. Since the break-up of his marriage there had been women, relationships. Discreet, orderly, controlled relationships that threatened no one, and he had certainly not had an affair with Dan's wife, despite Sir Alex's comment.

There was no one at the moment, but he had a single-minded ability to dismiss sex from his life when he felt it necessary. He had never been driven by his appetites, nor controlled by them.

Sometimes, when watching a competitor greedily consuming the meal he was paying for, greedily consuming the bait he was putting down…greedily anticipating what advantages might accrue to him through his involvement with him, Saul was filled with a sharp sense of disgust for that greed, for that wanton waste when so many were without.

It was his Scots blood, he told himself sardonically. All those generations of strict Presbyterians and their moral outlook on life.

Sir Alex was testing him, he knew that. His boss was sometimes laughably easy to see through, even though Sir Alex believed himself to be a master of subtlety.

Normally he would never have given Saul such a routine task. Normally they employed agents, at a distance of course, on this kind of business, keeping their own identity secret until they were ready to move in for the kill.

His stomach twisted. He was forty years old, fitter than many men fifteen years his junior, no grey as yet touched his dark hair, and yet sometimes he felt immeasurably old; divorced, distanced somehow from reality, completely alone and alienated from the rest of the human race.

At other times he felt a deep sense of resentment, of anger, of somehow having been cheated of something, and yet he could not quantify what.

Why had he warned Dan about the take-over? *Why* had he felt so much distaste about the thought of destroying the small old-fashioned company that had passed from father to son for five generations? After all, he had done it before without any qualms. Why now... now, when Sir Alex had virtually promised him that he would soon be stepping down and that he, Saul, would be taking over the chairmanship?

He could still recoup the ground he had lost. Sir Alex's speech today had confirmed that.

So why had he experienced that overwhelming impulse simply to walk away, to turn his back on Sir Alex and his own future?

There was a very deep and very intense anger inside him, he recognised, coupled with a fear of its overwhelming his self-control. Saul prized his self-control. It was his strongest weapon and now it seemed to be deserting him.

Cheshire. What the hell kind of game was Sir Alex playing, sending him out there? He loved manipulating people, pulling their strings and making them dance. Well, Saul had never responded to that kind of treatment. He might work for Sir Alex, but he had always made it clear that he would not be subservient to him. Sir Alex

was the kind of man who could only respect someone
he could not bully.

What exactly was he planning? Was it just because he
wanted to buy out this drugs company at the lowest
possible price that he was sending Saul to Cheshire, or
was there an additional motive?

Saul wondered sardonically if, like one of his prede-
cessors, he would return to London to find someone else
sitting at his desk. And if he did, would he really care?
Did he really *care* about anything any more? He cared
about his children, he told himself. He cared that they
rejected him, that they seemed to be more concerned
with material possessions. Had he been like that? Josey
was fifteen, Thomas nearly thirteen. They were very different in character, as different as he and Christie had
been.

He and Karen had been divorced for nearly ten years
and his children were strangers to him. Ten very busy
years for him. Too busy for him to make time for his
children?

The thought itched and stung like a burr under the
skin. Just recently he had been asking himself questions,
too many questions he could not answer, and why?
Because he had woken up one morning and suddenly
been sickened by himself, by his life. *Why* should he feel
like that? He had always made his own decisions, his
own choices.

From the past he heard Christie's voice, harsh with
passion, her young face angry with contempt as she slung
at him, 'You don't do anything for yourself, do you,
Saul? You just do things to please Dad. That's why
you're his favourite.'

He had laughed at her, dismissing her outburst. He
was a boy. It was only natural that he should be closer
to his father...his favourite...or so he had thought then.

Christie...passionate, turbulent, aching for freedom,
for full control over her own life even then.

And she hadn't really changed.

Not that they saw much of one another these days. He had visited her a couple of times since she had moved to Cheshire... a disastrous pair of visits when he had reluctantly... very reluctantly been accompanied by his children.

Christie, as a busy GP, hadn't been able to spare much time to spend with them, and Josey had been openly scornful of her aunt's disorganised home life, of the fact that meals were invariably eaten in the kitchen, of the fact that Christie hardly ever wore make-up and certainly never bought designer clothes, unlike her own mother.

The only thing Josey had approved of about her aunt was the fact that she was a single parent. Women no longer needed men, Josey had told Saul challengingly, and he had wondered if what she meant was that children no longer needed fathers, especially fathers like him.

Of the two of them, Josey had always been the more antagonistic towards him. He was surprised how much that hurt him. He had far more important things to think about than his relationship with his daughter, an inner voice warned him, but another challenged quietly, what... what *could* be more important than his own children? And he stood still in the street as the impact of his own thoughts hit him, unaware of the curious looks of passers-by.

Perhaps a week or so away from London, from Sir Alex, was what he needed, he reflected as he started walking again. A breathing-space... a time to reflect.

But what was there to reflect on? he wondered impatiently, frowning at the unease he could feel. He didn't like this dichotomy between what he knew he *should* feel and what he did actually feel. It was so out of character.

'You have to be single-minded to succeed, Saul.' That was what his father had always told him, his face shadowed by the disappointments of his own life, by the effects of his own inability to achieve the goals he had set himself.

Fate had been unkind to his father.

But it had been kind to him, he himself had seen to that, or so he had thought until recently.

CHAPTER THREE

'DAVINA, I know you're busy, but I wonder if you could spare me half an hour before you go home.'

Davina forced herself to smile.

'Of course I can, Giles. Would five o'clock be all right?'

As soon as he had closed the office door behind him her smile disappeared. There had been many challenges for her to face in the three months since the death of her husband Gregory, and now it seemed that she was going to have to face another one.

She suspected that Giles Redwood was going to tell her that he wanted to leave. She couldn't blame him. The company was on the verge of bankruptcy and she knew quite well that the only reason Giles was still here was because he was too gentle, too kind-hearted to leave her completely in the lurch.

And because he loved her?

She winced, her mind shying away from the thought, not wanting to admit its existence.

She had always liked Giles, but it was only since Gregory's death that she had become aware that he might have much stronger feelings for her. It disturbed her to have to acknowledge that she might have inadvertently played on those feelings in asking him to stay and to support her through the initial crisis of Gregory's death.

She hadn't meant to do so. Had, in fact, been motivated purely by panic, the panic of discovering that her father's company wasn't the thriving concern she had so foolishly believed, but was actually close to insolvency. That had shocked her more than Gregory's death in many ways.

It had been Giles who had comforted her, who had told her that she must not blame herself for the lack of awareness of the company's situation. And it was true that Gregory, and her father before him, had always refused to allow her to have anything to do with the company, to play any part in it.

But now she had no choice. Carey Chemicals was the largest local employer. If Carey's closed, people would be put out of work; families, whole households would suffer. She could not allow that to happen.

Giles had told her gently that she might have no choice. He had been warning Gregory for some time, he had added uncomfortably, that they must make some kind of provision for the time when their most profitable patent ran out.

Gregory had refused to listen to him. Gregory had had his own obsessions and they had nothing to do with the time and care it took to research and develop new drugs.

Gregory had liked playing the money markets. And, in doing so, Gregory had lost the company many millions of pounds.

Davina felt sick every time she thought about it...every time she remembered her own blind, wilful acceptance of all the lies Gregory had told her. She *ought* to have questioned him more closely, to have insisted on knowing more about the company.

She *ought* to have done a great many things, she told herself tiredly, including ending her marriage.

What marriage? There had been no marriage for years. Ever since... Her mind skittered back from a dangerous precipice.

She had married at twenty. Now she was thirty-seven. For seventeen years she had stayed in an empty, sterile marriage, and why?

Out of love? Her mouth twisted. Out of duty, then...out of necessity...out of cowardice. Yes, definitely that, or rather out of fear, fear not so much of being alone—that would almost have been a pleasure— but fear of the unknown, a fear that, once on her own, she would prove her father's and Gregory's contempt of her to be a true estimation of her character; and so she had stayed, too afraid to leave the security of a marriage that was a sterile mockery of all a marriage should be, hiding from life within its dead, empty embrace.

But now Gregory was dead. Killed in a road accident, his body twisted in the wreckage of what had once been his expensive saloon car. There had been a woman with him.

A woman who was not known to Davina, but who she suspected was very well known to her husband.

He had been consistently unfaithful to her and she had turned a blind eye to it, as she had to so many other things, telling herself that she was better off than most and that if her marriage had not turned out as she had hoped then she was not alone in her disappointment.

And always at the back of her mind had been the knowledge that her father would never have permitted her to divorce Gregory.

And of course Gregory would never divorce her. How could he, when in effect *she* owned the company? On paper, that was. Her father had made sure that effective day-to-day control of the company's affairs lay in Gregory's hands, but then he had tied those hands by ensuring that the shares were in her name and that Gregory could never sell them.

Carey's had meant a lot to her father. He had set up the company with his father shortly after the end of the war. Davina had never known her grandfather, he had died before she was born, but she had often wished she had.

It had been her mother who had told her the most about him. How he had had a reputation locally for making his own potions and cures, mainly for cattle ailments originally, but later for human ailments as well.

It had been his lifelong interest in such things that had led him to the discovery of the heart drug which had established the company right at the forefront of its competitors, although he himself had died shortly after the company had been established.

Her own father had been at medical school when war broke out. He had left to join up and had never completed his training.

As a girl, Davina had had dreams of following in her grandfather's footsteps, but her father had very quickly squashed them. Girls did not become chemists, he had told her contemptuously. They married and produced children...sons. Davina could still remember the look he had given her mother as he spoke. Her parents' marriage had not produced any sons...only one daughter. Davina.

And as for her own marriage... She frowned quickly. Giles would be coming back soon and she had no idea what she was going to say to him. His wife, Lucy, was one of her closest friends, or at least she had been. Recently Lucy had been behaving rather oddly towards her, and Giles had inadvertently let slip that it was partly because of Lucy that he still intended to leave Carey's.

Not that she could blame him. After all, if the bank manager was right, Carey's would not exist for much longer anyway. Unless she could find a buyer prepared to take it over and pump in enough money to save it.

It wasn't for her own sake that she wanted to keep the company going, and it certainly wasn't for her father's.

Carey's employed almost two hundred people, all of them local, and in a relatively sparsely populated country area that was a very large proportion of the working population.

More than half the workforce were women, and Davina had been dismayed to discover how poorly paid they were.

An economic necessity, Giles had told her. He had been unable to meet her eyes when he had added that Gregory had been able to maintain such a poor wage structure simply because they were the only major local employer.

Davina's stomach clenched as she remembered the anger, the guilt she had felt on hearing this disclosure. No wonder so many of the women watched her with stony-faced dislike when she drove through the village. She suspected that they would not have believed that Gregory had kept her as short of money as he did them, but it was true.

She had been shocked to learn just how much money Gregory had in his private bank accounts, but, large though that sum was, it was nowhere near enough to save Carey's.

As she had learned since his death, Gregory had run Carey's as an autocrat whose word was law. No amount of representations to him from the unions had persuaded him to increase his workers' wages, nor to provide them with anything other than the most basic of facilities.

Davina had been stunned when she had been shown the lavatories and wash-basins, the crude and unhygienic area that was supposed to be the canteen and rest-room.

Giles, who had escorted her around the company after Gregory's death, had been sympathetic and understanding, but not even his presence had been able to lessen her shock, her sense of despair and guilt.

And there was nothing she could do to put things right. There was barely enough coming in to pay the wages.

He himself was not a financier, Giles had told her. He was in fact the company's personnel manager, but even he had been able to see the financial danger the company was courting.

Gregory had refused to listen to him, just as he had refused to listen to anyone else who had tried to advise him, as Davina had learned.

Davina had no idea what on earth she was going to do to prevent the company from having to close down. Find a buyer, the bank had told her, or a backer. But how, and where? Her head ached with the constant tension and worry of suddenly finding herself with this kind of responsibility.

Only last week Giles had told her how much he admired her calm, her strength, but inwardly she felt neither calm nor strong. She was adept at hiding her feelings, though. She had had to be. Very early on in her marriage she had realised how much Gregory enjoyed hurting her. By then she had, of course, known how much of a mistake their marriage was. She had blamed herself, or rather her naïveté, for the failure of her marriage.

She had been a shy teenager, sent to a very small all-girls' boarding-school when she was eleven years old, and then abruptly removed from it at fourteen when her mother died suddenly from a brain tumour.

At first she had been thrilled because her father had wanted her at home. She had always been much closer to her mother than she had to her father. Theirs had never been a physically close household, but in her grief and shock at her mother's death she had gone up to him, wanting him to hold her.

Instead he had stepped back from her, rejecting her, his displeasure at her actions written on his face. Confused and hurt, knowing that she had angered him, Davina retreated into herself.

The rough and tumble of the local school confused and alarmed her. The other pupils made fun of her accent, the boys tugged painfully on her long plaits and even the girls ganged up against her, taunting and bullying her. She was an outsider, different, alien, and she was acutely aware of it.

She also soon discovered that her father had brought her home not because he wanted her company or because he loved her, but because he wanted someone to take over her mother's role as housekeeper. And, while other girls spent their teenage years experimenting with make-up and boys, Davina spent hers anxiously ironing her father's shirts, cooking his meals, cleaning his house, with what time she did have to spare spent on trying to keep up with her homework.

Of course, her schoolwork suffered. She was too proud, too defensive to try to explain to her teachers *why* she was always so tired, why she was always being accused of not concentrating on her lessons, and of course when her father read their end-of-term reports on her he was even more angry with her.

The dreams she had once had of emulating her grandfather, of exploring the world of natural medicines and remedies, died, stifled by her father's contempt and her teachers' irritation at her lack of progress.

'Of course we all know, Davina, that *you* won't have to work,' one of her teachers had commented acidly one afternoon in front of the whole class, causing her fellow pupils to shuffle in their seats and turn to look at her, while her face had turned puce with shame and embarrassment. 'Which is just as well, isn't it? Because you certainly won't be employable.'

One of the boys made a coarse comment that caused the others to laugh, and even though the teacher must have heard it she made no attempt to chastise him.

There were girls whom she could have been friends with, girls who, like her, seemed rather shy, but because she had come so late to the school they had already made their friends and formed their small protective groups, and Davina certainly did not have the self-confidence to break into them.

Everyone else at school looked different as well. The girls wore jeans or very short skirts, which were officially banned, but which were worn nevertheless. They had long straight hair and the more daring of them wore dark kohl lines around their eyes and pale pink lipstick.

Davina studied them with awed envy. Her father did not approve of make-up. The one time she had dared to spend her money on a soft pink lipstick he had told her to go upstairs and scrub her face clean.

At fifteen years old she knew that she still looked like a little girl, while her peers were already almost young women.

At sixteen she left school. There was no point in her staying on, her father told her grimly as he viewed her poor exam results.

Instead he paid for her to attend a private secretarial school in Chester so that she could learn to type and so do work for him at home when necessary.

And then just before her seventeenth birthday a small miracle occurred. Out of the blue one morning, while she was engaged on her bimonthly chore of polishing the heavy silver in the dining-room, a visitor arrived.

Davina heard the doorbell ring and went to answer it, wiping her hands on her apron as she did so. She was wearing a pleated skirt, which had originally been her mother's and which was too wide and too long for her, and her own school jumper, which was too small and too tight.

It would never have occurred to her to ask her father for new clothes. He gave her a weekly housekeeping allowance, but she had to provide him with receipts for the meticulously kept accounts he went through with her every Friday evening.

As she opened the door Davina blinked in surprise at the girl she saw standing there. She was tall, and very slim, and a few years Davina's senior. She was wearing a very, very short skirt; her long straight hair would have been the envy of the girls in Davina's class at school and in addition to the kohl liner around her eyes she was wearing false eyelashes.

Her mouth was painted a perfect pale frothy pink, and as Davina stared at her she smiled and said cheerfully, 'Hi, you must be Davina. Your dad sent me round with some stuff for you to type. I'm working for him while Moaning Martha is recuperating from her op. Honest to God, the instructions she gave me before she left . . . !'

The thick black eyelashes batted. She was, Davina recognised in awe, chewing gum. The thought of this girl working for her father, replacing Martha Hillary, her father's fifty-odd-year-old secretary, was almost too much for Davina to take in.

'I'm dying for a Coke. Not got any, I suppose?'

She was already stepping inside the house, while Davina apologised that all she could offer her was tea or coffee.

The thickly pan-sticked pale face contorted briefly, the long hair barely moving as she tossed her head. 'OK, go on, then. I'll make do with the coffee.

'What on earth do you do all day, cooped up in this place?' she demanded when Davina led her to the kitchen. 'It would drive me crazy. That's why I do temping. Just as soon as I can get a bit of money together, I'm off to London. That's where it's all happening.'

It was the start of a brief and wholly unexpected friendship.

Davina never knew why Mandy befriended her. Later on in her life she suspected that Mandy, beneath the outrageous clothes and make-up, had a very strong crusading and protective streak, for she could certainly think of no other logical reason why Mandy should have taken her under her wing.

Under Mandy's tutelage and because she was equally afraid of disappointing her as she was of angering her father, she forced herself to do as Mandy urged and to ask—Mandy had told her to *demand*—her father to give her a personal allowance.

When he agreed Davina could only assume that either she had caught him in a moment of unfamiliar weakness or that he had been so shocked by her request that he had acceded to it without thinking.

When Mandy heard how much she was to get she had pulled another face.

'Peanuts,' she had said scoffingly. 'You should have asked for at least twice as much. God, the typing you do alone would cost him hundreds if he sent it out to an agency.'

Several times a week Mandy would sneak out of Carey's and come racing over in her bright red battered Mini, entertaining and alarming Davina with her tales of her hectic and tangled love-life.

She consistently tried to persuade Davina to go out with her at night, but Davina always refused. Although often she envied Mandy her confidence and her worldliness when Mandy described in graphic detail the more intimate side of her life, Davina found herself recoiling a little. She was an avid reader, a dreamer, a romantic, who cherished ideals of the kind of man she would eventually love and who would love her, and he bore no resemblance whatsoever to the descriptions Mandy gave her of her boyfriends and their sexual demands.

And then, just over six weeks after they had first met, Mandy announced that she was leaving Cheshire and going to London.

Davina mourned her going and missed her. Mandy had brought colour and warmth to her life. She was the first close friend she had ever had, and without her life seemed dull and flat.

Her father, who had never approved of the friendship, made no bones about the fact that he was glad she had gone, even though he complained that she had left before his actual secretary was well enough to return to work.

It was summer. Working in the garden, keeping the flowerbeds and the lawn in the immaculate state her father demanded, had tanned Davina's body and firmed her muscles. She wasn't very tall, her body slim and delicate, and she had shoulder-length mousy fair hair. She hated her hair. It was neither one thing nor the other, neither curly nor straight, but possessed of an unwanted wave, so fine and silky that it was constantly falling in her eyes. It was a hot summer and the sun had bleached it a little, giving it blonde highlights, which emphasised the fragility of her small face with its sombre grey eyes.

Davina had never thought of herself as being pretty. Pretty girls looked like Mandy or like the models in magazines, and she did not look like them, but one Saturday morning, as she was weeding the front garden, dressed in her shorts and the cotton top she had made herself on her mother's sewing-machine, the paperboy abandoned his bike to stare admiringly at her and to tell her with a grin, 'Great legs, babe.'

He was seventeen years old and modelled himself on his American TV heroes. Davina blushed deep pink and hurriedly tucked her legs out of sight.

But even though his comment had embarrassed her, it had also in some complex way pleased her.

Sometimes now at night she lay awake in bed, confused by what she was feeling, aching for someone she could talk to...for someone to love.

She had started playing tennis with the local vicar's daughter, who was home from university for the holidays. They played together a couple of times a week.

Vicky Lane had a boyfriend, a fellow student, and the two of them were planning to spend a year backpacking once they finished university. As she listened to Vicky describing their plans, talking about the life they intended to live, Davina envied her. Compared with others, her life seemed so constricted, so dull and boring, but what could she do? She could not leave her father. How would he manage, and besides, how could she support herself? She had no skills. She could type and do some book-keeping; that was all.

She had tried to suggest to her father that maybe she could work at Carey's, but he had been furious with her. Who was to take care of the house and of him? he had demanded. She was becoming selfish, spoiled, he had added, and guiltily she had abandoned the subject.

The village they lived in was small, with very few other people of her age. Most of them had left to work elsewhere and those who remained worked either for Carey's or on their parents' land.

There was a certain pattern to village life, a certain hierarchy into which Davina and her father did not really fit.

There were the farming families, established over many, many generations, whose positions had been created not just by wealth but also by the length of time their family names had been associated with the area.

Davina and her father were outside that hierarchy. There were older people in the village who remembered her grandfather and who still made disparaging remarks about her father, saying that he had got above himself, reminding themselves and others that *his* father had been nothing but the local apothecary... one of *them*, in fact.

Now Davina's father was the wealthiest man in the area, and it was his wealth as well as her own shyness that isolated Davina.

Their house was outside the village, set in its own grounds, a large early Victorian building bought by her father when he married her mother, after the war, when such houses were cheap. When Davina's father brought senior members of his staff home with him for dinner he expected them to be impressed by the house's grandeur, and they were.

He had a keen eye for a bargain: the heavy old furniture, the Edwardian silver had all been sale-room bargains, and since it was Davina and not he who had to polish the carved wood and the intricately moulded silver he had no idea of the work entailed in keeping his home and his possessions as immaculate as he demanded.

He didn't love her, Davina knew that. He had wanted a son, and she always felt somehow to blame for the fact that she was not that son. She also felt guilty in some way because her mother had died, as though in doing so her mother had proved that her father was right to despise her sex as weak and second-class. Somehow Davina felt as though it was up to *her* to justify her sex's right to exist, but these were vague unadmitted thoughts and feelings that subconsciously shaped the way she behaved.

Yes, she had been very lonely in those years—and then she had met Gregory. Tall, good-looking, charming Gregory had been the ideal she had dreamed of secretly for so long.

A brief knock on the office door roused her from her thoughts. She wasn't using Gregory's office with its ostentation and luxury; somehow she hadn't felt able to. The contrast between it and the rest of the building had not only shocked her, it had also almost made her feel physically ill.

In her father's day Carey's had been austere enough, but it had been kept scrupulously clean and well painted. Gregory had discouraged her from visiting Carey's. And so the shock of discovering the conditions in which their employees were expected to work was something for which she had been totally unprepared.

And she was just as guilty as Gregory in that regard, guilty of taking the easy way out, of going along with

what Gregory wanted because she didn't want to argue
with him.

She felt responsible; she *was* responsible, even though
Giles had tried to comfort her and reassure her that she
was not to blame.

Giles! That would be him outside the office now—a
small square room at the rear of their premises without
a window, just a chair, a desk and a telephone, but it
was all she needed. There was no place, in a company
on the verge of bankruptcy, for plush, expensive offices,
for fax machines and computers that lay idle through
lack of orders. She had asked Giles innocently about the
fax machine in Gregory's office the first time she visited
it after his death. He had looked away uncomfortably
and when she pressed him he had blurted out that he
thought Gregory used it for his money-market dealings.

That had been the first she had known of her husband's disastrous gambling in the world money markets.

She called out to Giles to come in and smiled warmly
at him as he did so. Although he was almost six feet tall,
Giles always seemed shorter because he had a slight
stoop. His thick dark blond hair flopped endearingly over
his forehead and he was always pushing it back. He was
a quiet, studious-looking man who at forty still had a
boyishness about him. There was something gentle and
non-threatening about Giles that Davina found very
appealing.

She wasn't sure when she had first realised that Giles
was attracted to her. Last Christmas at their annual
Christmas party he had danced with her, and then, when
she was in the kitchen stacking used glasses in the dish-
washer, he had come to help her. He had kissed her
before he and Lucy left. A brief enough embrace, but
she had sensed the need in it...even though she had
firmly denied to herself later that it had existed.

She liked Giles and of course it was flattering that he was attracted to her, but she was married to Gregory, and Giles was married to Lucy.

Only now Gregory was dead.

'Giles—come and sit down.' She patted the spare chair and smiled warmly at him.

He looked tired, and she felt guilty. He was their personnel manager and was not really equipped to take over the running of the company, but there was no one else. Gregory had always refused to allow anyone to share control of the company, and now Davina knew why: he hadn't wanted anyone else to know how much money he was losing.

The sales director, their accountant, their chemist— all of them had reported directly to Gregory and had had no real power at all; the chemist had already left, telling Davina grimly that there was no point in his staying. The company was living on its past, he had told her, and Gregory had kept his department so starved of the money needed for research that their very existence was little more than a bad joke.

The sales director had said much the same thing, and their accountant was in reality treated as little more than an accounts clerk, dealing with the wages and day-to-day expenses.

The only person Davina had been able to turn to had been Giles, who at least knew something of how the company functioned.

She was learning, though, but what she *was* learning she did not like. The working conditions of her employees shamed her, as did their poor wages.

'You look tired, Giles,' she said sympathetically.

'Davina, I'm sorry... I hate to let you down, but I'm going to have to hand in my notice.'

He had been rehearsing his speech all day, dreading making it, but last night Lucy had given him an ultimatum. 'Leave Carey's or I leave you,' she had told him.

She was given to making tempestuous threats, and at one time the volatility of her nature had entranced and amused him. She was so different from him, so alive and vital, but gradually he had begun to find her unpredictability a burden; to find that he was longing to go home to someone who was calm and relaxed, who wanted to listen to *his* problems rather than to unload upon him the avalanche of her own. Someone, in fact, like Davina.

Davina, who was always so calm and so kind. Davina, who had never once in anyone's hearing criticised her husband, even though everyone knew that he had been unfaithful to her; Davina, whom, to his increasing despair and guilt, he was beginning to believe he loved.

'Giles, there's no need to apologise. I'm more than grateful to you for all that you've done. Without your support, your loyalty...' Davina made a wry gesture. 'I know what you think...what everyone thinks—that nothing can save Carey's now, that we're bound to go bankrupt.'

'You could trade on for another six months or so, but that's all,' Giles told her.

'I can't give up yet, Giles,' Davina told him. 'And it isn't for *my* sake. If Carey's closes down so many families will suffer.'

Giles remained silent. What she was saying was true. Carey's was the largest, virtually the *only* major local employer.

'If you could just stay for a little while longer,' Davina pleaded with him. 'We could still find a backer...a buyer...'

Davina could see the indecision in his eyes. She hated having to do this, but what alternative did she have? Without Giles the company would have to close. She was doing all that she could, but there was so much she had to learn. If Giles left they would lose what little credibility they still had, and it was all too likely that the bank would insist on her closing down the company.

'I know I shouldn't ask,' Davina continued. 'You've got your own future to think of, yours and Lucy's, but Carey's needs you so much, Giles...' She took a deep breath, and then looked directly at him and said quietly, '*I* need you so much.'

She saw the colour recede from his face and then flood painfully back into it. He moved as though he was about to get up and then settled back in his chair.

'Davina...'

'No, please don't say anything now. Think about it. Talk it over with Lucy,' Davina begged him. 'Philip Taylor at the bank has promised to do what he can to help us find a buyer.'

The overhead light highlighted the delicacy of her face. She had lost weight since Gregory's death, Giles thought and then wondered bitterly what it was about that kind of man that gave him a wife who was so devoted and loyal, so gracious and loving, while he...

He swallowed quickly. He must *not* think like that about Lucy. He loved her. He had been desperately in love with her when they married, and she had loved him... had wanted him. He flinched a little as he recognised the direction his thoughts were taking, shifting his weight slightly as his body was jolted into a sudden sharp and dangerous awareness of how alone he and Davina were, and how much he desired her. When he had kissed her last Christmas she had felt so light in his arms, so small. He had wanted desperately to go on kissing her... holding her.

'Please, Giles,' she repeated huskily now, and he knew that he couldn't refuse her.

Lucy often said things she didn't mean; often lost her temper and gave him ultimatums which within hours she had forgotten. In fact, he had been surprised that she actually cared what he did. Sometimes recently when she looked at him he felt almost as though she hated him, there was so much anger and bitterness in her eyes.

'I'll ... I'll think about it,' Giles promised her.

Davina smiled her thanks at him.

Outwardly she might appear calm, but inwardly her stomach was churning; inwardly she felt full of despair and guilt. How *could* she be doing this to Giles, using him ... using what he *felt* for her? But what alternative did she have? It wasn't for her own sake. Owning Carey's meant nothing to her. She felt no possessive pride of ownership in the company.

But what she did feel was a very powerful and strong sense of responsibility towards its employees, an awareness of how guilty she had been over too many years of turning a blind eye to what was going on.

She *could* have overridden Gregory's refusal to let her come to Carey's. She *could* have insisted on doing so, but she had, as always in her life, taken the easy way out.

Well, there was no easy way out now ... not for the people who depended on Carey Chemicals' survival for their living.

She was all right. She had the money her father had left her, money that had been left untouched since his death—a good deal of money, in her eyes, but Mr Taylor had explained patiently, almost a little condescendingly to her that, as far as Carey's was concerned, it was little more than a drop in the ocean.

He had told her then the extent of the company's overdraft, an overdraft secured by Carey Chemicals' premises and land, and she had blenched at the extent of it.

The money had been lent to Gregory some years ago by his predecessor, he told her grimly. An advance that should never have been made and certainly would *not* have been made in today's harsh financial climate.

That advance, together with Carey Chemicals' profits, Gregory had used to fund his money-market gambling.

Why had he done it? He had always been a man who enjoyed taking risks; who craved their dangerous excitement. That was, after all, why he had died. He had been driving far too fast for the road conditions, the police had told her, and yet there had been no need. He had not been expected anywhere. No, it had been the thrill of driving at such an excessive speed that had excited him, and killed him and the woman with him, just as his greed and reckless addiction to danger was now killing Carey's and threatening the livelihoods of everyone involved with it.

Davina stood up, and so did Giles.

They both walked to the door. Giles opened it for her. She thanked him, taking care not to stand too close to him, guiltily aware of the way his hand trembled slightly as he opened the door.

'Give my love to Lucy,' she told him. 'I haven't seen her for ages.'

She felt uncomfortably hypocritical for mentioning Lucy's name, as though she had no knowledge of Giles's feelings for her.

They left the building together, walking to their separate cars, Giles waiting while Davina unlocked and got into hers.

Carey's was within easy walking distance of the village, its two-storeyed buildings surrounded by the lush Cheshire countryside. The site on which her grandfather and father had originally set up the business had once been occupied by a corn chandler's. The original two-storeyed Cheshire brick mill was still there. It had a preservation order on it now, because of its age.

Face it: Carey's doesn't look like a profitable drug-producing company, Davina reflected as she drove off. She surveyed the jumble of buildings that housed the company, contrasting them with photographs she had

seen of the premises of the huge multinationals that
dominated the drugs market.

Carey's, she had to admit, was an anomaly. But for
her grandfather's discovery of that heart drug, Carey's
would never have existed. At home she had his note-
books with his meticulous descriptions of the drugs and
potions he had made up for his customers, human and
animal. When he had been a young man there had been
no National Health Service and very few ordinary people
had been able to afford the fees of a doctor, so men like
her grandfather had doctored them instead.

She thought it was a pity that her own father had been
so reluctant to talk about his childhood and his parents.
It had been her mother who had told her about her
grandfather, and she had only known him for a couple
of years, as he had died shortly after she and Davina's
father had married.

There was a portrait of Davina's father in the room
that was used as the boardroom, and Davina had always
thought that there should have been one there of her
grandfather as well.

There never would be now, of course. If she was lucky
enough to find a buyer, the last thing they would want
would be portraits of the original founders of the
company.

She drove home, worrying about whether or not Giles
would stay with the company, and trying to quell her
guilt at the way she had manipulated him.

And then, even more guiltily, she found herself wondering what her life would have been like if she had
married someone like Giles instead of Gregory.

CHAPTER FOUR

IT HAD been Davina's father who had been responsible for Davina's meeting Gregory.

Gregory had come to work for Carey's as their technical salesman and her father had invited him to one of the dinners he occasionally gave for certain members of his staff.

Davina had been busy in the kitchen when everyone arrived. These dinners were always something of an ordeal for her. Her father was a perfectionist and Davina dreaded his disapproval if everything was not as he wished it to be.

She had spent virtually all week preparing for this dinner, shopping, cleaning, polishing the silver, washing, starching and then ironing the table linen. And picking flowers from the garden and then arranging them. Her father would never countenance wasting money on buying flowers.

He personally selected the menus he wished Davina to serve, and they were always complicated. Her father was a fussy eater, preferring small, delicately cooked dishes, but on these occasions he liked to impress with lavish cordon bleu meals.

Sticky and uncomfortable from the heat of the kitchen, praying frantically that she had correctly judged the timing and that the hot soufflé her father had insisted on for the first course would not deflate before everyone was seated, Davina heard the kitchen door open. Expecting to see her father walk in to tell her that she could serve the soufflé, she was astonished to see instead a very good-looking young man.

He smiled at her, a warm flashing smile that showed the whiteness of his teeth. His skin was tanned; his brown hair shone. He was tall and lean, and there was a warmth in his brown eyes as he smiled at her that made her face burn even more hotly than the heat from the kitchen.

'Hello, I'm Gregory James,' he said to her, introducing himself and holding out his hand.

Automatically Davina extended hers and only just stopped herself from gasping out loud at the *frisson* of sensation that struck her as he slowly curled his fingers around hers and shook her hand.

No one had ever affected her like this before. In her naïveté her skin flushed darker, her whole body trembling as she succumbed to his sexual magnetism.

'I'm sorry. I didn't mean to disturb you,' Gregory told her smoothly as he released her hand.

For a moment Davina felt confused. There was something about the tone in which he delivered the apology that jarred on her, some falseness, some instinctive awareness of a mockery of her, as though he intended the words to have a double meaning, as though he was laughing at her for her reaction to him, but these feelings were so vague and unformed that they had vanished before she could really grasp them, leaving her to stammer a few incoherent words, while Gregory continued, 'Your father was on his way to tell you that everyone is ready to eat, and I asked if I might deliver the message for him. And to see if there was anything I could do to help.'

To help? Davina gave him an unguarded startled look. Her father believed that it was a woman's place to be subservient in every way to the males in the household, and the thought of any man offering her any kind of domestic help was a concept with which Davina was completely unfamiliar.

'Thank you, but there's really no need,' she began breathlessly, but he stopped her, looking at her until she could no longer meet the intensity of his gaze as he said slowly,

'Oh, yes, there is. There is *every* need. I've been wanting to meet you, Davina.'

He...this wonderful, good-looking man, had been wanting to meet *her*? She shook her head dizzily, wondering if she had fallen asleep and was having a dream, but no, it was real. *He* was real. She was so flustered that she could barely even breathe, never mind think of moving, and Gregory, watching her, allowed himself a small inner smile of satisfaction. Good. She was obviously as naïve and dumb as he had heard. He had met her. Now the rest should be easy.

Brought up by a widowed mother who had died while he was in his first year at university, Gregory had always bitterly resented the good fortune of others, a good fortune which had been denied to him. His mother was poor. He was clever and good-looking, but he learned early in life that that did not compensate for lack of wealth. Wealth was power, and power was what Gregory wanted. He had learned young to smile and say nothing when others taunted him or drew attention to his second-hand school uniform and the poverty of his possessions. His time would come. He would make sure that it came.

It was while he was at university that he realised how hard it was going to be for him to achieve his ambition. The best jobs, and with them the money and the power he craved, would not be offered to someone like him. They would go to others, youths with far fewer qualifications than he possessed, far less worthwhile degrees, but they had something more important than intelligence: they had family; they had position and power.

It had been a chance conversation he had overheard between two fellow graduates which had told him the path he must take through life. Both of them were unaware of his presence, and were discussing a third, absent friend.

'You know, his sister's getting married in June. He was telling me about it last week. She's in the club. His family are furious. Apparently she's been going around with some working-class type, who obviously knew which side his bread was buttered on. Now she's pregnant, the family have no option but to let them marry, and they'll have to support them, find him some sort of decent job. They're furious about the whole thing, but, of course, they're putting a brave face on it.'

'Nice work if you can get it,' the other man commented wryly. 'Marrying a rich girl.'

Marrying a rich girl. Gregory mulled the thought over in his mind, letting it lie fallow for a short time before finally allowing it to take root.

The problem was that he did not know any rich girls. He knew girls . . . plenty of them. He was a good-looking young man who had grown up in an environment where teenagers had begun experimenting with sex well under the legal age limit, and he had learned early the basic mechanics of sex. To those over the years he had added a variety of refinements which so far had ensured him as much success as he needed or wanted with the opposite sex.

When he wished he could be ingratiatingly charming and well mannered, surface attributes that went no more than skin-deep, as those of his sexual partners who had not immediately taken the hint that he was tired of them had very quickly found out.

Gregory had no real warmth about him, no real kindness; as far as he was concerned, they were weaknesses he could not afford.

A rich wife. He bided his time. The doors to the homes of his fellow graduates, or at least those who could have introduced him to the lifestyle he craved, remained firmly closed to him. He got a job and then another, and finally a third with Carey's.

He had chosen Carey's out of three possible employers because he had learned from eavesdropping on a casual conversation while waiting to be interviewed that the man who owned Carey's had only one child, an unmarried daughter.

Gregory had become very adept over the years at listening to other people's conversations. He had discovered it was an extremely profitable way of learning things.

He had been at Carey's now for six months. That was how long it had taken him to discreetly and cautiously bring himself to old man Carey's eye, without offending or arousing the suspicions of his co-employees.

He had accepted the accolade of the dinner invitation for one purpose only, and that had been to meet this small, naïve girl with the flushed face and untidy hair. He had made enough discreet enquiries into Carey's now to know just how rich Davina would one day be.

Physically she was not his type. He liked women with endless legs, generously curved bodies and with that look in their eyes which said they knew what life was all about.

Davina Carey was small and slight, her body girlish rather than sensual. Her eyes held naïveté and self-consciousness. And when they looked at him they also held awe and wonder.

As he accepted Davina's disjointed dismissal and left the kitchen—after all, he had never intended actually to help her; that had simply been an opportune method of meeting her—he was smiling to himself.

Physically, as a woman, she might not appeal to him, but as a wife, a rich wife, she would be ideal.

Davina served the meal in a daze of gauzy unbelievable daydreams in which all manner of impossible things suddenly seemed dramatically possible.

Now, she told herself breathlessly as she cleared the plates from the main course, scraping them into the waste-bin before soaking them in hot water and then hurrying to serve the pudding, she knew why there had never been anyone else in her life: it had been because fate had already chosen Gregory for her. Because fate had known that he was there, that he existed; that he lived and breathed...even if she hadn't.

Her body completely still, she stared out of the kitchen window, lost in her dreams, and then abruptly and painfully jolted herself back to reality by reminding herself that she was probably reading far too much into what he had said to her, in the way he had looked at her. Achingly she wished she had someone, a friend in whom she could confide, whose advice she could seek, with whom she could discuss the wonder and excitement of what had happened.

Gregory deliberately waited almost a week before getting in touch with her. A week was just long enough for her to have begun to lose hope, but nowhere near long enough for her to have even begun to forget about him.

He telephoned her, using his office telephone.

Davina had just returned from doing some shopping. She picked up the receiver and said the number, her heart shuddering to a frantic standstill of shock and pleasure when she heard Gregory's voice.

So many times over the last six days she had mentally relived those moments when he had walked into the kitchen, the things he had said, the way he had looked, and, with each day that passed, so her belief in herself, in the message his eyes had silently given her, had diminished.

And now, just when she had been on the verge of giving up hope, of accepting that she had foolishly read far too much into what had happened, he had rung her.

And then as abruptly as her hopes had swung upwards they were dashed again as he said formally, 'I'm sorry I haven't rung before. I've been away on business. I just wanted to ring to thank you for a marvellous meal last week.'

He was merely ringing to thank her. A polite bread-and-butter telephone call, that was all, Davina acknowledged dully.

On the other end of the line Gregory smiled to himself. He could almost taste her disappointment.

He waited a few seconds and then added casually, 'There's a very good musical on at the Palace in Manchester at the moment. I don't know if you've seen it, but I've been given some complimentary tickets and I was wondering if you'd care to see it with me. The tickets are for tomorrow evening. Rather short notice, I'm afraid.'

He was asking her out! *Her*. Like a rider on a roller-coaster, her hopes soared again. Both her hand and her voice were trembling as she thanked him and accepted the invitation, ignoring the small warning voice that reminded her that she would have to get her father's approval and that tomorrow evening was his bridge evening and he would expect her to provide a supper for himself and his cronies, since it was his turn to host it.

Well satisfied with his progress, Gregory made arrangements to pick her up the following evening.

He didn't live locally, but rented a small flat in Manchester, preferring to keep his work and his private lives apart. He had a company car, and one of the first things he had learned in his first job was how to ensure that his expenses claims covered his own personal motoring costs as well as the travelling he did for his employers.

Not that he overdid things. Gregory knew very well how to temper greed with caution. It was one of the things he was best at.

He was having a good day today. He picked up his paper and turned to the stocks and shares section. If he had one appetite that was not wholly under his own control, it was not, as with so many of his peers, sex; sex was something he enjoyed for the pleasure it gave him and the control over the women who enjoyed the benefits of his skill and experience. No, Gregory's weakness was the thrill of tension and excitement that he got from gambling.

Not gambling as in betting on horses, or visiting casinos. No, Gregory's gambling took the form of highly calculated risks in the buying and selling of stocks and shares.

Over the years Gregory had had some spectacular successes with this, his own private, very private game, and he had also suffered some heavy losses.

He frowned as he remembered the last one. It had all but wiped out the special fund he kept for his investments, and for a month or two he had had to live very meagrely indeed, but today he felt lucky. All the omens were good. He picked up the paper, studying it avidly.

For once fate seemed to be on Davina's side. When her father came home that evening, before she could mention Gregory's invitation, he said curtly to her, 'I shall be going out tomorrow night.'

'But it's your bridge night,' Davina interrupted him.

Her father's mouth thinned with displeasure. 'I wish you would allow me the courtesy of finishing my conversations, Davina, instead of interrupting me. Yes, it is my bridge night, but there has been a slight alteration in the arrangements. The Hudsons have decided to take a short holiday and visit their son next week, and because of this they have asked if the venue of tomorrow's meeting can be changed from here to their house, since it would have been their turn to host everyone the week they will be away.'

As she prepared her father's supper Davina hummed under her breath. She couldn't believe her good fortune. She closed her eyes, giving in to the temptation to let her imagination recreate for her a mental image of Gregory James. Tall, good-looking, and with a look in his eyes that made her ache with excitement.

She still couldn't entirely believe that he had actually asked her out.

She told her father about the invitation after he had eaten, picking her time carefully and cautiously, and then holding her breath as he frowned. 'Gregory James, you say. Hmm. A very bright young man. Well-mannered, as well. Not like some these days.'

Very slowly and carefully Davina released her pent-up breath. Her father, it seemed, approved of Gregory. She could scarcely believe her luck.

It took her virtually all afternoon the next day to decide what to wear for her date. Outfit after outfit was discarded as she went through her wardrobe, wishing she had had the courage to buy something as daring as the outfits Mandy had worn with such panache, and then being forced to admit that her father would never have permitted her to wear such short skirts, nor such striking colours.

In the end she settled for a cream linen skirt teamed with a neat floral blouse. Over it she could wear the cream mohair jacket she had knitted for herself the previous winter.

As an irrational extravagance, the last time she had been to Chester she had bought herself a pair of new shoes. They were all the rage, beige patent, almost flatties, with tiny heels and a large gold-rimmed flat buckle on the front. They matched her outfit exactly and she was lucky enough to have small enough feet to wear such pale-coloured shoes.

She was ready far too soon, of course, her hair combed as straight as she could get it, a defiant touch of blue eyeshadow on her eyelids, pale pink lipstick on her mouth. She ached for the courage to line her eyes with the black kohl that everyone was wearing, but cringed from her father's reaction should she do so. He didn't approve of make-up of any kind, but she defiantly refused to give in completely.

Her father was still at home when Gregory arrived. To her surprise and delight, he actually invited Gregory into his study and offered him a glass of sherry.

Davina, of course, wasn't included in the invitation, but she didn't mind. She went upstairs and surreptitiously checked her appearance, staring anxiously into the mirror. If only her hair were thicker, straighter. She wondered if it would look any better if she coloured it lighter or if somehow she could cut herself a thicker fringe. She wished too that she were taller. All the girls in the magazines were tall, with endless, endless legs.

She sighed fretfully. There were so many things about herself she'd like to change if only she could. What on earth could a man like Gregory possibly see in her?

Downstairs in Alan Carey's study, Gregory displayed the charm and good manners which so often had blinded people to his real nature. Alan Carey seemed as easy to deceive as all the rest.

It was a slow, careful courtship. Within weeks Gregory knew quite well that there was virtually nothing that Davina would not do for him, although it was not Davina who was important but her father. Davina was no use to him without her father's money. And so, in effect, although it was Davina he took out and dated, it was actually her father to whom he was paying court.

For six months they exchanged nothing more than relatively chaste kisses. Only occasionally did Gregory assume a mock passion, for which he always apologised, claiming to Davina that it was his love for her that threatened his self-control.

Davina, with no experience of any kind to illuminate her sexual darkness, accepted what he said, and, if when she left him and was lying awake in bed her body ached rebelliously for an intimacy that had nothing to do with the kind of kisses Gregory gave her, she told herself severely that she was lucky to have someone who treated her with so much respect.

It was a time when, although the media might have given out an image of teenagers eagerly and freely enjoying what was termed 'the sexual revolution', in fact in country areas, away from the freedom of cities like London, where young people lived away from home and their parents' watchful eyes, many of the old shibboleths still existed. And one of these was still that nice girls did not 'do it', or at least not until they were engaged, and then only very discreetly, so that it was something they discussed in nervous excited whispers, and only with other girls in the same situation.

So, while her body wantonly ached with a need whose fulfilment was only something Davina vaguely understood, her mind, her upbringing told her that it was right that Gregory should be so restrained with her, that it was out of love, out of respect for her; and she contented herself with rosy, breathlessly exciting daydreams of how different things would be if he actually asked her to marry him. Then there would be no need for restraint between them, then... She moved restlessly in her bed, turning over on to her stomach, her hand pressed against her lower body and then hastily, guiltily removed.

She had started waking up out of her sleep, brought abruptly from its depths by the intensity of the powerful rhythmic contractions of her body, shocked and disturbed by such a physical phenomenon, and yet at the same time delighted and awed by this glimpse of the pleasure it could afford her, naïvely assuming that, if her dreams of him could bring her so much pleasure, when Gregory did become her lover the pleasure would be even greater.

It was her father who announced that he had invited Gregory to spend Christmas Day with them, and, when after church on Christmas morning Gregory presented her with an engagement ring while her father looked on in approval, Davina was too thrilled with happiness and

love to question the fact that her father had obviously
known that Gregory was going to give her the ring before
she had, or that Gregory had not actually asked her if
she wished to become engaged to him.

The wedding date was set for the following summer.
Davina was pleased that her father approved of Gregory;
she was happier than she had ever believed possible.

They were married the following June. It had been
agreed that the young couple would move in with
Davina's father rather than buy their own home, an arrangement that had been made between Davina's father
and Gregory without either of them consulting her, but
Davina was too blissfully in love with Gregory to care.

They were honeymooning in Italy. She felt dizzy with
excitement at the thought of finally being alone with him,
alone and married!

On the way from the airport to their hotel all she could
think was that tonight she would lie in Gregory's arms.
Tonight she would become his truly and completely.

She looked towards him, wanting to reach out and
touch him, but Gregory hated public displays of affection. Suddenly she felt shy, nervous...very unsure of
herself.

It was hot in the coach and Gregory didn't seem to
be aware of her discomfort. He was talking animatedly
to the courier, a pretty blonde girl who had met them
at the airport.

Suddenly Davina felt very alone, very insecure. There
was a huge lump in her throat. She ached for Gregory
to turn towards her, to hold her hand.

The anticipation she had felt suddenly turned to a cold,
leaden feeling of fear and panic. It was a sensation that
persisted for the rest of the day, and she couldn't understand it.

Their room was smaller, much smaller than she had
imagined from the brochure. It had twin beds instead

of the double she had expected, and the balcony overlooked not the sea, but the rear of the hotel.

When she commented on this to Gregory he told her
that the courier had explained to him that there had been
a mix-up with the bookings. In actual fact, Gregory had
changed the booking so that he could pocket the difference between the room they had booked and this much
cheaper one. Davina's father had paid for their
honeymoon as a wedding present, and the difference between the two rooms would provide their spending money
while they were here.

The room felt airless and stuffy. Davina felt oddly
light-headed, sick almost.

Gregory was saying something about going down to
the bar for a drink.

Dusk was just falling, her body ached with tiredness
from the strain of the day, and nothing was happening
as she had expected. For one thing, she had somehow
imagined that they would be more alone, less surrounded by other holidaymakers *and* the efficient courier
who seemed to have attached herself to them. For
another, she had expected *Gregory* to be different. After
all, they were *married* now... *Now* there was no need
for him to treat her with restraint.

Her eyes were over-bright with foolish tears. What had
she expected? she asked herself as she heard the door
close behind him. That he would pick her up and carry
her to the bed, that he would undress her and then slowly
and thoroughly make love to her? Things weren't like
that these days. She was a modern young woman, she
told herself firmly. Of course Gregory wanted a drink.
It had been a hot, tiring journey, and while he was gone
she might as well unpack their things. She could have a
shower and then be all pretty and cool for him when he
came back. It never even occurred to her that Gregory
might have asked her if she wanted a cool drink in the
company of her new husband! Determinedly she pushed

aside her sense of somehow having been abandoned, and
unlocked their cases.

Gregory came back just in time to change for dinner,
and Davina, who, after her shower, had dithered over
whether or not to change into the ultra-feminine and
frilly broderie anglaise trousseau shortie robe she had
bought for herself, was glad that she had put on a dress
instead when Gregory disappeared into the bathroom,
firmly locking the door behind him.

When he came out fifteen minutes later his skin
gleamed; he smelled of soap, and, even slicked back off
his head, his hair still made her want to reach out and
stroke her fingers through it.

The sight of him, the smell of him, the reality of him
banished her earlier panic, and she ached to throw herself
into his arms, to have the confidence, the experience to
tease him with kisses and caresses until he growled that
what he wanted was not dinner but her, but she knew
awkwardly that she just wasn't that kind of girl, that
she did not *have* that kind of self-confidence, and so
instead she sat miserably through the dinner she had not
wanted, her throat closing up with a misery she could
not explain as the blonde courier hovered over their table,
chatting animatedly with Gregory while ignoring her.

It was late, almost midnight, when they finally went
up to their room. Gregory had been drinking steadily all
evening. He swayed slightly as he unlocked their
bedroom door.

The atmosphere inside the bedroom hit them like a
muggy hot wall. The room had no air-conditioning, and
the windows were screwed down so that they could not
be opened.

Davina showered quickly, trying to ignore the headache
tensing her scalp.

When she came out of the bathroom wearing her new
robe and its matching shortie nightdress, the broderie

anglaise threaded with pale blue satin ribbon, Gregory
was lying on one of the twin beds.

He looked up at her and pronounced, 'Very virginal.
What are you going to do? Take it home complete with
appropriate bloodstain to show Daddy?'

Davina stared at him in disbelief. She started to tremble
a little, aware that something was wrong, but not
knowing what.

After all her dreams, the reality of Gregory's lovemaking shocked her into a silence that prevented everything other than one brief, sharp sound of pain leaving
her lips as he possessed her.

She didn't even cry. Not then, not until she was alone
in her own single bed and Gregory was safely asleep,
snoring in the other bed.

Was *this* what she had waited for... wanted ... ached
for... dreamed about? Was this, then, sex? Where was
the exquisite build-up of sensation, the aching, consuming urgency of need, the quick, fierce pangs of sensation that exploded into that rhythmic starburst of
pleasure she had known in her dreams and in waking
from them? If this was sex, then what had *they* been?

When Davina returned from her honeymoon she felt
immeasurably older—and wiser; the scales had not so
much fallen from her eyes as been ripped from them.

After the fourth night of enduring Gregory's increasingly uncomfortable penetration of her now painful
body, on the fifth night she turned quietly and sadly
away from him.

Gregory made no attempt to coax or persuade her,
simply returning to his own bed with a small shrug.

Feeling shocked, distressed, and most of all guilty because she was not able to enjoy his lovemaking, not able
to respond to him since at times she almost wished she
were here on her own rather than here with him, she was
relieved to return home and to escape into the familiar
routine of her life there.

She had no close friends to whom she could confide her doubts and feelings of guilt and despair. Her family doctor was old, and a friend of her father's, and even if she had been able to pluck up the courage to consult anyone about her growing dislike of sex she could never have explained to him the way she felt, the tension she felt whenever Gregory touched her, the dread almost.

It was her fault, of course. It *had* to be, and she knew that Gregory must be as disappointed as she was herself, even though he made no complaints.

She was glad when she had her period and was relieved of the necessity of having to lie tensely in bed praying that Gregory would not touch her, and yet even in her relief she was conscious of other feelings, of a heavy, leaden sense of somehow having lost something; of having been cheated of something.

She refused to allow herself to remember those tormenting pre-marriage dreams, the feeling she had experienced. She had just *imagined* them; they hadn't been real. If they *had* been, she would have experienced them with Gregory, she told herself firmly.

It was on the night of their first wedding anniversary that Gregory told her that during their honeymoon he had made love to the courier.

The moment he told her she knew that it was the truth. He had come home late, too late for the special dinner she had prepared. Her father was out playing bridge. They had had a row. She had promised herself that tonight she would try, really try to overcome her dislike of sex, but then Gregory had come home late, and she had smelled the perfume on him immediately.

When she asked him whose it was he had told her about the girl he had been seeing. A girl who, unlike her, was good in bed and who knew how to please a man.

Shocked, distraught with despair, Davina had demanded to know why, then, he had married her.

Gregory had told her.

'For your father's money,' he said brutally. 'What the hell other reason could there be? Why the hell would a man...any man want you? And don't bother going running to your father over this, Davina. He thinks you're as useless as I do. Why do you think he was so keen to see us married? A divorce is the last thing he'd want.'

A *divorce*! The brutality of the ugly words hit her like a blow. Divorce was something that happened to other people. In Davina's world it was still seen as a stigma, as a sign of failure on the part of a wife, as a wife and as a woman.

The very sound of the word terrified Davina. It would be a public acknowledgement of her failure.

It was only later, curled up into a tight ball of misery on her own side of their bed, that she confronted the true enormity of what Gregory had told her.

He *did not* love her. He had *never* loved her. She felt sick inside...not at his lack of love, but at her own folly in believing that he might have loved her. From this point onwards Davina had had to acknowledge that their marriage was a sham.

Outwardly their lives went on as normal. Occasionally Gregory made love to her, and when he did Davina gritted her teeth and prayed that she might get pregnant. They both wanted children, but for very different reasons.

Davina's father had started dropping hints about grandchildren, but both Davina and Gregory knew that what he wanted was *grandsons*.

Gregory told Davina that it was her fault. She underwent a whole series of tests before a young and sympathetic female doctor suggested to her that the reason she had not conceived might lie with Gregory and not with her, since they could find no reason why she should not conceive.

Davina contemplated putting the doctor's theory to Gregory with a certain amount of grim mental despair. She had changed from the girl who had married Gregory in such blissful ignorance, even though barely twenty-four months separated the woman she now was from that girl.

No, she would not tell Gregory what the doctor had said, she acknowledged wearily as she drove home.

Slowly she started to forge a life for herself. A life apart from Gregory's. She was a married woman now, not a girl.

She ran the house smoothly and efficiently, and, since both her father and Gregory rejected any suggestions she tried to make that she could fill in some of her spare time by working for the company, she looked for another avenue to occupy her.

Davina needed to keep busy. That was the only way she had of keeping at bay her despair over her marriage. If she just kept herself busy enough she did not need to think about her marriage at all. She did not need to think about the fact that Gregory was unfaithful to her. She knew that because he made no attempt to hide it now.

In front of her father he used the pretext of work as an excuse for his absences. To her in private he didn't bother to conceal what he was really doing.

It shamed Davina more than she could bear to admit that she was actually sometimes glad, grateful that she was not the recipient of his sexual favours. Now she dreaded those times when he did touch her. Just occasionally, when her concentration lapsed, she sometimes remembered how she had felt before she married him, but she fought hard to keep that kind of weakness at bay. She was married to him, and at least he had the discretion to conduct his affairs outside their own small social circle. Davina had seen the way the other wives looked at Gregory, and she dreaded the day he returned any of their interest.

Sometimes she was sickened by her own weakness in staying with him, but she was too afraid, too conventional to break out of their marriage—and to what purpose, anyway? There was none. She was empty of all hope, all pleasure, all desire; a woman unwanted, unloved and undesired by the man to whom she was married.

But she was married and she must make the best of it. Behave like an adult and not a child.

Wryly Davina shook her head, dismissing her thoughts of the past. What was the point in dwelling on the past? She had *chosen* to marry Gregory, no one had forced her, and it was pointless wondering what her life might have been had she married someone like Giles. Gregory was dead now, and his death had brought her far more important things to worry about than the emotional barrenness of her own life.

It had been cowardice, and a too strongly rooted dread of offending against her father's idea of convention, that had kept her in her marriage; it was that which had trapped her just as much as Gregory's manipulation of her. She couldn't blame everything on him.

Not even the failure of the company?

She closed her eyes tiredly. That was a different matter. What on earth had prompted him to get involved in something as volatile and dangerous as the currency market, and with money that should have been used to secure the future of the company and of its employees?

How much real chance did she have of finding a backer...an investor? Virtually none, the bank manager had told her grimly. These were difficult times for industry; money was tight, especially the kind of risk-money involved in supporting something like Carey's.

Davina turned into the drive. She was home. Home; she smiled mirthlessly to herself as she stopped the car and got out.

She had lived in this house all her life and she felt very little affinity towards it. It had never truly been hers. During her father's lifetime it had been his, and after his death ... Well, he might have willed it to her, but she had never truly felt it belonged to her.

It had been Gregory, during one of his many affairs, who had produced the interior designer responsible for its present décor; she and Gregory had been having a passionate affair at the time, and even though she knew it was quite ridiculous, since she knew Gregory could never have had sex with her here at home, Davina felt somehow as though the very fabrics the woman had chosen were impregnated with the musky odour of sex.

She loathed the brilliant harsh colours the woman had chosen, the dramatic blacks and reds, the—to her—ugly rawness of so much colour and emotion. They made the rooms seem claustrophobic, reminding Davina of that awful honeymoon hotel with its cramped room and lack of air.

As she unlocked the front door and walked into the hall she wondered with a certain wry amusement if she was always to associate sex with a lack of breathable air. She also wondered even more wryly if, had it not been for Matt, she would ever have felt this faint stirring of curiosity about Giles. If all she had ever known was Gregory's lovemaking, somehow she doubted it.

It had been a long time now since she had finally recognised that Gregory might not have been the skilled lover he had always claimed. Five years, to be precise.

But now wasn't the time to think of Matt.

'Lucy, I'm home.'

Giles tensed as he heard the sound of pans being slammed in the kitchen. Increasingly these days he dreaded coming home, dreaded the inevitable row that followed his arrival.

Ducking his head to avoid the house's low beams, he walked slowly towards the kitchen. Outside the closed door, he paused, mentally willing away his involuntary mental image of opening the door and finding not Lucy, his wife, waiting there for him, her face sharp with temper, but Davina.

Davina, who always looked so cool and calm; Davina, whom he had never once heard raise her voice; Davina, who was always so relaxed, so easy to be with, her manner directly the opposite of that of his emotional, highly volatile wife.

He must stop thinking like this, he told himself fiercely as he took a deep breath and then pushed open the kitchen door.

Lucy was standing by the sink.

She was tall and slim, her thick, dark red curls a fiery glow of colour round her small pale face. Her eyes, green and almond-shaped, glittered with temper. Giles could almost see it vibrating through her tense body as she glared at him.

'Where the hell have you been?' she demanded. 'You were *supposed* to be back at half-past five.'

'I had to talk to Davina.'

'Oh, you did, did you? And did you *tell* her that you were leaving? That she wasn't going to have your broad manly shoulder to cry on for much longer?'

Giles winced at the bitterness, the acidity in her voice.

She had gone too far. She could see it from Giles's face, and for a moment she was afraid. She had thought she had learned to control these rages, these outbursts of temper fuelled by fear and insecurity.

'Well, I hope you've had something to eat,' she told Giles, 'because there certainly isn't anything here for you. Half-past five, you said. It's almost seven.'

'I'm not hungry,' Giles told her wearily. 'I'll make myself a sandwich later.'

'Why bother?' Lucy goaded him, driven relentlessly towards self-destruction by her fear and anguish. 'Why not ring Davina and have dinner with her? She's a wonderful cook... although rumour has it that she wasn't much good in bed. Still, that won't bother you, will it, darling? You haven't had much interest in that department yourself recently, have you? Or is it just *me* you don't want?'

'Lucy, please,' Giles begged her wearily. 'Not now. I——'

'You what? *You* don't want to discuss it. All right, let's discuss something else, then, shall we? Like your telling Davina that you weren't going to stay. You did tell her that, didn't you, Giles?'

Giles sighed. 'I... I tried. Look,' he said desperately when he saw Lucy's face, 'it won't be for much longer. Only another few weeks. She needs me, Lucy.'

He knew the moment he said it that he had said the wrong thing, but as he watched the way Lucy's face closed up, her eyes as hard and flat as dull river pebbles, he also knew it was too late to call back his words.

As Lucy slammed down the pan she had been holding and walked past him he said desperately, 'Lucy, please try to understand...'

As she opened the door she turned on him, feral as a maimed cat. 'I *do* understand,' she told him. 'I understand that Davina James is more important to you than I am.' As she slammed the door the whole house seemed to shake.

It was an old house, parts of it dating back to the fourteenth century, a long low-timbered building. They had bought it eight years ago when they first moved here shortly after their marriage.

They had been so happy then. So much, so passionately in love. When had it all changed? Why?

He had thought himself so blessed when he met Lucy, bemused by the way she had flirted with him, teased him and coaxed him, dazzled by her fire, by the life, the energy that filled and drove her. She had been a passionate lover, overwhelming all his hesitation, overwhelming him.

He had been thrilled, disbelieving almost when she had told him she wanted to marry him, shy, hesitant, unsure of him for the first time in their relationship. He had loved her so much then. And he still loved her now. At least, a part of him did; another part of him...

He tensed as he heard the front door slam and then the sound of her car engine starting up.

It had been unjust of her to accuse him of not wanting her any more. She had been the one to reject *him*, to turn away when he reached for her, to let him know without words that his body, his touch no longer aroused her.

Helplessly Giles sat down, his head in his hands. Maybe for the sake of his marriage he should have stood firm and told Davina that he could *not* stay on. Maybe he should have done, but the truth of it was that he hadn't wanted to. The truth was that he had looked at Davina and had ached to take her in his arms, to hold her, to protect her. Davina was that kind of woman. She did not, as Lucy had always done, challenge his masculinity, she complemented it. Where Lucy was all fire and passion, Davina was all loving, comforting serenity, and something within him ached to have that serenity wrapped around him.

He was so tired. Tired of Lucy's wild outbursts of temper, her volatility, of all the things about her that had once held him in such thrall. Including her passion? Her love for him?

Sick at heart, he groaned helplessly to himself.

CHAPTER FIVE

'I'M SORRY, Saul, but I'd forgotten when we arranged for you to have the children this weekend that we were going to stay with the Holmeses. Tom adores it down there. He and Charles Holmes are such good friends——'

'And Josey?' Saul interrupted his ex-wife grimly. 'Does she adore it too?'

It was pointless losing his temper with Karen. He knew that, but he could feel the emotion surging through him, battering down his self-control, demanding an outlet. What was happening to him? He had always been so sure of his self-control, of his ability to hide his real emotions, especially when they were unwanted ones.

'Saul, please. Don't be difficult about this. Josey's got her own friends. Her own life. She's growing up.'

And the last thing she wanted to do was to spend time with him, Saul recognised as he heard Karen out in acid silence. It was hard to remember now that they had once been married, that they had once shared all the intimacies of a married relationship, and sometimes it was even harder to recall *why* they had married, to recall the emotions he had once felt.

He was drained of those emotions now, incapable almost of experiencing them, even in retrospect. Increasingly he felt as though he had somehow lost pace with the rest of the human race, as though he was isolated from it, living in a void, a vacuum, where nothing existed other than his own unfamiliar, terrifying doubts.

'Why don't we arrange for them to come to you next weekend?' Karen was saying.

'I'm afraid next weekend is out,' Saul told her. 'I'm leaving for Cheshire next week.'

'You're going to see Christie?'

He could hear the astonishment in Karen's voice and just in time stopped himself from correcting her and telling her that he was going to Cheshire on business.

His body suddenly felt cold with shock at the thought of how easily he might have made such a self-betraying mistake. It showed how much his concentration was slipping...his control. The purpose of his visit to Cheshire was supposed to be confidential—not that Karen was likely to realise its significance if he had told her that he was going there on business, but that wasn't the point.

He ended his phone call without asking Karen if he could speak with either of his children, not because he hadn't wanted to, but because he had recognised that neither of them was likely to want to speak to him. His fault and not theirs. As a father he hadn't been much of a success, had he? He hadn't been 'there' for them.

Not like his own father. He had been there for him. He had always been there for him; through his childhood, through his young adulthood, and even after his death Saul had felt his presence, had been comforted by the knowledge that he was fulfilling his father's dreams for him, but just recently that closeness he had always felt had somehow slipped away from him. That inner conviction he had always had that in fulfilling his father's ambitions for him he was also fulfilling his own dreams had somehow become lost to him.

He and his father had always been so close. It was a closeness that Christie had resented and rebelled against.

He smiled wryly as he thought about his sister. She had always been a rebel and in some ways she still was. She was unorthodox, idealistic, tough, gritty, and so determinedly independent that he wasn't surprised she had never married.

She was also a marvellous mother. A much better mother than he was a father. He admired the way she had brought Cathy up herself, just as he admired the way she had doggedly pursued her chosen career and qualified as a GP.

Cathy had been born soon after she'd qualified, and even now, over twelve years later, he still had no idea exactly who his niece's father was, only that he'd been married and had wanted nothing to do with his child— or its mother.

He dialled her number, smiling as he heard the familiar huskily abrupt sound of her voice.

'You want to come and stay? Well, yes, of course you can, but why? What's wrong?' she demanded with sisterly candour.

'Nothing's wrong,' Saul told her. 'It's just that I've got some business to attend to there and I thought...'

'You'd save money on hotel bills by staying with me. Since when, Saul?' she scoffed. 'More like you're involved in something underhand and machiavellian for that precious boss of yours. I know you. There's no way you'd voluntarily give up the luxury and comfort of staying somewhere like the Grosvenor for the chaos of my place unless you had some ulterior motive.'

'Unless of course I just happened to want to see you and Cathy,' Saul told her grimly.

Her comment had caught a raw spot, rubbed against an inflamed patch of his conscience, but even as he became aware of it he was aware also of his inability to control or conceal his reaction to it.

'OK...OK...' he heard Christie saying wryly. 'Of course you can stay, Saul. As a matter of fact,' she added thoughtfully, 'you could be the answer to my prayers. I'm due to attend a conference at the end of next week. Cathy was going to stay with a schoolfriend, but the whole family's gone down with mumps and I can't inflict her on them as well.

'I don't suppose there's any chance of your extending your visit until after the conference, is there?'

'I don't see why not,' Saul told her. He had only intended to spend a couple of days in Cheshire, but there was no reason why he shouldn't stay a little while longer. The thought of putting some distance between himself and Sir Alex was one that appealed to him.

Alex was trying to manipulate him, to threaten him into submission. 'Get me what I want or else' had been implicit in his comments, and what the hell did he care about the damage he was about to inflict on the company he wanted to acquire?

Come to think of it, why should he care? Saul asked himself ten minutes later when he had finished speaking to Christie. He hadn't minded in the past, had he?

At least not until Alex had wanted to take over and dismantle Dan Harper's family company. *Then* he had minded.

He moved irritably from his desk to the fireplace. He had bought this apartment after the break-up of his marriage in what had then been an unfashionable part of London. The Georgian house was four storeys high and his apartment occupied the entire second floor. It was too large for a single man, but when he had bought it he had had the children in mind. The apartment had three good-sized bedrooms, each with its own bathroom.

He grimaced to himself. He could probably count quite easily on the fingers of both hands the number of times Josey and Tom had stayed with him for any period longer than one night, especially recently. Recently their visits had become even more spasmodic. Josey in particular seemed to be showing increased antagonism towards him.

Beside his bed he had a photograph of them, next to the one of his father.

His father. Why was it that, when he thought of his father these days, as well as all the love and the positive emotions he had always felt for him he now felt anxiety, a fear almost that somehow he was letting his father's dreams for him slip away from him?

His father's dreams for *him*. Wasn't that the crux of the problem, of the doubts, the anxiety, the increasing awareness possessing him that his whole life had narrowed down to a tunnel which had become a trap, and that in continuing down that tunnel he was going against his own instincts, his own desires? Wasn't *that* partially why there was so much antagonism between him and Alex? Wasn't it true that somewhere deep inside him an unwanted voice was beginning to question what exactly it was he wanted out of life, whether the ambitions he was pursuing so relentlessly were really what he wanted?

And didn't his thoughts always come back to this…this ongoing and increasingly stressful battle inside him to force himself to fulfil the tacit promises he had made his father?

For as long as he could remember, Saul had known that as his father's son it was his duty to succeed and do well in life.

His earliest memories of conversations with his father were of the tight, painful feeling he got inside his stomach when his father told him how much he regretted wasting his own opportunities, how hard it was to bring up a family on his modest income and how, if he was wise, Saul would not do as he had done and ignore the importance of becoming a success.

Saul had hated those conversations. They had left him feeling sore inside and afraid. He loved his father and he was proud of him, and he hated knowing that somehow his father was not proud of himself; that in some way he felt as though he were a failure.

And yet, when Saul looked for an explanation as to why his father should feel this, he could not find it. He was loved by his family, especially Saul himself. His parents had lots of friends; there always seemed to be people dropping in; the large kitchen was always full of

warmth and laughter, and, if his mother frowned sometimes and sighed anxiously when he tore his jeans, she
still hugged and kissed him and told him he mustn't
worry when he asked her if it was true that they were
poor.

Saul had not understood then why his father worried
so much about money. It seemed to Saul that there could
be no better place to live than here in their small, cosy,
well-filled house with its untidy garden; that there could
be no better feeling than the one he got when he came
home from school to find his mother waiting for him in
the kitchen with a smile and a warm hug. In fact, if it
had not been for the fact that his father was so often
worried and unhappy, Saul would have thought their
family was very lucky indeed. But he knew that he must
be wrong, because his father was not happy, his father
was always urging him not to make the mistakes he had
made, and that confused and worried him, because he
loved his father and he wanted him to be happy.

It worried Saul a great deal that a man like his father,
whom everyone liked and many people loved, a man
who was part of a family where there was such warmth
and laughter, should be so unhappy, and it made him
feel guilty and anxious because he could not always
understand what it was that made his father like that.

Saul knew that his father did not talk to Christie the
way he did to him. Girls, it seemed to Saul, did not have
to worry about things like 'doing well'. Girls were allowed
to be happy and not to have to think about things like
that. Saul loved his sister, but he understood as he listened to his father that it was his duty as a male to take
care of the females and to protect them, and most of all
to make sure that he earned enough money to look after
them properly.

Saul's father had had his chances, Saul knew that,
because he had often told Saul so, but he had not made
the most of them. Saul must not repeat his mistakes.

Saul must work very hard at school. There was no money in the family for him to inherit, no family influence to secure a safe future for him. He would have to succeed by his own endeavours.

The year Saul came third in the class in the end-of-term examinations his mother praised him but cautioned him to remember that there were other things, other gifts, other virtues that were just as important as being clever.

His father, on the other hand, told him that only the very best, the very cleverest children were given the chance to make the most of their lives, and Saul sensed that somehow he had let his father down. That being third was somehow not good enough.

The next year he was first. His father praised him, but still Saul felt empty inside. And not just empty, but lonely as well. He thought about all the football matches he had missed . . . all the times he had stayed in to work when his friends were out having fun, and he told himself again that he was wrong to feel that doing well and being a success had not made him feel happy in the way that his father had told him they would.

By the time he was ready to sit his GCEs Saul had dismissed those earlier childish feelings of doubt and pain. He was almost a man now, and he had absorbed his father's teaching so well that he no longer questioned how he felt. Feelings were for girls, anyway. He had more important matters to concern him.

Saul was going to do well. Everyone said so, and Saul could see how proud and pleased that made his father. He was going to be accepted for Oxford if he did as well in his exams as his teachers felt he could. He knew already what subjects he would read, and that he would leave Oxford to go to America to spend some time in Harvard, getting his master's.

After that the world, the commercial world, at any rate, would be his oyster. He would have the kind of qualifications that would make firms eager to employ him.

Saul saw his way ahead very clearly. A man with no money behind him and no family influence had to work, and work hard, to achieve... to make something of his life, and he intended to do just that... he *had* to do that... didn't he? His family, his father, were relying on him to do so.

When he was seventeen Saul fell in love. He was a handsome boy, tall, taller than his father, with strong bones and powerful muscles; looking after the garden had become his job, and all those winters spent digging over vegetable beds and all those summers pushing the old-fashioned non-electric mower had built up his muscles and weather-hardened his flesh.

The combination of his thick dark hair and pale blue eyes with their rimming of thick black lashes had already had a devastating effect on many of his sister's friends, but Saul had remained impervious to their flirtatious giggles and wide-eyed admiration.

Angelica, though, was different. In addition to looking after his parents' garden, Saul earned himself some much needed pocket-money by working in other people's gardens as well.

Angelica's parents' was one of these gardens.

Angelica's parents were a very well-to-do couple. Gordon Howard was away a great deal of the time on business. Amy Howard was a small, fragile-looking blonde woman with a vague manner. To Saul she always looked somehow as though she was about to burst into tears. Whenever he went to work there she appeared in the garden with glasses of fruit juice, tinkling with ice, and more often than not Saul could smell alcohol on her breath. He didn't like her very much. She was so very different from his own mother and yet in some way he felt sorry for her, and he had the same feeling in the pit of his stomach when she talked to him as he had had all those years ago, when his father had talked to him about his missed chances.

These days, though, Saul didn't allow himself to dwell on those kinds of feelings. He blocked them off, denying them. They were not male, and they were not going to be a part of *his* life. He was going to be successful and do well. He was not going to have any doubts...any regrets. When he married, his wife would never have that sad, despairing look in her eyes that he sometimes saw in his mother's.

The Howards had one child, Angelica. Saul had heard about Angelica from her mother, who, it seemed to him, appeared to adopt a very odd attitude to her daughter, one moment praising her to the skies, referring to her in such terms of glowing perfection that Saul frowned, secretly despising this wonder child, and then at other times complaining petulantly that Angelica did not love her, that she never spent any time with her, choosing to spend her holidays with her friends and their families.

Angelica was a year older than Saul. After leaving boarding-school, she had gone to an exclusive private college in Oxford, where apparently she was perfecting her languages and taking a very advanced secretarial course.

The half-term before Saul was due to sit his A levels Angelica came home.

Amy Howard was away in Miami, visiting friends. Gordon Howard was also away, on one of his business trips. Saul had gone round to the house to do the spring pruning and to dig over the formal beds which Gordon Howard had religiously filled with annuals every late spring, their precise colour patterns somehow re-inforcing Saul's awareness of the rigidity of the Howard home and the remoteness from one another of the people who lived there.

He had been working for a couple of hours before he realised that there was someone in the house, and he wouldn't have realised it then if he hadn't happened to turn his head and glance towards its windows just as the curtains at one of them were swished back.

The girl who stood in the window was definitely not Amy Howard. She had long dark hair that tumbled down on to her naked shoulders, and Saul felt his throat go dry with shock, and his muscles tense with something that was very definitely something else, as she stood there, stretching the suppleness of her body, apparently uncaring that he could see her.

Female nudity wasn't completely unfamiliar to him; he had a sister, after all, and there were magazines freely available to anyone who chose to look at them, depicting the female anatomy in far more explicit detail than anything he could see now as he stood motionless, staring up at the girl moving her body as languorously as a lazy cat, her stretching movement lifting her breasts so that he could see how firm they were, how narrow her ribcage, how softly rounded her hips, how fascinatingly erotic and enticing the small patch of hair between her thighs, how long and supple her legs.

As he stood transfixed, staring at her, he knew he should look away, but he simply could not move. A raw, scorching heat seemed to spread through his body, a sharp, pulsing ache that made his face burn with embarrassment and confused his mind.

He had made forays into exploring the technicalities of sex, of course, and had thought himself well aware of what did and what did not turn him on, but this girl, with her wild, gypsyish mane of hair, her strong, lithe body, her apparent indifference to her nudity and to his observation of it, excited his senses in a way that wasn't solely sexual.

He wanted to take hold of her, to run his hands over her skin, to close his eyes and absorb its silky texture, to breathe in the scent of her, to stroke her with his tongue, to...

He groaned out loud, aware that he was almost shivering with the intensity of what he was feeling. He closed his eyes, trying to blot out her image, trying to deny his need to reach out to her, to touch her face, to explore its delicacy, to see if the full smoothness of her lips felt as soft and silken as it looked. They reminded him of the petals of a poppy, vulnerable, rich, drawing the eye and enticing the touch, but all too easily bruised if treated' too roughly.

He gave another deep shudder, his body racked by the physical torment of his desire, by the emotional impact of his reaction to her. He felt somehow awed, and humbled, his mind a jumble of conflicting sensations and needs. He had an unfamiliar urge to throw himself at her feet, to tell her she was the most perfect, the most beautiful human being he had ever seen. He wanted to hold her, to cherish her, to tell her how much she moved him and in how many ways, and he wanted also to crush her body beneath his own, to enter her and possess her and hear her cry out with the same elemental, savage urge that pulsed through him.

That he should feel this way made him both elated and ashamed.

Saul's father was a very moral man, and, despite what Saul had observed happening in the world around him, a part of him retained his father's earliest teachings: that women were to be cherished and revered, protected and treated with tenderness and care. It confused him now that he should experience both that tenderness and at the same time an alien and very sharp physical desire that he could only translate in his own mind as somehow pagan and dangerous.

When he opened his eyes, trying dizzily to clear his mind, she had gone. The curtains were still drawn back, fluttering slightly in the breeze.

She had, he realised, opened the window. Had she seen him . . . watching her? A dark red tide of guilt and embarrassment burned his skin. He turned to his work, resolutely keeping his back to the house.

Half an hour passed, longer, but he still could not relax, his muscles taut and stressed.

He heard the back door open but he dared not turn round. The grass muffled the sound of her approach, but he still knew that she was there, even before he heard the slow seduction of her voice saying, 'Hi. You must be Saul. I'm Angelica.'

He *had* to turn round. He couldn't ignore her. She was tall, but nowhere near his own height. Her body was now clothed in jeans and a dark grey baggy sweater with a neckline that left her collarbone exposed and with it the graceful, delicate curve of her shoulder and throat.

She was close enough for him to catch her scent. He could feel the heat searing his body, the ache of wanting. She smiled at him, perfectly composed, perfectly at ease.

She had long, slanting hazel eyes...cat's eyes, and close to her mouth was just as full, just as enticing as it had seemed at a distance. Her skin was matt and smooth, her nails, when she lifted her hand to push the tumble of her hair off her face, free of lacquer and yet somehow glossy and attractive.

He had a shocking second's vision of them lying against his skin, digging into it, the kind of vision he had never had in his life, and with the heat of embarrassment that poured through his body came a sharp sense of surprise that he who had never experienced such a thing should know so clearly and so unequivocally how it would feel to have the fierce rake of her nails against his flesh, the passionate twisting of her body beneath his own.

'I'm just having a drink. Want one?'

The casual words focused his attention on reality, although he couldn't quite bring himself to look directly into her eyes, just in case she was laughing at him. Instead he looked round as though somehow expecting to see the usual glass of juice materialising out of thin air. He *was* thirsty, he recognised, his throat raw and dry. He nodded, still unable to trust his voice.

'Come on, then.' She turned back towards the house, plainly expecting him to follow her.

He dug the spade into the earth and did so.

He had been inside the house before on many occasions, but this time it felt different...almost as though in some way he was trespassing...or walking into danger. He felt the hairs on his arms lift as he paused on the threshold of the kitchen to remove his boots.

His socks were old heavy-duty ones he wore when he was working. There was a hole in one toe and he blushed furiously as he saw it. He couldn't imagine her ever wearing anything with holes in it...ever looking less than the picture of immaculate perfection she presented now. When his sister wore jeans they looked like jeans. On this girl... And that sweater...

He felt himself go hot as into his mind slipped a mental image of his tugging it down over her shoulder to expose her flesh to the exploration of his mouth. He imagined her winding her arms around his neck, pressing herself up against him, making small excited noises of pleasure in his ear.

'Coffee do, or would you prefer something stronger? Always supposing you're old enough to drink it.'

Her words brought him back to reality. He swung round and then flushed as he saw the way she was looking at him. 'Coffee will do fine,' he told her thickly.

He watched, fascinated, as she lit herself a cigarette. He had never been able to understand why anyone should want to poison themselves with nicotine, but now, watching as she perched on the edge of the kitchen table, supporting her weight with one slender hand, arching her back so that her breasts were clearly outlined beneath her sweater, he suddenly wished that he too was

a smoker; that he could go up to her and lean close to
her as he lit his cigarette from hers.

'Coffee's over there,' she told him, gesturing towards
the filter machine but not making any attempt to help
him. 'Help yourself.'

He moved awkwardly across the kitchen, conscious
of his mud-stained jeans, his holey socks, the sweat
drying on his body in the warmth of the room.

'Not much to say for yourself, have you?' she commented mockingly. 'Will you be working here all week?'

He nodded, his body tensing as he saw the way her
nipples were pushing against the wool of her sweater.

Feverishly febrile images tormented his senses.
Mentally he pictured her naked body as he had seen it
earlier. Beneath her sweater she was naked now. He knew
it. He ached to go over to her, to reach out and touch
her, not in lust but with all the aching emotion, all the
weakening need, all the unexpected reverence for the
perfection of her body that he could feel tormenting him,
sweeping aside all that he had previously thought he believed about sex.

Within three days they were lovers. Angelica was the one
who initiated their intimacy, laughing at his hesitancy,
his shyness and his inexperience, and then suddenly
heart-stoppingly ceasing to laugh at him when she
touched his naked body, stroking it with her fingertips,
and then with her soft open mouth, doing to him un-
imaginable, unbearable things that made him forget his
inexperience and his hesitancy as he took hold of her
and possessed her, making her cry out with sharp
pleasure.

By the end of the week it was as though he had known
her all his life, as though she had always been a part of
him. Each time, he tried to find some new way to please
her, to show her how much he loved her.

She had no inhibitions, knew no boundaries, and if
at first he was semi-shocked by her lack of hesitation or

shyness, that shock quickly disappeared under the expert ministrations of her hands and her mouth.

One afternoon when it was unexpectedly mild she insisted on making love outside, in the wild, overgrown section of the garden out of sight of the house.

Afterwards she smiled languorously, showing her teeth like a stalking cat as she whispered to him, 'Mm...very D.H. Lawrence, but I think I prefer doing it inside, and there are still some things we haven't tried.'

As he held her close, wanting to prolong the intimacy they were sharing, she leaned towards him, telling him explicitly what she would like to do.

It still had the power to shock him, this almost aggressive sexuality she possessed, but he was too besotted with her to question why he should want to recoil from any evidence that this was not her first experience of sexual pleasure. He knew that she was twelve months older than he was, but he was tall and well built and could easily have passed for a youth of nineteen or twenty rather than one of seventeen.

He had been disconcerted to discover that her favourite place for making love was her father's study. At first he had felt uncomfortable, inhibited, being there, but his desire for her and the way she touched and aroused him quickly subdued those feelings.

She had a game she liked to enact with him, a fantasy, which she played out in the study. She was, she told him, his secretary, and he was to summon her into the room and then order her to make love to him. For this fantasy she would dress up in a neatly formal little suit, but under it she would be completely naked, or sometimes she would simply wear stockings. On other occasions she was the one who was the aggressor, sitting on the desk in front of him, peeling off her clothes, stroking her hands over her own skin but forbidding him to touch her until she said that he might.

Often by the time she finally allowed him to touch her he was so aroused that he could do little other than give in to his need to possess her, so quickly that afterwards he felt cheated almost, aching for an opportunity to show her how much he loved her, to touch her with tenderness and love, to spend as long as he could savouring every aspect of her and his love for her before that final act of possession.

Sometimes when he left her he experienced the same feeling he had as a child when his father had told him about the importance of success; an empty, hollow feeling as though something wasn't quite right... as though there was something absent... missing.

He had ten days with her before she told him she was going back to college.

'I'll write to you,' she promised, and foolishly he believed her. Even more foolishly he spent so much time aching for her, yearning for her, that he failed two out of his four A levels and had to resit them.

His father's disappointment was the hardest to bear, the feeling of having let him down, of having allowed himself to forget his main goal, and because of that he set up barriers to protect himself from making the same mistake a second time. Emotions, he warned himself, must never be allowed to take priority over ambition. He had seen what could happen when they did. He had almost ruined his entire future, and for what? A girl who had not even written him one letter, a girl who, he saw with retrospect, had simply been using him... who had never been emotionally involved with him in the way he had been with her.

To punish himself for his weakness he concentrated exclusively on his work, studying so far into the night that his mother protested. His father shook his head and said that sometimes in order to succeed sacrifices had to be made; that he was young and could afford to miss out on a few hours' sleep...that he wished *he* had Saul's chances...that, given his life again...

Saul escaped to his own room, unable to bear the look of pain and sadness he knew would be in his mother's eyes.

This time he passed his A levels with exceptionally high grades. He had learned an extremely valuable lesson, and all the time he was at Oxford he took care to avoid getting himself into any kind of situation that would make him emotionally vulnerable.

He dated girls, even slept with one or two of them, but he always made it clear that, while physically he found them desirable, that was all he wanted, and all he had to offer.

He got the reputation of being remote and unemotional. 'Clever as hell,' was the way one girl described him, 'cold as Siberia and so sexy that just looking at him makes you ache inside.'

When Saul heard this description he smiled grimly to himself. He was a lot wiser now than he had been at seventeen, and a lot less naïve. He knew a come-on when he heard one, but he wasn't going to respond. His finals lay ahead of him, and after that, hopefully, a year at Harvard. And this time he wasn't going to forget all the important things he had learned from his father; this time he wasn't going to make the mistake of allowing his emotions to get in the way of his ambitions.

The phone rang. Saul frowned as he picked up the receiver.

'Ah, Saul. Glad I was able to catch you in.'

His frown intensified as he recognised Sir Alex's voice. It was like the man that he should feel no need to introduce himself; that he should assume autocratically that he needed no introduction.

'I was half expecting you'd be on your way to Cheshire by now.'

Subtlety, at least when it came to people rather than business, had never been Sir Alex's strong point, Saul reflected. His tools of persuasion veered more towards the verbal bludgeoning and threatening school than the delicate hint.

'You haven't forgotten our discussion, have you?' Sir Alex queried sharply when Saul made no response. 'Or are you suffering another crisis of conscience?'

'I shall be leaving for Cheshire once I've tied up some loose ends here,' Saul told him coolly.

There weren't really any loose ends for him to tie up. He knew already as much as he was going to know about Carey's without being on the spot to do some far more in-depth research, but he could feel himself bristling inwardly at Alex's bullying tone. The older man's manner was beginning to jar on him. There were many things about him that Saul genuinely liked and admired, but he had never been more conscious of how little he wanted to be like him.

And yet for years he had worked patiently towards that one goal: to take over from Sir Alex when he retired. To take over from him, but not to be him.

On Sir Alex's desk was a photograph of his daughter, taken when she graduated from Cambridge. Sir Alex had not been there for her graduation. He had been away on business. He and his wife had divorced over twenty years ago, and as far as Saul knew Sir Alex's contact with his daughter was now limited to the exchange of cards at Christmas. Was that what *he* wanted? Was that the kind of relationship he wanted with his children?

For the first time behind the slightly hectoring tone of his employer's voice Saul was suddenly aware of, if not exactly a loneliness, then certainly an aloneness. Two men, both of them, in the eyes of the world, successful and to be envied, but take away their work and what was there really in their lives?

For quite a long time after his conversation with Sir Alex was over he sat motionlessly where he was.

Beside him on his desk was the small file containing the basic facts about Carey Chemicals. He picked it up, flipping it open as he started to read.

He read quickly, pausing only a handful of times, once when he read how the company had originally come into being, a second time when he read of Gregory James's heavy losses on the money markets, and a third time when he read that the company was now in the hands of his widow, the founder's granddaughter, Davina James.

She would want to sell. She would have to. There was no other option open to her. The business was on the verge of bankruptcy. Saul suspected he knew the kind of woman she would be. The investigating agents Sir Alex had employed had been thorough. There were no details of Gregory James's many affairs, just a couple of paragraphs stating that his unfaithfulness was a constant and ongoing situation and that it would seem that his wife must have been aware of it.

Saul thought he knew the type. He had met enough of them over the years; elegant, brittle, too thin, too tense and too expensively dressed, they reminded him of fragile china ornaments. You always had the feeling that if they were asked to participate in anything real they would crack and fall apart.

Some of them turned to sex as a means of solace for the uninterest of their husbands, some of them turned to drink, some to good works, but none of them, it seemed to Saul, seemed prepared to take the simple step of freeing themselves from the humiliation and destruction of their marriages by divorcing their husbands. Wealth, position, appearances, it seemed, were always more important than pride, self-respect or self-worth.

He had once made the mistake of saying as much to Christie and she had turned on him immediately, challenging him to put himself in their shoes, to be what life and circumstances had forced them to be.

He winced a little as he remembered her anger, her vehemence about the fact that so many members of her sex were taught almost from birth to accept second best, to put others first, to give instead of to take. Many of them were held in those marriages by their children, she had told him fiercely.

But Davina James did not have any children. He frowned as he lifted the last sheet of paper from the file and saw the photographs pinned neatly behind it.

There were several of Carey Chemicals, showing the run-down state of the buildings and how totally ill equipped it was to compete with even the poorest of its competitors. Without that all-important heart-drug patent which had been revised over the years to create a second patent it would have disappeared decades ago.

There was another photograph. He stiffened as he saw the name written on the back: 'Davina James'.

He turned it over.

She was nothing like what he had imagined. The file quoted her date of birth, so he knew that she was thirty-seven years old, but in this photograph she looked younger and vulnerable in a way that made his body tense with rejection.

There was none of the glossy sophistication that he had expected about her. She was dressed in jeans and what looked like a man's shirt, one hand lifted to push a strand of soft fair hair out of her eyes. She was wearing gardening gloves and there was a smear of dirt along one cheekbone, a fork in the ground at her feet. Her skin, free of make-up, looked clear and soft, and without even realising what he was doing Saul suddenly discovered that his thumb was touching her face.

But it wasn't the living warmth of a woman's flesh he could feel, just the hard glossy texture of the print.

He withdrew his hand as though the print had scorched him.

CHAPTER SIX

GUILTILY aware of how long it had been since she had last seen Lucy, and of the discomfited look on Giles's face whenever she mentioned his wife to him, on Saturday afternoon, knowing that Giles would be playing golf and that Lucy would be on her own, Davina decided to call round and see her.

She had done nothing wrong, she assured herself as she drove through the village. It was her duty to do all she could to protect the livelihoods of those who worked for Carey's, and without Giles's help she could not do that.

But Giles was Lucy's husband, and one of the reasons she had been able to persuade Giles to stay on had been his feelings for *her*. Feelings which neither of them had discussed...admitted, but which both of them knew were there. Did Lucy know as well?

Davina's heart sank. The last thing she wanted to do was to hurt anyone, and she genuinely liked Lucy. Oh, she knew that there were those in their small, tight-knit local circle who disapproved of her; Lucy wasn't like them. She was flamboyant, outspoken, turbulent and passionate. She was also extremely attractive, Davina reflected as she drove through the soft Cheshire countryside.

And extremely unhappy?

Davina pushed the thought away. Lucy's obvious disenchantment with her life and with her husband had nothing to do with her. Lucy was not a woman's woman. She had no interest in cosy, gossipy chats over cups of coffee, comfortable womanly discussions on the failings of men in general and husbands in particular, rueful,

sometimes too dangerously honest admissions that there
came a point in a relationship when sex was no longer
its prime motivating force, when, as one long-married
wife had once put it in Davina's hearing, she 'got more
excitement out of watching *Neighbours* than making love
with her husband'.

Lucy was openly, too openly sometimes, scornful of
that kind of female intimacy. Lucy was different, and,
because she *was* different, other women found her
dangerous.

Davina didn't find her dangerous. Davina liked her,
and when Giles had first come to work for Carey's
Davina had envied her. Things had been different then.
She had not yet met Matt, and Lucy and Giles had been
so obviously, so passionately, so blindingly in love with
one another that it had made Davina's empty heart ache
just to see them.

She remembered calling round early one afternoon just
after they had moved in. Giles had come to answer the
door, his face flushed, his hair untidy, apologising for
keeping her waiting, and then behind him on the landing
Davina had seen Lucy, and she had known immediately
that she had interrupted them making love.

She had felt so envious then, so alone.

And now she felt guilty, even though she told herself
she had nothing to feel guilty about.

Davina parked her car on the Cheshire brick
herringbone-patterned drive and walked up to the front
door.

She remembered the first time she had visited the house
and how stunned she had been by the way Lucy had
decorated and furnished it. The whole house had seemed
to sing with harmonious colour and warmth, soft peaches
and terracottas which complemented Lucy's dark red
hair, cool blues and greens and creams, the colour of
her eyes and skin; the house *was* Lucy, Davina had
thought, right down to the femininity of the soft cushions

and the voluptuous way in which she had used her fabrics. It was a house in which even on the greyest of days the sun always seemed to be shining.

Today the sun was shining, but when Lucy opened the door Davina was shocked to see how pale she looked, how withdrawn her manner was in stark contrast to her normal ebullience.

'Lucy, it's been ages since I saw you,' Davina told her nervously. 'It's the company. It seems to eat into my time.' As she followed Lucy into the kitchen Davina was aware that she was speaking too fast, gabbling almost.

'Funny, that's always Giles's excuse,' Lucy told her harshly. 'The company. Odd that you never seemed very interested in it while Gregory was alive, isn't it?'

There was outright hostility in her voice now and Davina's heart sank. This was what she had been dreading; that Lucy would resent her for persuading Giles to stay on.

'Lucy, I know how you must feel,' she began awkwardly. 'But——'

'Do you? I don't think so,' Lucy interrupted her bitterly. '*You* aren't the one who has to sit here alone all day waiting for your husband to come home, are you? Why are you so anxious to hold on to Carey's, Davina? You never cared about it while Gregory was alive.'

'I didn't realise then the problems they were having,' Davina told her. On that subject at least she could be totally honest with Lucy. She owed it to her to be totally honest with her. 'I have to try to keep Carey's going, Lucy. I can't let the company close down.'

'Why not? *You're* financially secure, aren't you?'

Davina winced at the accusation in her voice. 'Yes,' she agreed. 'It isn't the money, Lucy. It isn't for me...'

'Then who is it for?' Lucy asked sarcastically. 'Giles?'

Davina winced again.

'If Carey's closes, over two hundred people will lose their jobs, and there are no other jobs for them to go to.'

'Giles can get another job,' Lucy told her stubbornly.

'Giles isn't free to throw his career chances away for Carey's, Davina. Giles is my husband.'

'I know that.' Davina couldn't look at her. She could see how angry Lucy was, how upset, but there was more than anger in her eyes; there was pain, as well as vulnerability. Davina wasn't used to seeing Lucy vulnerable, and doing so now made her ache a little inside.

She had always envied Lucy slightly, envied her insouciance, her self-confidence, her brilliant, glowing sensuality, her way of living life to its fullest, and most of all, if she was honest, she had envied Lucy the love that existed between her and Giles. Not because she had wanted Giles for herself, never that . . . No, what she had envied Lucy was the state of being loved, of being wanted, needed, of being the centre of someone's world.

Once she had known a little of what that was like, once and very, very briefly, but what she had known had merely been a shadow of the brilliance of the love that Lucy and Giles had seemed to share.

What had happened to them? What had happened to that love? She could understand why Lucy was resentful and angry that Giles was staying on at Carey's, but surely she must know that it was Giles's very nature to stick loyally to those to whom he believed he owed that loyalty?

'I was wondering if you fancied a day in Chester, shopping?' Davina asked her, trying to change the subject to something less painful.

'Shopping? While Carey's goes bankrupt and people lose their jobs?' Lucy demanded gibingly.

Davina flushed, with irritation, not guilt. Lucy was being deliberately difficult . . . childish almost. For the first time Davina realised that there was still a lot of the child about Lucy, and that it was this combination of a child's faroucheness and a woman's sexuality that made her so powerfully appealing.

She tried again.

'Lucy, I'm sorry if you're angry because Giles has decided to stay on a little longer at Carey's.'

'So it was Giles's decision, was it?' Lucy demanded tauntingly.

Davina heard the bitterness in her voice and her own heart suddenly felt unbearably heavy. It had been wrong of her to persuade Giles to stay, but what alternative had she had? If he left, the company would collapse. There was literally no one else who could take over. She tried to explain as much to Lucy, but Lucy did not want to listen.

'Giles isn't doing this for Carey's, Davina,' Lucy interrupted her angrily at one point. 'He's doing it for *you*. You know it and I know it. Even Gregory knew it.'

Davina couldn't hide her shock. It was reflected in her eyes, in the way her body tensed, her colour fluctuating as she demanded huskily, 'What do you mean?'

'Oh, come on, Davina. Giles must have told you about the arguments he and Gregory had about the way Gregory was running the company. Giles didn't approve of the way Gregory was playing with the firm's money. He was concerned for *your* future ... *your* security. He even threatened Gregory that he would tell you what was going on. If Gregory had lived he would have sacked Giles, and Giles knew it. Do you honestly think Giles did any of that because of Carey's? It isn't Carey's Giles cares about, Davina. It's you.'

'No ... no, that isn't true,' Davina denied, but she felt like Judas, not only denying Giles, but also denying Lucy the right to express her bitterness and pain.

When she left it was with the feeling that all she had done was to make things worse. The last thing she would do would be to have an affair with another woman's husband, especially when that woman was a friend; surely Lucy knew that? She liked Giles, of course she did. And yes, she was flattered...comforted even by his obvious concern for her, but that was as far as it went.

Except that she had used Giles's concern for her to persuade him to stay on at Carey's. Except that, in being concerned for her, Giles was very obviously hurting Lucy. And hurting other people was the very last thing Davina wanted to be responsible for.

From an upstairs window Lucy watched Davina drive away. She ought to hate Davina, but she couldn't. She felt too afraid. What would she do if Giles did leave her? She loved him, she had always loved him and she always would, but so much had changed between them, and she knew that she herself was sometimes guilty of almost deliberately trying to drive him away, but she hurt so much inside. The pain was unbearable, eating into her, driving her into a frenzy of despair so that she had to lash out at someone, and that someone was inevitably Giles.

No, she couldn't blame him if he left her for Davina. Davina was older than her but she was still young enough to give him children...sons.

The scene beyond the window blurred as her eyes filled with tears. Sons. Men needed them...craved them. They were always more important to them than daughters. Lucy had learned that when she was six years old. The day her mother told her that her father had left them to go and live with someone else.

Lucy hadn't understood at first when her mother had told her that she wasn't her father's only child. That she had half-brothers, two of them, five years younger than Lucy. Twins...two boys...two sons. How could one daughter ever be important enough to a man to hold him against competition like that?

'When is Daddy coming home?' she had asked her mother over and over again until at last she had turned on her and screamed,

'Never! Do you understand? Never. He doesn't want *us* any more. He doesn't want *you*. He has other children now...two sons, and they're more important to him than you and I could ever be.'

Lucy had been afraid then; afraid because she knew that somehow being a girl meant that she would never, ever be loved as much as if she had been a boy.

She was a rebellious child, difficult, her mother said. Her teachers complained about her wilfulness and blamed it on her red hair. Lucy didn't care. When she was naughty people couldn't ignore her. When she was naughty she was almost as important as if she had been a boy.

Tall for her age, thin and gawky, she was almost fifteen when suddenly, overnight almost, she was transformed from an ugly duckling of an overgrown schoolgirl into a stunningly sensual young woman.

Suddenly she had a figure, breasts, a waist, hips. Suddenly her legs, so thin and coltish, were enviably long and slender. Suddenly her eyes seemed to develop a mysterious slant, her mouth a soft pout. Suddenly Lucy discovered the power of her sexuality, and equally suddenly boys discovered her.

Now things were different. Now Lucy discovered that one look from her bewitching eyes, one toss of her red curls, one tantalising pout was enough to have every boy in the neighbourhood at her feet.

Suddenly she had something that others wanted, and because of it she was valued...loved...or so it seemed to the emotionally starved child who still lived inside the quickly developing body of the new Lucy.

For a while Lucy was happy. People...boys...wanted her and said they loved her, and then three months before her seventeenth birthday her mother announced that she was remarrying. The man she was marrying did not, it seemed, want a seventeen-year-old stepdaughter, and it had been decided that Lucy would go to live with an aunt of her mother's in London.

Lucy told everyone at school that London was 'quite definitely the place to be', and she even pretended that *she* had actually persuaded her mother to let her go and live with her great-aunt.

Lucy had become very good at pretending, like when the boys who said they loved her fumbled clumsily with her clothing, their hands hot and sweaty on her body. She pretended to herself that she enjoyed what they were doing; that she liked the way they touched her...wanted her, when in fact what she really felt inside was very afraid and very alone. She would never admit that to anyone, though. Not to anyone.

At eighteen Lucy left school and then drifted casually from job to job. Jobs were plentiful in London and Lucy was too busy enjoying herself to think about things as dull and boring as the future.

She was no longer living with her great-aunt. Now she shared a flat with three other girls; and not always the same three other girls. Life was casual, careless; Lucy was popular and sought-after. By the time she was twenty-one she had been engaged three times and had turned down several other proposals.

But deep down inside, despite her popularity, Lucy was afraid...afraid that somehow she was not worthy of being loved, afraid that when men said they loved her they did not mean it. Her father had said he loved her but it had not been true. He had left her. And so had her mother.

Lucy was determined that if there was any more leaving to be done she would be the one to do it, and she did.

She had turned from a pretty girl into a stunningly beautiful and sensual young woman. Men were fascinated by her. She was more cautious now, though, more wary; less inclined to give anything of herself. She had learned that men valued best that which was the hardest to obtain. Lucy took care to make sure that she was very hard to obtain. Impossibly hard, in most cases.

And then she met Giles.

She was working for an upmarket London PR firm. Giles worked for a recruitment agency which was head-hunting for a new advertising director for the company.

He came in one afternoon to see Lucy's boss. And then he returned, the next day and the next, for the rest of the week in fact, until he finally plucked up the courage to ask her out.

He wasn't Lucy's type at all, too shy, too quiet, but he continued to besiege her until finally, out of a mixture of exasperation and amusement, she went out with him.

It was only after her fifth date with him that Lucy admitted to herself that, while he might not be her type, she was enjoying the way he treated her, the way he spoiled and pampered her. Not in the financial sense— Lucy wasn't particularly impressed by money as money, although she had a love of rich things that made her sensually materialistic. No, it was the way Giles bathed her in his obvious love for her, the way he surrounded her with it, wrapped her in it; the way when they were out together he so patently never even thought of looking at anyone else.

Lucy was a beautiful young woman but her up-bringing, her insecurities and the type of men she had dated before had taught her that, while she might be valued and wanted for her physical appearance, her es-corts were constantly and sometimes not even very tact-fully checking to make sure that she, their date, was the most attractive woman in the room; that the other men were aware who she was with, that they were envying them because she was with them.

With Giles there was none of that, and yet it was plain that he was totally bemused, totally head over heels in

love with her. Lucy, starved all her life of such unques-
tioning love, responded to it.

The sharply clever manner she adopted with other men
softened when she was with Giles. When they were
together she started to shed the outer of her many layers
of protective cynicism. When he kissed her and she felt
his body tremble, instead of inwardly mocking him for
his weakness she found that she wanted to cling to him
and hold him.

She had assumed from his manner towards her that
Giles would be a tentative, hesitant lover, but when he
stumblingly invited her to spend a long weekend with
him she discovered otherwise.

He did not, as others had, take her to an expensive,
prestigious hotel where he could show her off during the
day to the other envious male guests, and where at night
he could make love to her in the anonymous surroundings of their hotel bedroom.

Instead Lucy discovered that he had rented what he
hesitantly described as 'a cottage', though not some
rough, ill-equipped and damp affair as she had dreaded.
No, he had displayed far greater sensitivity than that,
and what intrigued and tantalised her even more was
that he had also displayed how keenly aware he was of
what pleased her. Because the cottage was, in fact, a
small country house, not very far from Bath, since, as
he told her hesitantly when they arrived, he had thought
she might like to visit Bath while they were staying in
the area.

'I believe there are some very good shops,' he told
her, clearing his throat a little uncertainly and looking
hesitantly at her in the half-light of the evening.

Shops! Lucy smiled to herself. Giles was far more per-
ceptive than she had realised. There was nothing she enjoyed more than shopping. She remembered for the first
time with a faint touch of self-dislike the occasions in
the past when she had subtly manoeuvred a previous

unwilling escort into taking her shopping, and when she had normally also managed to inveigle him into buying her something.

Her machinations had never bothered her in the past, so why did she feel this unexpected dislike at the thought of cynically coaxing Giles into buying her something? She dismissed the thought, wondering if the 'cottage' would be as presentable inside as it was out.

It was set in its own large gardens, and, from what she could see of them in the dusk, they were softly pretty with flowers, climbing roses and clematis, a perfect complement for the softly washed pink-tinged front of the house.

She wasn't disappointed.

Inside, the house smelled of polish and fresh flowers, which were everywhere, and in her favourite colours as well, she observed as she walked silently through the downstairs rooms and the hall, with its polished floor and rugs, its circular polished table with the huge display of delphiniums, and larkspurs in their lavender-blues and lilacs spiked with white.

The sitting-room was large and elegantly furnished, off-white settees with mounds of cushions, sofa tables with displays of flowers, this time in creams and soft pinks, huge overblown roses that looked as though they had come straight from some country garden.

She touched the petals of one of them. It was still slightly damp, as though it had actually just been picked.

A log fire, a *real* one, burned in the hearth, the faint smell of seasoned logs mingling with the scent of the roses.

Behind her she heard Giles saying roughly, 'They reminded me of you, of the colour and texture of your skin, of the way you smell,' and then he was holding her, burying his mouth in the nape of her neck and then the side of her throat, and she realised that he had actually chosen the flowers himself.

Something inside her, some hard, tight part of her which had never been breached, swelled and ached with the emotion she had locked away inside it. Astoundingly she felt her eyes prick with tears and her heart... her *heart*, not just her body, ache with feeling.

Giles was pressed up hard against her back. She could feel him trembling, knew how much he wanted her, and yet he still released her, apologising rawly, 'I'm sorry. That was crass of me.'

Lucy looked at him. One of her flatmates had commented on how attractive he was, how solid and male-looking. She herself hadn't really been aware of it before, but now suddenly she was.

Angry with herself and for some reason a little afraid, she reacted instinctively, adopting her normal manner of protective cynicism, shrugging as she flicked the petals of one of the roses with her polished fingertips and commenting, 'Well, there certainly isn't any need to rush, is there? I mean, we've got the whole long weekend. Four whole days.'

The look in Giles's eyes stunned her.

'A lifetime wouldn't be enough for me, Lucy,' he told her hoarsely.

After that, to be allowed to go upstairs on her own while he unpacked the car threw her a little.

The house had five bedrooms, two with their own bathrooms. She chose the smaller of these, oddly drawn by its softly pretty country décor. The ceiling sloped down to a pair of dormer windows, and it had been papered with a pretty cottagey paper. The bed was high and old-fashioned, with proper bedding instead of a duvet. The floor was carpeted in such a pale peach carpet that it made the whole room seem full of warmth and light.

The bathroom off the bedroom was simple and functional. The sanitary-ware was white and old-fashioned, the bath huge with enormous brass taps. As a con-

cession to modern-day living, a wall of neat cupboards
had been installed with, Lucy was pleased to see, mirrors
set above them and decent lighting. The floor was polished and sealed, a proper door on the shower instead
of the plastic curtain they had in the flat.

She heard Giles coming upstairs and opened the
bedroom door.

'I haven't booked dinner anywhere for us this evening,'
he told her awkwardly. 'I wasn't sure what you'd feel
like doing.'

It was obvious what he felt like doing, Lucy reflected
to herself. She was torn between irritation and a sudden
and sharply unexpected *frisson* of tension, of ner-
vousness almost. *Her*, nervous . . . and of *Giles*? Impossible.

'Well, what I feel like doing right now is having a
shower,' she told him coolly. 'And what I shan't feel like
doing afterwards is . . .' She hesitated deliberately,
watching him, waiting for him to become either angry
or hectoring, but instead he simply looked steadily back
at her. 'I'm hungry,' she told him pettishly, suddenly
unsure of herself, and afraid because of it. 'And I certainly don't intend to play the little woman and start
cooking.'

She reached out, took her case from him, and then
retreated, closing the bedroom door on him. She waited
for several minutes, wondering what he would do, and
then she heard him going back downstairs.

As she stripped off her clothes and showered she wasn't
sure whether she was pleased or disappointed that he
had taken her dismissal so calmly. Most of the men she
knew would have been demanding their pound of flesh
by now and no mistake.

She eyed herself in the mirrors as she stepped out of
the shower. She had a good body; her breasts were
perhaps a little fuller than fashion dictated, but her waist
was enviably narrow, her legs long and slender, her bone-

structure that of an expensive, fragile racehorse. Her skin gleamed with health and with the scented moisturiser she was fanatical about using. She had the beginnings of a soft peachy tan.

There was a hectic flush along her cheekbones and her eyes looked huge, as though she had been on drugs, she recognised tensely. She dried her hair and then took her time dressing and reapplying her make-up.

There was no sign of Giles. The house was so quiet that she even wondered if he had perhaps gone and left her, but when she went to the window and looked out she could just about make out the outline of the car in the darkness.

She opened the bedroom door and walked out. She had been through this often enough before to know what it was all about, she reminded herself as she walked downstairs.

So why was she feeling so nervous...so on edge?

She had almost reached the bottom step when the kitchen door opened and Giles appeared. He had changed too, and his hair was damp as though he had showered. He must, she realised on a small spurt of shock, have used one of the other rooms.

'Supper's ready,' he told her.

Supper was ready. Lucy stared at him. What had he done? Certainly he could not have sent out for a take-away, not here.

'I thought we'd eat in the sitting-room,' he added a little uncertainly.

Lucy nodded, for once lost for words.

An hour later, greedily eating the last of her chocolate mousse, she admitted to herself that she was impressed.

The food, which, Giles had told her shyly, he had brought with him in a hamper from London, had been wildly delicious and, she suspected, wildly expensive. There had been champagne, pink champagne, which she knew others looked down on, but which she loved.

They had started the meal with tiny wild strawberries, and then there had been delicious cold salmon served with delicately flavoured salads, a sorbet laced with something alcoholic, and then proper, darkly bitter chocolate mousse, and she had greedily eaten both hers and Giles's.

It had been food chosen not for a man but for a woman, and again she was confused by Giles's sensitivity in so accurately gauging her tastes.

Now, curled up on the settee while Giles removed the remains of their meal, she felt relaxed and replete. She felt, she recognised on a sudden startled stab of awareness, happy.

The scented candles Giles had lit while they ate still burned, filled the room with their fragrance, warm and musky. She breathed it in sensuously.

She was wearing a simple shift dress, simple in design, that was. It had been perilously expensive, so soft and fragile that all she was able to wear underneath it was a tiny pair of briefs.

Now as she moved into a more comfortable position on the settee she was aware of the sudden sharp peaking of her nipples, and the slow unfolding ache of desire inside her.

When Giles came back she smiled languorously at him, her eyes narrowed and mysterious. He came across to her, leaning over her. His hand cupped her face. It felt good against her skin, cool and firm. His thumb brushed the corner of her mouth, tentatively, hesitantly almost. She let her lips part, rubbing the tip of his thumb with her tongue, her eyes closing sensuously, but there was nothing calculated or deliberate about the gesture, she *was* genuinely aroused, and as she arched up towards Giles she heard him mutter thickly. 'Oh, God, *Lucy* . . .'

He had never kissed her so fiercely before, so hungrily. She heard him telling her unsteadily that she tasted of chocolate, but then she teased him with her tongue and he stopped saying anything.

She had never, she realised breathlessly later, wanted to make love so much with any man. Suddenly she couldn't wait to be rid of her clothes and for Giles to be rid of his. She could feel how aroused he was and that knowledge excited her.

She tugged impatiently at the buttons on his shirt, spreading her hands flat against his chest, licking and nuzzling his bare throat and then his chest, laughing softly as she heard him groan and felt the sweat springing up on his skin.

He fumbled with the zip on her dress the first time he tried to unfasten it, but instead of irritating her his hesitancy only seemed to sharpen the excitement coiling inside her. When he finally unfastened it and the dress slid to a silky heap at her feet, leaving her body virtually naked, gilded by the light of the candles, its sheen enhanced by the soft cream backdrop of the settee, the dark arousal of her nipples as perfect as the deepest of the velvet-petalled roses, Giles didn't touch her. He simply looked at her.

Men had looked at Lucy before, but none of them had ever looked at her like this, as though they were beholding a miracle, a vision; none of them had ever looked at her with heaven in his eyes.

And then he started to touch her, to kiss her, not hesitantly or half clumsily, as she had expected, but with a true lover's sensitive awareness of every minute response she made, so that when she quivered as his mouth touched the sensitive cord in her neck he kissed it again slowly and lingeringly. And when her nipple swelled tautly in the moist heat of his mouth he knew that she wanted him to caress her there, without her having to say or do anything to tell him so.

His knowledge of how to please her was something that shocked her almost as much as her own quick, almost avid sexual response to him. She found that she was piqued, jealous almost of where he might have gained that knowledge, of the woman or women with whom he had learned such unexpected skills.

But, as Giles told her later, his sexual experience was far less than hers, and what had guided him, motivated him had been his need to please her, to love her.

The climax that shook her body long before he entered her caught them both off guard, Lucy doubly so because it was an alien sensation to her to have her body so completely out of her own control.

Giles was not a selfish lover, nor a demanding one, and nor, she discovered to her astonishment, would he allow her to even the score with the quick, deft manipulation of her hand.

When she drew back from him, startled to have her hand gently but very definitely removed from his body, he told her quietly, 'When it happens I want it to be when I'm inside you.'

She made a brief, automatic inviting movement, but he shook his head.

'No,' he told her huskily. 'I want you to want it as well.'

Later she did, laughing a little at him when it was over so quickly, recovering the control she felt she had lost when her body had responded to him so completely earlier.

She fell asleep in his arms, something so alien to her that to wake up and discover that she was in bed with him, and to know that he must have carried her upstairs while she slept, sent a *frisson* of apprehension along her spine.

To quell it she woke him up and made love to him passionately, almost angrily, her anger dissolving into tears of release when her body was overwhelmed by the intensity of her orgasm.

When she woke up in the morning she was alone. She turned her head, glancing at where Giles had slept, the pillow smelling faintly of him. She moved, turning her face into it, her emotions torn between a helpless awareness of how different he was from anyone else she had known and an instinctive fear of that difference and what it was doing to her.

He came back while she was lying there. He had, she realised when she saw the tray he was carrying, brought her her breakfast... *her* breakfast, she noticed, and not his: orange juice, which looked as though it had been freshly squeezed, warm croissants, honey and tea—proper tea, not the insipid tea-bag variety they normally had in the flat, and all served on a tray with a cloth and proper china, and, instead of the too perfectly tightly furled hot-house-grown rosebud which always seemed *de rigueur* in the hotels in which she had stayed with previous lovers, Giles had picked from the garden a jugful of fully open, softly petalled roses.

She buried her face in them, breathing in their scent, not wanting him to see the stupid tears burning her eyes.

'Where's *your* breakfast?' she asked him when she judged that her voice was steady enough for her to do so.

The smile he gave her was rueful, boyish almost. 'I had bacon and eggs,' he told her. 'I didn't think you'd appreciate the smell. I thought I'd walk down to the village and get some papers—let you eat in peace.'

It shocked her that he should know her so well already, that he should know that after the intimacy they had shared she now needed some time to herself, to distance herself a little from the intensity of that intimacy, to recover the emotional isolation that was so necessary to her.

She was a sensual woman, but she was also one who had absorbed too many of the sexual insecurities suffered by her mother when she was abandoned by Lucy's father.

Although when making love she had no inhibitions at all about her body, she preferred to perform the ritual of cleansing her skin, of preparing herself for the world, on her own.

While she could enjoy the love-play that went with sharing a shower or a bath with her lover, she did not like to share what was to her the greater intimacy of preparing herself to face the outside world. No man had ever realised that so immediately and instinctively as Giles had known it.

After he had gone she pictured him making her breakfast, squeezing the oranges, picking the roses. So much care...so much planning must have gone into every fine detail of this weekend with her. She liked that. She liked knowing that he had gone to so much trouble. Where another woman might have disliked his lack of spontaneity, Lucy did not. To her spontaneity equalled fecklessness, the same restlessness which had driven her father to leave her mother. Giles wasn't like that. Giles was careful, thoughtful. He made plans.

It was a magical weekend, extended by an extra two days because neither of them could bear to break the spell.

Once Giles could add knowledge to his love for her, his lovemaking took on a special quality that took it worlds beyond anything Lucy had known before.

And it wasn't just in bed that he surprised and delighted her. He took her out, sightseeing, shopping, entrancing her with his determination to spoil and indulge her.

It was only when they were driving back to London that he confessed to her that he hadn't hired the house at all, but that it belonged to his godmother.

Lucy already knew that both his parents were dead. He had been born to them late in their lives, an only child maybe, but one who had still had the love of both his parents.

When he said he loved her he meant it, Lucy recognised, and she was beginning to suspect that she loved him as well.

Strangely, that did not terrify her as it might once have done, and when three months later he proposed, she accepted.

They were idyllically happy. Secure for the first time in her memory, gradually Lucy let her defences down.

Children, he must want children. She had tested him before they were married, but he had shaken his head and told her roughly that *she* was all that he wanted.

'Maybe one day, if you want them,' he had told her. 'But girls, Lucy, not boys, otherwise I shall be jealous of them.'

She had laughed then. His words seemed to set the final seal on her happiness.

And they had been happy, Lucy remembered achingly. Too happy perhaps. Perhaps the very quality and intensity of her happiness ought to have warned her.

She had never intended to become pregnant. It had been an accident; a brief bout of food poisoning which had nullified the effect of the contraceptive pill she was taking. By the time she realised she was pregnant it was too late for her to opt for an early termination.

She had been frantic at first, angry and resentful, with Giles as well as with the child she was carrying. She was thirty-three years old and the last thing she wanted was a baby.

Although she tried to suppress them, all the fears she had had before she fell in love with Giles resurfaced. She was alternately anxious and emotional, angry and depressed, but stubbornly she refused to explain to Giles what was wrong. He thought it was because she was pregnant without wanting to be and that she blamed him for it, when in fact she was suddenly terrified of turning into her mother; of producing a child which Giles would reject along with her.

She couldn't analyse her fears and she certainly could not discuss them with anyone. Her doctor was old-fashioned and disapproved of mothers-to-be being anything other than docilely pleased with their condition.

The more her pregnancy developed, the more afraid Lucy became, the more trapped and angry she felt. And as the weeks went by she could almost feel Giles withdrawing from her. Where once he had always slept as close to her as he could, now he turned away from her in bed.

Her body was changing. She was carrying a lot of water with the baby, which made her seem huge. It was no wonder Giles didn't want her any more. He denied it, though, and claimed that it was for *her* sake, because he could see how tired she was, how great her discomfort.

She couldn't sleep at night, twisting and turning. She woke up one night and Giles wasn't there. She found him sleeping peacefully in the spare room. She woke him up, furious with him, blaming him for everything, telling him how much she hated him . . . how much she hated the baby.

She felt more afraid and alone than she had ever felt in her life. She was so used to having Giles to lean on, having Giles to love her, and now suddenly it seemed as though he didn't any more.

She couldn't bear people asking her about the baby, and when they did her whole body would tense with rejection, but some instinct she hadn't known she possessed drove her.

She found she was instinctively adjusting her diet; exercising her body less vigorously, sleeping for longer; it was as though some part of her outside her control was ensuring that, despite her conscious resentment and misery, her baby was being well looked after.

The first time she felt the baby kick she was in the garden picking flowers for a dinner party. She dropped them in shock and stood there, her eyes suddenly brilliant with tears, but when Giles came home she didn't say anything to him.

A gulf seemed to have opened between them. He couldn't even seem to look at her these days without wincing, and when he kissed her it was a chaste, dry peck on the cheek.

The people they were entertaining that evening were a local solicitor and his wife. Giles was well established at Carey's now, even though he detested Gregory James. He was not the kind of man who enjoyed pushing his way up the corporate ladder, and as long as he was happy Lucy had been happy as well. He was a good husband financially, generous, giving her her own allowance. His godmother had died just after their marriage and the money he had inherited from her he had invested to bring them in an extra income so that they lived very comfortably.

The solicitor's wife was a couple of years younger than Lucy but looked older. She had three young children, around whom her entire life revolved.

'Has the baby kicked yet?' she asked Lucy over dinner. 'I remember the first time John did ... I couldn't wait to tell Alistair. We spent all evening with me with my tum exposed and Alistair's hand on it just so that he wouldn't miss it if it happened again. And it was the middle of winter.'

Lucy's hand shook as she tried to eat her food. Giles couldn't bear to look at her now, never mind touch her, or at least that was how it seemed.

When Lucy was just over six months pregnant she went into premature labour. Giles was away on business for Carey's and so there was no one to accompany her when the ambulance screamed to a halt outside the house, summoned by the alert doctor's receptionist's response to her frightened telephone call.

The baby, a boy, was born before Giles arrived. She wasn't allowed to hold him. He was taken away to be placed in an incubator. He was very frail, the hospital told them when Giles arrived two hours later, white and strained, having received a message relayed from the hospital via his secretary.

Lucy was too shocked and drugged to take in much of what was being said. It had all been so unexpected. There had been no warning signs, nothing she had felt or done.

It happened like that sometimes, the nurses soothed her, but Lucy couldn't let it rest. She felt guilty that somehow *she* was the one responsible for the baby's too early birth. She wanted desperately to see him, but had lost a lot of blood and they didn't want her to move.

In the morning she could see her son, they told her, and Giles, who had been terrified when he walked into the ward and saw how pitifully small and frail she looked, tried awkwardly to describe their child to her.

His halting, terse description seemed to reinforce to Lucy that she had failed, and that he was angry with her because it was her fault that the baby had been born too soon, when in reality what Giles was trying to do was to blot out his mental image of the appalling fragility of the little figure he had seen through the screen that separated him from the premature-baby unit, and the wires and tubes that had been attached to his son's minute body.

He hadn't realised until he saw him just how much the sight of his own child would affect him. He had known that Lucy did not want children, and he loved her so much that he had been happy with that. He had seen how angry she was when she found out she was pregnant, and he had known that she blamed him.

All through her pregnancy his guilt had increased. He had seen the discomfort she was in. He had tried his best not to exacerbate things for her. He had even started sleeping in another room in case his need for her overwhelmed him. He ached so much to touch her, to explore and know the rounding contours of her body. He was amazed at how very sensual and arousing he found the visible signs of her pregnancy, at how much he wanted to make love to her, a reaffirmation of all that he felt for her and for the child they had made between them, and then he had been ashamed of his need, reminding himself that Lucy did not share the joy he was beginning to feel in the coming baby.

Now, in the hospital, trying to describe their son to her, he ached with the love the sight of him had stirred up inside him, and with the fear. He was so small ... so fragile. He could feel the tears clogging his throat, burning his eyes, and he knew he mustn't cry in front of Lucy. He turned away from her, unaware of the hand she had stretched out towards him as she tried to find the words to plead with him to tell her more about their child.

She ached inside with the loss of him. A feeling she had never known she could experience overwhelmed her. She wanted her child here with her, in her arms, at her breast, and that need was a physical pain that wrenched apart her whole body.

In the end, hours after Giles had gone home, they let her see him, afraid that if they didn't she would work herself up into a fever anyway.

The nurse who wheeled her down to the prem unit warned her what to expect.

'He's very small,' she told her quietly. 'And very frail, I'm afraid.'

Lucy didn't hear her. 'My child ... my son.' Her body tensed, aching with love and fear.

The small room seemed so full of equipment that the five incubators were almost lost among the paraphernalia of monitors and tubes.

The nurse on duty stood up, frowning a little as Lucy was wheeled in, but Lucy was oblivious to her presence. All her attention was concentrated on the tiny baby in its incubator; the sole occupant of the small ward, her baby...her son. Without realising what she was doing she stood up, her body trembling as she left the wheelchair, ignoring the protests of the attendant nurse, the weakness of her own body forgotten as she stumbled across to the incubator.

The baby was lying on his back, his head turned towards her, his eyes open. She shuddered as she saw the mass of tubes attached to him and the way his tiny, fragile body fought to take in oxygen. His entire body from head to toe was only a little longer than a grown man's hand, his limbs so delicate and fragile that his vulnerability made Lucy tremble with anguish and love.

Her impulse to reach into the incubator and pick him up was so strong that she could barely resist it. Her body ached with tenderness and despair. The intensity of the emotion that gripped her was like nothing she had ever experienced or imagined experiencing. Every other aspect of her life faded into oblivion as she looked at her baby and saw him look back at her. The pain of wanting to reach out and touch him, to hold him, and of knowing that for his sake she could not do so, that to even attempt to do so would be to endanger his life, filled her whole body.

As she watched him she prayed for his survival and knew that she would sacrifice anything, even her own life, for him, and the fact that she had once not wanted him or any other child was forgotten in the wave of love that swamped her. She stood motionlessly watching him, pleading silently.

Please God, let him live. Let him live. The sin, the guilt is mine. Please don't punish him because I thought I didn't want him.

But her prayers went unanswered. He was a strong baby, they told her compassionately later, but just not strong enough. He had been born too soon and his body was just not developed enough to sustain him outside the womb.

Lucy knew before they came to tell her that he had gone. She had spent every moment they allowed her in the unit, watching over him, afraid even to look away from him, silently, fiercely supporting him with her strength and her love, willing him to go on living, but finally the staff overruled her protests that she must stay with him, and she was wheeled back to her bed. She had lost a good deal of blood, they reminded her, and she was still far from fully recovered herself.

When Giles arrived she wept and begged him to make them let her stay with Nicholas, and when Giles told her that he agreed with the staff that she must recoup some of her own strength she turned away from him and refused to speak to him.

The rift that had developed between them while she was pregnant seemed to have deepened with Nicholas's premature birth.

Although she did not know it, Giles blamed himself for not being there with her when she went into labour. At the back of his mind lay the feeling that somehow, if he had been, things might have been different.

It had shocked him when he arrived at the hospital to see how ill Lucy looked. He had been so desperately afraid then that he might lose her that for a moment he had actually forgotten their child.

Their child. His heart ached with the weight of his love for Nicholas. A love he couldn't find the words to express, especially not to Lucy.

Nicholas's birth had changed her completely. The girl who had so fiercely resented her pregnancy had become a sad-eyed, haunted woman who seemed barely aware that anyone other than her child existed. She seemed to have distanced herself from him completely. When he touched her she winced away from him. He could see in her eyes now her anger and bitterness.

'Giles, please. I must be with him . . . I must.'

Her voice had started to rise, panic flooding her as the need inside her fought against her physical weakness, her inability to get up and go to her child.

Tears filled her eyes. She didn't want to cry, she wanted to scream, to rage, to vent her anger and her fear, to somehow make them understand that she must be with her child, but already a nurse was hurrying towards her bed, holding her wrist, telling her firmly that she must not upset herself.

She tried to fight off the drug they gave her, forcing her weighted eyelids not to drop, focusing bitterly on Giles's blurring face as she lost her battle.

She woke up abruptly hours later, her heart pounding, her mouth dry. It was just gone two o'clock, and she knew immediately why she was awake.

She heard the door to the ward open quietly and saw the nurse coming in, heading for the small curtained area at the end of the ward. She wanted to cry but she couldn't; the pain was too great for that.

Giles. Where was Giles? Why wasn't he here with her? Didn't he care?

Outside the premature-baby unit, Giles leaned back in his chair, blinking his eyes rapidly. He couldn't believe it was over. They had told him to go home after they had given Lucy the sleeping drug but he hadn't been able to do so. He could still see the way she had pleaded with them to let her be with Nicholas.

Had she known? He shuddered, weighed down by his sense of guilt and failure, and the ache of loss. Their child, their son... his son. Born and now dead.

He stayed until a doctor gently insisted that he must leave; that he must go home and rest because Lucy would need him when she woke up and was told the news.

Giles wanted to tell her how much he wanted to hold his child... how much he wanted to lift him from his cradle of plastic and metal—after all, they could not save him now—and hold him against his body, flesh to flesh, father to child. That he wanted to pour out to him all the love he felt for him, but he just could not find the words, and so instead he nodded and stumbled out of the hospital into the cold of the pre-dawn summer morning.

They would not wake Lucy until nine, they told him kindly. That would give him time to have a brief rest and get back to be with her.

It was not his fault, nor the hospital's, that Lucy did not need to be wakened.

She waited until the nurses changed shift. There was a new nurse, a trainee, the ward was busy, and it was easy for Lucy to convince the girl that she could manage to get to the bathroom unaided.

It took her a long time to make her way to the prem unit. She was still very weak. They hadn't told her just how much blood she had lost or just how much danger she had actually been in, and Lucy assumed that it was the drug they had given her that made her feel so unsteady.

The nurse in charge of the unit didn't see her until it was too late. The tubes had been removed from the incubator and Nicholas had been dressed in a set of minute doll's clothes, a white knitted romper suit embroidered with teddy bears in pale blue and yellow.

The mother of another premature baby had given the clothes to the hospital, and the nurse, who knew that she should have the strength to detach herself from her emotions, had cried a little as she dressed him in them.

She saw Lucy and knew immediately that there was no need to tell her anything, and she marvelled, not for the first time, at the power of maternal love. Silently she settled Lucy with Nicholas in her arms and then went to her office to ring Lucy's ward.

His body felt soft and warm so that it was almost possible for Lucy to believe that he was simply asleep. She touched his face. His skin felt so soft. He looked like Giles. She was sure of it. It was only when she kissed him that her control broke, her body racked by the shudders of pain that ached through her.

By the time Giles arrived they had sedated her, and, what with his concern over her and the arrangements for the funeral she insisted on holding, it never occurred to Giles to tell her how he had watched over Nicholas for her, or that he had been with him when he died.

In order to save her pain, Giles stripped the nursery and had it repainted while she was still in hospital. When he visited her he never mentioned the baby, and Lucy took this as a sign that he blamed her for Nicholas's death. But, no matter how much he blamed her, he couldn't blame her as much as she blamed herself. She hadn't wanted her baby and so fate had decreed that she shouldn't have him.

At the hospital they offered her counselling, but she refused it. The other mothers who had lost their children *wanted* them. She deserved the pain she was suffering now. She wasn't like them.

At home with Giles she didn't discuss Nicholas. She had a Polaroid photograph of him, which she studied obsessively when she was on her own.

Giles was spending more and more time at work. When he came home he looked drained and exhausted, but Lucy was barely aware of him. She had shut herself away from him, from everyone, retreating to a place where no one could reach her, possessed by a pain and a guilt so deep that they left no room for anything else.

It was over six months after Nicholas's birth before Giles attempted to make love to her. She turned away from him immediately, unable to bear the thought of allowing herself the comfort of his lovemaking. Why should *she* have any comfort? She didn't deserve any. What comfort had Nicholas had? Denied his right to life by his own mother.

Giles, not understanding what she was feeling, thought she was rejecting him and that she still blamed him because she had not been with Nicholas when he died.

Neither of them talked about what was happening. Giles felt too heart-sick and alone, and Lucy could only think of Nicholas. If she had carried him to full term he would have been three months old by now. Sitting up, smiling, laughing, his eyes wide and dark, their pupils dilated and out of focus as he suckled at her breast.

Her body still ached for him and she knew that it always would.

The months passed and slowly Lucy became aware of how much Giles had withdrawn from her. They still shared the same bed, occasionally they made love, but all the old joy and sharing had gone from it. Giles no longer told her how much he wanted her, how much she aroused him, how much he loved and desired her.

She began to suffer feelings of intense panic and rage, a growing fear that Giles would be taken from her like Nicholas, a growing conviction that she deserved to lose him just as she had deserved to lose their child, and, being Lucy, she kicked out against that fear, fighting it with furious outbursts against Giles for spending so little time with her, with passionate demands for his love-making, alternated with weeks when she was cold and distant with him.

This was what she had always feared . . . what her mother had told her was the fate of any woman who did

not give her husband sons. When Giles grew impatient
and irritable with her she told herself it was because of
Nicholas. When she saw the way he smiled at Davina,
when she heard the affection in his voice when he talked
about her, she told herself that he was turning against
her because she had lost his child...his son. That he
was rejecting her in the same way that her father had
rejected her mother and ultimately her.

Lucy's violent mood swings, her outbursts of temper,
confused and dismayed Giles. The more Lucy panicked
and tried to reach out to him by raging verbally at him,
the more he retreated into the silence of his own
confusion.

He loved her still, of course he did, but he was
exhausted by the uncertainty of her moods, and he
dreaded the anger that would boil up inside her and ex-
plode into a rage of screaming invective against him.

Looking at the past was like looking back down a long,
dark tunnel, Lucy reflected wearily. She knew that once
Giles had loved her, that his whole world had been built
around her, but now that love was lost to her, and soon
Giles too could be lost to her.

She didn't want to lose him. She still loved him, she
ached to be able to tell him so, but every time she tried
she remembered Nicholas and her guilt and misery would
paralyse her.

She didn't deserve Giles's love. She had killed their
baby and she must be punished for it.

Davina would never scream that she did not want a
child. Davina would never deny the child her body was
carrying. Davina would sail through her pregnancies as
calmly and placidly as she did everything else. Davina
would give Giles healthy children; sons.

She knew that Davina had not consciously done anything to come between her and Giles but she was there,
and Giles admired and desired her.

What was she supposed to do? What could she do?

CHAPTER SEVEN

SAUL had not planned to make any breaks in his journey, but a hold-up on the motorway had delayed him and he had rung Christie from his car to warn her that he would be arriving later than they had arranged.

She had laughed, telling him not to worry, adding drily that she hoped he wasn't expecting to arrive to find a cordon-bleu-standard cooked meal waiting for him.

'I'm working on my notes for this damned conference,' she told him, adding ruthlessly, 'besides, eating heavy meals after four in the afternoon isn't good for the digestive system.'

'Don't worry, there's no need to apologise,' Saul assured her, grinning to himself as he caught her sharp intake of breath and heard her fierce and immediate,

'I wasn't *apologising*.'

She had always risen quickly to the bait, as impulsive and sometimes as ungoverned as he was controlled and careful. They had quarrelled fiercely sometimes during their growing years, Christie accusing him of benefiting from their father's favouritism to her disadvantage.

He had denied it then, too full of youthful male arrogance to see the pain behind her anger. Now he understood her far better. She had far more ambition than him and it was channelled into her own beliefs and goals, unlike his.

He frowned as he hung up. What was the matter with him? It was too easy to blame his father for his present dissatisfaction with his life, too easy and unfair. His father had never forced or coerced him into doing anything.

He realised just in time that he was approaching his motorway exit. He would be at Christie's sooner than he had expected after all.

Half an hour later he drove through Thresham. The small market town was virtually deserted. Too small to attract the attention of the planners of the sixties, it still had its narrow streets and its huddle of timber-framed and small Georgian houses.

He winced though to see the neon sign of a fast-food restaurant in the town square, although, to judge from the group of teenagers gathered outside it, not everyone shared his aversion. Fast food wasn't a wholly new invention after all, he mused. One only had to think of the pie and sweetmeat sellers who would have thronged this square on a busy market day.

He couldn't be very far away from Carey Chemicals, he realised, and on a sudden impulse he pulled to the side of the road and opened his briefcase, searching for the map and plan that had accompanied the investigator's report.

He had virtually to drive past Carey's on his way to his sister's. It was gone nine o'clock and going dark. A good time to take a discreet and unofficial look at the place.

Carey's had long ago ceased to need to run shift work, and as far as he knew from the report there was no official nightwatchman. What was the need? Carey's had precious little left to steal. Gregory James had seen to that.

He found the lane easily enough. It was bumpy, untarmacked, and in the glare from his headlights he could see the signpost indicating 'Walkers, this way'. He had forgotten that the site was bisected by a right of way that ran virtually through its centre.

Alex would not like that. Or at least he would not have liked it had he genuinely been intending to run the company as a going concern, instead of merely using it in order to take advantage of the proposed government grants.

Saul could see the purpose of the government's scheme. It would be a good way of both furthering research into new drugs, and at the same time ensuring that the expense of successful ones was kept to a minimum for the National Health Service. But how many people would see it as Alex was doing, as a means purely of boosting their own profits?

Why should he concern himself over that? It was more Christie's territory than his. She was the guardian of the family's morals, not he.

He would have to be careful about what he told her, he admitted wearily as he parked his car and switched off the engine. He frowned to himself, aware of a growing sense of distaste for what he was going to have to do.

But what was the alternative? Give up his job. He would never get another. Alex would see to that. He had an ex-wife and two children. He couldn't afford moral scruples.

But could he afford not to have them? Could he go on the way he was, with the canker of self-dislike eating into him, destroying him?

As he got out of his car he heard an owl hooting. When he looked up he saw the small bodies of tiny bats swooping and darting around the upper storey of the old corn mill.

He paused for a moment to study their busy movements. As a boy he had lived in East Anglia, flat, open countryside where in those days it had been safe for a child to roam at will. In his imagination he had travelled the secret fens with the free traders, evading the government's excise men sent to hunt them and their illegal cargoes of French goods down, and then when he was older he had spent endless hours studying the wildlife with his father.

He felt a sudden ache deep inside. He had loved his father so much, wanted to please him...wanted to make up to him for all that his own life had lacked; to give him the success he had wanted so much. But his father was dead and had been for nearly ten years, and there was no one in his life to whom he could offer the gift of attaining his father's ambitions for him.

A feeling of intense melancholy, of loneliness swept over him. He was tired of the way he was living, of the cynicism that had eroded the brightness of his dreams. He was tired of the constant power struggle with Alex, but most of all he was tired of himself, he acknowledged as he turned on his heel and walked over to the buildings.

Davina sighed as she closed her office door. The corridor lights were off but she knew her way well enough, and there was just enough light from outside to lessen the darkness.

It had been a long day. This morning she had had a deputation from the shop stewards representing the unions. They had wanted to know what was going to happen to the company.

She had answered them as honestly as she could, and she had seen the fear in their eyes when she was forced to admit the possibility of the company's having to close. She was hoping that they could find a buyer, she had told them.

'Who the hell would want to buy this place?' one of the men had demanded sourly. 'We're working in conditions that aren't fit or safe.'

Davina flushed at the accusation in his voice. There was nothing she could do to refute it. She had seen their working conditions for herself and had been appalled by them.

'I'm sorry, but there just hasn't been the money to re-equip,' she had told them, but her voice had faltered as she thought about the money that Gregory had gambled away.

She was a rich man's daughter, and, although she had learned young to be frugal, over the last few years she had indulged herself with the luxury of good, well made clothes, expensive clothes; and she had been acutely conscious of the fact that the suit she was wearing had probably cost more than many of her employees earned in a month, even though it was several years old.

She had seen in the eyes of the two women shop stewards present that they were equally aware of the disparity in their situations, and again guilt had engulfed her.

A buyer. Would the bank be able to find one? The manager had warned her that he had grave doubts.

She had reached the reception area, which was empty and in darkness. The air smelled stale and faintly dirty. While no expense had been spared in fitting out Gregory's office, the reception area, the first place a potential customer saw on his or her arrival, was shabby and unappealing. Davina's nose wrinkled in faint distaste as she hurried through it, opening the door and stepping out into the pleasantly fresh evening air.

She locked the door and then turned round. Her car was several yards away. As she hurried towards it she turned the corner of the building without looking up, her mind on the company and her problems, so that the totally unexpected sensation of walking straight into another person, when she had believed herself to be completely alone, sent her body into an automatic physical reflex action of panic.

The man—she knew it was a man even before she was able to look properly at him—caught hold of her as she tried to step back from him. She tensed as she felt his fingers gripping her arms, all the warnings she had read and heard about the danger of being a woman out at night on her own suddenly flooding terrifyingly through her.

The man was holding her too tightly for her to break free, and so instead she beat frantically at his chest and heard the surprised exhalation of air he gave.

That calmed her a little, making him suddenly seem less powerful, making it obvious that the contact between them had shocked him as much as it had done her.

At the same time Saul realised how much he had startled her. He had seen her coming round the corner, walking quickly, her head down, but it had been too late for him to call out a warning to her and she had walked straight into him.

Now he reacted instinctively to her panic, pulling her close against his own body and holding her pinioned firmly there while he told her quietly, 'It's all right. I'm not going to hurt you.'

She looked up at him then, a quick, startled, questioning look that fully revealed her face to him.

Davina James.

He recognised her immediately from her photograph, but what the photograph had not told him was how oddly fragile she was, how large and brilliant her eyes, how vulnerable the soft fullness of her mouth.

She was trembling slightly. He could feel the fast race of her heart, and to his own surprise he reacted instinctively to the subliminal messages of her body, tightening his grip on her, realigning his body slightly so that there was less distance between them, and then stopping abruptly as he realised what he was doing, halted by the sudden sharp awareness of how quickly and unexpectedly his physical responses had changed from an instinctive reaching out to fend off her unsuspecting collision with him, an action he would have used to anyone, either man or woman, to something that was only just a hair's breadth away from outright physical arousal.

What was the matter with him? He was daily in just as close physical contact with dozens of women, beautiful young, desirable women. No one who worked in a city environment could not be. Every day there were countless small incidents of accidental close physical contact, in lifts, on the Tube, in offices. The accidental brushing together of human bodies in the close, confined spaces of modern living was a fact of life, and it was certainly not something that normally disturbed him.

In fact... He grimaced to himself, unwilling to admit how long it had been since he had even fleetingly thought about sex, never mind had it. There just wasn't the room in his life to form that kind of relationship and just lately there hadn't even been the need.

'Let me go.'

The furious words brought him back to reality. He stepped back a little, flexing his fingers, thinking quickly.

Now that she was over her initial shock, she was furiously angry; angry enough, he recognised, to jeopardise all his plans before he had even begun to put them into action. The last thing he needed now was to be reported to the police as a potential prowler or worse.

'I'm sorry,' he apologised, smiling at her, using the techniques of body language and control he had learned over the years, stepping back from her but trying to keep his face in the shadows, lifting up his hands, palms open.

Davina's heart was still beating too fast. He was well spoken, calm and authoritative, and now that he had released her her intuition told her that she was not in any physical danger from him.

'What are you doing here?' she demanded quietly. 'This is private property.' He might have apologised, he might have released her, but the adrenalin was still surging through her veins; shock and fear had turned to anger laced with the feeling of insecurity that came from

being in a situation that was not fully under her own
control.

She knew that she was probably over-reacting, but she
couldn't help it. Beneath her anger lay the uncomfortable knowledge that for a handful of seconds,
as he held her, she had felt an unmistakable *frisson* of
sexual awareness . . . of sexual need?

This was ridiculous. She wasn't some sexually deprived widow, desperate for physical contact with a man,
any man, because she had lost her husband.

If she wanted sex she could have it with Giles, couldn't
she?

The earthiness of her own thoughts blunted her anger,
filling her with self-distaste.

'I must have missed the footpath,' she heard Saul
telling her calmly.

It was a good job he had remembered that footpath
sign. It gave him a perfect excuse for being where he
was. He saw the hesitation in her eyes, and the quick
searching glance she gave him. Luckily he was casually
dressed.

A walker who had missed the signpost for the
footpath. It was quite feasible, of course. In fact, it did
sometimes happen, but it was already virtually dark. Too
dark for someone who didn't know where the footpath
lay to risk following it?

Contrarily, although she wanted to press him, to challenge him, something made her hold back. Caution. . .the
sense of self-preservation and hesitancy she had developed as a child; an awareness that it might not be
wise to ask questions whose answers might provoke the
still, placid waters of safety.

'The footpath is over there,' she told him curtly, gesturing towards the open fields.

'Thank you.' There was nothing in his voice to give
rise to the sharp quiver of tension that touched her. His

face was obscured by the shadows, but she caught the reflective glitter of his eyes as he answered her.

He was a tall man and lean, but unexpectedly hard-muscled. She shivered a little. It had been a long time since she had been in such close, intimate contact with a man's body.

Not really since Matt.

Matt...what on earth had made her think of him? There was no similarity between the two men at all. Matt had been just over average height, fair-haired, solid, an amiable, easygoing man, full of laughter and warmth, and her instincts told her that, quite apart from their physical differences, the last thing this man would be was easygoing.

But he had still, however briefly, made her sharply aware of her body's sexuality.

He was turning away from her now, walking with a long, well paced stride. She watched him until he was out of sight before heading for her car.

The unexpected encounter had disturbed her more than she wanted to admit.

Saul waited until he was sure she had gone before returning to his own car. There was no point in risking looking around now. She might just decide to come back.

As he started his car the file on the front passenger-seat slid forward, the contents coming out. As he reached out to pick them up Saul saw the photograph of Davina.

On paper Davina James had seemed the least important of the elements surrounding Alex's desire to buy out Carey's, but in the flesh... In the flesh she was threatening to complicate matters in a way that made him instinctively fight to suppress his awareness of those complications.

Anger, irritation and the familiar surging panic of somehow no longer being totally in control of every aspect of his life tensed his body.

He pushed Davina's photograph to the back of the other papers and stuffed them all quickly back into the file before driving off.

She supposed she ought to make herself some supper but she really wasn't hungry, Davina admitted as she let herself into the house. Instead she felt charged with an unfamiliar, disconcerting physical and emotional energy, a restlessness that matched her quickened heartbeat and tense movements.

It came to something when an accidental run-in with an unknown man could put her into such an advanced state of reaction, she thought grimly as she stared at her reflection in her bedroom mirror. Her face was slightly flushed, her eyes huge and dilated. Even her mouth seemed softer, fuller. As though she had been kissed.

She banished the thought, irritated that it should have formed at all. What was the matter with her? The last thing she had time for now was idiotic wayward thoughts of that kind. Hadn't she got enough to worry about without imagining...?

Imagining what? That he...the walker had kissed her? Thank God he hadn't done. The whole incident had been difficult enough for her to handle as it was.

She stripped off her suit and blouse. Being at Carey's always left her feeling grimy.

Matt had once told her that, per capita, English women had the best bodies in the world. The trouble was, he had added, that they were also the best at concealing that fact. He had then gone on to describe eloquently and erotically the visual delight a man might enjoy in observing the way an Italian woman wore her clothes and moved her body, or the subtle sensuality of cool hauteur that matched a Frenchwoman's immaculate grooming and posture.

It had been shortly after that that he had taken her to London shopping, exhausting her with his energy and his enthusiasm, and astonishing her with his concentration on even the smallest detail of not just how clothes were constructed but how they felt to the touch, how they moved, how they embraced a woman's body.

But then, of course, as an artist, such things had been important to him.

He was dead now, an accident in California. She had read about it in the papers and had quietly mourned his loss. Not as her lover, but as a gifted and talented man who had also possessed great humanity and generosity.

In her bathroom she stripped off her underwear, glancing briefly at her body in the mirrors. It had been Matt who had taught her not to be ashamed or embarrassed about her femininity, not to seek out its imperfections but instead to celebrate its individuality.

He had been a good man, a kind man, a man she had been lucky to know and whom she had never regretted knowing, but why on earth that walker tonight should have reminded her of him she had no idea.

She tensed as she saw the immediate sexual tension change her body, her breasts swelling slightly, lifting, her nipples erect, flushed with heat, her stomach muscles clenching, her stance altering infinitesimally in the way a woman's stance did when she thought about the intimate physical contact of standing close to a man she desired.

Irritated, impatient, and too much on edge, she turned away and stepped into the shower, lathering her body with quick efficiency and rinsing off the soap, reaching for her towel, firmly refusing to give in to the temptation of looking at herself in the mirror again.

What was she afraid of seeing?

Defiantly she stared into the mirror, throwing the damp towel to one side. Her body was slim and firm, her skin smooth and unblemished.

If she closed her eyes she could still remember how it had felt to have Matt's hands touching her, Matt's mouth on her skin. *Matt's* hands, *Matt's* mouth, not those of tonight's stranger, she told herself fiercely.

Matt. Not him ... *Matt*!

The first time she had met Matt had been one sultry afternoon when she'd returned from shopping to find him lifting the heavy stone slabs that formed what she had always privately considered to be a particularly ugly patio. She had mentioned a month earlier to the owner of the local garden-maintenance company they used that she would like to have that part of the garden re-designed, and he had promised to send someone round to look at it.

Matt, it transpired, was that someone. He had stopped work when he saw her and as her eyes had flicked uncomfortably away from his bare, sweat-damp torso he had reached easily for his discarded shirt, pulling it on, taking care to allow her to stay a comfortable distance away from him as he showed her the sketches he had prepared for a pretty paved sunken garden.

He had taken a temporary job on the landscaping side of the business, he told her later when she took him a cup of tea. Later still she learned that he and Owen Graham, who owned the company, had been at public school together. She also learned that Matt was a wanderer, a traveller, a man who could never be tied to one place or one person for very long.

She had been drawn to him immediately. There was something open and warm about him that touched her starved senses. She had no awareness of him in the sexual sense, not then. She had long ago abandoned any thoughts of herself as a sexually functioning woman, and especially as a desirable woman. She and Gregory no longer had sex, and she felt no desire to experience with another man the misery and sense of inadequacy she had suffered on her honeymoon.

Gregory had his other women. She had learned to recognise the signs and, while inwardly she ached with the pain of disillusionment of all that she had once thought her marriage would be compared with what it actually was, she told herself that in many ways Gregory was no worse than other women's husbands.

It was true that they might not be as persistently unfaithful as Gregory but, all too aware of her own inability to respond to him, she felt guiltily that she must just accept that he would seek sexual solace elsewhere.

The thought of divorcing him and perhaps beginning a new relationship with someone else was as alien to her as the thought of flying to Mars...

And it wasn't even as though she was particularly unhappy. Not now... she had been at first, but now she had learned to accept the limitations of their relationship and to live within them. She just wasn't the adventurous or independent type, she told herself when the small voice of despair and disillusionment deep inside her broke through the defences she had put up against it.

It had been at Gregory's insistence that she had handed over the care of the garden to Owen's company. She suspected that Gregory's insistence had more to do with appearance than because he wanted to spare her the hard work. Hard work which she had actually enjoyed, and which she still enjoyed.

She was trying an experiment with a group of pink hydrangeas in one of the borders through which she was growing a darker pink clematis, and she was just studying the effect of the first opening flowers of the clematis against the paler pinks of the hydrangeas one morning when she looked up to see Matt walking across the lawn towards her.

For some reason she suddenly felt oddly embarrassed and nervous. She flushed a little as he approached her, but he hadn't seemed to notice, remarking pleasantly, 'A good combination. You have a good eye for colour.'

'Not me,' Davina admitted, his calm words relaxing her. 'I'm afraid I'm only a copyist.'

'The effect is good none the less, and there's nothing wrong with being a copyist. That's how I've earned some of my best commissions.'

From her brief conversations with him, Davina had learned that Matt was an artist, who supplemented his small income from commission by doing casual work for a variety of friends.

He was a man of odd contrasts, physically sturdy and slightly heavily built, and yet unexpectedly deft and gentle in his movements; he worked manually, but his accent betrayed his upper-class origins.

She knew that he had never been married, and suspected that he cherished his freedom. He seemed to have travelled all over the world, and he was obviously intelligent as well as extremely articulate. But what surprised her most of all about him was his obvious lack of material ambitions.

He didn't run a car; he lived in a small cottage he was renting from a local farmer, laughing about its lack of facilities, its ancient stove and even more ancient hot-water system.

Davina laughed too as he described to her the rough shower arrangement he had rigged up in the yard, and then abruptly her stomach tensed, her body stilling with shock as she suddenly had a sharply clear-cut mental image of him standing there, his solidly muscled body glistening with moisture, his skin, water-sleek, tanned, furred by the soft golden hairs visible to her now on his arms.

Her mouth went very dry. She tried to swallow and was shaken by a fierce *frisson* of sensation that was so unexpected, so unfamiliar that the shock of it froze her. And then, as the mortified colour flooded her skin, she was frantically glad that Matt had had his back to her.

After that she kept away from the garden on the days when he was working, disturbed and distressed by her physical reaction to him, terrified that he might become aware of it and of embarrassing them both.

She missed the conversations she had had with him. She had recently discovered the books of Gertrude Jekyll and become a devoted fan of her work, and Matt had been a fund of knowledge about her colleagues and peers, especially the architect Sir Edwin Lutyens.

And then totally unexpectedly one morning when he was not due to work at all he arrived at the house with a brown-paper-covered package.

'I spotted this in a bookshop in Chester,' he told her as she invited him in.

Flustered, Davina offered him a cup of tea. He moved very easily and lightly for such a solidly built man and the realisation that he was standing directly behind her flustered her even more.

'What is it, Davina?' he asked her quietly, very gently taking hold of her and turning her round so that she was facing him. 'Is something wrong?'

She shook her head. Tiny thrills of sensation were running up her arms and down her body, sensations that sprang directly from the sensation of his hands on her bare arms.

'So you haven't been avoiding me as a means of telling me that you know how much I want you and that my wanting isn't reciprocated, then?'

Davina stared at him, as confused as though he had spoken to her in an unfamiliar language, which indeed he had. Davina was not used to hearing men telling her that they wanted her.

'Now I *have* shocked you.'

He was smiling. She could hear the rueful amusement in his voice, the total lack of embarrassment or self-consciousness.

'You're blushing,' he told her, releasing her arm to brush his knuckles gently across her hot face. And then he saw the tears filling her eyes. 'Davina, my dear, what is it?'

He was holding her now, holding her as a child and not a woman.

'Please don't cry. I never intended to upset you or offend you.'

'It isn't... You haven't...' she managed to tell him, and then, like the lancing of a too painful, too long-concealed inner wound, she was telling him about Gregory, about her marriage, and even, most astonishingly of all, about her own deep and humiliating fears that she was somehow unable to function properly as a sexual woman.

Matt let her talk, not trying to halt the tumultuous flood of half-sentences and words, letting the pain spill out of her to be soaked up by the comfort of his physical closeness, his gentle, accepting, uncritical silence.

Later, recalling the event, she would marvel at the extraordinary way in which she had so easily and so speedily cast aside the caution of a lifetime and confided to Matt things she had barely been able to allow herself to admit even in the privacy of her thoughts, but it was as though once she had started it was impossible for her to stop, impossible for her to stem the impulsive disjointed torrent of words that carried with them in their fast flow all the detritus of pain and insecurity she had carried with her for so long.

Matt let her speak, not trying to interrupt or stem the flood, and when the words had finally ceased to pour from her he produced a large crisply clean white handkerchief and commanded gently, 'Come on, blow.'

He was so calming and relaxed after the high emotion of her outpourings that it made Davina laugh.

'That's better,' Matt told her approvingly, and then while she was still looking up at him, laughter mingling with her tears, his expression changed, a subtle but somehow very distinctive change that made her heart beat faster and her body become charged with a different kind of emotion.

'I can't tell you why your husband doesn't want you, Davina,' he said softly. 'But what I *can* tell you is that it isn't any fault of yours, and as for your being sexually undesirable...' He smiled at her again, a rueful, slightly crooked smile that made her breath catch in her throat and her heartbeat rocket into sudden acceleration. 'Come and have supper with me tonight. I've had some ideas about the garden I'd like to discuss with you.'

He saw her expression and his smile deepened.

'It's all right,' he told her. 'I shan't try to seduce you. In my book, desire must be a mutual need in order to make it a mutual pleasure. I want you, Davina, and there's nothing I'd like more than to take you to bed and to show you all the reasons why that husband of yours is wrong, but until you tell me that you want me as well I shan't do so. You've nothing to *fear* from me, Davina.'

But everything to fear from herself, Davina acknowledged shakily. Common sense and caution told her to refuse his invitation, but recklessly, wantonly, she ignored their chiding voices.

Her father was away on a golfing holiday, and tonight, as with most nights unless they were entertaining, Gregory was unlikely to return home until the early hours of the morning, so there would be no one to carp or question where she was or with whom.

Even so, she couldn't quite meet Matt's eyes as she said huskily, 'Thank you...I'd...I'd like that. The garden *does* need a lot of replanning,' she added quickly, guilt making her underline the purpose of her visit. 'I've been wondering about separating the garden into different sections...' Her voice trailed away and she knew she was flushing, even though what she was saying was perfectly true.

'I've got some books you might like to look at,' Matt told her. 'I could make some preliminary sketches incorporating different features.'

'You're ... you're very kind,' Davina told him, swallowing hard, wishing her voice wouldn't tremble so betrayingly nor her skin flush so hotly.

He was laughing a little now, his eyes bright with amusement as he leaned towards her, his fingertips touching her hot skin, just brushing the corner of her mouth. 'You're trembling,' he told her, watching her, watching her mouth. 'You'll tremble even more when we're lovers, when you cry out my name at the apex of your desire.'

She couldn't conceal the effect his words were having on her, and nor could she control the fine thrill of pleasure that ran through her as her body reacted physically to the heady sensual promise of his words.

The oddest thing of all, she reflected dizzily later, having gone over and over a hundred times or more the entire incident in the hours since he had left, was not just that he had actually *said* that he had desired her, but that she had *believed* him, and had actually responded to him; had actually felt her body's physical response to all that he had said.

She could feel it even now, could even conjure up a sharply erotic echo of that fiercely thrilling sensation just by closing her eyes and imagining the sound of his voice, by visualising a mental image of him; by recalling everything he had said to her; everything he had done, everything he had promised.

Her heart jerked nervously. What on earth was she contemplating? They could not possibly become lovers. It was totally out of the question. She simply was not that kind of woman. She was married, for one thing, and if her marriage was not the relationship she had hoped for, well, that did not mean that she should fling herself headlong into the arms of the first man to approach her.

Where was her common sense, her caution, her self-restraint, her pride? Did all the things she had lived her life by suddenly mean nothing because a man had told her he *wanted* her? She had never felt like this before; never felt particularly deprived because of the paucity of the sexual side of her marriage. In fact, she had been guiltily relieved when Gregory had stopped having sex with her. She was not highly sexually motivated, she knew that. She did not feel intense sexual desire, so why, suddenly and totally contrarily, had she experienced that wholly unfamiliar and sharply thrilling surge of need and awareness?

Hot colour burned her skin as she closed her eyes in self-distaste. She ought to be ashamed of herself. She *was* ashamed of herself, and she certainly wasn't going to go and have supper with Matt tonight. He would understand, of course, when she didn't turn up. But what would he understand? That she was disappointed because he had said that he would not attempt to seduce her? Her face burned even more hotly at the thought.

Even so, it wasn't until she was actually getting changed that she was prepared to admit to herself that she was going to go.

She drove to the cottage slowly and nervously, fiercely reminding herself that nothing was going to happen, that they were merely going to discuss replanning her garden, but that didn't stop her heart from beating nervously, nor her body from tensing in nervous anticipation.

But it was too late now. She had reached the cottage, and there was Matt, opening the door and waiting to welcome her.

Her heart literally feeling as though it had lodged somewhere in her throat, blocking it, she got slowly out of her car and walked even more slowly across the

cobbled yard, pausing briefly as she felt the soft
cushioning of something underfoot and looked down to
discover that someone had planted a variety of mosses
in the cracks between the cobbles.

Her tension momentarily forgotten, she studied them,
entranced by the subtlety of the soft greens and yellows
against the grey of the stone, realising that only Matt
with his artist's eye could have chosen such a delicate
and yet effective colour scheme.

'Like it?'

She had been so absorbed that she hadn't heard him
move, and now suddenly she felt breathless and dizzy
as she lifted her head and realised how close to her he
actually was.

He smelled clean and fresh, of soap rather than any
artificially created scent, and she was suddenly acutely
and keenly aware of him as a man. He was dressed
casually in jeans and a soft faded cotton shirt and, like
him, his clothes smelled of clean fresh air and soap.

Dizzily she stared at him, helplessly caught up in the
tide of her own awareness, fighting to remember why
she was here as he led her towards the cottage.

The front door opened straight into a small sitting-
room, where a log fire burned in the grate, casting
softening shadows over the room so that at first one
didn't notice the shabbiness of its furnishings, only the
warmth of their colour.

Old faded rugs softened the bleakness of the stone
floor, woven throws disguising the splits in the leather-
covered chesterfield. A variety of plants in pots cluttered
the window-sill, and almost every inch of wall space
seemed to be filled with shelf after shelf of books.

Thoroughly bemused, Davina simply stood absorbing
her surroundings, both drawn to and fascinated by their
alienness, by their total contrast to her own home. Here
nothing was rigid or formal; here nothing shrieked too
self-consciously and gratingly of wealth and status; here

everything was soft and mellow, inviting one's touch, soothing one's senses.

Matt, watching her, marvelled at her naïveté and her innocence. She had absolutely no awareness whatsoever of her own overflowing sensuality. He had never seen a woman respond so quickly nor so enticingly to the visual stimulation of her senses. He had witnessed it first while he watched her in her garden, his artist's eye immediately aware of the way she touched her plants, of the way she responded to the texture and colour of them.

It was the same now in this room. He could almost see the way her senses were responding to its warmth and colour.

She was starving inside, he recognised. Not for the crude physical appeasement of mere sex, but for the true fulfilment of the sensuality she had been forced to suppress. He would teach her to enjoy that sensuality, to appreciate and to laud it. He would make love to her here in this room in front of the fire, which would cast its warming glow over her pale satin skin; where its curves and hollows would glow, mysteriously pale and vulnerable in the shadows and where she would cry out tremulously beneath his touch.

He would make love to her in the sunshine as well; in the long sweet grass of the cottage's small neglected orchard, where her skin would smell of sunlight and where she would protest a little at the brilliance of that sunlight on their entwined bodies until he showed her the delight of its warmth on their skins.

And if he stayed long enough he would make love to her in winter, their bodies locked together in the warmth of the high old-fashioned brass bed upstairs in the cottage's single attic room, while outside the snow would lend an eerie delicacy to the light and her breasts would glow rosily pink from the roughness of his skin against their soft tenderness as he suckled on her nipples.

Davina, totally absorbed in her wondering visual exploration of the room, had no idea of his thoughts. When she looked at him he was watching her quietly, smiling slightly at her.

'You've made it so...' she shook her head, searching for the right words, and could only say helplessly '...so...so you.'

He grinned at her, and as she watched him she realised that she had never known this with anyone, man or woman; that she had never shared laughter with anyone before; that she had never wanted to share laughter, nor indeed thought of herself as the kind of woman who did laugh very much; but suddenly with Matt it seemed easy to laugh, easy to kick off her shoes and to curl up on the chesterfield, as he suggested, while he brought her the books he wanted her to see.

They were well worth seeing, and very quickly she was engrossed in their contents, exclaiming enthusiastically and enviously over the photographs of the gardens they detailed.

When she lingered wistfully over a photograph of a pergola heavy with fat pink old-fashioned roses Matt produced a sketch-pad and quickly showed her how such a feature could be used to break up her own garden. As she pored eagerly over his sketch Davina forgot how hesitant and doubtful she had been about spending the evening with him, watching in awed pleasure as his pencil quickly created for her a visual image of how her garden might be transformed.

'It looks wonderful, but I doubt if either my father or Gregory would agree,' she sighed wistfully.

'Why ask them?' Matt challenged her, and suddenly her heart thumped heavily and disturbingly. 'You're an adult, not a child, Davina,' Matt told her. 'You have the right to define your own life, to make your own decisions and to be held responsible and accountable to no one but yourself.'

Again her heartbeat quickened. They were not, she knew, merely discussing any changes she might want to make to the garden, but before she could say anything Matt put down his sketch-pad and got up.

'Suppertime,' he told her cheerfully, and then when she too would have risen he shook his head, his hand on her shoulders, gently pressing her back into the chesterfield. 'No, you stay here,' he told her.

He wasn't gone very long, and when he came back he was carrying a tray with a platter of meats and cheeses on it.

'I've discovered a marvellous deli in Chester,' he told her as he put down the tray. 'Hang on a sec and I'll get the wine.'

The wine was clear and cold, misting the plain glasses into which Matt poured it, glasses that Gregory, with his love of heavily cut expensive crystal, would have disdained, but Davina knew the moment she tasted it that this cool, clear liquid with its sharp burst of taste was far superior to anything her husband would ever have served.

'Like it?' Matt asked, watching her.

She nodded.

'Good. It's Italian, from a small family-run vineyard. They don't produce much commercially,' he added carelessly, not telling her that the vineyard belonged to an uncle who was one of his godparents, nor that the wine they produced was not sold commercially because its production was the hobby of the aristocratic Italian *conte* who owned the vineyard, and that to be given a bottle of his cherished wine was an honour accorded to few people.

When he had given Matt the wine he had told him eloquently that its bouquet was as delicate and erotic as a virgin's first tremulous climax, and it seemed very fitting to Matt that he should share it with Davina James, who, while maybe no virgin in the strict physical sense, was still unawakened in a way that very few modern virgins could claim to be.

The wine, the unexpected and unfamiliar textures and tastes of the spicy meats and the soft cheeses, were all so new and different to Davina that her enjoyment of them filled her senses. She only drank one glass of wine, knowing that she was driving, but even that one glass seemed to warm her body, sending a singing vibrancy through her veins that made her suddenly, acutely and nervously aware of Matt and the fact that they were alone.

When she put down her plate and protested huskily that she had stayed too long and must leave, Matt made no attempt to stop her. Gravely he helped her on with her jacket, making no attempt to do anything other than formally and carefully assist her with it, before walking with her out to her car.

When he opened the door for her he did so without any flourish or sexuality, and she told herself that the small shiver of sensation she felt as she got into the car was one of relief and gratitude rather than disappointment.

She was actually about to drive away, when he leaned down and said to her through the open window, 'Davina... remember, if you want me, or need me for anything, you can always find me here.'

CHAPTER EIGHT

SHE was glad that nothing had happened. Of course she was. But, even though Davina had told herself the same thing over and over again in the four days since she had had supper with Matt, she still seemed to need to reassure herself as to their veracity.

And why? Why did she need to mentally repeat the words over and over again, as though they were some kind of protective chant? Why, when she knew she had done the right thing, did she wake up in the night, her body aching with a tension that refused to be ignored or suppressed? Why did she constantly think about the small sitting-room of Matt's cottage, the sharp, clean taste of the wine he had poured her, the rich taste of the food, sensual pleasures that could, if she had chosen to let them, have led to even greater pleasures?

She imagined Matt holding her, kissing her, undressing her. She imagined them sharing a single glass of wine, Matt licking the drips from her skin, his tongue hard and warm, and as she was caught up in the helpless spiral of her own arousal she was also filled with the most acute sense of shame and guilt.

She wanted him. She could not pretend to herself any more that she didn't. But she was ashamed of that wanting, ashamed of her own need, and she was ashamed as well that he had recognised it.

But the ache inside her still refused to go away, even though she worked herself so hard that she ought to have been too physically exhausted to do anything other than fall into a grateful numbing sleep.

On the day Matt was due to do the garden she went out shopping. There was no point in putting herself in the path of temptation, she told herself bitterly, not when she apparently had so little self-control.

Her father was still away on holiday, but Gregory had come home early for once, surprising her by arriving just as she was unpacking her shopping.

She was just about to ask him what he wanted for supper when the phone rang. To her surprise, he said instantly, 'I'll get it,' lifting the receiver and then keeping his back to her so deliberately and pointedly that she knew he expected and wanted her to leave the room. Automatically she did so. There was, after all, nothing to be gained from antagonising him.

The phone call was brief, but when he came into the kitchen his face was slightly flushed, and she immediately recognised the air of scarcely suppressed excitement that made his eyes glitter so betrayingly.

'I shan't be in for supper after all,' he told her. 'I've got to go out.'

She knew, of course. How could she not do? Although it wasn't his usual practice to allow his women to telephone him at home, perhaps because he was afraid her father might take the call.

She said nothing—what was the point?—but there was a bitter, corrosive taste in her mouth as he drove away. Not because his obvious infidelity hurt her. She had sealed off those feelings years ago. No, it was his total lack of any attempt to treat her with courtesy or compassion that galled her so bitterly.

He didn't care whether or not she guessed what was going on, she recognised. He didn't care enough for her, nor respect their marriage enough to even attempt to pretend or to conceal the truth from her.

She didn't go to Matt then. She couldn't. She felt too raw, too sore emotionally and mentally, but as she lay sleepless in bed she remembered him telling her that she was an adult, that she could make her own choices, and suddenly she wondered what was worse: despising herself for craving the physical possession of another man, or despising herself because she didn't have the courage, the guts, to accept that she was a human being with every human being's frailties and with the right to choose for herself whether or not she would indulge those frailties.

If she had an affair with Matt, who would it harm? Who would it hurt? Would giving in to the physical need he aroused within her really be any more contemptible than living with a man who treated her the way Gregory treated her?

Which was really the more dishonest: allowing herself to admit that she wanted Matt, or allowing herself to be used the way Gregory used her?

She was not a girl, a teenager any more; she was a woman. A *woman*—she smiled mirthlessly to herself. *She* was no woman...not really...not inside. But with Matt she could learn to be...with Matt she could discover what it really meant to be a woman. With Matt...

Was that really what she wanted, a brief, transitory affair with a man who did not love her and whom she herself did not love?

But what *was* love? There were many different ways of loving, and in Matt she had recognised a man who *did* love her sex in a way that men like Gregory and her father never could.

She knew any relationship she might have with Matt could never be permanent. He was a wanderer, she had already recognised that even if he had not stressed it to her. But he would never deliberately hurt her...and he would certainly never abuse her, either emotionally or physically.

So what was holding her back? Surely only a lack of honesty, a lack of the courage to look closely at herself and to admit that she wanted him. Any time you want or need me, he had said, and she told herself grimly that she only hoped he had meant it.

At least she wouldn't have to explain the purpose of her call, she reflected as she got in her car and fastened her seatbelt. Eleven o'clock in the evening was hardly the usual time to make a conventional social visit.

As she drove towards the cottage half of her was hoping that he would be there and half of her was praying that he wouldn't. She had been rehearsing over and over again what she would say to him, but in the end there was no need for words.

He must have seen her arrive because he had opened the door before she had stopped the car, coming across the yard to open the car door for her, the touch of his hand on her cold, tense arm warm and reassuring as he helped her out and said simply, 'Davina...I was just thinking about you.'

She waited until they were inside to speak to him, taking a deep breath and then saying quickly, 'I've come because...because I'd...I'd like you to make love to me.'

Was that really admiration she could see in his eyes? There was certainly tenderness in his touch as he held her arm, tenderness and sympathy, as though he knew how hard she had to fight to confront her need with honesty and to admit it to him.

Very gently he led her further inside the cottage. The familiarity of the small sitting-room helped to ease her tension, as did the calm, easy way Matt was holding her hand, his thumb brushing gently against her knuckles, soothing and relaxing her a little.

He hadn't said anything in response to her statement and in another man she might have taken this as a sign that he no longer wanted her, but not with Matt. Somehow she knew that that kind of cowardice, that kind of cruelty, was not part of him.

Now, as the nervous trembling of her body died down a little with the hurdle over of actually telling him why she had come to him, he turned her towards him and told her, 'You're a very courageous woman, Davina, and—even more rare—a very honest one.'

'Honest?' Her face mirrored her disagreement. How can I be honest when I'm about to break my marriage vows? she wanted to ask him, but she couldn't frame the words, didn't want to be guilty in her own eyes of thrusting the responsibility for her decision on to him instead of taking it upon herself.

'Yes. Honest,' Matt persisted gravely as he raised her hand to his mouth, palm upwards. The light brush of his lips made her stomach quiver with nervous anticipation but that was nothing to the sensation she felt when his tongue began to lightly trace erotic circles against her skin.

How on earth was she going to cope when he touched her more intimately, when merely the touch of his tongue against her palm had this effect on her? she wondered faintly.

'Honest,' Matt repeated huskily. 'And very, very desirable.' His lips caressed the inside of her wrist, and she couldn't hold back the tremors of pleasure any longer.

Instinctively she leaned towards him, her body unfamiliarly pliant. Before he finally kissed her he slid his hands into her hair, letting it slide luxuriously through his fingers.

'It feels like silk,' he told her huskily. 'And your body will feel and look like the finest French satin, rich and soft, gleaming in the light.'

She had started to shiver, unable to hide the effect his words were having on her, her eyes huge and dark, mirroring all that she was feeling.

His hands touched her face, the pads of his fingers slightly rough against her skin. The sensation of being touched by him was so acutely pleasurable that she forgot to be apprehensive and self-conscious.

When his mouth touched hers her lips parted automatically, her body instinctively seeking the warmth and proximity of his. It wasn't a passionate, demanding kiss, but rather one of greeting and welcome, a slow, gentle exploration of her mouth, which allowed her senses to absorb the taste and pleasure of him. His hand supported her neck, his thumb stroking gently just behind her ear. She could feel the pleasure filling her in a slow, warm tide, relaxing her, restoring to her the feminine self-confidence, the ability to believe in her sensuality, which Gregory had taken from her.

Slowly Matt released her, kissing her mouth briefly and rather hard before telling her huskily, 'I think this calls for another bottle of Uncle Paolo's wine, don't you?' He led her over to the settee and pushed her gently on to it before excusing himself, 'A fitting celebration of a very, very special event.'

As he went to get the wine, Matt admitted that it wasn't to celebrate her coming to him that he was delaying things a little, not even purely to help her relax and push aside the crippling burdens her husband had placed on her sexuality, so much as to help him retain enough self-control to ensure that he could lead her gently and carefully through this all-important threshold into true awareness and appreciation of her sensuality.

He had known that ultimately they would be lovers; but he admitted that he had not expected her to come to him like this; that he had not recognised how fine and brave her spirit actually was.

As he uncorked the wine he realised that, had he been a man who wanted permanence and only one woman, Davina James could very, very easily have been that woman.

When he came back he handed one glass to Davina and then raised his own in a brief toast. 'To you, Davina.'

As she drank she trembled a little so that the wine spilled over the side of her glass and down on to her hand, and immediately she remembered how she had fantasised about Matt licking it from her skin, and her face grew hot at the memory. What would Matt say if she told him about that fantasy? Would he laugh at her or would he...?

Matt had emptied his own glass, and now he was reaching for hers, taking it from her, drawing her to her feet and into his arms.

He made love to her slowly and carefully, and with an awareness of her fears and lack of self-confidence which she only later recognised. When he undressed her he allowed her to keep herself half concealed from him in the shadows. When he caressed her body his touch was soothing, stroking, coaxing her body to relax, not asking anything of her other than that she allow him to show her pleasure.

Her senses numbed by the years of Gregory's contempt and malice, Davina was too aware of her own inexperience anyway to reach out and touch him; too conscious of her lack of ability and knowledge. It was ridiculous that a woman married for as long as she had been had no real awareness of how to arouse a man; of how to touch or caress him.

As he stroked her Matt spoke to her, soft, soothing words of praise and appreciation, which at first startled and confused her. Gregory never spoke when they had sex, and he had certainly never, as Matt was doing, told her that the taste of her skin reminded him of the warmth of the Greek sunshine, nor that when she trembled as he touched her it made him feel as powerful and omnipotent as a Roman god.

'Look what you're doing to my body, Davina,' he whispered against her mouth. 'Feel how hard you make me, how hungry for you.'

As he spoke he took her hand and placed it on his body. Initially she recoiled slightly; not because the intimacy repelled her, but because she was shamingly aware that she had no real knowledge of how she should respond. That he was inviting her to caress him, to arouse

him, she did know, but how? On the few, very few occasions she had tentatively attempted to touch Gregory
intimately, he had pushed her away, deriding her, his
rejection underlining her own inadequacy.

Her mouth went dry with the panic and despair filling
her, her throat ached with the burden of her ignorance,
but Matt seemed to know what she was thinking and
feeling, because he covered her hand with his own, his
voice comforting and reassuring as he told her, 'I like it
this way best,' and his hand moved over her own, guiding
her, teaching her.

It was like learning to dance, she discovered dizzily;
once one knew the rhythm, to move to it and with it was
the most easy and natural thing in the world.

'Mm...' Matt muttered against her mouth. 'That's
good, Davina...so good. Let me show you.'

And then he was touching her as intimately as she was
him, and her body was responding to him, her tension
melting from her to be replaced by another, different
kind of tautness.

It crossed her mind dizzily as his fingers moved
erotically against her that she had imagined that this kind
of love-play was something indulged in only by teenagers, that it was a form of intimacy scorned by adults—
it was certainly not something Gregory had ever shown
any inclination to do; and then, as Matt's mouth touched
her breast, she forgot about Gregory, forgot everything
but the feelings Matt was arousing within her, ceasing
to caress him as she lifted her hands to cling frantically
to his shoulders, her back arching as the heat within her
grew and Matt's tongue licked at the dampness of her
skin.

The sensation of him within her was totally different
from anything she had known with Gregory. In awed
wonder she experienced her body's desire not just to
accept him, but to embrace and absorb him, to urge him
deeper and deeper within it to savour and encourage each

powerful rhythmic thrust as the need within her built
and went on building.

When he suddenly ceased moving, the shock of it made
her cry out in protest, and then abruptly she realised
what had happened and flushed with shame and mortification. Her body ached and pulsed still with need,
but she tried to ignore it, ashamed of her wantonness in
the face of Matt's satiation, but he was still holding her,
still kissing her, his hands stroking her as he slid from
her.

'It's all right. It's all right,' he told her as he kissed
her, and then his hand was holding her, touching her,
and, while her brain was ashamed and appalled that he
had recognised her need and was seeking to ease it, her
frantic body achingly welcomed his awareness of its need
for the fulfilment it craved.

The orgasm that engulfed her left Davina trembling
and tearful, embarrassed at what it had been necessary
for him to do for her, and yet at the same time overwhelmed with happy relief that he had done so.

Later, as she sat curled in his arms while they finished
the wine, he told her firmly, 'Never be afraid to tell your
lover what you want from him sexually, Davina. A man
wouldn't be, and you, as a woman, as his partner, have
an equal right, an equal need to enjoy fulfilment and to
reach orgasm.'

He smiled a little as he saw the way she flushed.

'Does it embarrass you when I talk so frankly? It
shouldn't. Why is it that human beings find it so comparatively easy to be physically intimate and yet so hard
to tell one another vocally about the pleasure they want
to give one another? Very few of us are mind-readers.
Every lover that ever existed wants to know that he or
she is giving pleasure.

'It's one thing to know that a woman is responding
to you, to see it in her eyes and in her body, but when
she tells you how she feels when you do this...' He bent

his head and gently licked her bare breast, covering her
nipple with his mouth and suckling on it, while she tensed
and gasped, not just at the unexpectedness of the gesture
but at her body's swift reaction to it.

'You see,' he told her as he released her. 'I can tell
from your physical reaction that my touch pleased you.
But if you were to whisper to me that you loved the feel
of my mouth against your skin, that it made you ache
with pleasure and need to have me caressing you that
way...'

His voice had grown rough and husky, and just the
sound of it made her shiver, her body suddenly fiercely
aroused.

'Let me show you,' he told her thickly. 'Come here
and kiss me, Davina, and I'll tell you how good it makes
me feel when you do.'

It was almost light when she finally left him, refusing
his offer to drive her home, knowing that it would mean
he would have to walk the five miles back.

'This isn't the end of it for us,' he told her as he kissed
her. 'It's just the beginning.'

'But we don't...we don't love one another,' Davina
protested, shivering a little in the cold pre-dawn air, the
words more a shocked acknowledgement of her own
ability to enjoy him so intensely physically than because
she expected or wanted any denial of her comment.

'We are not "in love",' Matt corrected her. 'But with
this kind of pleasure there is always love, of a kind. You
must have felt it when we touched one another. I know
I did.'

He kissed her again.

'There's only one person whose love should ever be
really important to you, Davina, and that's your own,'
he told her.

It took her a long time to truly understand what he
had meant, and she didn't really do so until their affair
was over and he had gone and she recognised what a

truly wonderful gift he had given her, not just in showing her the reality of her own sexuality, but in giving her the ability to value and appreciate her own self.

They were together for the whole summer. Fate was kind to them and aided them in keeping their relationship a secret. Gregory was too engrossed in his own affair to concern himself with what she was doing, and her father, totally unexpectedly and uncharacteristically, announced that he was going to retire and spend a couple of months in Scotland golfing.

Later, when she looked back on the summer, Davina was often awed and faintly incredulous when she remembered how quickly and startlingly intensely her sensuality had developed.

Matt was intuitive as well as knowledgeable about her sex, and he encouraged her to explore her own sexuality as well as his, the desire he expressed so openly and freely for her giving her the self-confidence to lay claim to her own desires.

And then, in October, she began to notice a change in Matt. Sometimes he seemed to withdraw mentally from her and he was oddly edgy and tense.

She had always known that their affair must end, and because she had learned now to be honest with herself and with her needs and her emotions she recognised that Matt could never be wholly satisfied with the kind of life that most appealed to her. She was no traveller, no wanderer. She wanted roots, security, permanence.

At the end of October Matt told her that it was time for him to leave.

'Owen doesn't really have a job for me any more, and if I stay much longer...' He looked at her, and then touched her face. 'I'm more tempted than you know to take you with me, Davina, but my life wouldn't be right for you, and sooner or later...' He sighed and shook his head. 'Will it make it better or worse if I tell you that I love you?' he asked her.

'Better,' Davina told him shakily, and then added rue-fully, 'And worse.'

They both laughed; something else she had learned to enjoy and share with him.

'Don't stay with Gregory,' Matt urged her. 'We both know that ultimately I couldn't give you the things you need, but Davina, somewhere out there there *is* a man who can. You'll never find him if you stay married, and you *deserve* to find him. You *need* to find him, not just for yourself, but for him and for the children the two of you will have together.'

They had one last night together, a feast of cel-ebration of all that they had shared and a fitting way to end their affair, Davina thought. She knew already how much she would miss him, but that knowledge did not cause her to despair. She had learned so much with him, grown so much.

Leave Gregory, he had told her, and she knew that he was right, but she also knew that Gregory would not let her go easily. He could not afford to. And her father was wholly against divorce, violently disapproving of it. He would certainly not support her.

But why should she *need* his support? She was an adult, fully capable of directing and controlling her own life, of making her own decisions. With her father back from Scotland, fussily critical and demanding, she had little time to mourn Matt. It was only at night when she was in bed alone—she and Gregory had permanently separate rooms now—that she allowed herself the luxury of remembering, of conjuring up in the darkness the touch of his hands and the warmth of his mouth. She missed him, yes, but she accepted his going because she had always known that he would go.

And then, less than a month after Matt had gone, her father suffered his first stroke. In the months that fol-lowed, as she nursed and cared for him, Davina was forced to accept that it was not now possible for her to divorce Gregory.

The doctor told her that her father was unlikely to make a full recovery; he had become irascible and so demanding that Davina was the only person he would tolerate around him. His body might have failed him but his brain was still sharply keen and there seemed to have arisen a deep resentment between her father and Gregory. Davina, as the buffer between them, suffered the worst of their mutual aggression.

Trying to maintain some form of calm and peace was more exhausting for her than having to nurse her father and run the house, and cravenly she often wished she had had the foresight to announce her desire for a divorce before her father had had his stroke. Now it was impossible for her to leave... to escape.

With care, there was no reason why her father should not live for many more years, his doctor had told her cheerfully, and those words had snapped tight her prison gates, trapping her inside them. She could not leave her father and she could not divorce Gregory; not while her father lived.

Drearily she acknowledged that it was unlikely that Gregory would divorce *her*. Why should he? He enjoyed the financial security their marriage gave him. If he ever managed to gain full control of the company it might be a different story. She had heard him trying to persuade her father to give him a majority shareholding, but her father had refused. Not out of concern for her or her future, Davina recognised, but out of resentment and spite, out of his desire to ensure that he maintained some form of control over Gregory.

'Why the hell doesn't he just die?' Gregory had demanded viciously after a particularly violent argument with him, but in the end Gregory himself had barely survived her father by more than a year.

And now, with both of them gone, she had the freedom she had once craved, or at least she would have had it had it not been for Carey's.

Freedom. Did anyone really have it? Davina wondered as she dragged her thoughts wearily from the past.

That man this evening, did *he* have it? There had been a solitariness about him, an aloneness, but somehow it had been a solitude that spoke of a certain grimness and austerity rather than the carefree warmth she had always associated with Matt.

So why had he so immediately and so alarmingly reminded her of Matt? Surely not just because he had touched her body?

The thought disturbed her. Why should *his* touch, the casual, clinical touch of a stranger, have anything to do with Matt, her lover, a man with whom she had shared every sensual intimacy? There had been nothing sensual about that man tonight. On the contrary, however, her heartbeat jerked unevenly as though in betrayal of her self-deception.

There *had* been something; something which her body had recognised even if her brain refused to accept its existence.

She moved uncomfortably, physically shying away from her own thoughts, disliking the idea of her body's being sexually aware, however briefly and subconsciously, of that of an unknown man, irritated and alarmed by this sudden unwanted reinforcement of her sexuality.

Perhaps it was some kind of displacement effect, she decided grimly; her friendship with Lucy and her own moral code made it impossible for her to respond to Giles's as yet undeclared desire for her, so perhaps she had somehow become over-sexually aware of that man tonight as some form of compensation.

Or perhaps she was simply using his unwanted intrusion as a means of deflecting her attention from the

far more serious problems she had to contend with. Like
the future of Carey's and those who worked there. The
union officials had made it clear that they were anxious
to know what was going on, and she couldn't blame
them, but both Giles and the bank had warned her that,
once she publicly admitted that the company could not
continue in business for much longer, she would find it
even harder to find a buyer. For that reason Giles and
the bank had warned her that she must keep up the pretence that the company's future was secure.

Davina hated imposing that kind of deception on the
workforce. They had a right to know what was happening, to have the opportunity to look around for other
jobs.

Not that they were likely to find any. There was no
other major employer in the area, which was why Carey's
had been able to get away with paying such low wages
and imposing such poor and sometimes dangerous
working conditions on its employees, Davina recognised. Guiltily she closed her eyes. She had been appalled when she visited the factory after Gregory's death
to discover just what conditions their employees *were*
working under.

When she had in all innocence and outrage questioned them she had been informed grimly by one of the
foremen that he had complained on any number of occasions in the past to Gregory personally about the
physical danger of their working conditions, never mind
the aesthetic unpleasantness of them.

Davina had flushed with mortification as she listened
to him. She was as much to blame as Gregory, she decided. She should not have accepted his ruling that he
was the one running Carey's, nor his insistence that his
business and his personal life were to be kept strictly
separate and that that included her having nothing
whatsoever to do with the day-to-day running of the
company.

She had her dividends and her shareholding, and that was all she needed to concern herself with, he had told her dictatorially, and because she had hated the use-lessness of arguing with him she had weakly allowed him to have his way.

She ought to have been stronger, more insistent . . . she ought to have been more concerned; she ought simply to have been far more responsible, and it was no good making excuses for herself now by going over and over all the reasons why she had just never realised that in taking the easy option for herself she had wantonly con-demned many, many other people to Gregory's domi-nation and abuse.

She wasn't going to allow it to continue, though. In her desk at home was a document she had roughed out and drawn up herself, outlining all the improvements she considered essential to provide Carey Chemicals' employees with not merely adequate but good working conditions, the kind of working conditions she would want to work under herself; the kind of working con-ditions that showed respect for their employees as human beings.

Attention to the safety aspects of their work was at the top of her list, but there were other things on it as well: a decent canteen; clean, attractive rest-rooms and wash-rooms; better social facilities to engender a good relationship between company and employees that ex-tended into leisure activities; and, most important of all, good crèche and nursery-school facilities for those em-ployees with under-school-age children.

Davina had said nothing of this charter to either Giles or the bank, but she was determined that she would not sell the company until she was sure that any prospective buyer was agreeable to putting her proposals into effect.

She would rather sell the company for a pittance and secure these benefits for its employees than sell it at a profit to herself. It was, after all, the least she could do for those to whom she owed such a heavy debt of responsibility and neglect. However, she accepted that Giles and the bank were unlikely to share her views.

No matter. They must *learn* to share them, she decided firmly. After all, the company belonged to her, and it was up to her now to stand firm, to be strong and determined on behalf of everyone who worked for her, if only to make up in some part for her weakness in the past.

Matt had once told her teasingly that she had a very Calvanistic moral outlook: every debt to be repaid, every promise to be honoured.

Matt. He had given her so much. Taught her so much.

'You know now what it means to be a woman, Davina,' he had told her before he left. 'Don't waste that knowledge, and most of all don't waste your womanhood. Find a man who will love you as you deserve to be loved.'

She hadn't done so, of course. How could she? Her father's stroke had kept her chained to Gregory and their marriage. Find a man... She laughed a little savagely. What she needed to find right now was not a potential lover but a buyer for Carey's. Please God, let there be one. Not for her... but for all those who depended on the company for their living.

The phone rang, the sharp, demanding sound sending a thrill of tension along her nerve-endings. She stared at it for several seconds before reaching for the receiver, glancing at the clock as she did so. It was late, gone midnight. Who could be calling her at this time of night?

'Davina?'

Her muscles tensed even harder as she recognised Giles's voice. He was breathing slightly heavily, as though he had either been running or was under some kind of strain.

'Giles.' She said his name awkwardly, uncomfortably aware of the contradictory messages flashing from her brain.

'Davina...I need to see you...to talk to you.'

Her heart raced as she recognised the husky, aching need in his voice. She couldn't allow him to come round now. Not while she was feeling so emotionally and physically vulnerable, not with her body still soft and aching slightly from her memories of Matt. It was too dangerous.

'Not now, Giles,' she told him huskily. 'It's late and I was just on my way to bed.'

She could almost feel his disappointment, her fingers clenching as she gripped the receiver. Would it really do any harm to let him come round? He was obviously very distressed. Both of them were adults. She knew that he was married.

Fiercely she pushed aside the shallow excuses, quietly saying goodnight and replacing the receiver before Giles could plead with her to change her mind.

It was all his fault...that man tonight...If he hadn't set her off thinking about Matt...remembering...She shuddered, folding her arms around her body.

She wasn't going to allow herself to be drawn into an affair with Giles simply because her body was aching to be touched...to be loved; simply because tonight, when a strange man had held her, she had suddenly remembered exactly how it felt to be held by a man who desired her and whom she desired in return...was she?

CHAPTER NINE

MUCH to his irritation, Saul discovered that Davina James was still on his mind twenty minutes later when he pulled off the main road and into the quiet lane that led to his sister's house.

Christie had bought the sturdy four-bedroomed Victorian villa when she'd first moved from the city to Cheshire. It was on the outskirts of the small market town, it and its neighbours initially looking slightly out of place in their rural setting, their design being more in keeping with a commercial city environment than a country one. It would have been easier to picture them in a prosperous Victorian suburb of Liverpool or Manchester than out here on the edge of this very small town, but they had been built by a Victorian entrepreneur who had slightly overreached himself, thinking to follow the example of those who had so cleverly anticipated the effect of extending the railway system.

In his case, the venture had not been a success, but the moment she saw the house Christie had pounced gleefully on it, announcing that with its proximity to the town centre and the surgery, its very large gardens, and the spaciousness of its rooms, plus its very reasonable asking price, it was exactly what she wanted. Saul, invited down to give her the benefit of his advice, had wryly pointed out that the reason for the low asking figure was undoubtedly connected with the vast amount of remedial work the house needed, but Christie had refused to be put off. The house had character, potential, she told him, ignoring his suggestion that something smaller and more modern with lower running costs might suit her better.

In the event, Saul had to admit that the house *did* suit her. True, she had never actually got round to putting into effect all the renovations she had planned, but, as she had teasingly remarked to him the last time he had visited her, she had lost nothing by not rushing into modernising the house. The bathroom, for instance, with its plain white sanitaryware, was now back in vogue, as were all the original detailings such as the huge original fireplaces, the dado rails and cornices.

They might be, Saul had agreed wryly, but the antiquated heating system fuelled by the monster of a boiler with the temperament of a prima donna, which crouched so malevolently and sulkily over the kitchen, was most certainly not, and he for one preferred to know that when he turned on the hot water for his shower hot water was exactly what he was going to get, not a thin rusty dribble of something that could be anything from ice-cold to red-hot, frequently veering balefully from one to the other without the least warning.

Christie had laughed at him, telling him that he was getting soft on his rich, cosseted lifestyle, reminding him of when they were children and central heating of any sort had been an unknown luxury. Saul remembered all right. He also remembered how he had learned to be careful about mentioning at home the luxuries enjoyed by the families of some of his peers. He had once made the mistake of commenting enthusiastically on the new car acquired by the father of one of his schoolfriends, and had then realised from the set, tight look on *his* father's face that he had somehow hurt him. After that he had been careful never to comment on the material possessions of others, just in case by doing so he might cause his much loved father any pain.

Christie, so much less close to their father, had suffered no such qualms, and yet, for all her often expressed envy of more affluent schoolfriends when she was growing up, she was now scattily and happily totally unmaterialistic.

People didn't need wealth, she was fond of saying, they needed love and good health; the chance to fulfil their potential as human beings. They needed to give and to receive respect from those around them, to feel that their lives held purpose and meaning. Too much money blunted the human spirit's ability to enjoy the pleasure of self-achievement almost as much as too little, although, of course, Christie being Christie, her sympathies were far more with the have-nots than the have-too-muches. People with wealth had the opportunity to do something about their handicap, such as using it for the benefit of others. Those who lived in poverty had no such opportunities.

Saul grimaced a little to himself as he drove slowly towards Christie's house. What would his sister make of Davina James? They were two utterly different types. Christie was hard-working, independent, stubborn and determined in her support of the underdog, her only real vulnerability her daughter Cathy, followed perhaps by her own passionate involvement with what she believed in. Christie was passionately intense in her beliefs and in supporting them.

Davina James, on the other hand, was completely the opposite: the rich man's daughter who had never worked, never had to support herself; who had gone from protected girlhood to equally protected wifehood; a woman who had such little emotional passion in her nature that she had calmly turned a blind eye to her husband's numerous affairs.

Saul moved uneasily in his seat, frowning. There was no reason why that should fill him with such anger. She wasn't on her own. He could name several couples among his own acquaintance who had exactly that kind of marriage; the kind of marriage which on the surface seemed all calm compatibility and politeness but which in reality cloaked sour indifference and mutual lack of any real feelings. Why did such people stay together? His frown deepened as he turned into Christie's drive.

What the hell did it matter why Davina James had stayed with her husband? Their personal relationship had no bearing on Alex's desire to acquire the company. But it had disturbed him to feel that intuitive unwanted thrust of awareness of her as a woman, soft, vulnerable, her body tensing against his in the classic defensive reaction of a woman to the physical threat of an unknown man. Not that he had been threatening her.

How could a woman like that, a woman with such sensitive and intense reactions, armour herself into the cynical indifference of being married to a man consistently unfaithful to her? Or was it that she was so physically cold that she welcomed his sexual infidelity?

His senses, his body rejected the thought so quickly that it shocked him into a fresh surge of anger. Forget the woman, he told himself as he stopped his car. She isn't important. Just as his own awareness of his discontent, of his despair almost, over the direction of his life wasn't important?

Getting out of his car, he slammed the door with more force than was necessary. Security lights flashed on as he walked towards the house; the front door opened and Cathy came running over to him, flinging herself into his arms. How different she was from his own daughter. It amazed him sometimes that his volatile sister should have produced this serene, loving child, whose contentment and joy in her life were so immediately obvious, while he...while Josey...

As he bent to return her hug he suppressed the sharp pain of self-knowledge. How much was he to blame for the cynical materialism that was becoming so much a part of Josey's personality? All right, so she was older than Cathy, and lived in a different environment; but that did not change the fact that Cathy was happy while his daughter, his children were not.

'Mum's had to go out on an emergency call,' she told him as they walked back to the house together. 'She said she shouldn't be long, though.'

'I suppose that means the gorgon is here, then, does it?' Saul mock groaned.

It was an old joke between them; a private name they had for the severely respectable and outwardly formidable widow whom Christie employed to sit with Cathy when she had to be out.

Beneath her formidable exterior Saul knew that she was devoted to both Cathy and Christie, but she was one of that apparently dying breed of women who exuded disapproval of the male sex. Impossible as it was to imagine that she had actually been married, she always spoke very severely of her husband as 'the late Mr Lynch,' causing Saul to wonder if she had ever addressed the man during his lifetime by his actual Christian name.

Christie derided him for his attitude, telling him that if Agnes Lynch was repressed then it was because of the rules of behaviour imposed on women by the male sex; because she had probably been taught from childhood to suppress her sexuality; because she had been taught that it was a woman's responsibility to exercise a civilising influence over the men around her.

'You men, you're like children,' she had scoffed at Saul. 'Always refusing to take responsibility for your own behaviour. You're sexually promiscuous…well, that "isn't your fault". It's "up to the woman to say no for you". Rubbish! A man is just as capable of controlling his sexual urges as a woman, and a woman has just as much right to the freedom to enjoy her sexuality as a man.'

Saul had said nothing. He often wondered how much his sister's voluble championing of women's sexual rights had to do with the fact that Cathy's father, the married man who had seduced her and then calmly told her that he wanted neither her nor her child, had treated her so cruelly, but he knew his volatile sister too well to ever lay that charge at her.

'I'm to make you some supper,' Cathy told him importantly. 'It's all ready in the kitchen, but I expect you'd like to go upstairs first.'

Saul hid a small wry smile at her young motherliness. Where had she picked that up from? Certainly not from his independent sister, who was far more likely to direct him to the fridge and tell him to help himself.

An hour later when Christie arrived home she found the two of them at the kitchen table, playing Scrabble. She kissed her daughter and then hugged Saul, releasing him to demand drily, 'So what *is* this important business that brings you to our part of the world, big brother?'

'Who said anything about its being important?' Saul countered. Christie might be volatile, but that did not mean that she was unintelligent. Far from it. Uncomfortably he acknowledged that he had no wish for his sister to know exactly why Alex wanted to obtain Carey's.

But why should he care *what* Christie thought of his actions? The differences in their moral viewpoint and outlook had never bothered him in the past. No, because in the past he had been bolstered, protected from her acerbic dismissal of the materialism and greed that turned the wheels of his world by the knowledge that he was fulfilling his father's dreams for him. Now he no longer had that protection.

'You're Sir Alex's right-hand man. You wouldn't be here if it weren't important,' Christie told him, watching him.

'Ah . . . I'm afraid I've suffered a slight fall from grace and that this is more what Alex deems to be a subtle form of punishment than anything else. There's a local company he's interested in acquiring.' He gave a brief shrug and deftly made up another Scrabble word, trying to give the impression that his concentration was fixed more on his game with Cathy than on the purpose of his visit to Cheshire.

Christie was frowning. 'Which local company?' she demanded. 'I shouldn't have thought that there was anything big enough here to interest Sir Alex. There's only really Carey's.' She stopped and stared at him. '*Is* it Carey's?' Her frown deepened. 'But why on earth would Sir Alex want them?'

Saul shrugged. 'I'm not really sure that he does,' he lied.

'Well, something needs to be done about them,' Christie told him grimly. 'They've got a very poor accident record, and I'm very concerned about the number of people working there who've consulted me recently with contact dermatitis. The wages they pay are horrendous, and none of his employees seemed to think very highly of Gregory James.'

'Did you know him?' Saul asked her.

She shook her head. 'No... and from what I've heard about him I doubt we'd have had anything in common. I've met his wife a couple of times.' She frowned. 'She's the quiet, docile type, although...'

'Although what?' Saul pressed her. As he waited for her response he suddenly realised how tense he had become, the small lettered squares in his hand biting into his flesh as his fingers closed too tightly over them. He could feel the sudden acceleration in his heartbeat, and he knew he was waiting for Christie's answer with a very dangerous blend of anger and hostility.

'Well, she and I were on the same fund-raising committee a couple of years ago, and she was the one who actually managed to persuade the hospital authority to agree to look into certain types of alternative treatments and therapies. I'm still not quite sure how she did it...'

'You mean she's not perhaps as docile as she appears.'

Christie shrugged. 'I don't know the woman well enough to pass any real judgement on her; all I *do* know is that the general local consensus is one of surprise that she's become so involved in the business since her husband's death. Come on, Cathy,' she added, turning to her daughter. 'Time for bed. How are Josephine and Thomas?' she asked Saul over her shoulder.

'Fine,' he told her shortly, tensing a little as she turned round to give him a thoughtful look.

'Sore subject?' she asked softly.

Saul shrugged, unwilling to admit even to Christie how much of a failure he felt as a father, and how frustrated and unhappy he felt at not being able to get closer to his children. 'They're growing up,' he said. 'Especially Josey. They both have their own lives, their own friends.'

Christie said nothing, but later, when Cathy was in bed and they were alone, she caught him off guard by returning to the subject.

She had just made them a nightcap; she had been telling him ruefully about one of Cathy's small misdemeanours, and then quietly she asked him, 'How do you *really* feel about Josey and Tom, Saul? They *are* your children.'

He put down his cup, angry with her for raising the subject and even more angry with himself for what he was feeling. 'Biologically, yes,' he agreed tersely. 'But if they don't want me in their lives I can't force them to accept me, Christie.'

'Have you thought that they could just be testing you?' she asked him. 'Josey especially is at an age where her emotions are very vulnerably poised between childhood and womanhood. You *are* her father, and she's bound to——'

'To what? Want me in her life?' Saul demanded bitterly. He got up and wheeled around, leaning down towards her. 'And what about Cathy, Christie; does *she* want *her* father in her life?'

He was cursing himself before the words were out, hating himself for his cruelty as he saw the blood drain from his sister's face.

'God, Christie, I'm sorry...' he apologised instantly. 'I shouldn't have said that.'

'No. It was a question you'd every right to ask,' Christie told him shakily. 'And, believe me, it's one I never cease to ask myself.

'Cathy is young for her age. I've always tried to be as honest as I can with her, without hurting her. She knows that her father was married when we met, that he has a wife and family, other responsibilities, and so far she's always accepted that he isn't free to play any kind of role in our lives.

'What I haven't told her is that he wanted me to abort her; that I know he would never want anything to do with her and that if she ever tried to approach him he would reject her. What I also know is that one day she is going to want to make that approach—she wouldn't be human if she didn't—and I know I can't protect her from the hurt she *will* suffer. That's my guilt and my burden, only Cathy is the one who will have to bear their pain. As she grows up I keep on asking myself if I should prepare her...warn her...but then I wonder, even if I *do* tell her, will she believe me...will she still not want to find out the truth for herself? I know that, in her shoes, I would.

'All I can do is to make sure that she's strong enough; that she grows up surrounded by enough love; that I give her a strong enough belief in herself as a human being to sustain her through that pain.'

As he saw the tears standing out in his sister's eyes Saul felt sick with shame and self-contempt. He reached out and took hold of her, rocking her in his arms.

'Christie...forgive me. I envy you so much, you know,' he added truthfully. 'Whenever I'm with you, you make me so sharply aware of my own shortcomings.'

Against his chest Christie laughed. 'Shortcomings! *You!* I never thought you had any.'

Saul laughed with her, both of them acknowledging the truth that had dominated their shared childhoods, which was that their father had loved his son to the detriment of his daughter.

Saul marvelled that Christie had always been large-spirited enough never to resent him for that; that she had been strong enough to somehow find her own way through life.

'I'm glad Cathy's father didn't really want me, you know,' she told Saul now as she pushed herself away from him. 'It would never have worked out. I realised later that what I wanted from him was his approval, his admiration...that what I wanted from him was all that Dad withheld from me. I put him up on a pedestal, virtually worshipping him, and when he rejected me and Cathy, when I realised the truth...well, let's just say that by the time Cathy was born I was glad he was working on the other side of the Atlantic.'

'Is he still there?' Saul asked her.

She shrugged. 'Who knows? It would be easy enough for me to find out, I suppose, but I can't see the point.' She touched his arm briefly. 'Don't give up on Josey, Saul. She needs you in her life. They both do.'

'Not according to Karen,' he commented sardonically.

Christie gave him a quick look. 'I'm going up to bed,' she told him. 'I want to check over my notes for the conference.'

'I'll stay down here for a little while longer, if you don't mind,' Saul responded.

She shook her head, smiling at him as she opened the door and left.

Once he was on his own he sat down again.

Was Christie right? *Did* his children need him? Not according to Karen.

Karen... It seemed impossible now that they could ever have been married. Had she ever loved him? Had he ever loved her?

He closed his eyes, leaning back in his chair, thinking back to the past, to the year he had left Oxford to begin his course at Harvard. Two things of almost equal importance had happened to him as a result of going to Harvard: the first was that he met Karen Manners, and the second was that he was head-hunted by one of New York's most prestigious and old-established firms of financial analysts.

He met Karen soon after he arrived at Harvard. She, like him, was a Brit, doing a fill-in course at Vassar. A tall redhead, she had a sharp-boned elegance, a wickedly keen wit, and an almost masculine attitude towards sex, which drew him to her like metal to a magnet.

They met first at a party given by a mutual acquaintance, and in the crowd of American women Karen stood out immediately as being different. There was, Saul recognised, something about her that drew him to her, although it wasn't until later, much, much later that he recognised that what he saw in her was a mirror image of his own ambition and drive.

Outwardly all cool control, all elegance, she was, as Saul discovered the first time they went to bed together, a very accomplished lover. Accomplished and controlled. He liked that in her. It made him feel safe. It seemed to underline her support and her approval of the way he had chosen to run his own life. She was not like other women of his acquaintance, a creature of emotions and needs that he was supposed in some way to satisfy. Karen had no needs, made no demands on him other than sexually.

It was she who suggested they move in together, but he had no qualms about doing so. He already knew her

well enough to know that living with her would not mean
that she would impinge on his life in any way that would
prejudice his ambitions. She was, after all, as ambitious
as he was himself.

They rented a tiny apartment in a block that had a
resident husband and wife team who took care of the
domestic chores—an essential, not a luxury, as Karen
pointed out to him when he suggested that they could
probably find somewhere cheaper. Money was always
on Saul's mind. He was deeply aware of how much the
lack of it, of how having to economise had pressured
and depressed his father.

'After all,' she told him calmly, 'neither of us will have
time to waste on domestic drudgery.'

It was true, and before too long Saul was agreeing
with Karen that they had made the right decision; that
it would not have helped either of them to have to go
home at night to such mundane tasks as doing the dishes
and playing at house. They both had studying to do,
both of them had groups with which they were very involved, a very important part of campus life; it wasn't
enough simply to do well academically—one had to prove
that one was socially adept as well. The Americans placed
great importance on social address, and Saul had already
decided that his best career move lay in getting a job in
the States. Not only was the money better, the prospects
were as well, which were far more important. He had
already discussed this with Karen and she was in complete agreement with him. She intended to go into advertising, and she had already drawn up what she called
her attack plan, listing those agencies she most wanted
to work for.

She would succeed in her objectives, Saul never
doubted that. While not perhaps beautiful, she had
something striking about her, something that caught the
eye and the mind . . . a coolness, a stillness, an awareness
of her firm resolve and her strong belief in herself.

They made a good couple; everyone said so. Physically they were well matched; two elegant, lean creatures, whose bodies complemented one another, whose desires ran in tandem, and who found nothing wrong in their being together in a relationship that had begun with carefully mapped-out boundaries. There was no question of either one being unfaithful to the other; they had everything they needed in their neat, well defined anti-septic togetherness.

At home in England they might never have met. Karen came from what could be termed a privileged back-ground. There was no money in the family, she told him openly, just a succession of titled and impoverished re-lations who luckily had had enough influence to get both her and her brothers into decent schools.

'I have enough maiden great-aunts to form their own convent,' she had told him once grimly. 'All victims of the First World War; all living on dreams of what could have been. That is never going to happen to me. I shall never rely on a man to complete my life.'

Saul had praised her foresight, admiring her drive, recognising how alike they were in so many ways.

She had had other lovers before him, but no one who had been important. Her view of sex was that it was as vital to develop a good skill in that as it was in any other activity one wished to undertake. She was a good skier, she rode well, she could converse on virtually any subject with almost anyone she met, all skills which had been honed and practised until they reached the standard she had set for herself. And it was the same with sex.

She complimented Saul on his own expertise, and had no hesitation about telling him what she liked and what she did not like. It was important to her that when they made love she reached a climax, and on those rare oc-casions when she did not she seemed to blame herself for some lack of ability and purpose, rather than being frustrated and upset because she had been denied physical satisfaction.

There was, Saul recognised, an almost clinical precision about their lovemaking, but he told himself he preferred that to the hot, dangerous excitement he had known with Angelica. He remembered all too well how dangerous that had been, how vulnerable it had made him, how often she had left him aching to tell her how much she meant to him . . . aching to give her so much more than merely the satisfaction offered by his body.

With Karen it was different. For a start they shared a mutual respect, a mutual awareness. They each knew the limitations set down by the other.

As an example, they each had their own bedrooms, and, although when they made love they invariably slept together, on some occasions Karen would retire to her own room to work, and Saul knew that when her door remained closed it meant that she wished to be left alone and that unless she opened the door to indicate otherwise she would want to sleep alone as well.

But then, after all, as they both agreed, sex wasn't everything.

All in all, Saul considered that he was very fortunate.

And then he was head-hunted by McCaine, Abbott and Drury. Of course, Karen was the first person he told, once he had given himself a day to think it over in his own mind, to list the pros and the cons and to give due consideration to all that was involved.

'They're a very prestigious firm,' Karen had pronounced when he finally told her.

'Yes,' he agreed.

'But not *the* most prestigious, and you still have to get your master's.'

Both of them knew that, if his results were as good as his tutors indicated, the chances were that he would have more than one offer to choose from, and yet there was a certain security in knowing that he could walk away from Harvard and straight into such a good firm. After all, he was not the only pebble on the beach and some of the other pebbles had some very influential boulders indeed standing behind them; they were WASP students from families whose names and connections would virtually guarantee them entrée into the best jobs. An advantage which Saul did not have.

'There's still time yet,' Karen said at length.

Both of them knew what she was saying. Saul nodded in agreement and added, 'Best not to seem too eager... too hungry.'

'Quite,' Karen agreed.

Karen flew home for Christmas. Saul did not. He could not afford it. Instead he worked, both on his studies and to earn money. Picking up his cue from Karen, he got himself a job in Aspen, and while he was there he learned to ski. The wages were poor, but the perks, including free ski passes and tuition, more than made up for the wages.

Skiing was the 'in' winter sport. If Saul had not already known that, he was intelligent enough to pick it up from the conversation of his fellow collegiates when the winter season approached.

Several of the female holiday-makers made it plain to him that he was welcome in their beds, but he had no wish to get involved. He had other more important things to do.

The physically hard activity of skiing, the long hours spent outside, honed his body after the softening influence of the months of study. The sun bronzed his face, further dramatising the contrast between the darkness of his hair and the lucid lightness of his eyes. He returned to Harvard half a stone lighter and a good deal fitter.

Yes, she had had a good Christmas, Karen confirmed when he picked her up at the airport, but she had missed him. Saul had missed her too, and suddenly the sexual appetite he had kept so rigorously under control while he was in Colorado burst into life.

If Karen was taken aback at being rushed straight through the front door of their apartment and into the bedroom she didn't show it, responding to his need with an expertise that made him shudder against her in aching pleasure, almost immediately reaching orgasm.

He told himself that the sensation that gripped his stomach when she turned over and whispered firmly in his ear, 'My turn now, I think,' wasn't really an unpleasant sense of somehow having broken some unwritten rule, but later on, after he had made love to her again, he watched her sleep, irritated with himself for the negative feelings that kept him awake.

He got his master's with distinction and, although he was offered several prestigious jobs, he was aware that the most prestigious of them were all going to others, others who were not as academically well qualified as he was himself but who had other advantages. He accepted the most promising of all offers, and then used the time before taking it up to fly home to Britain to see his family.

His father seemed to have shrunk physically since he had last seen him. He looked greyer and more worn down. He was pleased that Saul had done so well and very proud of him, but even while he was accepting his praise, Saul felt let down...empty...as though something was missing. He told himself it was because he knew that the very best job offers had passed him by, and he swore that when he got back to New York he would work until he had proved to those who had passed him over that they had made a mistake. He was, he assured himself on the flight back, going to be the best in his field...the very best.

Karen too had got her master's and a job with one of the leading agencies. Like him, she had her sights set on the very top of the career ladder.

Since they were both going to be working in New York, and in view of the terrifyingly high cost of living it seemed only sensible that they look for an apartment they could share. There was a comfortable familiarity about their relationship now, a steady, easy pattern to their sex and social life.

As they had done at Harvard, Karen insisted that they manage to afford a maid to come in and clean for them. Saul protested that surely between the two of them they could keep the small apartment clean, but Karen had shaken her head. *He* might choose to turn himself into a domestic drudge if he wished but she had no intention of doing so. Her career was far too important to her. She simply wouldn't have the time to spare for that kind of work. Saul gave in. His salary was a good one, but living expenses were high and he soon discovered that his firm expected a certain social standing from its young executives. Saul was quickly aware that he was the only new recruit who did not have a moneyed WASP background.

It was discreetly and subtly suggested to him that he should join certain clubs, take up certain interests. The firm was rather an old-fashioned one, unlike the agency where Karen worked.

Saul had been working for Adams, Adams and Hewitson for six months when he first became aware that the senior partners were not too happy about the fact that he was living with Karen.

At first he misunderstood the point of the discreet queries that followed his appearance with Karen at an obligatory dinner-dance given to celebrate the sixtieth birthday of one of the partners, but then broader hints were dropped, and to his astonishment he realised that he was gently but firmly being warned that his progress within the firm could be impeded by the wrong kind of personal life, but that correspondingly the right kind of wife was extremely beneficial to an ambitious young man. Karen, with her family background, was, he was given to understand, very much the right kind of wife.

He gave Karen the gist of their conversation later that evening over dinner. They ate out most evenings, sometimes locally, but more often than not in places favoured by people of their own type, up and coming young executive couples with a certain social standing to maintain.

Karen paused and looked reflective but offered no comment. It was only later after they had made love and were lying relaxed in bed together that she referred to their conversation again, startling him by commenting, 'You know, Saul, I think it might be worthwhile thinking about getting married.'

'But I thought you didn't want marriage.'

She shook her head. 'Not originally—but now... However, it would have to be a specific type of marriage. A marriage to someone who understood the importance to me of my career. Of course, if you don't care for the idea...'

Saul looked at her. There was no doubt that she would make him an ideal wife, and although at first the idea had taken him by surprise, for he had not thought of their relationship in terms of marriage, once he *did* think about it he had to admit that it had a good deal in its favour.

'There's no need to rush into any decision,' Karen pointed out, but it seemed that the senior partners were anxious Saul should conform to the way they believed things should be done, and within a month of the subject first being broached Saul told Karen that if she still favoured the idea he would like to get married.

Karen took a week to give him the answer, during which time she flew back to England and then returned to tell him that she did want to marry him, but, in view of her family's penurious state, she felt that a quiet New

York wedding would be in the best interests of all concerned.

'Daddy simply can't afford to give me the kind of wedding the family would expect. There just isn't the money. Much less embarrassing all round if we just get married quietly and discreetly over here, don't you think?'

Saul agreed, and yet somewhere at the back of his mind it was there again, that tight, painful sensation he remembered from childhood, that sense of disappointment...of pain almost. He dismissed it, of course, and accepted the approving congratulations of his employers.

To celebrate their marriage Saul and Karen gave a party at one of their regular restaurants. Karen chose the venue and the menu, both of which were a careful and well judged balance that allowed her to mix her colleagues from the agency with the new WASP friends they had made, and the older generation of partners from Saul's firm.

It was the general consensus of opinion among the senior wives that Karen was an ideal wife for an ambitious young man; that her obvious breeding and impressive lineage would be an asset to one who lacked the wealth and strength of a firm WASP background to support him.

Approving invitations to a variety of events were issued. Karen was asked if she would care to join several sub-committees for a variety of charities. She complained to Saul that she could not really spare the time, but nevertheless accepted the invitations.

'Charity work is a big part of the social scene here,' she explained when Saul protested that since their marriage he hardly ever seemed to see her. 'It's a good way of meeting the right sort of people...people with influence. Which reminds me, we'll have to think about joining a more up-market country club. I've heard on the grapevine that one of your senior partners is going to retire early. That means that someone will be moved up to take his place, which means that someone from lower down in the firm will also be promoted, and it's your particular field, so...'

'They've taken on four new analysts so far this year,' Saul pointed out to her. 'And I suspect that I'm the one on the lowest salary and——'

'All the more reason for making sure *you're* the one who gets the promotion,' Karen told him crisply.

They didn't make love that night. Karen was too tired, so Saul did some work instead.

They hadn't made love in over a week, but as his body registered this fact Saul picked up the files he had brought home and was soon immersed in them, his earlier desire to wake Karen up and take her in his arms so that he could make love to her pushed to one side.

CHAPTER TEN

SAUL got his promotion, and a large increase in salary. He planned to take Karen out to dinner at Le Circe to celebrate, but when he telephoned her she told him that she had to go away for a week on business. 'A brainstorming session to put together a new campaign for one of our largest clients.'

Karen's voice was full of unusual excitement. She had been picked to head the team chosen to come up with something innovative. It was a breathtaking opportunity, one she hadn't expected to come anywhere near getting at least until she was a few more rungs up the ladder.

In fact, she had been told that it was a testimony to her talents that she *had* been chosen. Brad Simons, the director who dealt with the account, had summoned her into his office to give her the news, and that evening he was taking her out to dinner so that they could discuss the client's particular foibles.

Saul tried not to feel disappointed. As he replaced the receiver he told himself that Karen had every right to feel pleased and that it was unfair of him to feel that somehow his promotion had been pushed into second place.

Everyone considered them a fortunate...even an ideal young couple; they had more social invitations than they could fulfil; their company was always in demand. They had the approval of Saul's senior partners, and he had even been mentioned in the *Wall Street Journal* as someone to watch. He had earned praise from the partners for the work he was doing, and he had received

several tentative, subtle enquiries from other organisations inviting him to join them.

And yet he still woke up in the night with that tight,
aching pain in his chest and the awareness that, somewhere in his dreams, a child had been crying. And while
he lay there, with Karen asleep beside him, he fought to
dismiss the feeling he had that somehow his life was
empty. How *could* it be? He had met all the targets he
had set for himself at this stage of his life and more. He
had a wife he knew was a good partner for him. They
were the envy of their friends, and he could tell from
his father's voice whenever he rang home how pleased
and proud he was of his progress.

Yes, he had everything he had ever planned to have.
Everything he had ever wanted. But inside there was still
that sense of loss, of a dimly perceived awareness that
something was missing.

And then Karen lost her job.

He came home one Friday to find her in the apartment,
her face white with rage as she paced the floor.

She had been sacked . . . fired, she told him. And why?
Why? Because those bastards had deliberately set her
up. They had known they were going to lose the McCall
contract and so they had set her up for a deliberate
fall . . . handing her all those lies . . . giving her all that
praise, and the whole time knowing . . .

At first she was so enraged that she could barely speak
coherently, and then slowly the whole story came out.
How the agency had slowly been losing some of its best
clients, and how Brad Simons had known that they were
going to lose their most important and biggest client,
McCall's . . .

'He set me up. I should have guessed. He never liked
me. He wanted me to fall on my face. He used me to
get out from under himself.'

Saul had never seen Karen so angry. Her eyes blazed
with the intensity of it; her body was so tense that he

was afraid to touch her, her face as white as the chic modern minimalistic walls of their living area.

'It isn't the end of the world,' he told her. 'You'll get another job.'

She rounded on him then, contempt spiking the look she gave him. 'You mean it isn't the end of *your* world,' she threw back at him. 'And as for getting another job...what agency would touch me now? I'm dead, Saul...poisoned meat. The ad exec who lost the McCall account—*that's* how I'll be remembered. Do you know when I walked out of my office today not a single soul looked at me...never mind spoke to me?

'Of course, they've always resented me because I'm not one of them...because of my background.' She was pacing the room again, bitterness corrosive in her voice, her eyes darkening with resentment.

Saul tried to comfort her, to tell her that there would be other jobs, other successes, but she refused to listen to him, deriding him as being naïve, asking him how he would have felt in her shoes. When he tried to take hold of her she pushed him off.

'Oh, for God's sake, Saul, don't touch me,' she told him. 'Can't you see that sex is the last thing I want right now? Men.' Her mouth curled with disdain. 'You really can't think of anything else, can you?'

The charge was so unjustified, the criticism and the contempt in her voice so acidic that Saul immediately stepped back from her. Sex had been the last thing on his mind. He had simply wanted to touch her, to hold her, memories of how, as a child, he had been comforted by his mother's arms somehow motivating him.

But Karen was making it plain that she didn't want his comfort...that she didn't want *him*.

That night she slept in the spare room.

He had work to do over the weekend. He offered to stay home with her, but she laughed bitterly and told him there was no point. For a month she stayed in the apartment, refusing to go anywhere or see anyone.

Saul's immediate boss commented to him that his wife was concerned because she had been trying to reach Karen by phone about a committee they were both on but had not been able to get in touch with her. He said nothing about her sacking from the agency, although everyone knew about it. The agency's loss of the McCall account had made news in the financial Press.

That night when Saul got home Karen was waiting for him. Bob Lucas's wife had called round to see her, she announced. Bob Lucas was Saul's boss, and he felt his body tense as he searched her face, looking for clues to see how she had reacted to this visit.

'I think it's time we moved out of New York, Saul,' she told him. 'There are some very nice properties available in Westchester and——'

'Westchester?' Saul stared at her. She had always claimed that she could never live anywhere but in the heart of the city, deriding those who chose to move outside it.

'After all,' she continued without looking at him, 'once we start a family we'll need more space.'

'A family? But I thought you were going to look for another job...'

'No,' Karen told him evenly. 'No, I'm not going to look for another job... How can I?' she demanded savagely. 'How can I after the way I've been humiliated and made to look a fool? What agency in their right minds would want me?'

'Karen, you're taking all this too personally,' he told her gently. 'I know what happened hurt, but... but everyone knows the agency was just using you... that they'd lost McCall's account long before you——'

'Before I what... before I really messed up for them? Oh, yeah, everyone knows that... and everyone's laughing at me for being such a fool as to fall into their trap. I can't go back, Saul... I can't and I won't.'

Nothing he could say would change her mind. They could afford to move out to Westchester, she told him. It was the right kind of career move for him to make. She was twenty-five... the right age to start thinking about a family.

All of what she said was quite true, but it still made Saul feel on edge and uneasy. Karen had always claimed that she wanted a career, she had always told him how important that was to her. It was not that he didn't want children, he did, but he was afraid that in starting their family now they would be doing so for the wrong reasons, and he was also afraid of telling Karen so. There was something dangerously brittle about her these days...something that made him feel that he had to hold back... to move cautiously so as not to upset her.

And so he gave in. They bought a house in Westchester, a move that was firmly applauded by the senior partners and rewarded with another increase in salary plus a slightly freer hand with his work and more responsibility.

His peers, those other graduates from Harvard, who had the WASP advantages that Saul had not, and who had at first been inclined to rather look down on him, now watched him enviously and sometimes even a little resentfully. He was gaining the reputation not just of having an astute brain, but also of being prepared to use it and to devote himself exclusively to any given task. Dedicated, hard-working, ambitious—those were the words used to describe him. And more and more often Saul found that he was being approached by friends and acquaintances outside the firm for his advice, discreet, off-the-record advice that they could use to further their own careers. Saul was also gaining the reputation of being a good person to know.

The house in Westchester was only small, but in one of the best residential districts, and it had a good-sized garden, or 'yard', as the Americans called it.

Karen was soon pregnant and apparently content. She was kept busy with her charity work and assured Saul that she was happy.

Saul could not be with her for Josephine's birth. He was away on business. He hadn't thought too much about how it would feel to become a father until he saw his small daughter for the first time.

She was three days old, and as he looked at her he fell in love for the second time in his life, but this was a very different emotion from the one he had felt for Angelica. This was for his child ... his daughter, a new life that was so much a part of him that when he reached out to touch her his eyes filled with tears and his body with protective pain.

Karen was a perfect mother. Everyone said so. She wanted the best ... the very best for her child. And so, of course, did Saul. He remembered his father telling him that one day he too would have a family to support ... He remembered everything his father had warned him about the importance of doing well and achieving success. He earned a good salary but they had heavy expenses. He started to work longer and longer hours.

Karen complained that he was never at home, and yet in the same breath she told him she had put Josephine's name down for an exclusive and expensive nursery school.

When Josephine was two years old one of the graduates who had been taken on at the same time as Saul got his partnership. Karen was bitterly resentful on Saul's behalf. That partnership should have been his, she complained, but of course Saul did not have John Feltham III's family connections.

Something about her comment rubbed Saul raw inside. Was Karen blaming *him* because he had not been offered a partnership? Had he failed in some way... failed to meet the standards, the targets he had set himself? It was not good enough simply to do reasonably well; his father had told him that much. He had to succeed, to excel.

Saul started looking around for another job. He found it in a thrusting, go-ahead new firm that had recently set up in business.

On the strength of his increased salary they moved house, and when Josephine was two and a half years old Thomas was born.

'Of course, it should have been the other way round,' Karen complained petulantly after the birth. 'Thomas should have been born first.' And somehow, as he listened to her, Saul felt as though she was actually blaming him; that he had somehow failed her in giving her first a daughter and then a son instead of the other way round.

Karen was once again the perfect mother. Saul, who had tried his best to involve himself with Josephine after her birth, but who had been firmly excluded from the nursery by his wife, found that with Thomas he was hanging back, allowing Karen to take charge, and, besides, he was away such a lot. The firm had so much business out on the West Coast that they had jokingly said that they might as well send Saul out there full-time.

When he had time to think about it, which wasn't very often, Saul was aware that he and Karen were drifting further and further apart; that they now virtually lived separate lives; that Karen seemed impatient and irritated by him when he was at home; that the children, especially Thomas, seemed not to respond to him at all.

When he could spare the time for a holiday, a vacation, it always seemed as though some all-important

business would come up and that he would be forced to
turn what should have been a complete break into a
working holiday. But then, what option did he have if
he was to succeed? And success was even more important to him now that he had a family to support.

It was when Thomas was still a baby that, on a fleeting
visit to Britain, a business visit into which he had
managed to squeeze some time out to see his family, he
discovered that his younger sister was pregnant...
pregnant by a married man who, it seemed, had no intention of leaving his wife.

She was so close to the end of her medical training,
and he couldn't stop himself from asking her,
'Why...why, Christie? You could have had an abortion.
You——'

'I didn't want one,' she told him fiercely. 'This is *my*
child, Saul,' she went on, holding her stomach. 'My
child.'

'But your career...'

She gave him a painful smile. 'Yes, I know.'

'Mum and Dad...do they know?'

She shook her head. 'No, not yet. I'm dreading telling
them. They were so proud of me, especially Mum. I don't
think Dad ever really felt that it was quite the thing for
a woman...to want to be a doctor.'

It all seemed such a waste...such a crime. To have
to give up all that she had worked for. Saul contemplated the future that lay ahead of his sister and her child,
the child she was determined to have, and knew there
was only one thing he could do.

When Christie went home to tell her parents about her
pregnancy, Saul went with her. Christie must not give
up her training, he told them, and before he left to return
to New York it was arranged that Christie would return
home to live; that their mother would look after the baby
once he or she arrived and that Christie would continue
with her studies and take her final exams.

'I don't know how to thank you,' she whispered weepily to him as she saw him off at Heathrow.

'Thank me by succeeding,' he told her quietly. 'Thank me by working hard and qualifying.' He hugged her and kissed her, but went back to New York with a hard lump of undissolved pain burning inside him.

Karen was not pleased when she heard what he had done. With two children of their own to bring up and educate, they could hardly afford to take on the responsibility for a third—a fourth if you counted the cost of supporting his sister through what remained of her medical schooling.

Her voice became shrill and sour as she yelled at him. She had lost weight, and, where she had once looked elegant, she now looked thin, her face and voice marred with dissatisfaction.

As he looked at her and recognised that dissatisfaction Saul knew that it was his fault, that he had somehow failed as a provider...a husband...a man. That he had not been successful enough.

He started to look around for a better job. After all, they needed the extra money. What he wanted now was to find a business where ultimately he would be the one in control. When he was head-hunted by Sir Alex, he thought that he had found it.

Sir Alex owned the Davidson Corporation. He had no son to succeed him, he told Saul openly, and he was looking for someone he could groom to one day take over for him. In Saul he thought that he might have found that someone.

Saul thought so too. He brought all his formidable intelligence and skills to bear on attacking the problems of turning Davidson's from a company that was reasonably successful to one that was the most successful in its field.

The financial Press showered him with plaudits and praise. Sir Alex rewarded him with a generous profit-

sharing scheme, a large office, a new car and a very generous salary, but he did not relinquish control.

What he did do, though, was to agree to one of Saul's
suggestions that it might be an advantageous time to re-
organise the London office. Sir Alex had two power-
bases: the office he ran from New York, and the London
end, which was not performing as well as could have
been hoped. What Saul had not bargained for was that
he would be put in charge of that office.

By now he was well versed enough in office politics
to listen, narrow-eyed, to Sir Alex's suggestion and to
wonder cynically if this was Sir Alex's way of demoting
him. As he had quickly discovered once he joined the
company, he was not the first ambitious young man in
whom Sir Alex thought he might have found his 'natural
successor'. Not the first. But he intended that he should
be the last.

Karen was furious when he gave her the news. She
and the children were established in the American way
of life. She had neither the intention nor the desire to
move to London, she told him flatly.

Saul was stunned. He tried to reason with her, to point
out the advantages of the move, but Karen refused to
listen. Saul was baffled and infuriated by her attitude.
He was doing this for her, he told her furiously, for her
and for their children. Karen remained adamant. She
was *not* going to London. Saul would have to go without
her. After all, there was no real guarantee that the venture
was going to be a success.

Saul interpreted her comments as a lack of belief in
his ability to succeed; a questioning of his ability to
protect the financial future of herself and his children.
It resurrected all his old feelings of anxiety and tension.
He had to prove himself; to prove that he was successful
and that he could be even more successful.

Perhaps Karen was right to refuse to go with him.
Perhaps she was right to demand that he prove to her

and to the world that he could achieve the targets he had
set himself.

Saul went to London without Karen. Six months later
she filed for divorce. Their marriage had been failing
for a long time, she told him calmly when she made her
announcement at Christmas. Saul had flown home on
Christmas Eve. The Westchester house, the new one
Karen and the children had moved into when Saul got
his first year's profits from the company, had a long
shrub-bordered drive, and was well set back from the
road, a 1920s Tudor Gothic edifice made respectable with
its coating of ivy. Discreet outdoor lighting sprang to
life as he drove towards the house. When the front door
opened he could see the Christmas tree in the large square
hallway. It was illuminated with a myriad tiny plain white
lights, the tree itself decorated in traditional reds and
golds, satin ribbons tied to the branches, no trace of
inelegant glitter anywhere in sight. The rich red carpet
in the hallway gave the room a warm glow, subtly pat-
terned heavy curtains hung at the windows either side
of the doorway, and in the ornate wooden-frame fireplace a log fire glowed.

The room was full of the rich, warm scent of
spices...of Christmas itself, and yet as he stepped inside
the house Saul felt cold; felt a deep inner iciness, a chill
of foreboding that took him instantly back to his
childhood, back to his memories of those confusing,
painful things he had felt when his father talked to him
about the importance of success.

Over dinner Josey was subdued, turning to her mother
before answering his questions. Even baby Tom refused
to hold out his chubby arms to be held by his father.

When Saul pushed away his meal, barely touched,
Karen raised an eyebrow, her mouth compressing with
irritation. He shook his head. He had suddenly lost his
appetite; he felt alien, out of place, an intruder. The doll
he had bought for Josephine in London was, he realised,

far too impersonal a gift for the withdrawn girl sitting watching him with such cool, wary eyes, and as for the train set he had bought for Tom... Obviously the boy was still too young to appreciate that present, and there was every likelihood that Saul wouldn't be around to see him eventually start to play with it. Saul wasn't happy with his thoughts.

'Uncle Richard said he would come by to take me to the park on Tuesday,' Josephine announced to her mother. 'He said to tell you that he'd drop by on Boxing Day and that you weren't to forget that he was taking you to the Feldmans' for drinks.'

A faint glow of colour seemed to illuminate Karen's pale face as she removed Saul's plate. She was still thin; she had never regained the weight she had lost before the children's births, and the sport she played had given her a taut suppleness that somehow Saul found depressing. As he watched her he contrasted her almost boyish figure with the round softness of the girl she had been when he first knew her.

She was wearing her hair in a different style and she had changed her make-up. She looked, he realised with a small start of shock, far more American than British; she had lost that difference, that individuality which had once so clearly marked her out. She was wearing a silk shirt and a plain wool skirt, and her skin had the cool year-round tan of someone who spent time and money on maintaining her appearance. She looked...she looked groomed, he decided as he hunted for the right word... Too groomed. Impossible to think of taking this elegant, disdainful woman to bed and making love to her. If he did, it would no doubt be an antiseptic, unappealing process, a dutiful coupling after which she would retire to her bathroom to fastidiously and thoroughly remove the physical evidence of his intimacy with her.

There was a raw, uncomfortable sensation in his chest, a sense of being weighed down...a depression...an awareness of pain...of failure.

Karen was saying something about taking the children to Aspen during the Christmas vacation. Saul frowned and started to tell her that he doubted that he would be able to go with them; that he would have to return to London virtually before the New Year.

'Uncle Richard's coming with us.'

He focused on Josey's face as the girl delivered the aggressive statement, suddenly sharply aware of the hostility emanating from everyone else in the room.

'Josephine...I want to speak to your father on my own. Why don't you take Tom and go down to the den and watch television for a while?'

Quietly, without looking at him, Josephine slid out of her seat, gathered up Tom and headed for the door.

Almost as soon as it was closed Karen told him coolly, 'I want a divorce.'

He stared at her, his heartbeat suddenly accelerating, his body reacting to the threat by going into an adrenalin-boosted fight mode, but Karen wouldn't let him speak.

Their marriage had been failing for a long time, she told him...in fact, she should never have married him in the first place. Should never have given up her career in New York.

Saul listened in silence as she told him how she felt about the way she had been forced to abandon her own career to bring up his children, the way she had been forced to stay in the background, a stay-at-home wife, while he neglected her and their children in favour of his career. There was, she told him, someone else. Someone who was more than prepared to accept that she had other needs beyond and above those of merely being a wife and a mother...someone with whom the children had already bonded in a way they had never bonded with him.

There was to be no fuss, no squabbling, she told him. That would be bad for the children. The children he had proved were not important to him by the way he had left them and her when he took up the job in London, a job she had pleaded with him not to take. Financially there need be no problems. He . . . her lover was more than prepared to support both her and the children. The Westchester house could be sold and the proceeds split between them.

'You can keep the damned house,' Saul had told her savagely when he was at last allowed to speak.

Later that night, alone and wide awake in the anonymity of his motel room, he reflected helplessly on all that he could and should have said, and cursed himself for his ineptitude.

He spent Christmas Day alone in his motel room, asking himself over and over again where he had gone wrong. He had done as his father had told him, hadn't he? He had worked . . . achieved . . . succeeded.

Karen could not be dissuaded from going ahead with the divorce and in the end, rather than upset the children, who, she told him cruelly and clinically, did not really consider him to be their father at all, he gave way.

She and 'Uncle Richard' were married almost as soon as the divorce was final. Under pressure from Karen's lawyers, Saul had agreed not to demand access to the children. It would only upset and distress them, Karen had told him, pointing out that he rarely saw them anyway, and for their sakes, remembering how they had turned away from him at Christmas, how they had rejected him, Saul felt bound to agree.

Richard had his own business. A year after he and Karen were married he went bankrupt. Karen got in touch with Saul, reminding him that the children were his. Saul agreed to support them, but Karen still refused to allow him any real contact with them. It would only upset them, she said, and during the one meeting his

lawyers managed to arrange for him to see them they
were so antagonistically aggressive towards him that he
had to agree, and, besides, he was rarely in the States
these days.

Ironically, the British arm of Davidson's was thriving
and succeeding way beyond his original forecasts. He
was commonly and sometimes enviously known as Sir
Alex's 'blue-eyed boy'.

Over the years he had discreet sexual liaisons with
several women, but made it plain to all of them right
from the start that he was not looking for any kind of
emotional commitment and that he could most certainly
not give one. None of them believed him ... at first. The
business was his life, its cut and thrust life's elixir. He
neither wanted nor needed anything else.

And then, totally out of the blue, Karen and Richard
moved to Britain. Richard was working for a West-Coast-
based computer firm, which had opened an office in the
south of England. He was transferred there with certain
other key staff.

Saul knew of this because he was still financially supporting his children, and of course Karen had to write
to him requesting him to redirect his monthly cheques.

'Why don't you try to make some kind of contact with
them?' Christie had suggested to him when he'd told her
what had happened. 'They *are*, after all, your children,
Saul.'

'Not as far as they're concerned,' he'd told her bluntly,
but whenever he thought about it, which he tried not to
do too often, there was an ache inside him, a
hunger ... the same kind of ache and hunger he had
known as a child. He knew that people found him in-
timidating and that they withdrew from him, all except
Cathy.

Cathy loved him. Right from being a small child she
had loved him. Running up to him whenever he could
make time to visit, holding out her arms to him, de-

manding to be picked up and cuddled. And he loved her too, loved her with an intensity that sometimes confused and disturbed him. How could he love this child of his sister's so much when, as his ex-wife had so bitterly told him, he had not loved his own children? But he had loved them. When they were born... He could still remember so vividly how he had felt the first time he'd seen Josephine, the first time he'd picked her up in the hospital.

A nurse had come bustling in, he remembered, snatching the baby out of his arms, telling him that he must not touch her.

Karen had done much the same once Josephine was at home. He remembered once, when Karen had gone out shopping, Josephine had been crying. He had picked her up and had realised she needed changing. He had done his best, but his hands were large and the baby so tiny, and when she lay there, looking up at him so trustingly, he had felt so clumsy, so incompetent and yet at the same time so proud, so full of love.

What on earth did he think he was doing? Karen had demanded, pushing him out of the way. Josephine had immediately burst into tears, causing Karen to pick her up and croon to her, 'Never mind, darling. Mummy's here now...Mummy's here.' And Saul had left the nursery, knowing that somehow he had transgressed...that he was not needed.

With Cathy, though, it was different. From the time she was a baby she had crowed with joy when Christie, weary from the long hours she spent at the hospital, had picked her up and thrust her into Saul's arms, telling him, 'Here, Saul, you hold her, otherwise she's going to think the world is completely made up of females, and I don't want that for her.'

Unlike Karen, Christie seemed to have no qualms at all about leaving her baby with him, and when Cathy was wet he changed her nappy for her and received a big beam of delight and a crow of pleasure in return. He found that he was spending more and more of his spare time with his sister and her child.

And then their father died. At the funeral Saul stood apart from the others, trying to come to terms with his confused feelings. He felt sorrow and pain, of course, and guilt as well ... guilt because somehow he still had the feeling of having failed, of somehow not having met enough targets, of not having done enough to prove to his father that he had listened to everything he had told him, of not having done enough to make it up to him because he had not got all he had wanted out of life. And then shamingly allied to that emotion was a frightening well of anger.

Anger against his father! His father, who had loved him. His father, who had only wanted the best for him ... the very best. His father, who had brought him up to know how important it was to be a man, how heavy a man's responsibilities were and how strong he needed to be to carry them ...

With Karen and Richard living in England, Saul made sporadic attempts to see his children. Sometimes Karen agreed, sometimes she did not, but what was constant was that the visits were never a success. Neither child seemed able to talk to him. Of the two of them, Josephine was the more antagonistic and aggressive. She seemed to hate him, whereas Thomas simply shut him out.

Thomas was now at boarding-school, the fees paid by Saul, of course, while Josephine attended a private local girls' day school. Both of them were doing well. They had to. After all, one day they would have to support themselves, Karen commented bitterly.

She had, Saul noticed, become a very bitter woman, who seemed to lose no opportunity of telling them her marriage to him had contributed to the destruction of her own career plans and hopes.

Saul said nothing. After all, what was there to say?
He had no regrets about the divorce, but when it came
to his children... Every time he saw them his sense of
failure increased. He found that sometimes he was actually avoiding having to see them because of that guilt.

But Davidson's continued to thrive. At Saul's insti-
gation they had taken over several weaker rivals, deadly,
precise take-overs that stripped the fallen rivals of their
assets and which left their managements stunned and
disbelieving. But still Sir Alex remained in control; still
Saul felt that the final prize, the ultimate success was
being withheld from him.

And then, the Christmas after his thirty-ninth
birthday, Cathy had looked across at him, her eyes alight
with love and excitement, her face glowing with the
happy pleasure of the day, and she had said to him, 'I'm
so happy, Uncle Saul. Are you?'

He had started to assent automatically, but for some
reason he had stopped; for some reason the simple untidy
warmth of his sister's sitting-room had momentarily
dimmed and he was once again standing listening to his
father telling him how important it was to succeed,
watching with pain and apprehension as he saw the unhappiness in the older man's eyes, and then, as he blinked
away that vision, he had another one: the hallway of the
Westchester house, the tree with its red and gold satin
bows, the set, bitter face of his ex-wife, the taut, withdrawn expression of his daughter and the lack of recognition in his young son, and he had experienced a
sensation within himself that left him bereft of words,
a spasm of pain contorting his face so that Christie, who
was watching him, had asked anxiously if he was feeling
ill.

Her cooking was a joke between them, and he had
complained last Christmas that her roast potatoes were
more like cannon balls, more for Cathy's benefit than

anything else. She loved it when he teased her mother and was mocked in return.

'No. It's nothing,' he told her and he told himself the same, but after that nothing was the same. It was as though his whole world had somehow subtly shifted its axis so that he was looking at things from an unfamiliar and often unwelcome angle. He found himself questioning things he had never questioned . . . he found that he was aware of feelings, emotions that he didn't want to be aware of . . . he lost track of what was going on at an important meeting. He couldn't sleep; he was irritable with his staff; he was frighteningly aware that somehow his life was slipping out of his own control, and that knowledge generated further fear, further anger, terror almost, as he fought desperately to regain all that he felt he was in danger of losing.

He was afraid . . . more afraid than he could ever remember being in his entire life; more afraid than he had been when as a child he had looked into his father's eyes and seen the pain there, more afraid than he had been when he'd failed his A levels, more afraid than he had been when he'd held his small daughter, more afraid than when Karen had asked him for a divorce; and yet he could not analyse why he should experience that fear, or what there was to fear.

He had everything he had ever wanted, didn't he? All right, so there had been some sacrifices, but he wasn't the only man to be divorced and lose contact with his children . . . that was what happened these days. It was sad, but it was a fact of life. He was successful. Sir Alex had intimated six months ago that he was virtually ready to step down. There was no one else on the board to challenge Saul's right to step into his shoes. So what was happening to him? Why, when he woke up in the morning, did he have the sour taste of bile in his mouth? Why, when he looked in the mirror, did he experience revulsion? Why, when he pictured the faces of his children, did he feel such violence... such anger?

Stress, the doctors said. Stress! The ultimate accolade... the ultimate acknowledgement that he had made it. What successful businessman did not know the meaning of that word, did not thrive on the adrenalin-based narcotic it produced? But his stress wasn't like that. His stress did not fuel him; it destroyed him... it was as though in some way his own body, his own senses, his own perceptions had turned on him and attacked him.

And then Sir Alex had told him that he wanted him to use his friendship with Dan Harper to enable them to take over his company in an asset-stripping exercise which would have left it as picked clean of every ounce of flesh as though carrion had devoured it, and something within him, something he had hitherto not known existed, refused to let him do it.

For the first time in his adult life he experienced the realisation that his brain could not always have domination over his emotions. That awareness had produced a shock effect as cataclysmic to him as a complete nervous breakdown might have been to someone else.

It had been weeks, months almost, before he had been able to accept what was happening to him, and since then he had been experiencing the most acutely painful kind of self-analysis and self-inspection he had ever endured.

He had looked at himself for the first time in years; had seen himself not in the image cast for him by his father, and the long shadow of his father beside that image dominating it, but as the man he actually was, an individual with a right to his own feelings and needs, and he had experienced the deep soul-sickness of someone who knew that spiritually and emotionally he had been denied something deeply necessary to his life.

He had tried to ignore his feelings, of course, dismissing them, fighting them, even ignoring them, but stubbornly they refused to let him go; they were his accusers, his tormentors, his judge and jury, and they never seemed to tire of drawing for him comparisons between what his life was and what it might have been.

Another, weaker man might have tried to blame his father, but Saul had loved his too strongly for that, and still loved him. But did he still believe that his father's ambitions for him had been right?

Tiredly he got up. It was late. He should be in bed, not sitting here, indulging himself in useless introspection.

Tomorrow he would have to start making some discreet enquiries about Carey's. It was one thing to know that the company was looking for either a buyer or an investor; it was quite another to get them to accept the kind of offer Sir Alex wanted to make, and, more important, to accept the consequences of that offer.

Sir Alex was no philanthropist. He would run the company on the smallest shoestring he could; that would mean wholesale redundancies, and a virtual closing down of production, leaving the company as a mere shell, to be reactivated when it suited Sir Alex to do so, and then only so that he could take advantage of the government's new grants package.

None of that need necessarily influence the company's shareholders, of course. The bank, for one, would be only too glad to see it sold off, if only to clear their outstanding loans.

Control of the company's shares lay with Davina James, and everything written in the reports he had on her indicated that she would be only too pleased to sell.

So why did he have this niggling *frisson* of awareness that obtaining Carey Chemicals was not going to be as easy as he had first assumed?

CHAPTER ELEVEN

LEO got the phone call from the Schloss at four o'clock in the afternoon. He had just come out of a particularly difficult and aggressive board meeting during which he had only just managed to hold on to his temper when Wilhelm had deliberately obstructed every one of his proposals.

Torn between a helpless desire to laugh at his brother's sheer cussedness and refusal to accept that their father's decision to give him control of the corporation was as much an anathema to him as it was to Wilhelm, and an equally dangerous surge of almost savage resentment at Wilhelm's obstinacy—after all, what real objection could Wilhelm genuinely have to Leo's proposals to increase their intake of university graduates to include more young people from their fellow EC countries?—the sheer effort of controlling his irritation and ignoring his brother's constant, relentless needling had left him with the beginnings of a sharply painful migraine.

Migraine was something he thought he had stopped suffering from years ago, and it struck him now as ominous that he had started having them again almost from the moment he had had to take over running the corporation.

His father would have told him that it was a sign of weakness. Leo thought otherwise. If they were caused by any one emotion, that emotion was most probably guilt. Guilt at having, no matter how unknowingly, deprived his brother of the role he had always believed would be his.

So why not simply step down and let Wilhelm take his place? He grimaced to himself. Wilhelm knew as well as he did himself that that simply wasn't possible, not under the terms of his father's will, which were extraordinarily specific and detailed. Indeed, they were so detailed that when Leo had been read them the fact that struck him most forcefully had been not so much that his father wanted *him* to take control, but that he wanted to prevent Wilhelm doing so.

At first when he recognised the familiar voice of his grandmother's housekeeper on the other end of the line he wasn't unduly concerned, but when he heard the anxiety in her flustered words his stomach muscles tensed and coiled, his fingers tensing as he gripped the receiver.

His grandmother was ninety-two years old; she had outlived her husband, her sisters, and even her daughter, and now it seemed that she was reaching the end of her own long life.

Her nurse had asked that the baroness's grandsons be informed that the old lady was approaching death, the housekeeper told him, her voice thick with tears. He would be there just as soon as he could, Leo told her, promising, 'I shall leave immediately, Helga.'

As soon as he had replaced the receiver he rang through to Wilhelm's office, only to be told that his brother had left the building without telling anyone where he was going.

Leo's mouth compressed. That usually meant that Wilhelm was going to see his latest mistress. Like father, like son, and Wilhelm was as brutally contemptuous of keeping his marriage vows as their father had been, but at least Wilhelm didn't physically abuse his wife, Anna... As far as Leo knew.

Broodingly Leo stared towards his office window. Beyond it lay the familiar Hamburg skyline of the industrial side of the city and the river. Wilhelm had never shared the rapport with their grandparents that had done so much to alleviate the misery of Leo's childhood. Wilhelm had looked upon the holidays spent at the

Schloss as a form of incarceration, although he was keen
enough to drop their grandfather's title into his conversation if he thought it was likely to impress, and Leo
knew that, like their father, Wilhelm bitterly resented
the fact that it was their mother's family that held the
title, the long centuries of tradition; the blue blood that
went back to the times of the great Charlemagne.

Their parents shared a very distant family connection;
in effect, Leo's paternal grandfather had been a cousin
many times removed of his maternal grandfather, and
his parents had originally met when Heinrich von Hessler
had come to the Schloss while tracing his family ancestry.

That had been early on in the war, and Leo had always
wondered a little at his father's apparent freedom to
travel at such a time, but, like so much else, he had
quickly realised that it was yet another subject which
must not be broached.

As he explained to his secretary why he had to leave
he put a call through to Wilhelm's wife. Anna was an
elegant, almost too frail woman, whom Leo privately
pitied. She had been a model when Wilhelm first met
her, but her youthful beauty had long since faded into
gaunt despair as the reality of marriage to Wilhelm took
its toll on her.

Keeping his voice as neutral as he could, Leo explained the situation, asking if she would tell Wilhelm
what had happened when he came home.

'Don't you mean *if* he comes home?' she asked bitterly.

There was nothing Leo could say. He put down the
receiver just as his secretary walked into his office to
announce that a company helicopter was being prepared
for his flight to the Schloss. It was corporation money
that kept the Schloss in the hands of the family, and Leo
had always sensed how much his grandparents had felt
the burden of their son-in-law's 'charity'. His grandfather was dead now. He had died when Leo was fifteen.

Stopping off at home merely to collect a change of clothes, Leo headed for the private airstrip that housed the company's two helicopters.

The pilot was waiting for him. Leo acknowledged his greeting and followed him out to the waiting machine.

His grandmother was still conscious, but growing very weak, the housekeeper had told him during her telephone call. What were her thoughts as she came to the end of her long life? Leo wondered. Were they of her past, or were they of what might lie ahead? She had lived through so much. Seen so much. He ached inside at the thought of her death, a part of him a small boy still afraid of being left alone, even while the majority of him accepted the inevitability of what had to be.

From the air, the ravine of the River Neckar looked like a toyland, the river itself glinting in the early-evening sun, the steeply wooded escarpments dappled in various shades of green apart from where the sharp sheer sides of its medieval castles rose from the ground like jagged rough-edged teeth.

Their own *schloss* was small by comparison, its original medieval structure overlayed by its later seventeenth-century façade. Leo could see it up ahead now. The family flag, the standard bearing the ancient arms bestowed on the family by Charlemagne, still flew at full mast, but ominously there was no breeze to stir the canvas, until the descent of the helicopter made it rattle wildly in the down-draught.

Helga was waiting for him. She had been with the family for as long as Leo could remember. Her husband was in charge of the Schloss's maintenance and had for many years been his grandmother's chauffeur. He knew how fond they both were of his grandmother. There were those who did not know her well who considered her to be autocratic and withdrawn, but Leo knew the real warmth that lay behind her formal manner.

'My grandmother,' he began, his heart catching at the sight of Helga's tears.

'She still lives,' Helga told him. 'But the nurse feels that it cannot be long.'

Silently Leo patted her hand, his eyes taking a few seconds to adjust to the dimness of the huge silent hall. This, the original great room of the medieval castle, always seemed to him to hold echoes of its origins, despite the panelling with which his eighteenth-century ancestors had cloaked it. Faded rugs, surely very like those that must have once been brought back from the Crusades, were dotted here and there, adding dull patches of colour to the vastness of the stone-flagged floor. A stone staircase rose grimly upwards, its harshness only slightly softened by the carved wooden banister.

On the second floor was a huge window, the family's arms and honours picked out on it in richly coloured stained glass. The window overlooked the Neckar. During the Second World War the commander of the SS regiment stationed locally had insisted that the window be destroyed to allow his troops to properly survey the river and the skies above it.

The story went that his grandmother had announced that if the SS commander wished to employ his men in carefully removing the stained glass piece by piece in order to replace it with clear glass then he was perfectly at liberty to do so, but that she would not stand by and see her country's heritage destroyed simply so that his men might obtain a view of the Neckar that might just as easily be obtained by stationing themselves in one of the Schloss's many attic rooms.

It had been Helga who had told Leo this story, and he had been far too overawed by this evidence of his grandmother's puissance to even dare to think of questioning her about the event.

Now the evening light shone through the glass, making a golden halo around the cherubic features of the small child who was said to represent the infant son of a medieval baron who had handed the child over to his enemy as a hostage for the safety of his overlord, only to receive the child's body back in place of his living son.

Yes, the Schloss had known its fair share of violence, both given and received. He could still remember the repugnance he had felt on being shown, by Wilhelm, of course, the site of the oubliette where once their family had imprisoned its hostages.

And yet, for all the violence of its past, now the Schloss breathed tranquillity, as though somehow its great age had conferred on it an absolution for all that had happened within its walls. It was as though the Schloss, having known all the injustice and cruelty of which human nature was capable, had somehow weathered and endured man's weaknesses and flaws and had emerged from the experience to offer its benign serenity and acceptance to all who came within its walls.

He had always felt the atmosphere of the Schloss very strongly, unlike either his father or Wilhelm, who, while prone to boasting of its existence, were also somehow resentful of that existence, fearing perhaps that it overshadowed them and their achievements.

He went upstairs alone, too familiar with the warren of corridors and blank wall endings to have to think where he was going.

His grandmother's bedroom in the west tower was the room she had come to as a new bride. Her only daughter had been born there, and her husband had died there in the vast bed, which had cradled the bodies of so many generations of his family in life as well as in death.

He knocked briefly on the door before entering. His grandmother's nurse, who had been sitting beside the bed, got up as he walked in. A tall, statuesque woman in her later thirties, she moved with that apparently effortless glide developed by professional nurses.

Although she wasn't wearing a uniform, Leo could almost hear the starched crackle of antiseptic clothing as she walked.

He looked towards the bed. His grandmother lay there motionless, her eyes closed. His heart gave a tremendous bound of fear and pain, but the nurse quickly reassured him, telling him in a soft monotone, 'She still lives, although I do not think it will be long. You will want to be alone with her.'

She had a formal, distancing manner that could sound cold, but Leo knew she was deeply devoted to his grandmother. She had been with her for the last five years, and he made a mental note to make sure that, if his grandmother had not thought to do so, her devotion was properly rewarded.

There was no money in his mother's family, a fact which his father had never ceased to use as a means of taunting and deriding his in-laws. Once, when Leo had been foolish enough to leap to his grandparents' defence and to announce hotly that money was not everything, the force of the blow his father had dealt him had knocked him to the floor and left him bruised for over a week afterwards.

He took the chair vacated by the nurse. His grandmother lay still beneath the covers, her fragile body barely discernible. Her hands lay on the coverlet, the skin withered and puckered, the gold of her rings worn thin. Instinctively Leo reached out, covering her hand with both of his.

'Leo.'

The shock of hearing her speak his name made him jump. She opened her eyes and smiled at him.

'So, my time has finally come, has it?'

She must have seen his distress because she smiled again.

'No. It is all right. I am ready to go. More than ready. Is Wilhelm with you?'

He could hear the exhaustion in her voice, but he had not expected that she would be so lucid...so much the woman he had always known. He had been afraid of coming here, he admitted. Afraid of what he might see, but she was just as she had always been.

'No. He... There was a meeting. I have left a message. He will be here soon.'

'You mean he is with one of his women.' As Leo watched, her eyes hardened. 'Who can ever know the tricks fate will play? That you should be so like Wilhelm's father and that he should be so like yours.'

Leo stared at her. His heart had started to pound with sick, heavy shock, his brain telling him that his ears were playing tricks on him. His body suddenly felt cold and heavy, clammy with fear and awareness.

His grandmother had closed her eyes again. He leaned towards her.

'Grandmother.'

She opened her eyes and looked at him.

'Tell me,' he begged her urgently. 'What do you mean? Wilhelm and I have the same father.'

'You mean that you believe that I am a senile old woman who cannot separate truth from fiction. Oh, Leo, if only that were so. Perhaps I should have said nothing to you, but since your mother's death it has lain so heavily on my conscience. I should never have allowed her to marry your father. It would have been easier to bear the disgrace of her illegitimate child than to suffer the pain of knowing how she suffered through her marriage, but things were different in those days and we were already under suspicion from the SS. Your grandfather had made his views on Hitler too clear. It was only our name that protected us, and for how much longer? Your father...' She closed her eyes as though silencing herself, and then said slowly, 'He had already approached your grandfather to ask for Elizabet's hand, but she...there was someone else . . . a young man she had met at university. They were very much in love.

'He was very gentle, a pacifist, I imagine you would call him now, but he was not a coward. He had great spirit, and he loved your mother as she did him.

'Heinrich hated him, and I have often wondered if it was Heinrich who betrayed him to the SS, but perhaps it is best that there are some things that we never know. He was taken prisoner . . . executed. Your mother begged Heinrich to try to help him, but it was no good.

'I didn't know then that they had been lovers. Your mother was very young, barely eighteen.

'When less than six weeks after his death she announced that she wished to marry your father I could not believe it. It was then that she told me that she had conceived her dead lover's child. She must marry Heinrich, she told me, she must have a father for her child. She could not face the disgrace she would suffer if she did not. No one but I knew she was pregnant. She had already, she told me fiercely, given herself to Heinrich, and I saw then that there was no price she would not pay to protect her lover's child.

'They were married quickly and quietly, and when Wilhelm was born it was here at the Schloss. Fortunately it was an easy birth so that we were able to pretend that Wilhelm was a seven-month child, a child conceived on the night of his parents' wedding, so to speak.

'Your father never questioned that Wilhelm was his. I suspected, although I have no proof, that your mother took care to deceive him into believing that he was her first and only lover. They moved to Switzerland shortly after the birth.'

Her voice had started to fade, and as Leo looked at her she closed her eyes. He hated to press her any further; to question her when she was so obviously close to death, but there was something he had to know, a suspicion as cold as the lack of love he knew his father had always had for him.

He leaned over the bed, his voice low and tense, his hand enfolding that of his grandmother, stroking the aged fragile flesh.

'Grandmother...my father...did he know, in the end?'

At first he thought she could no longer hear him; that she was already slipping into a pre-death unconsciousness, but then she turned her head and opened her eyes.

'Yes,' she told him. 'Your mother, before she died ... He had been so cruel to her, Leo; so unkind. Many times I wanted to beg her to leave him, but I knew she would not. She was afraid, you see... afraid for you... afraid that your father would persuade the courts to give him custody... and afraid for us as well... afraid of your father's vengeance, and so she stayed, but in the end she exacted her own payment from him for all the unhappiness he had caused her.

'She knew she was going to die. She had insisted on the doctors' telling her the truth. She told me what she intended to do. She could not die with the secret of Wilhelm's true fathering on her conscience, she told me.'

As Leo watched, his grandmother took a deep breath and then shuddered.

'She was my daughter, my only child, and I had watched your father abuse and destroy her. I knew that it was not out of guilt that she wanted to tell him the truth but out of anger and hatred. He came to see me afterwards...'

She closed her eyes and then opened them again, and Leo could see that they were bright with tears.

'He asked me if what she had told him was true. I told him it was. I think he would have disinherited Wilhelm publicly then, had his pride permitted it.'

'"Wilhelm is your son," I told him. "You have moulded him in your own image."'

'"He is not my son," he told me, and I shall never forget the way he spoke, the way he looked. "I have no son. No true son. That bitch your daughter has seen to that."

'"Leo is your child," I told him.

'"Leo... the seed which gave him life was mine, but that is all he has of me. Your daughter took good care to make sure of that. She has cheated me... deceived me. May she rot in hell for eternity for it."'

Leo saw his grandmother shudder as she closed her eyes. 'If anyone is to have that fate, if indeed such a place as hell actually exists, it will be my father,' he said painfully. His own eyes ached and burned with the tears he could not shed. Suddenly like a child again, he yearned to be able to unburden himself of the fear and pain of his own thoughts, to tell this woman he had always been so close to of his own discoveries about his father's past, but as he blinked fiercely the frightened child within him was subdued and the man took control. How could he add to what she had already suffered, the pain she had already known?

'So that is why he left control of Hessler Chemie to me,' he said instead.

'Yes. Because *you* are his son.'

His son. 'My son... *My* son.' Now he understood what his father had meant with those final bitter, hating words.

There was still one question he had to ask.

'Wilhelm... does he know the truth?'

His grandmother shook her head.

The baroness died at two o'clock in the morning. Leo was with her, holding her hand as she slid from one last shallow breath into infinity. He knew immediately that she had gone, even though he continued to hold her hand within his for some time afterwards.

Wilhelm arrived in the morning, heavy-jowled, his jaw nicked where he had shaved, his temper savagely on edge. He still smelled of sex, Leo recognised nauseously as he listened to him cursing the inconvenience of their grand-mother's death.

Even now, knowing the truth, it was difficult to accept that Wilhelm was not Heinrich's son. His attitude, his manner, his temper were all so much Heinrich's, but then, he had been taught to model himself on the older man almost from the moment of his birth, and his mother had probably not even realised what was happening in her desire to protect her new-born child—her lover's child—from her husband's wrath if he ever discovered the truth. How glad she must have been, how relieved to see the way Heinrich had totally accepted Wilhelm as his own. When had she started to realise what he was doing to the child... her child...?

Leo remembered the way she had always kept him close to her. Because she had seen what Heinrich had done to Wilhelm?

Sickened, he turned away from his brother, full of pity and compassion for him. What might he have been if Heinrich had not distorted and maimed his personality, fostering within him all the arrogance, the greed, the selfishness which made him the man he was?

And how could he tell him the truth? Leo knew that he could not; that to do so would totally destroy him.

'She's gone, then, has she?' Wilhelm demanded aggressively.

'Yes,' Leo acknowledged heavily. 'She's gone.'

Later, reflecting on what he had discovered, Leo wondered how any man, even one like his father, could reject a child he had brought up as his own the way Heinrich had finally in his will rejected Wilhelm. To love a child was surely to love the *child*, and not the seed that had given him life?

But then, his father had never actually loved either of them. Leo doubted if he had ever loved anyone, including himself. And Leo knew how all-important it was to love oneself, to accept one's flaws and weaknesses, because without that capacity for self-compassion, how could one truly love or show compassion for anyone else?

As a young man, disturbed by the pattern of Wilhelm's marriage, so closely echoing that of his parents' with its infidelity and disharmony, he had wondered if perhaps his genes were better not passed on to others. He had brooded over the question of marriage, the vulnerability of it, wondering if he too might somehow copy the relationships of his father and brother.

He had been in love several times, but always his love was tinged with fear that he might somehow harm or hurt those he had loved.

While he was at Heidelberg there had been a girl, a fellow student. He had loved her deeply and had ached to tell her so, but his fear had made him hold back. She had accused him of simply using her, of not wanting to give a real commitment.

Just before his death his father had been urging him to marry, telling him that it was his duty.

Because he had discovered that Wilhelm and therefore Wilhelm's sons were not of his fathering.

The baroness was buried with due pomp and solemnity four days after her death.

The Schloss felt empty without her. For one family to own such a place was surely an anachronism, Leo reflected. It had been built to house a feudal lord and all his dependants, not a modern nuclear family.

He was not surprised to discover that this unentailed estate had been left to him, and neither, thankfully, was Wilhelm.

'You're welcome to it,' he had told Leo before he returned to Hamburg.

Leo stayed on for another few days. There was nothing really for him to do; his grandmother's papers were meticulously in order; her preparations for her death made with the care and precision which had hallmarked her whole life. *Noblesse oblige*.

Leo knew he was delaying his return to Hamburg. In two days' time he was due to attend a conference in Edinburgh. He had decided to combine the trip with a visit to Cheshire to see Alan Carey's daughter. He knew that unless he did see her, unless he did everything he could, searched as hard as he could for whatever evidence might exist about his father's past, he would always wonder if he had not actually deliberately tried to avoid learning the truth.

His enquiries in Germany had revealed nothing that he did not already know. If his father had ever been in any way connected with the SS he had successfully ensured that no one else would ever know. Even the tentative enquiries he made through a tortuously circuitous route in Israel had produced nothing to show that they had any awareness of what his father might have been or might have done.

But those newspaper cuttings could not be ignored; he could not now forget he had seen them.

He had been unwilling to delve too deeply into Alan Carey's past; in his position there was only so much he could do without exciting other people's interest and curiosity, which was why he would have to see Davina James personally.

The tentative enquiries he *had* made had revealed more about Davina than her father. She was popular and well liked, a quiet, calm woman who had apparently stoically borne the infidelities of her husband and the burden of nursing her father.

Now, it seemed, she had taken on another burden: that of an almost bankrupt company.

She appeared to be used to carrying burdens, but did he have the right to inflict yet another on her? And yet if he didn't see her... didn't at least try to uncover some evidence...

What more evidence did he need? Didn't he already
know the truth in his heart...hadn't it already made
him soul-sick enough without his adding to that sickness?

There was no going back, no altering what had happened. But Leo knew that he wouldn't be able to rest
until he had seen Davina James.

If Alan Carey had confided in anyone he was far more
likely to have done so to his son-in-law rather than his
daughter, Leo acknowledged wearily. They had been two
of a kind, those two, both of them now dead...like his
father...thank God.

In Hamburg he went straight from the airfield to his
own home. He had bought the small town house in the
old part of the city over ten years ago, but it had never
truly seemed to him to be a real home.

The woman who came in daily to clean for him had
kept it aired and polished in his absence. There were
fresh flowers on the table in the hallway, and the soft
glow from the buttermilk-yellow walls should have felt
welcoming to him as he stepped inside.

Was it the house that was at fault or was it him? he
wondered. He tried to think when he had last shared the
intimacy of waking up in a bed disturbed by a night's
lovemaking...when he had last opened his eyes to look
into the sleeping face of his lover, when he had last ached
so much for her body that he had cried out in ecstasy
just to feel her naked warmth in bed beside him.

His last relationship had finished quietly and discreetly just after his mother's death. He and Elle had
been lovers for just over two years. She was slightly older
than he was, a tall, elegant natural blonde whom he had
met at a dinner party. Her husband, a government official almost twenty years her senior, apparently turned
a blind eye to her affairs provided they were conducted
with discretion and tact.

She had been the one to instigate their relationship.
She had called round to see him on some pretext or other,

subtly making her real purpose clear, but carefully allowing him the opportunity to ignore her sexual invitation if he chose. He had almost done so, but she was intelligent as well as attractive, and his desire for her had overruled caution.

There was no question of her wanting to end her marriage or to leave her husband, she told Leo frankly. Hans suited her as a husband.

'I know that, no matter how wonderful and exciting the sex between us is now, Leo, there will ultimately come a time when that excitement no longer exists. Marriage is not about sexual desire, or even about love. At least, not for me. Hans understands me. Our marriage works and I intend to ensure that it goes on working, but in the meantime there is no reason why you and I should not enjoy one another...provided we are discreet.'

Which was exactly what they had done. Until just after his mother's death, when Elle had announced quietly and casually, as though she were discussing nothing more personal than the weather, that she thought it was time for them to part. 'We are becoming staid...almost middle-aged,' she had told him, wrinkling her nose. 'It is time for us both to move on to new partners.'

He *had* missed her, but not as much as he had expected, and when he had seen her several months later with the man who he suspected had supplanted him he felt no jealousy, only a wry envy of her ability to skim so lightly over the surface of life.

Physically, as a lover, she had been exquisitely skilled, but a part of him had always known that it was not enough and had hungered for more than the mere physical coupling of their two bodies, no matter how sexually pleasurable their lovemaking was.

Wryly he admitted that for him mere sex was not enough and that he would have found it more erotic, more arousing to have been needed and loved rather than merely sexually desired.

A case of role reversal? It had certainly opened his eyes and made him see himself in a new perspective to know that he, the man, needed more emotional input into their relationship than Elle, the woman, who needed him only to satisfy her sexual hunger.

He went upstairs, stripping off his clothes in his bathroom and got into the shower.

It still shook him to know that Wilhelm was not Heinrich's child; they had been so alike, so much more so than he and Heinrich, and yet *he* was Heinrich's son.

Perhaps after all he had been wrong to fear that he might have inherited his father's genes, his viciousness and cruelty, and that, while these traits were dormant in him, he might somehow pass them on to his own children.

Having seen the effects of his father's personality, he had come to believe that it was as potentially destructive to pass on to one's children flawed personality traits as it was to conceive a child one knew would inherit a physical disorder.

Now couples carrying the genes of hereditary physical diseases received counselling and screening. Would there ever come a time when those carrying known character disorders might receive the same benefits, or would that be carrying man's interference with nature too far?

Once he had not thought so, but now, realising that Wilhelm's mirroring of Heinrich's vices might have come simply from living with him, rather than from a flaw carried in the blood, he began to wonder if he had not made too harsh a judgement; a judgement based on fear rather than reality.

He turned off the shower and stepped out on to the floor, reaching for a towel. His body was powerfully muscled, his torso rough with soft thick body hair. He exercised when he could, swimming in the pool at the private health club of which he was a member. In the winter he skied, and occasionally, when he had time, he played squash, although he was beginning to think of himself as too old for the sport.

Elle had once told him teasingly that he had the body of a Greek god and a profile from a Roman coin. She had laughed at his embarrassment, dragging her nails delicately along the inside of his thigh so that the fine hairs were set on edge and his flesh broke out in a rash of goose-flesh as his muscles quivered under the strain of trying to control his reaction to her. She had laughed again then, pouting a little as she glanced downwards at his body. They had already made love, but her deliberately tormenting touch was making it difficult for him to stop himself from having an erection.

When Elle played games she liked to win, and he wasn't entirely surprised when she bent her head and took him in her mouth, skilfully playing with him until his self-control broke and his penis swelled to hard rigidity.

She had enjoyed being the one who controlled their relationship. Sometimes Leo wondered if she was deliberately trying to push him to the point where he physically dominated her, but that was something he had promised himself he would never do to any woman. Down that road lay the dangerous path of violence and abuse taken by his father and brother, and he was never ever going to follow them. If he ached sometimes to stop Elle's deliberate torment by rolling her over on to her back and taking her angrily and quickly, he told himself that the brief satisfaction of giving in to that need would very quickly be outweighed by the self-contempt that would follow.

Elle had been an aggressive lover, often leaving his flesh marked with bruises and bites, his back and arms lacerated with raw scratches inflicted by her long nails. To Elle violence seemed to be an integral part of sex— perhaps, in a way, it was—but if so it was a violence he had never felt he dared allow himself to experience.

Instead he had learned to turn Elle's own need against her, to skilfully arouse her to the point where she would cling demandingly to him, begging him for his penetration of her body, often with words, pleas that used the language of the gutter. The first time she screamed during orgasm he thought he must have hurt her.

He grimaced as he rubbed himself dry now. No doubt she had thought him very naïve.

Well, their affair was over now, and since they had parted he had met no one for whom he had felt any real kind of desire. He was a sensual rather than a sexual man, he had decided. The mere act of penetration on its own was not sufficient to motivate him. When he thought of making love to a woman he thought of touching her slowly, of running his hands over her skin, of caressing her with his mouth, feeling that first sensitive quiver beneath her flesh that meant he was arousing her, feeling her body tense in his arms as she moved closer to him when he kissed her, feeling her tremble against him when she trusted him enough to let him see her need. The scent of her skin, her hair, the warmth of her body, its pliancy and softness, the way she smiled, talked or simply looked—all these were just as erotic and arousing to him as the thought of his body moving within hers as she opened herself to him and shared with him the mystery of her womanhood.

Two days later, when he boarded the Lufthansa flight for Britain, Leo's spirits were weighed down by the knowledge of what lay ahead of him. He closed his eyes, not wanting to think about what might happen if he proved that his father had not come by the original chemical equations as innocently as he had claimed.

Times, opinions, *morals* were changing. The generation that had lauded his father's success and shared his hunger for it had given way to one that was held far less in thrall to materialism, that questioned motives of profit-making far more deeply than the one that had gone before. Drug companies, once hailed as the saviours of the people, were now often viewed with suspicion, accused of putting profits before people, of experimenting on and exploiting humanity.

There was no corporation on earth, even one as powerful as Hessler Chemie, that could not be destroyed by the same people for whom it had been created. If people turned their backs on their drugs... boycotted them, as could very well be done... How short a time ago was it that the fur trade would have laughed in the face of anyone who might have claimed that the views of a few animal activists could destroy them? Now they were becoming as extinct a species as the animals they had once hunted down for their pelts.

Look at the way public opinion had turned against smoking and was now turning against alcohol. It was never wise to assume that one was in an unassailable position, and, whatever his own views might be on some of the methods his father had employed to increase the power of the corporation, it was his duty, his responsibility to ensure that Hessler's survived, for the sake of all those whose lives it supported.

If at the same time he could introduce a different approach to research and development, an awareness of the benefits of kinder, milder drugs, then he would certainly do so, but his prime duty now was not to ease his own conscience but to ensure that the corporation's reputation was safe, that it could not be damaged or tarnished by anything his father might once have done.

CHAPTER TWELVE

'Now remember,' Christie told Cathy mock seriously as she hugged her, 'no letting Uncle Saul stay up too late watching television.'

Cathy giggled, hugging her back.

She was so dearly precious to her, this child she had borne in such anger and bitterness, Christie acknowledged as she smoothed Cathy's soft hair back off her forehead.

Over Cathy's head she looked at Saul. He was lost in thought, staring out across the airport concourse. Much as she loved him, she had always been aware of how very different they were, not just in temperament but in their whole outlook on life.

As she grew up she had been constantly both infuriated by and resentful of the way his male superiority armoured him from all her small gibes and made him impervious to the self-doubts that tormented her.

As adults they had taken completely different paths in life, but she had never forgotten or ceased to be grateful for the way he had supported her when Cathy was conceived.

Now, abruptly, she was aware of a change within him, an unfamiliar introspection and withdrawal. She wanted to reach out and touch him, to ask him what was wrong, but she knew instinctively that he would rebuff her. Their father had been a man who was afraid of emotions because they made him feel vulnerable. He had taught Saul that emotions were something a man should always contain and control. Sadly she wondered if Saul was beginning to realise that their father might not always have been right. Sadly, because she knew how much Saul had idolised him and that to bring him down from his pedestal would be to destroy the strongest motivating force in her brother's life.

Their father had been a subject they had never been able to discuss calmly or logically, Christie acknowledged as she gave Saul and Cathy a final hug before turning to board her flight for Scotland.

When she was a teenager, adoring Saul and yet at the same time resenting him, sometimes even hating him, her feelings had confused and upset her, causing her to wonder if she was in some way abnormal. She already knew that her father was not really interested in her. Her mother, quiet, calm, apparently content with the confines of her marriage and her life, was not the role model her churning, fierce youthful ideals and beliefs wanted. She loved her mother dearly, but at the same time, watching her, seeing the way she always seemed to be smoothing her husband's path through life, soothing his irritations, boosting his ego, she had known that she could never settle for such a subservient role.

She had yearned, ached sometimes to ask her mother if she really truly was satisfied with a relationship, a life, that allowed her only to fulfil someone else's expectations of her and never her own; but somehow she had never felt able to do so. Perhaps because she had been afraid to hear the answer?

Her mother was a loving, gentle woman, the kind of woman to whom others constantly brought their problems. As an adult Christie had learned how highly respected and loved her mother had been, how much her judgement and wisdom had been appreciated by those around her, and quite clearly she had seen that, of the two of them, it was her mother whom others valued the most, but during her lifetime her mother had always taken care to ensure that she never in even the smallest way outshone her husband.

How much effort and suppression of her own needs must that have taken? How much self-restraint? How much love? *She* could never love anyone like that. She was too selfish, and she would certainly never denigrate herself, her own ideals, her own ambitions simply to pacify a man who was either too petty or too immature to recognise and accept her right to be an individual and to strive to succeed.

Her father had never wanted her to become a doctor. Surely nursing was far more suitable work for a woman, he had asked, frowning at her. Heatedly she had started to argue with him, angry when her mother quickly hustled her out of the room.

'Why won't he listen to me?' she had demanded tearfully, alone in the kitchen with her mother. 'Don't I have as much right to use my brains as Saul?'

'Your father is a little old-fashioned about these things,' her mother had soothed. 'Just give him some time to get used to the idea, Christie. You know how he hates things being thrust on him.'

'You mean how he hates anything that wasn't his own idea,' Christie had challenged, her eyes stormy, her body tight with tension. 'Just because I'm a girl he expects me to do as I'm told and not to have any ideas of my own. Well, I'm not like that.'

'No,' her mother had agreed.

Tears had burned her eyes then. Tears of anger and frustration, and tears of pain as well, because her father could never love her as he did Saul and because he could never accept her as she was. In the end it had been Saul who had persuaded him that she be allowed to train as a doctor, and it had been Saul who had supplemented her meagre grant.

Those years of young adulthood had been very difficult for her, very chaotic, the pain and confusion of her father's attitude towards her still sharp and sore. With hindsight she often wondered if the main thing that

had attracted her to Cathy's father had been the fact
that he was somehow a substitute for her father, and
that initially in seeking his approval what she had subconsciously been seeking had been the approval of her
uncaring parent.

David hadn't been her first lover; there had been the
usual teenage forays into sexual exploration, during
which she had quickly learned to feel contempt and resentment for teenage boys' apparent belief that *she* was
there to please *them*.

With David it had been different.

She had been a student when she'd met him. He had
just been appointed to the hospital. He specialised in
heart surgery and was spoken of in tones of awe by those
who knew him.

Forty-two to her twenty-two, he had dazzled her more
quickly than she could have believed possible. She had
always prided herself on her judgement of others and
on her ability to see people for what they really were,
but David had very easily deceived her, or had she simply
deceived herself?

Since he was devastatingly attractive in that way that
a certain type of mature man could be, she had been
overwhelmed and tongue-tied when he first started
singling her out from among the other students.

She had known, of course, that he was married. It
was no secret that he owed at least some of his meteoric
career rise to the influence of his wife's father, an eminent
Harley Street surgeon, but he had very quickly and subtly
given her the impression that his marriage was little more
than a worn-out legality. His wife was presently living
in America, he told her carelessly, as were his two sons,
and she, besotted fool that she had been, had not had
the wit to question him further. She had thought he loved
her and she had certainly believed that she loved him.
Sexually he had dazzled her into dazed disbelief that it
was possible to feel such intense pleasure. That was how

naïve and inexperienced she had been. She was on the Pill, of course. Pregnancy, a child, had no part in any of her plans.

Being loved by David acted on her like an adrenalin-boosting drug, increasing not just her physical desire for him, but also her enthusiasm for her work. It was doubly important for her to succeed now. Now she wanted to show David what she could do. She wanted him to see how different she was from his spoiled socialite wife who never did anything other than shop or sit on charity committees.

'I love women with brains,' he had told her once as he entered her. 'They're always such a challenge.' And she, infatuated as she was, hadn't realised until much, much later that what he had meant was that he loved reinforcing his own belief in his male superiority by reducing her to a mass of aching, pleading flesh—by, in fact, short-circuiting the brain he claimed to admire so much. But of course that knowledge had come a long time later. After Cathy's birth, in fact.

High on the euphoria of being with him, of the intense pleasure of discovering her sexuality, of knowing how much he wanted her, it had been easy to ignore the future, to live simply for the present.

Of course one day she would want far more of him than the brief secret meetings they presently shared. Of course one day she expected to be able to stand proudly side by side with him . . . of course in her rare moments of leisure she indulged in daydreams where the two of them, hand in hand, stood solemnly to receive the plaudits of their colleagues . . . a renowned surgical team. But she was too content living in the present to dwell overmuch on the future, and then had come the moment she had been waiting for.

David told her that he had arranged to borrow a friend's cottage for the weekend. He'd collect her. He'd meet her after work on Friday, he told her, picking her

up at their usual place, which was a discreet half-mile
from the students' home where she lived. He himself
would be away for the rest of the week, since he had
some business to conduct. 'What kind of business?' she
asked him innocently.

He seemed to pause for a long time before answering,
'It's nothing. Nothing that need concern you,' he told
her, and then went on to describe to her exactly what
he planned to do once they were alone, and as her body
tensed and ached with excitement she forgot all about
his unimportant meeting.

A whole weekend together... She closed her eyes,
leaning blissfully against the wall. She could hardly wait.

She almost didn't make it. On Friday morning she
woke up with a stomach-ache and was violently sick, but
she forced herself to get dressed and to attend the
morning lecture. Throughout the morning she felt distinctly ill, and at lunchtime, unable to face the sight and
smell of food, she went outside for some fresh air.

It was at further classes in the afternoon that she
learned that there had been an outbreak of food
poisoning among the students. Grimly she told herself
that nothing... nothing was going to stop her being with
David, and headed for the pharmacy to get a pre-
scription made up for a calming drug. Luckily she only
seemed to have a mild version of the poisoning and,
although she still felt shaky and weak, by the time she
finished lectures the nausea and stomach cramps seemed
to have ceased.

She mentioned nothing of her illness to David when
he picked her up; already instinctively she was mim-
icking the behaviour patterns of her mother.

The weekend, so much anticipated, so much longed
for, somehow didn't quite live up to her expectations.
Her fault, she told herself, for being unrealistic, and yet
it still hurt when David had to drop her off out of sight
of anyone who might have recognised them, reinforcing

the awareness she had had all weekend of how important it was to him to keep their relationship a secret. Too important? She didn't have time to dwell on her unease; this was her final year and she was studying hard.

David was away for three weeks, not just one, and then when he came back it was another week before she actually managed to see him.

By then she knew that she was pregnant. The fault of her bout of food poisoning negating the contraceptive pill? It had been a shock, of course. A child wasn't something she wanted. A termination would be the most sensible answer, but that was something she must discuss with David. It was his child too, after all.

Again it was only later that she could acknowledge to herself how much subconsciously she had been relying on her lover to take the burden of responsibility from her, hold out his arms to her and tell her how much he wanted both her and their child. But of course he had done nothing of the sort.

'I thought you were supposed to be on the Pill,' had been his first comment, the shock and anger in his eyes making her stomach muscles clench in misery. 'If this is some silly trick to blackmail me into marrying you, Christie...'

The words hit her like stones, blunting her capacity to think, pain oozing like blood from her pride and self-respect.

'You *know* I'm a married man. I can't afford the kind of scandal it will cause if this gets out. Are you *sure* that it's my child and not someone else's?'

She must have made some kind of sound, some verbal betrayal of her anguish, because he stopped then and looked at her. Suddenly he looked old, she recognised, old and stripped of the glittering robes in which she had foolishly clothed him. Suddenly she saw him for the shabby creature he really was.

'Christie... You must be sensible about this. I can help you... arrange a termination.'

She was starting to feel sick and giddy. 'An *abortion*, don't you mean?' she challenged him, her voice shaking, rejecting the easy clinical term for the harshness of reality.

'You must be sensible,' he stressed. 'Think of your career——'

'Think of *yours*, don't you mean?' she demanded. She was beyond pain now, beyond everything but somehow trying to contain the huge, gaping, life-threatening wounds in her pride and self-respect.

She no longer loved him. How could she after what he had said... after what she had seen in his eyes? Sickened, she stepped back from him and said quietly, 'It's all right, David. I understand exactly what you're trying to say.' She saw the craven relief in his eyes and her contempt both for him and for herself increased.

'So you're going to do the sensible thing. Have a termination.'

She gave him a brittle, proud smile. 'What I choose to do with *my* body and *my* child is *my* affair, don't you think?' She heard him calling her name as she walked away from him, but she didn't look back.

She knew she couldn't go back to the students' home, not in her present state, and so instead she booked herself into a small, shabby hotel, something she could not really afford, where she locked herself in her room and wept out her grief and disillusionment.

Never, ever again would she allow herself to be this vulnerable... this naïve. David had never really loved her. He had merely wanted her... had merely fed his own ego on her innocence and naïveté. Distantly she wondered how many other girls there had been like her in his life before her, and how many more there would be after her.

What hurt her the most was not the discovery that he had not loved her, but the realisation of what he was, of how she had deceived herself, of how she had betrayed herself in believing that she loved him.

She placed her hand on her stomach. His panic . . . his rejection had been so betraying and so unnecessary. She had already decided to end the pregnancy.

And yet somehow she found herself putting off doing so, and, the longer she put it off, the more frequently she found herself shying away from making any real decision. It was new territory for her, this indecision. In fact, she was suddenly experiencing a good deal of bewilderment at the unfamiliar emotions and tensions that gripped her. She told herself that it was just the trauma of discovering the truth about David, about the prospect of her looming exams, about everything, in truth, other than the fact that she was pregnant.

She did not *want* a child. She had never experienced any desire for motherhood and, besides, it was impossible. How *could* she have a child and continue her studies?

She heard the gossip that David had accepted a job in America at Johns Hopkins and that apparently it had been on the cards for some time because his wife had been out there with her father, doing some canvassing on his behalf. The news barely touched Christie. She had other matters to occupy her thoughts.

Later she wondered if she had deliberately made that mistake over the date, which had resulted in her failing to realise that she had left it just that little bit too late for an early termination, but at the time she was filled with panic and despair, blaming the stress of her coming exams for causing her to lose that all-important final week.

And it had been while she was in the middle of that panic that Saul had arrived and quietly but firmly taken charge of everything, including her.

When Cathy was born the intensity of the love that drenched her stunned her. David was forgotten, pushed into the past, where he belonged, his weakness and her own self-deceit merely one more of life's hard-earned lessons. Cathy, her child, her daughter, was all that mattered now.

Thanks to Saul's financial support and the pressure he had brought to bear on their father to accept the situation, she was able to continue her training and to qualify.

She was a changed person now, aware, mature, with a keenly honed social conscience. Where once she had wanted to go into surgery and had seen herself rosily successful and admired, now she accepted that for her the patient was a complete whole, not merely an isolated set of symptoms.

She had chosen to go into general practice and she had also chosen to work in one of the most deprived areas of the city of Manchester. The practice's patients were drawn largely from the dilapidated tower blocks on the outskirts of the city. Christie rented a flat close to them because she felt it was important that as a doctor she should live in the same environment as her patients.

The social and financial deprivation in which the majority of her patients lived appalled Christie. It was the women who suffered, the women and the children, imprisoned in their small flats, isolated from one another by the fear that kept them separated, mothers with small children often living in flats at the tops of tower blocks where the lifts were broken and prams, children and shopping had to be carried up umpteen flights of stairs. Stairs that were often smeared with filth and rubbish, excrement sometimes, the territory of gangs of youths who roamed the tower blocks, jobless and often homeless, living by the only asset they had—the physical domination of others, petty theft their only source of income.

Drug addicts were another hazard, as were drunks both male and female, and, watching the exhausted young mothers who came to her surgeries with their pale-faced, fresh-air-starved children, she ached with compassion. What chance did they really have, any of them?

Those children she saw with the blank faces and uninterested stares, those who were hyperactive and violent, those who showed their frustration by becoming withdrawn—all of them suffered from the same things.

'What the hell are we doing here?' she demanded furiously of her colleagues. 'We give them drugs and send them home *knowing* that what those children need, what their mothers need, is somewhere decent to live, fresh air and space...stimulation of their senses, something to give them a chance of achieving self-worth.'

'By doing what?' one of the men had asked her grimly. 'We're living in a world where man is being replaced by machinery. When they grow up there won't be any jobs, any futures for them, just as there haven't been for their parents. What we should be doing is persuading them not to have children. They're not——'

'Not what?' Christie interrupted him, fury blazing from her eyes. 'Not fit to have them? Is that what you were going to say? Perhaps *we're* the ones who aren't fit. Because *we're* the ones who are condemning them and their unborn children to this miserable quality of life. Because *we're* the ones who refuse to publicise the truth and to make others act on it. So little Tracy has had a cold for the last six months...well, let's just give her some antibiotics, shall we, and her mum some tranquillisers, even though we *know* that what they both need is a decent home, a garden for Tracy to play in...security for her mother so that she isn't so terrified of going out that she and Tracy don't see anyone but each other for days on end?'

Her despair exhausted her. Her anger left a hard lump inside her chest, but there was so little she could do.

She organised a crèche, a meeting place for the mothers and their children, persuading the council to allow them to use an empty flat. She bullied and coaxed paint and brushes out of a local DIY centre and motivated the mothers out of their apathy, insisting that *they* were the ones to redecorate the flat, encouraging them to use their own ideas, and then marvelling with genuine humility at the unexpected skills of the women who painted the murals on the living-room walls, watching with growing pleasure and hope as they gradually built up their own and the others' confidence, watching as they organised themselves into groups to find ways of raising money to equip the nursery.

She found places for three of the women on short-term nursery-nurse teaching courses. She encouraged them to organise outings for themselves and the children; the practice and Cathy absorbed all her time and attention, and when the women teased her slyly about the fact that she had no man she shrugged and told them honestly that she had no need of one.

And besides, they were in fact wrong. She had been having a relationship with someone for several months. They had met through her efforts to persuade the local authority to do more for the tower block inhabitants. He was divorced with two children and a partnership in an architectural practice, which kept him almost as busy as her work did her. He made her laugh and he was a good lover, something she had discovered was more important to her than she would once have wanted to admit, but she was firm about keeping him at a distance. Their relationship suited her exactly as it was and she did not want any closer emotional commitment with him.

She had learned her lesson with David. When a woman loved a man she lost a very vital part of herself. She had once suffered the pain that went with that loss, that abandoning of self for someone else, and she was not going to suffer it again.

When Peter started to press her for a closer relationship she cut herself off from him completely, refusing to either see or speak to him. She missed him sexually but not enough to change her mind. And besides, she needed her independence. It was very important to her; she recognised that now. With it went her self-respect and her feeling of self-worth, and she was never going to risk losing them again.

Her life was full and busy. She had her work, and she had Cathy, her wonderful, precious daughter. The extent of her love for her child was something that still had the power to surprise her. Never thinking of herself as maternal, she was sometimes shocked to discover just how fiercely protective of Cathy she actually was. There were problems, of course. Twice she had had her car broken into while attending a bogus call to a patient, the thieves patently after drugs, but on each occasion she had been lucky and had had her bag with her. The police warned her not to come out to any night calls unattended, and she was duly cautious even while she was infuriated by her vulnerability as a woman.

Cathy was growing up quickly. She was at playschool now, taken there and collected by a childminder.

There were increasing reports of violence among the local youths and talk of rival drug gangs. Christie began to notice a new mood of fear among her patients, an awareness of them withdrawing from her. The police issued warnings to all local GPs and chemists about the dangers of drug-motivated thefts. Christie observed all the necessary precautions. It was not just herself that she had to consider now. There was Cathy as well.

A fact that was brought sharply and sickeningly home to her one afternoon when she returned home to discover that her flat had been broken into. There was little doubt that whoever had done it had probably been after drugs, the police told her. As a doctor, she was an obvious target. It had probably been out of sheer frustration that they had wrecked the place, destroying her furniture. The items they had stolen, her television, her clock and various other small things, would be sold to buy the drugs they had not been able to find in the flat.

Christie had always considered herself to be a strong person, not given to emotional weakness, but when she walked into Cathy's room and saw what had been done the fear that chilled her totally overwhelmed her. As she looked at Cathy's bed, its quilt torn, the mattress gaping open from the jagged knife wounds ripped into it, all she had been able to see was Cathy lying on that bed...

It was the hardest decision she had ever had to make, far, far harder than deciding not to abort her child, but for Cathy's sake she had to make it.

When she told the other partners that she was leaving they accepted her decision philosophically. 'City practice is no place for anyone with small children,' she was told gruffly by the senior partner.

Tears burned her eyes, but she refused to shed them. One half of her felt as though she was a deserter, a traitor, as though in leaving she was abandoning those who needed her. She felt she owed them a responsibility, a duty.

But she owed Cathy those as well. What if Cathy had been in the flat when it was broken into? The thought turned Christie cold with fear, and yet she ached inside with the knowledge that she was turning her back on people who needed her.

She had already found a new partnership; this time in the country, somewhere quiet and safe where Cathy could grow up enjoying the kind of environment that every child should have.

Oddly, for all the differences between them, it was Saul who seemed to understand best what she was going through, how torn she was between her desire to help those who had the most need of her and her desire to protect her child.

'You *are* doing the right thing,' he told her quietly, and then added with a sideways smile, 'Cheer up. There's bound to be some cause for you to champion, even in the depths of rural Cheshire. How about starting up a refuge for abandoned tractors?'

He had made her laugh, of course; that at least had been something they had always shared: their sense of humour.

With a start Christie realised that the plane had started to descend. It wasn't like her to dwell on the past, and, as she had soon discovered, poverty and deprivation were not restricted merely to the city. Look at the way, for instance, that Carey's had so flagrantly broken the safety laws, the way they had blackmailed the workforce into accepting criminally low wages, the way that Gregory James had somehow managed to use his influence and position to squash the attempt she had made to set up an inquiry into the incidence of contact dermatitis among his employees.

She frowned as she reached for her hand luggage. She had become increasingly disenchanted over the last few years with the large drug companies and the methods they employed to influence the medical profession to use their products, products in some cases which had the potential to cause more harm to certain patients than good.

The drug companies were supported by a very powerful government lobby, and she, as a doctor, did not believe that their motives came anywhere near being altruistic enough. 'Profits before patients'—that was the title of the speech she was to give the small group of doctors attending the conference who supported her beliefs. With luck they might just make it into one of the local papers. The dailies would, of course, be dominated by revelations about the promises of new wonder drugs which the drug companies would make use of the conference to announce.

The plane touched down. Christie waited until nearly everyone was off before vacating her seat and then smilingly thanked the stewardess as she got off.

The airport building was packed, a large proportion of her fellow travellers quite obviously other delegates. She sighed a little as she saw the queue for the taxi rank but joined it nevertheless.

As she did so she was aware of the man joining the queue behind her, catching sight of him out of the corner of her eye and instantly aware of his height and of the confident, very male way in which he moved.

A discreet glance over her shoulder, in a pretence of checking the heel of her shoe, gave her the opportunity for a more thorough look. Good-looking as well, somewhere in his mid to late thirties, she would guess. Apparently unaware of her subtle scrutiny, he was glancing at his watch, frowning slightly. Obviously a man in a hurry. A wealthy man, to judge from his clothes. Somehow she did not think he was a doctor, although she had no idea why she *should* think that.

As she turned back to face the head of the queue she amused herself by imagining how he might look without those expensive clothes. His hair was the colour of warm toast, apart from that striking blond streak at the front. Would his body hair be the same colour? Would it be soft, in toast-coloured fuzzy curls, or sleek to his torso, or even perhaps slightly wiry and abrasive to the touch?

She favoured the first, and her mouth curled into amused sensuality at the direction of her own thoughts. Well, why not? Women were as at liberty as men to entertain themselves by discreetly mentally stripping an attractive member of the opposite sex. Men, after all, did it all the time. But not just for pleasure. There was a sense of power as well in what she was doing, and with it an awareness of the darker side of human nature, especially male human nature.

Quickly she diverted her thoughts to other less emotive channels. Thankfully the queue was quickly growing shorter. Soon it would be her turn, but when it was, to her fury, the taxi driver ignored her, pulling up to the man behind her, inviting, 'Jump in, sir.'

'I think this lady was before me.' His voice was pleasantly pitched, his English accentless and easy, and yet she was immediately aware that it was not his first language.

The taxi driver was glowering, no doubt recognising that his preferred passenger was a good deal more likely to tip generously than she was herself. Another few seconds and he would ignore them both, Christie realised.

'Perhaps we could share the taxi,' she suggested quickly. 'I'm heading for a medical conference in Edinburgh.'

'Me too.' They smiled at one another, and then he reached past Christie to open the door for her. Unlike her, he had a suitcase as well as a small piece of hand luggage. The raincoat he had over his suit swung open as he moved and she saw the label—German. She gave him a swift appraising look, admitting a small *frisson* of surprise.

He did not *look* German, but there was a Lufthansa tag on his luggage. Derisively she asked herself how a German was *supposed* to look: all Teutonic stiffness and blue eyes? Scoffing at her own outdated preconceptions, she got into the cab.

As he followed her into the taxi and closed the door he suggested, 'Perhaps we should introduce ourselves? I am Leo, and you?'

Leo what? Christie wondered idly as she gave him her own name. Was it a German custom to only introduce oneself by one's Christian name?

'Are you familiar with Edinburgh and the conference centre?' he asked her as the taxi set off.

Christie shook her head. 'Are you?'

'I have visited Edinburgh before, but it was several years ago. The conference centre is new since then, I think. You are a doctor...a chemist...a scientist?' he questioned.

Christie liked the way he did not automatically assume, as so many men would have done, that she was either a secretary or someone's PA. She liked the fact that he had automatically conferred on her the status of a qualified professional.

'A doctor,' she told him. 'And you?'

He paused fractionally and then told her. 'A chemist.' As he glanced out of the window at the traffic Leo wondered why he had felt it necessary to withhold from her both his name and his true position. As a doctor, she was bound to have heard of Hessler Chemie, and once the conference was under way she could not avoid discovering his connection with the corporation. So why try to separate himself from it? Because he wanted her to *accept* him, to judge him as himself rather than as the head of Hessler Chemie.

He had only met her five minutes ago. What importance could her opinion of him possibly have? He did not know. He only knew that it would be important, and he knew that as intuitively as he knew that if he had told her who he really was she would have immediately withdrawn from him. He had no idea why or how he should sense that, he only knew that he did.

She was a very attractive woman, stunningly vibrant and alive, her dark hair thickly glossy, her body firm but feminine, not beautiful in the strict sense, perhaps, but there was something very compelling about her, a very real and true sensuality which he had noticed the moment he saw her.

He had also noticed that quick assessing sexual scrutiny she had given him. Had she liked what she had seen? Inwardly he mocked himself for his susceptibility.

She too was now looking out of the opposite window. He glanced quickly at her. There was nothing socially contrived or deliberate about her; rather she had a natural fresh earthiness. He sensed that she was a woman who knew how to enjoy and appreciate the pleasure of her own body; that as a lover she would give herself generously and demand equal generosity in return.

As *a* lover? Or as *his* lover?

CHAPTER THIRTEEN

'No...no.'

Davina sat up in bed, shivering as she tried to control the fine tremor of fear convulsing her body, the intensity of the dream that had woken her too real to be easily dismissed.

She hugged her arms around herself and glanced at the alarm clock beside the bed, groaning as she realised how early it was and how unlikely that she would be able to go back to sleep.

She got out of bed, her mood lightening briefly with wry self-mockery as she caught sight of herself in the dressing-table mirror. The nightshirt she was wearing was probably too young for her, too juvenile, and no doubt it was the fact that her eyes were still blurred with sleep that gave her that brief sense of *déjà vu*, of stepping back in time and momentarily seeing in the mirror a much younger reflection of herself, her hair tousled and hanging down her back, its normal smooth neatness untidily ruffled by her disturbed night's sleep, her legs looking oddly coltish and slender beneath the brief cotton shirt.

As she pushed back the curtains and studied the clear blue sky she was briefly reminded of another morning, another bedroom, another Davina standing in front of the window wearing a man's shirt, Matt's shirt, her body bare beneath the faded chambray cloth, her hair tousled not from her dreams but from Matt's lovemaking.

She remembered how Matt had come up behind her, sliding his arms around her, pulling her back against his body, kissing the nape of her neck and then her shoulder,

slowly turning her round to face him as he felt her body's
response to him.

She shivered, suddenly aware of the disconcerting ache
of need she could feel now, knowing that it had been
caused not by her memories of that early morning lovemaking but by the darker forces of her subconscious
thoughts and the dreams they had caused her. Dreams
in which she had been following Matt as he walked down
a narrow path ahead of her, oblivious to her presence,
to her voice as she called out to him. And, no matter
how fast she had walked, the distance between them only
seemed to increase. She had felt panic and fear, dismay,
loneliness, grief and anger all rolled into one as she
fought to keep up with him, to make him turn round
and see her, to make him wait for her, and then suddenly
he *had* stopped. Only when he turned round it hadn't
been Matt's face she had seen but that of a stranger…the
stranger, she acknowledged tensely as she stepped back
from the window.

As she went downstairs to make herself a coffee she
told herself that it was probably not as illogical as she
had first imagined for her to dream about him. After
all, it had been a shock to walk round that corner and
into him, and what woman these days could view that
kind of experience with equanimity? Her sex was only
just beginning to discover that real freedom of choice,
real parity in life, real equality was as much an illusion
as it had always been.

A woman might now *technically* be able to achieve
the highest academic, political and professional echelons
there were, but they were not free to walk in safety along
their city streets; they were not free to drive with confidence and security from one end of the country to the
other; they were not free to open the door to the male
stranger who knocked on it; so was it really any wonder
that that small and unimportant encounter should have
had such an intense effect upon her?

These days a woman had to treat any man who was a stranger, and often many of those who weren't, with suspicion and caution, and if she didn't . . . If she didn't, the world of men ruled that she must accept that she had voluntarily contributed to any violation of her home, her privacy and her body.

But the *frisson* of sensation she had felt in her dream when the man turned round and it wasn't Matt had not been *that* kind of fear. There had been apprehension, yes, but it had been a sensual, sexual apprehension, a dangerous spiralling excitement that had plunged her sharply from the anxiety of wanting Matt to turn round and see her and to wait for her to one of acutely searing need combined with an equally searing resentment of that need and of the man who had caused it.

The coffee was ready. She breathed in deeply, firmly switching her mind to other and far more important matters; she was almost out of coffee and she had other shopping to do. She wanted to make an appointment with a local estate agent with a view to getting the house valued and up for sale; it was much too large for her to live in alone, and although she would miss her garden she would not miss the house itself, despite the fact that she had lived in it all her life.

At the back of her mind was the thought that perhaps she could use whatever money there might be left over, after she had bought herself something smaller, to keep the company going for a little while longer. She tried not to let herself dwell on the fact that such funds might be needed to cover the redundancy monies due to Carey's employees if she had to cease business. The bank manager and Giles had both pointed out to her that, if the company went into liquidation, no such payments would be due.

Gregory had always been very careful about preserving his own finances, the bank manager had told her; although Carey's had borrowed a good deal of

money from the bank, Gregory had somehow or other
managed to persuade his predecessor that it wasn't
necessary for Gregory to give any personal guarantees
as a director to secure this borrowing, and Davina suspected that Philip Taylor had had a rather begrudging
admiration for Gregory's financial far-sightedness.

It was a view she did not share. Gregory might not
have broken any actual law, but he had broken nearly
every moral law there was, and she felt almost as guilty
by association as though she had known about it and
encouraged him to do so.

'It's just sensible and cautious business practice,' Giles
had told her uncomfortably when she had initially expressed her shock and disgust, and she had begun to
perceive then that perhaps men, even the best of them,
operated within a different framework of ethics from
her own sex.

She had recently read a brief article in one of the
Sunday papers propounding the theory that men were
goal- and achievement-orientated, while women were
people- and emotion-orientated.

Certainly neither the bank manager nor even Giles
seemed to share her view that the most disturbing conse-
quence of Carey's going bankrupt would be the effect
it would have on its employees.

No company these days was in a position to guarantee
its workforce long-term employment, Giles had told her
when she had confided to him her concern. It was their
investors, their shareholders, their competitors and the
City who mattered.

Davina had very little knowledge of the business world
and how it worked, he had added gently, and, although
she had said nothing, she had been irritated by his
attitude. His area was personnel, and surely he should
have expressed a more sympathetic attitude, although
Davina had to concede that he was sadly right in his
assessment.

She was intelligent enough to perceive that if she wished to be taken seriously, her view of what was important given respect and attention, she must learn to adapt her arguments so that she could put forward her viewpoint in such a way that it would not receive the instant dismissal, the derision almost, she had seen so clearly in the bank manager's attitude towards her.

Because it was an issue that was so important to her, and because she did not intend to allow anyone to bully her or confuse her into doing something that went against her own moral codes, she had gritted her teeth and done what she now told herself she ought to have had the sense and the courage to do years before: she had insisted on learning everything there was to learn about Carey's; about the way it was run; about the way it was financed; about the way its products were sold and distributed, the way they were presented to the members of the medical profession who used them; and what had initially shocked her more than anything else, after her discovery of how badly Gregory had treated their employees, had been the realisation that there had been so little spent on research and development of new drugs.

Gregory, her father even, *must* have known that once the renewed patent ran out on their market-leading heart drug their profits would drop sharply, but it was obvious to her that even during her father's lifetime little or no attempt had been made to invest those profits in research to preserve the company's future.

It was true there was a laboratory, but, as Giles had been forced to admit to her, it was hardly up to the standard of a second-rate university's and none of the work carried out in it could ever have led to the production of a new market leader.

Her father had known that and so had Gregory. But why had that happened? Her father had been a student of medicine, surely educated by *his* father to take full advantage of the benefits of the drug he himself had discovered almost by accident, and to lead Carey's into the new age of modern drugs?

Her father had, Davina was forced to admit, remained as much a stranger, an enigma to her in his death as he had been during his life. She knew that during the war, partly qualified and obviously idealistic, he had enlisted as a medical orderly with the army.

How could a man with those sort of ideals then become the same man who, it seemed, had ignored all the advantages, all the challenges his training had given him, all those opportunities to benefit mankind, and instead simply lived off the profits of the company?

Had he perhaps been afraid that no matter what he did he might never match the achievements of his own father? But her grandfather's discovery of the heart drug had been more by accident than design; he had been an untrained explorer in a world which her father's education should have mapped out so clearly for him that it would have been easy for him not just to follow in his father's footsteps, but to continue that journey even further.

There was no point now in looking back into the past for answers to questions that could never be answered, she told herself as she drank her coffee. What she had to do was to concentrate on the problems of the present. And those of the future? If Carey's *had* a future.

She finished her coffee and went upstairs to shower and get dressed.

Despite the warnings of the environmental lobby concerning the detrimental effect of the motor car on the quality and health safety of people's lives, and even in spite of the fact that driving was an increasingly stressful activity, with the roads becoming more busy and more hazardous every year, people, including herself, still continued to ignore all the disadvantages of driving for its one simple heavyweight advantage, Davina reflected as she parked her car in the car park that surrounded her local food hypermarket.

And what woman, having endured the discomfort and sheer physical effort involved in lugging heavy bags of grocery shopping on and off public transport in all kinds of weather, having carried that same shopping from the bus-stop to her home, more often than not having to cope with small children at the same time, would willingly go back to such a protracted means of carrying out what at best was an unattractive and stressful chore?

No wonder the car park was full, and Davina suspected that, until someone came up with a truly viable alternative to the motor car, this and other car parks like it all over the country would continue to be full.

The years of living first with her father and then with Gregory had taught her to be an economical and thrifty shopper, but these days, with only herself to cater for, Davina found she was becoming less and less inclined to cook. She liked simple meals—fruit, crusty bread, cheeses and pasta rather than the heavy meat, potato and vegetable main courses her father had always insisted upon.

She shopped quickly and methodically, her mind on other things. The check-outs were busy, and she sighed a little to herself, knowing that whichever queue she chose it would be the wrong one. For once, though, she seemed to be in luck. The girl on her check-out was quick and efficient, pleasant too, Davina noticed as she watched the way the girl smiled and responded to the person she was serving.

Davina was just about to unload her own trolley when she noticed that the woman standing behind her was only carrying a few items, and, moreover, that she was rather obviously glancing at her watch.

Even though she suspected that she was being deliberately manipulated, Davina gave in, wryly inviting the woman to precede her in the queue. As she stepped back to allow her past she saw the man standing in the next queue.

Her heart gave a ferocious bound as against all the odds she recognised him immediately. It might have been growing dark then and bright neon-lit daylight now, but she hadn't just recognised him with her sight, she had somehow known him with her senses as well. He wasn't looking at her. He was talking to the young girl he had with him. His daughter? Certainly they were close, the girl leaning confidently and lovingly against him as she said something to him.

An unfamiliar emotion gripped Davina as she watched them. Once, a long time ago it seemed now, she had hoped for children, when she had been young and naïve. She had years ago come to accept that Gregory was the last man she would have wanted as a father for her child, a role model, and that, in denying her children, life, or fate, had been generous to her rather than cruel.

But suddenly, seeing *him*, with that child . . . she was overwhelmed not just by a sense of deprivation and loss, but also by a feeling of resentment, of dislike almost, so sharp that it was an actual physical pain.

She turned away abruptly, not wanting to see any more, quickly attacking the tangled mountain of shopping piling up at the other end of the conveyor.

It was only once she was back at home, feeling calmer, that she was able to ask herself just why a man who was a stranger to her should cause her to react to him with such intense antagonism. Surely not merely because he had given her a bit of a shock, thrown her off guard and made her feel vulnerable for a handful of seconds?

Was it, then, because for some inexplicable reason he had reminded her briefly of Matt, or rather because that momentary accidental physical contact with him had stirred up memories of Matt?

It wasn't a line of self-investigation she felt it wise to pursue.

She had work to do, she reminded herself as she put away the last of the shopping. And surely enough tangible things to worry about without adding any foolishly unnecessary intangibles.

'Where are we going now, Uncle Saul?'

Saul's frown disappeared as he looked down into Cathy's expectant face. She always had such a shining happiness about her, this niece of his, a warmth and the kind of innocence that belonged to those who genuinely loved their fellow humans and who saw only the good in others and never the bad.

As he stowed away their shopping in the boot of his car he couldn't help contrasting her loving openness with the cynicism and materialism of his own children, especially Josephine.

True, she was older than Cathy, and perhaps more exposed to the kind of lifestyle that encouraged materialism. But her cynicism, the deep-rooted contempt and disdain he could see in her, not just for him but for almost everyone she came into contact with—how had she come by those? Was it *his* fault, not perhaps by example—he had never spent enough time with either of his children for that—but maybe by omission?

His children needed him, Christie had told him. He doubted that they would share that view. He and Karen should never have had children, he decided savagely. Neither of them had turned out to be even adequate parents, never mind good. It would have been better if he and Karen had remained childless like Davina James and her husband.

Davina James! It had startled him to see her in the supermarket this morning, dressed casually in jeans and a loose cotton top. He had watched her, unobserved, while she shopped, noting her neat, methodical movements, the quick, intent way she made her choices, her

manner efficient and contained, controlled, and
somehow very much at odds with the way she had to
pause occasionally to push her hair back off her face
when it swung forward, obscuring her view, as she bent
to take something from a lower shelf. That gesture had
betrayed a vulnerability that for some reason had reminded him of Cathy. He was irritated with himself, and
his frown deepened.

Davina James meant nothing to him other than
through her connection with Carey's and the fact that
she was its main shareholder.

He realised that Cathy was still waiting for an answer
to her question. 'I don't know,' he responded. 'We could
have lunch somewhere if you like.'

Vigorously Cathy nodded her head. As he drove
through the town Saul had noticed a family pub-cum-
restaurant which was part of a nationwide chain, and
when he suggested this to Cathy as a lunch venue she
beamed responsively.

The place was quite busy, mainly with family groups,
and a smiling waitress quickly showed Cathy and Saul
to a table.

Saul hid his amusement at the very adult air Cathy
assumed when she was handed a menu. A quick glance
at its contents made him suspect that his sister would
not have entirely approved of what was on offer as an
example of nutritious healthy eating, but he stifled his
conscience by telling himself that it was only a one-off.

The table next to them was occupied by a couple with
two early-teenage children, both boys, both enjoying
large plates of some kind of battered fish and chips, and
Saul grimaced a little to himself as he saw Cathy eyeing
the contents of their plates lustfully. There was nothing
on the menu that really appealed to him, but he ordered
from it nevertheless, his attention suddenly caught when
he heard the woman at the next table saying grimly to

her husband, 'I tell you, Bert, it makes my blood boil. Everyone at Carey's knows that it's the stuff the girls have to handle that gives them these rashes, but will they do anything to stop it? No. Too damn mean to care what happens to those who make their money for them.'

'Carey's... Carey's... Come on, love, you're not at work now,' her husband retorted, clearly irritated and bored by a conversation he had obviously heard over and over again. 'You're the shop steward. It's up to you to get them to do something about it. There's no point in complaining to me. I don't even work there.'

'No, thank God. It looks as if the lot of us will be out of work anyway before too long.'

'Has she told you that?'

The woman shook her head, chewing a mouthful of food before responding.

Saul's own meal had been served, but he was too interested in listening to what was being said at the next table to do more than pretend to eat it.

'No. She seems to think she's going to get someone to buy her out... at least, that's what we've heard, although she's not admitting it.

'Mind you, I've got to say that at least she does seem to take more of an interest in us than that husband of hers ever did. Never saw him down in the packing sheds or on the assembly line unless he'd got his eye on one of the girls working there. A right one, he was. Always at it, and never cared who with either. He was with someone else the night he was killed. It's no wonder she's taken up with Giles.'

Her husband put down his knife and fork. 'Has she, now? Well, she wouldn't be my type, and I'm surprised she's his with a wife like he's got. Now, she's——'

'Bert,' his wife warned, glaring at him and then looking towards their two sons, who were both oblivious to their parents' conversation.

'Don't worry, I'm quite happy with what I've got at home,' Bert told her with a grin, and Saul suspected from the brief silence that followed and the way they were looking at one another that the hand Bert had slid under the table wasn't entirely innocently occupied.

So Davina James was having an affair with Giles Redwood.

He pushed away his meal virtually untouched, causing Cathy to give him a brief uncertain look.

The couple at the next table had finished eating and were chivvying their two sons to finish theirs. The woman was small and vigorous-looking, with thick dark red hair, the man taller and more relaxed. Saul observed the way the man's hand rested momentarily on his wife's buttock as they left the restaurant. Karen would have poured scorn and contempt on their behaviour, her voice acidly derisive as she criticised them, but momentarily Saul found himself envying them.

They were just an ordinary couple, an ordinary family such as one might see anywhere, a couple without many financial or educational advantages, but they had something that he had never had: they had a closeness not just with one another, but with the two boys who had now joined them, a family closeness and a personal awareness of and for one another which he and Karen had never truly known. And which he never would now know?

He shook off the heaviness of his thoughts as he waited for Cathy to finish the chocolate-laced ice-cream dessert she was battling with. Too much introspection, too much dwelling on self-pity was an affliction peculiar to modern-day man and woman, according to a doctor friend he knew. But his chief fault over the years had not been too much delving into his own motivations, but too much sealing himself off from them.

Because he had been afraid of looking behind the shadow over his life which his father had cast in case he might not recognise the reality of the self that stood behind it?

'I'm finished, Uncle Saul.'

Saul spent the rest of the day rereading the file he had brought with him and adding to it the snippets of information he had picked up since his arrival in Cheshire.

Christie rang to check that everything was all right. She sounded preoccupied and distant when Saul spoke to her, almost edgy, in fact, but he put this down to the fact that she was probably caught up in the self-generating tension such conferences always seemed to produce.

His own next logical step was to get in touch with the manager of the local branch of the bank that Carey's used and to make sure that he won them over to his, or rather Alex's, way of thinking.

It shouldn't be too difficult. Carey's were heavily in debt to the bank and he had no doubt that in the present financial climate the banker would be only too pleased to offload its liability on to Alex.

Gregory James had been very clever when setting up the original loans in managing not to give the bank any personal guarantees for them; and, with the value of commercial property of any sort so very low, the bank would be lucky to realise even half of its borrowing if it forced Carey's into bankruptcy and sale.

Yes, he suspected the manager would welcome him with open arms and do everything he could to persuade Davina James to sell out.

He frowned a little to himself, drumming his fingers on the table. Davina James was no businesswoman; so little so in fact that she had had to plead with Giles Redwood to stay on and to take over running the company for her.

By sleeping with him? Or had that merely been a bonus, for both of them? Had they in fact been having an affair *before* Gregory James died? And how much did the fact that they *were* having an affair affect his own initial assessment of the situation?

If she did prove stubborn, in view of that relationship, it might not be a possibility to consider applying leverage by bribing Giles to leave. It depended which one of them needed their affair the most. It *had* to be her, surely? A lonely, probably insecure woman whose husband had been openly unfaithful to her for years...

He frowned briefly. It irritated him that she was proving so difficult to slot neatly into the place he had made for her; there were too many conflicting components... too many things about her that didn't tie in together neatly, and yet what was there really about her to cause him all this unwanted consideration? She was a widowed woman of thirty-seven, forced to step into her husband's shoes on his death; a woman who could not really have the slightest interest in the company of which she was the main shareholder, a woman who on the face of it should not have caused him even a second's deviation from the path he had set himself. Not young, not beautiful, not brilliantly clever. So why had she lodged in his thoughts with all the irritation of a small pebble in a tight-fitting shoe?

He shrugged it off, denying the reason for its existence. Just as he had denied for too many years that he was playing a role in life which rightly belonged to someone else. That they were not *his* choices, *his* goals he was reaching for. That the need which had driven him had never been to achieve financial success and recognition but simply to receive his father's approval and love?

Why did he feel so demeaned by having to admit that need? Why did it make him feel so vulnerable, so afraid... so angry?

Because it was wrong for a man to admit that he needed *anyone's* love, much less a parent's.

He glanced across at Cathy, her head over the book she was reading. No need to question if Cathy felt secure in her mother's love. It was obvious that she did. But what about his own children? Did he want his son, his daughter to repeat his mistakes, to waste their lives questing for something every child should have as a birthright? What kind of father was he anyway, that he might have denied that need, might not even have recognised it?

He moved restlessly in his chair. He was letting Christie get to him. His children had no real need of him, and they certainly did not want or need his love; they had demonstrated that to him often enough.

But what if they did? What if beneath the indifference, the cynicism, the apparent contempt and disdain, they too ached for his approval, his time, his attention, his unequivocal acceptance of them as they really were, as he had done for his father's?

His eyes had started to blur. He lifted his hand to rub away the exhaustion clouding them and discovered with a sense of disbelief that it wasn't tiredness or strain that had blurred his sight, but tears.

Tears. For his children or for himself?

He needed time to think things through properly, he told himself wearily. To allow himself to be pressured by his emotions into any kind of impulsive action was simply not sensible. Not possible either. Before he could give any attention to his personal affairs he needed to get this business of the purchase of Carey's sorted out. Well, hopefully, with the bank to bring pressure on Davina James, if it was needed, it shouldn't take too long.

Davina James.

Where was she now? With her lover? Another woman's husband, by the sound of things. Odd—he hadn't somehow thought of her as the type. But then, what *was* the type? Did there have to be a type? As far as he could see from his own cynical observation of heterosexual relationships, there were only two main reasons for those relationships breaking up, both related to control and power. And within most relationships there were only two bases for that control: one was money, and the other was sex. And in the past it had, as a generalisation, normally been the man who controlled the money and the woman the sex, and, like any kind of transaction in which mankind indulged, it very quickly became common currency for one to barter with his or her power-base for what he or she wanted from the other.

Equally, it never took long for one and often both of them to discover that anything that was not freely and generously shared with full equality soon became not worth having, or so loaded down with resentment and hidden anger that it came to be used as a means of punishment rather than a reward.

Saul remembered the distaste and contempt he had felt when he first heard an American client disclose a view he had later come to realise was shared by a large proportion of his own sex. 'Sure, we have a good sex-life. I pay her a hundred dollars every time she sucks me off—that way we both get something we want and I get the added bonus of knowing every time she goes out and buys herself a new outfit that it's cost her as well as me.'

Admittedly it took two people to devalue a relationship to that point, but with hindsight he could see how close he and Karen had come to getting caught in the same trap.

Was that why Davina James had stayed married to her husband? Because of the money? He frowned. What the hell was he doing, dragging *her* back into his thoughts? And, besides, he acknowledged irritably, Davina James was the one with the money. Her father

had seen to that. That must have galled her husband.
He was the one who ran the business, but she was the
one who had the real control.

Control...yes, it all came back to that one word...that
all-important source of power.

Lucy examined her perfectly made-up face carefully in
her mirror, searching for any betraying evidence of tears.
There was still a slight puffiness beneath her eyes, a slight
pinkness, but not enough for Giles to notice.

Face it, she told herself bitterly, Giles wouldn't
notice...wouldn't care if he came home and found her
stripped and spread-eagled on the sitting-room floor with
some other man.

She closed her eyes tightly to prevent the tears welling
and ruining her make-up, tears not of misery but of
anger. Last night Giles had come home late. Again. And
drunk. Well, maybe not drunk, exactly, but certainly he
had been drinking and, she suspected, not alone,
although he had denied it when she accused him of being
with Davina.

She had been in the sitting-room when he came in,
pretending to be engrossed in her magazine. He had
hesitated in the doorway for a moment as though surprised to see her there. As though he would have preferred not to see her there?

He had come over to her, leaning clumsily over her
as he aimed a kiss at her forehead and missed, and then
trying to take her in his arms. It was the first time he
had touched her in weeks...in months, and immediately she had pushed him away, infuriated and bitterly
hurt that he could only face the thought of doing so
when he was drunk enough to forget who she actually
was...when he had anaesthetised his lack of any desire
for her with drink.

To her chagrin, he had refused to let her go, and today
she had bruises on her arms from where he had held her.
Giles had never been a violent man, not even a rough

one, but last night ... She shuddered as she remembered the way he had held her, the way he had kissed her, trying to force some kind of response from her.

'Don't touch me,' she had spat at him when she had finally managed to push him off. 'I am not Davina. She——'

'No, you're not, are you?' he had agreed, interrupting her grimly, not allowing her to finish what she was saying. 'She's a real woman, not a phoney copy. *She* doesn't play at loving.'

His accusation, all the more hurtful because she had sensed that it was what he actually felt, had driven her into a frenzy of temper, hurling insult after insult at him, telling him that he was useless as a lover, a husband, a provider, telling him that as far as she was concerned he was free to go to Davina and that she wished he would.

'You're two of a kind, both of you,' she had screamed at him. 'Both of you useless in bed ... sexless.'

It had been then that he had grabbed hold of her, taking her off guard by the speed of his attack. What had followed had been squalid and destructive, the complete opposite of the tenderness and intimacy they had once shared, but there had been a point where her body, aching for him, needing him, had overturned her rage and hurt to respond helplessly and eagerly to the driving force of his, matching the intensity of his angry possession of her.

This morning she had still ached a little from that possession, her flesh slightly bruised, slightly tender, so that somehow that small physical ache seemed to echo the greater and far more damaging ache inside her heart.

Afterwards, trembling as much with sexual release as actual shock and pain, she had accused him of raping her, had reminded him that a man no longer had the right to sexually abuse his wife.

Just for a moment the stricken, sickened expression in his eyes made her hesitate, made her want to open

her arms to him and tell him that she was sorry; sorry
for having goaded him, sorry for having lost him, and
most of all sorry for having lost their child; but his eyes
had hardened and the impulse was lost, buried beneath
the burden of her grievances and betrayal.

'Go to Davina, if she's the one you want,' she had
screamed at him. 'Go to her, because I damn well don't
want you. Go and rape her and see how much *she* likes
it.'

She had heard him storming out of the house, and
then the sound of his car engine firing, and was left to
spend the rest of the night wide awake; she had watched
the hours tick by, forcing herself to resist the impulse to
pick up the phone and dial Davina's number. Of course
he had gone to her. Where else would he go? And
Davina, of course, would succour and sympathise with
him, Davina, whom no man would ever be driven to
abuse and rape, Davina, the perfect wife...the perfect
woman, at least as far as Giles was concerned.

Davina was in the shower when she heard the telephone
ring. She had been outside, working in the garden for
most of the afternoon, a means of clearing her head and
organising her thoughts as well as completing a necessary
chore. Now her body ached from kneeling and weeding,
and she hesitated, frowning as she waited for the caller
to get bored and hang up, but instead the ringing persisted, so that finally in exasperation she put down the
sponge and reached for a towel.

'Davina...at last. Davina, I need to see you...now.'
Her muscles tensed as she recognised the desperation
in Giles's voice. He sounded as though he had been
drinking, although surely that was hardly likely at this
time in the day, especially since he was normally a rather
abstemious man? Now, however, his voice was slightly
slurred, and her tension increased as she heard the background noise of voices and music.

'Giles, where are you?' she demanded.

'I'm at the motel, the one by the motorway. I stayed there last night. It's over, Davina. My marriage is over. I can't——'

'Look, Giles, stay where you are. I'll come and collect you. No, don't drive,' she cautioned him as he started to protest. She wasn't one hundred per cent sure but she suspected he was in no fit state to be behind the wheel of a car.

It took her ten minutes to dry herself off and dress. She didn't bother with any make-up, simply running a comb through her half-damp hair before hurrying out to her car.

The motel was only fifteen minutes' drive away. She found Giles in the reception area, his eyes bloodshot, his whole appearance dishevelled and so unlike his normal clean neatness that she felt an almost maternal pang of sadness for him.

He hadn't seen her come in, and when she went up to him and touched him lightly on the arm he swung round, his whole face briefly alight with pleasure as he saw her.

'Davina.' He made a move to take her in his arms, but instinctively she stepped back from him, and then wished she hadn't as she saw the look in his eyes. 'I'm sorry,' he muttered awkwardly. 'I . . .'

'It's all right, Giles,' she told him. 'Come on. Have you checked out?'

He hadn't, of course, and while she did so for him he stood behind her. He was like a man suffering from some kind of shock or trauma, she recognised as she ushered him out to her car.

She kept the windows open as she drove, and by the time she had reached home he seemed rather more sober, his face white and strained.

'What's happened?' she asked him gently once they were inside and she had made him some coffee. They were in the sitting-room, Giles's dishevelment even more noticeable against the backdrop of the immaculate, elegant room.

She waited as he leaned back, closing his eyes. She saw the way as he swallowed that his Adam's apple moved in his throat. He needed a shave, and when she moved close to him he smelled faintly of stale sweat. Normally these things would have, if not actually disgusted her, certainly not have sexually attracted her. With Matt she had discovered the sensual pleasures of every kind of intimacy, especially those very special ones that came from recognising and appreciating the scent of a lover's arousal, but Giles was not her lover and now, as her senses observed these signs of self-neglect, she was moved to pity and an odd sort of almost maternal compassion.

She reached out and touched his hand, frowning as he stiffened and flinched back from her, his eyes opening, shocking her with their stark anguish.

'Oh, God, Davina. I've done the most dreadful thing. I couldn't stop myself. She made me feel so humiliated... and so... so angry...'

Davina's stomach lurched with shock and dread. She wanted to stop him from saying any more, from making her a party to whatever it was that had happened, from making her shoulder any part of his guilt.

But why shouldn't she? Wasn't she just as guilty? By association if nothing else.

Subduing her own instinctive desire to escape, she said huskily, 'Giles... what is it? Please tell me what's happened.'

His eyes were wide open, but he didn't seem to be looking at her even though his attention was focused on her. He seemed to be looking past her... through her.

'It happened last night. I... I wanted to come and see you but... I couldn't go home. Not at first. So I'd gone to this pub... just to have a few drinks... to try and sort myself out... but then when I got home Lucy was waiting for me. We had a row.' His mouth twisted. 'Nothing unusual in that. That's all we do have these days.

'All I wanted to do was to stop her from saying those things... I never meant...' He groaned, covering his face with his hands. 'I don't know what came over me. It's just that it's been so long, and she...she... I raped her, Davina,' he told her rawly. 'I raped my own wife. I wanted to kill myself afterwards. I've never been that kind of man. I've never... Oh, God. No wonder she told me she wants a divorce. Say something, even if it's only that you think I ought to be shot...'

Davina forced a small, twisted smile. 'No. No, I don't think that.'

'But you are shocked...disgusted.'

She took a deep breath. Yes, she was shocked, and yes, it was not the behaviour she would have expected from a man like Giles, and she certainly did not subscribe to the theory that certain women deliberately invited and even incited male violence, but, looking at him as he sat slumped in her armchair, his guilt and despair so plainly obvious, she also felt not so much disgust as intense compassion, for him and most of all for Lucy. She reached out hesitantly and then stopped as he drew back from her.

'For God's sake, don't touch me,' he cautioned her. 'I shouldn't even be here like this, inflicting myself on you.'

'You could always go home,' she told him quietly. 'Talk to Lucy. Try to...'

'Go home... She's probably got half the local police force waiting there for me. It's a crime now for a man to rape his wife, you know. Dear God, I never thought it would come to anything like this. All I wanted to do was... I never thought I could lose my control like that. I used to love her so much, Davina. She meant everything to me, but since we lost Nicholas she's turned completely against me. She blames me for what happened... For her pregnancy... for everything.

'I've tried to be patient... to understand... to wait. I never meant what happened last night to happen.'

He made an abrupt uncoordinated movement, standing up and turning his back to her, but not before Davina had seen the tears in his eyes. Instinctively she got up too and walked over to him, taking hold of him, motivated by an automatic feminine urge to offer comfort and compassion.

At first he resisted her, his body tight with tension and withdrawal, but then abruptly he held on to her, wrapping his arms around her, his body shaking with emotion as she held and rocked him. She could feel the dampness of his tears against her skin, his head a heavy weight on her neck.

'Oh, God, Davina, how can you bear to be near me, after what I've done?'

'Shush... shush... it will be all right,' she comforted him.

'Davina.'

She felt his mouth touch her skin, the caress light and sweet, conjuring lingering memories of another man and another time.

'Davina.' He said her name more huskily this time and the pressure of his mouth was stronger, more sensual. She felt his hand against her breast and was sharply reminded of how much larger the male hand was than the female and how very easily, how very naturally it could cup a woman's breast.

It was not his fault, not even hers, she tried to comfort herself later. Her body's physical response to his touch was simply that of flesh whose need had been denied a natural outlet for too long. He was, after all, a man she liked, a man with whom she felt comfortable and at home; and, whatever had happened between him and Lucy the previous night, she had no fear that there was any real violence in him. In fact, his touch was almost faintly hesitant, questioning and uncertain rather than demanding. Perhaps it was that which caused her own body to yield and in doing so incited the subtle alchemy that led to mutual physical arousal.

Certainly making love with Giles or anyone else had been the last thing on her mind when she had brought him home with her, but now, with his hand hesitantly caressing her breast, his body hard and aroused against her, his mouth slowly exploring the warm curve of her throat, and that tiny, betraying and so erotic faint trembling within her own flesh, instead of moving away from him she found she was actually moving closer to him, her muscles, her flesh subtly accommodating itself to him, as though it had been merely days and not years since she had last been touched like this... held like this.

He kissed her slowly, lingering over the caress so that she could taste the whisky he had drunk and somehow become ever so slightly intoxicated by it herself.

She ran her hand along his arm and up to the nape of his neck, sliding her fingers into his hair, splaying them against his scalp, holding him against her mouth as she felt him shudder, his tongue thrusting eagerly against hers.

'Davina... Davina.'

He was touching her more impatiently now, one hand moving down her spine to rest flat and hard at its base, urging her closer to him, while the other caressed the curve of her hip and then tugged at the cloth of her skirt.

He wasn't as skilled a lover as Matt had been, but there was still a sharp surge of excitement and awareness within her. Perhaps because she was older, more knowing, his slight clumsiness and lack of expertise caused her to feel tenderness and compassion rather than discomfort and unease.

She took hold of his hand, guiding it back to her breast, holding it there as she murmured softly against his mouth. He trembled violently against her, his thumb rubbing fiercely against her nipple.

She had a momentary, sharp aching memory of Matt undressing her, caressing her breasts, his mouth tender and controlled against her untutored flesh. Her spine started to arch, her body moving to invite and support the heavy weight of his head against her. She could feel him tugging impatiently at the buttons on her shirt and was just about to help him when she heard the doorbell ring.

'Lucy!' Giles breathed as they automatically froze and then stepped guiltily back from one another. 'For God's sake, don't answer it, Davina.'

'I have to,' Davina told him. 'We can't just leave her outside.'

Lucy was her friend, and guilt warred with female solidarity, with the knowledge of how she would have felt in Lucy's shoes. She could not humiliate her by refusing to acknowledge her presence, her right to demand her own part in what was happening.

Hurriedly buttoning her shirt, she went to answer the door, knowing as she did so that her guilt was plainly written not just in her eyes but on her body as well, her nipples tight and hard, thrusting against the fabric of her shirt. The last thing she had ever wanted to do was to break up anyone's marriage, especially a friend's, and it increased her guilt to be forced to acknowledge that what had motivated her actions had not been love for Giles but simply physical desire.

As she swung open the door she was already mentally rehearsing her excuses and explanations, but they were not necessary, because it wasn't Lucy who had rung the bell.

As she stared blankly at him Saul realised immediately what he had interrupted. Her flushed face, her eyes, her tension and guilt would have betrayed it to even the most obtuse visitor even if her body had not. He felt his own body tense in recognition of the meaning of the aroused thrust of her nipples. He even wondered savagely at what point he had interrupted their lovemaking. Certainly she had barely had time to fasten her shirt—two of the buttons were mismatched in their buttonholes.

'Davina... Lucy...'

Saul switched his attention from Davina to Giles as the other man came into the hall, his mouth curling in disdain as he took in his unshaven face. They had obviously made rather a night of it, although to judge from their contrasting appearances Davina had recovered from their lovemaking rather faster than her lover; certainly fast enough to have been at the supermarket earlier.

'I've obviously called at an inconvenient time,' he said sardonically, and as he looked at her Davina suddenly became conscious of the fact that her blouse was incorrectly buttoned and half hanging out of her skirt. She felt the hot embarrassment scorching her face, and wondered why on earth she should actually be wishing that her visitor *had* been Lucy.

Who was this man, and what on earth was he doing here outside her front door, looking at her with those ice-blue eyes of cold disdain? With one look he told her that he knew exactly what he had interrupted. Indeed, for one appalling second it was almost as though he had actually *seen* Giles fumbling with her buttons, had actually *seen* into her own mind and witnessed her own visual image of a man's head at her breast, his mouth on her nipple.

A cold shudder of self-disgust galvanised her body. She stepped forward to ask what he wanted, but he had already turned his back on her and was walking over to his car. Caution warned her to let him go.

'Who the hell was that?' Giles demanded, watching him drive off.

Davina shook her head. 'I don't know.' She was frowning. What was it that had brought him, a stranger, to her door? Coincidence? Or... or what?

The desire she had felt earlier had gone. In its place she felt cold with self-disgust and shock. What if it had been Lucy at the door? Lucy was her friend and had every right to expect her loyalty.

Giles was eyeing her uncertainly, his own expression faintly sheepish.

'I... I think I should make us both another cup of coffee and then I'll drive you back to the motel to pick up your car,' she suggested.

'Can I come back here with you?' Giles asked her.

Davina shook her head. 'Oh, Giles. I... Lucy is my friend.'

'She doesn't want me,' he told her stubbornly. 'She said so herself. She wants a divorce. For God's sake, Davina, I love you.'

She shook her head again, trying to clear her thoughts. 'Everything's happening too quickly, Giles,' she told him. 'I can't——'

'You want me to go home to Lucy... to my wife, is that it?' he demanded bitterly. 'To share her bed, when what I really want is to be in yours?'

Davina winced at the passion in his voice, her guilt increasing. 'I... I need time to think, Giles,' she told him.

'All right. I'll book back into the motel. I'm not going back to Lucy, Davina. I can't,' he told her flatly.

CHAPTER FOURTEEN

As THE clapping died down, Christie walked sedately back to her seat with the other speakers.

'Great speech,' the man seated next to her told her. 'You really made them sit and think. And with any luck it will make the dailies. There's nothing they like more than the combination of a controversial subject and an attractive woman.'

Christie acknowledged his comment with a half-smile, her attention not on him but on the audience. This wasn't the main lecture hall, of course; subjects such as hers that seemed to cover all the more outrageous and un-scientific elements of fringe and alternative medicine had been relegated to an old mission hall on the outskirts of the city, some distance from the main conference centre, but nevertheless her lecture had been well enough attended.

It hadn't been a first for her, speaking to an audience; her subject was very dear to her heart and she was a powerful orator, making up with emotion for what she lacked in manipulation and subtlety.

She felt the man seated next to her edging his chair slightly closer to her own. The next speaker was now standing at the podium, and as he announced his subject Christie noticed that several people got up to leave. 'It's not as hot a topic as yours,' her companion told her. 'And he isn't as attractive.'

Christie could feel the irritation beginning to edge up under her euphoria. She turned her head, giving him a cool, assessing look that told him quite categorically that he was wasting his time. She knew the type far too well: forty-something, married, full of his own self-importance, thinking himself God's gift to the female sex and looking for a temporary—very temporary—bit on the side.

She saw that he wasn't pleased at her visual rejection, but she didn't care; her attention was already back on the audience, her eyes scanning the seated figures below her. What was she actually looking for? Confirmation of what she already knew? That *he* wasn't here? Her mouth twisted with self-mockery. What had she expected? What had she *wanted*?

She had behaved more like a schoolgirl than a woman after their taxi had disgorged them outside their hotel, hanging back deliberately and trying at the same time to pretend that she was not doing so, while she watched him at the reception desk.

He seemed to be having some trouble with his reservation, or was it simply that the receptionist, an over-made-up brunette with pan-sticked skin and a full, sulky mouth, was deliberately keeping him there? In the end pride had won out over desire; the reception area was full and she was being jostled by the busy crowd. The last thing she really wanted was for him to turn round and see her standing there, too obviously waiting for some sort of recognition or contact with him.

After all, if he *had* been interested in her he had had ample opportunity to do something about it on their taxi journey here, she reminded herself as she fought her way through the crowd and headed for the lifts.

This hotel was rather more expensive than she had wanted, but she had left her booking rather late and had been unable to get in at anything cheaper. Even so... She had wrinkled her nose a little, unimpressed by its bland décor; it was, she'd reflected as she unlocked the door to her room, to the hotel business what fast-food chains were to the food industry.

The air in her room had been overheated and stale, the windows locked down so that she had to ring through to Maintenance to get someone up to open them, her mind not really on the non-opening windows, nor even on her purpose in attending the conference, but on the man who had shared her taxi journey here to the hotel.

He had introduced himself to her as Leo, but Leo who? There were heaven alone knew how many hundreds of delegates here in Edinburgh; what were the chances of running into him again, even if they were booked into the same hotel?

Christie considered herself to be neither naïve nor inexperienced. She had made a decision long, long ago that just because she was a woman she was not going to be forced into the conventional mode of only allowing herself to enjoy sex once she had convinced herself that she was 'in love'. The human need to enjoy sex was a physical urge, an appetite which, like any other appetite, should be indulged and enjoyed, and which should also be subjected to a certain amount of sensible self-control. She would not, for instance, gorge herself on food she had no real appetite for, which did not really please her, simply because it was there; and it was the same with sex. She was careful, choosy... but that did not mean that she could not and should not enjoy sex simply for what it was.

She did not want a permanent relationship in her life, a man who might try to curtail her freedom, who would almost certainly expect her to put his own needs before hers, who would demand adjustments and alterations in her lifestyle, who might even seek to change the way she thought and felt. She had seen far too often what happened when women committed themselves to men, and it wasn't going to happen to her.

Saul had once pointed out to her that she seemed to have no difficulty in committing herself to Cathy, in putting *her* needs before her own, but Christie had told him that that was different; Cathy was her child and depended on her, and another dependant in the form of a permanent male partner in her life was something she just did not want, either emotionally or physically.

It had been a long time, a very long time now since any man had had that kind of physical effect on her—immediate, sharp, hungry, clawing at her flesh, making her ache, making her so aware of him that long before the taxi journey had ended she had been conscious of the betraying softness within her own body, the beginnings of a wetness that had made her fight against the urge to tighten her muscles and cross her legs in rejection of what was happening to her.

If she had had any corresponding physical effect on him, he had kept it well hidden, she'd admitted wryly.

The bedroom window was open and the cool fresh air blowing into the room had made her shiver a little.

The serviceman had glanced admiringly at her as he left. Christie had responded with a cold stare. It always irritated her that men felt that their sex conferred on them the right to express the sexual side of their natures without any kind of thought for whether or not the woman wanted their awareness of her.

Now, as she surveyed the audience below her, she told herself she was a fool for looking for that certain male face. If he had wanted to make contact with her he could have done so in Reception. It was hardly likely that he was going to turn up here.

There were only another two speakers to go before the end of the afternoon session. Tomorrow was the really big day, with an important set of speeches being given by various representatives of the drug industry, including a huge multinational concern which less than five years ago had only just managed to buy itself out of a potential scandal by paying out large sums of compensation before any case could ever reach court.

One of Christie's patients had been a victim of that particular drug. Its side-effects had caused severe pain and then semi-paralysis of one of her arms. She had been pathetically grateful for the compensation she had received. As a pensioner, she could never have afforded to take Hessler's to court, she had confided to Christie.

The drug had been withdrawn from the market, of course... at least officially. Christie suspected that it would be marketed again at some point under a different name, and maybe even via a different company. Too much money would have been spent on its research for its producers completely to write it off.

Half an hour later as she walked off the stage several people came up to congratulate her on her speech, including a local reporter who wanted to do a piece on her. A local TV crew arrived and she found herself being interviewed by them as well.

'That's great,' their reporter told her when she had finished. 'This natural health thing is really hot at the moment.' He gave her a cynical smile. 'Personally I prefer to go for the doctor's cure every time, but if folk want to believe that drinking herb tea is going to help them, who am I to argue with them?'

Christie gritted her teeth and gave him a feral smile. 'You do realise, don't you,' she challenged him, 'that almost *every* modern synthetic drug has its equivalent in nature, that many of them are simply chemical copies of a drug first derived from nature?'

'Yeah, yeah,' he agreed flippantly. 'So if Mother Nature's so hot on curing things, how come they never found anything to cure the plague and that sort of stuff?'

Christie gave him an exasperated look. 'They couldn't cure it because they lacked proper sanitation, proper... And as a matter of fact some of the things they used for smallpox, for instance, like hanging red cloth at the windows, has actually been scientifically proved to be effective.'

'Yeah? Well, me, *I'd* prefer a good dose of antibiotics every time,' he told her. 'Mind you... it could make a good item for the local news round-up. What's your name again?'

Grimacing slightly, Christie gave it to him before he turned away to interview someone else.

She wanted to get back to her room to ring Cathy. She knew that she would be fine with Saul, but already she was missing her.

She didn't see the small white envelope someone had slipped under her door until she had finished her phone call. Frowning, she replaced the receiver and then went to pick it up. The front was blank, the envelope sealed down.

She broke the seal with her nail and withdrew a piece of paper from inside.

If you are free perhaps we could have dinner together this evening.

Leo

P.S. My room number is 11a.

Her heart was beating far too fast, the sense of let-down and exhaustion that had followed her speech instantly banished, elation and a swift surge of adrenalin taking its place.

How had he managed to discover her room number? Well, that didn't matter now, she told herself as she reached for the telephone and punched in the appropriate numbers.

He answered almost straight away and she had said no more than a slightly hesitant, 'Leo?' before he recognised her voice and responded warmly.

'Christie, you got my note. Good. *Are* you free for dinner this evening, or——?'

'Yes, yes…I…' She bit her lip, conscious of sounding almost over-eager.

'Perhaps we could meet in the foyer at, say, eight?' he suggested easily, making her feel less self-conscious.

'Eight would be fine,' she confirmed.

It was only when she had replaced the receiver that she discovered that she was actually physically trembling a little, the palm of her hand damp, her pulse-rate far, far too high.

What was the matter with her? She was acting like an idiot, she warned herself as she went into her bathroom and held her wrists under the cold tap. He was just a man, for God's sake. A man...a fellow human being...not some Olympian god.

What would he be like in bed? Her body shuddered, her nipples suddenly peaking under the erotic stimulation of her imagination. Calm down, she warned herself, adding wryly under her breath, 'Just because he looks good and physically he turns you on it doesn't necessarily mean he's a good lover. Remember, the proof of the pudding...' Her mouth curled up at the corners, amusement darkening the colour of her eyes, her heartbeat quickening. Would he be a sensual lover, enjoying touching her, stroking her, kissing her...licking, sucking and biting her skin and inviting her to do the same to him?

Already she could feel the heady mixture of anticipation and sensual languor taking over her body. That his invitation to dinner was merely a precursor to their spending the night together she had no doubt.

She went over to the window, breathing in the clear cool air, throwing her head back and laughing as the excitement gripped her, suddenly feeling more alive, more adventurous, more impetuous than she had felt in a long time.

As honest in the way she felt about her body and her appearance as she was in her attitude towards sex, Christie was not the kind of woman who prepared herself for her lover by dressing herself in the kind of clothes historically thought to appeal to the male sexual appetite. To her that was a form of bondage as outdated as the image of the submissive, obedient, dutiful wife whose one goal in life was to please her mate.

No, a man must take her as he found her, accept her on equal terms, accept her body as that of another individual and unique human being and *not* see it only as some kind of cruel caricature of the unfortunate models who posed for the so-called 'male' magazines, their flesh lifeless and inert, a receptacle for the physical fruit of man's lust without either giving or receiving any enjoyment from it.

In his own suite of rooms, Leo continued to hold on to the receiver for several seconds after Christie had hung up.

It had been difficult to track her down, but not as difficult as getting himself a room here in her hotel. The receptionist had told him huffily that they simply did not have any rooms free, until for the first time in his life he had used the power of the von Hessler name.

The look on her face when she'd realised that he was willing to forgo the suite that had been booked for him at the city's top hotel to take an ordinary double room with them had made his mouth twitch a little with amusement. Flushed and uncertain where she had been lofty and all-powerful, she had gone to find the manager.

A suite had been found for him, and Leo hoped that no one had actually been ejected from it. He had protested that an ordinary room would be fine. In fact, he would have *preferred* an ordinary room, but the manager had been so shocked at the thought of his occupying anything other than their best suite that he had wryly given way.

Christie Jardine. He knew quite a lot about her now. His PA, baffled by his non-appearance at the hotel suite originally booked for him, had only just about managed to conceal his curiosity when Leo had casually asked him to find out which room Christie was in.

One of the few advantages of his power, Leo recognised, was that he did not have to give anyone any reasons or explanations for what he chose to do.

His PA, for instance, had not been able to ask him either why he had booked into another, less luxurious hotel, nor why he was interested in Christie Jardine. Jürgen was a Hessler man through and through, though, and Leo realised that he had thought he had found the answer to his own curiosity when he'd reported back that Christie was one of that as yet mercifully small band of doctors actually daring to question the morals of the huge multinational drug companies.

Leo had been wryly amused by Jürgen's obvious disapproval of Christie, gravely thanking him for his report and then feeling a little ashamed of himself for taking advantage of him and his own position. He wondered what his PA would have thought had he known that his interest in Christie was personal and had nothing to do with her antipathy towards corporations such as Hessler's.

But would she be similarly able to accept him, or would she reject him because of who he was?

He frowned as he looked out across the city. From his penthouse eyrie, only the castle on its granite perch overlooked him, a frowning edifice that dominated the city sprawled at its feet.

How grimly this place must have struck the young spoiled Mary, Queen of Scots, returning here from her cocooned life of soft luxury in France. How cold and dour both it and its people must have appeared to her, judging her, rejecting her.

As Christie Jardine would reject him if she knew who he was. He turned away from the window, frowning. Sooner or later he would *have* to tell her. It wasn't in his nature to enjoy any kind of deception and certainly not the kind that involved deliberately withholding from another person information he knew might be drastically important to them.

He reached for the telephone receiver, picking it up and punching in the number he had written down on the pad beside the phone. Once again thanks to his PA, he had the name and number of what he had been assured was one of the city's best restaurants. Best not in the sense of being patronised by a certain 'in' crowd, but best in the sense of being somewhere that was richly rewarding on a much more sensory level.

You could learn a lot about people from the kind of restaurants they favoured and the food they chose to eat. He frowned again, the old habit of self-regulation of his thoughts and actions making him pause to ask himself why he was taking Christie there…as a means of testing her? Or himself?

Neither. He was simply taking an attractive and very sensual woman out to dinner. That was all.

If that *was* all, why hadn't he told her who he was?

In her own room, Christie showered, rubbing the sponge firmly over her skin so that it glowed from the friction. She had good skin, firm and sleek, olive-tinged and healthy. It clung firmly to her bones and muscles. As she rinsed herself off she reached for her towel and then changed her mind, padding naked into the bedroom to study her image thoughtfully in the mirror there, trying to view herself as a man might.

Her legs were long and elegant, her body a woman's rather than a girl's, her breasts well shaped but soft from having breast-fed Cathy, her nipples dark and surrounded by large and slightly swollen areolae.

On holiday, sunbathing topless, she had seen the way a certain kind of man had looked at them and, while she had pitied the men for their sexual repression and inadequacy, she had been sharply irritated by their furtively expressed sexual immaturity. She had no more control over the shape of her breasts than she had had over the colour of her eyes; they had been encoded within her at her conception, but to some men it was as though she had deliberately chosen them as an advertisement of her sexual availability.

She had her own scale now for judging how men reacted to them, a private test, which disappointingly few men managed to pass.

There was, after all, as she had pointed out to the distraught woman patient who had come to her requesting a breast-implant operation because of her husband's attitude towards her neat and perfectly normal pair of thirty-two As, far more to a woman's sexuality than a pair of oversized boobs. 'Try telling your husband you want him to have his penis extended,' Christie had told her.

The woman had stared at her. 'Is there such an operation?' she had asked doubtfully.

Christie hadn't known whether to laugh or cry. One thing she did know was that, if there were, ninety-five per cent of the world's male population would no doubt be queueing up for it. Perhaps, after all, a sex that still could not accept, despite overwhelming evidence to prove it, that as far as women were concerned it was not the size of the equipment that was important but what you actually did with it, and, even more important, what you did before and after you even got around to using it, could be forgiven for its fixation on large breasts.

She placed her hand flat against her midriff. Her waist curved in, her hips round and smooth, her stomach a small gentle swell above the dark tangle of her pubic hair.

Christie knew that she was fortunate in her easy acceptance of her own body and her own sexuality. Every day in her surgery she listened to women patients who were not, and ached for them in their lack of self-love, wanting to urge them to thrust aside their ingrained sense of lack of self-worth and somehow to replace it with pride in their sexuality, with self-confidence in their womanhood, with the right that surely belonged to every human being to value themselves ... to love themselves.

It had taken her a long time and a lot of self-searching before she had been able to cast aside the image of herself she had seen in her father's eyes and to stand tall and proud in her own individuality; an individuality she was fiercely determined to protect and see thrive.

She was perfectly happy to share her body, her pleasure in her own sexuality, her desire and even some of her vulnerabilities with a lover; what she was not and never would be prepared to do was to submerge herself in him, abasing herself for him, demoting herself to second place for the sake of his needs, his ego. If he was not man enough to accept her as an equal, to understand that for her there would always be times when her own needs, her own ambitions must be set above his and he must accept that fact, then there was no place for him in her life, not even as a lover.

Which was probably why she had been celibate for these last several years, she acknowledged humorously as she finished her tally of her physical self and briskly dried her still damp skin, extracting clean underwear from the drawer, a plain fine silk bra and equally plain briefs to go under the warm tobacco-brown of the simple silk dress she was going to wear.

No need for tights; her legs were smooth and lightly tanned, and the silk fabric of her dress wasn't happy over man-made Lycra and nylon.

She had washed her hair. Now she dried it, brushing it vigorously. It was thick and shoulder-length with a strong curl. When she was a child her father had always complained that it looked wild and untamed. She remembered that now as she plaited it into elegant control. She shivered, acknowledging how much she already wanted Leo; knowing that the imagination of his mouth against her own, against her breast, her stomach and the sensitive female flesh where a small pulse was already beating excitedly, was tensing her stomach and making her body soften and ache so that she could feel its sensual swell pressing against the constriction of her clothes; those who believed that it was only male arousal that caused such an immediate and visible physical swelling of the body were woefully ignorant of either their own or their partner's reaction.

But then, how many of them ever actually looked? She had been mystified when a man had moved uncomfortably away from her as she studied his erection, sensually enjoying its effect on her senses, on her awareness of the pleasure that awaited her in having him inside her.

It put him off, he told her uncomfortably. Women were supposed to close their eyes.

It had done more than put him off, and after that it had been another test she had subconsciously used on her would-be lovers. They had not only to enjoy having her look at them, but to enjoy looking at *her* as well.

After all, sex, good sex, should surely employ the use of all of one's senses; the physical penetration of one body by another was, to her, only the climax of what should have been a banquet, a feast of all the senses. A man who did not enjoy watching her, seeing how much his touch aroused and pleased her, was in her opinion a very poor kind of lover.

Christie wasn't a fool. She knew that many of her feelings, her beliefs challenged some of the most dearly held male beliefs, challenged them too dangerously in many cases, but she refused to be bullied or cowed into a sexual stereotype because that was the only way some men's egos could accept her.

And yet she was very much a woman, secretly acknowledging that part of her sexuality that wanted at the height of her desire to be passive, penetrated, possessed, but knew that in being all those things there re-

mained a subtle strength and power, an elemental mystery
that held the kernel of the atavistic male drive to possess
the female.

Very few men could understand that in a woman. But
the few that could and did...

A wry smile curled her mouth. Don't get too carried
away, she warned herself. Just because he looks good
and turns you on, it doesn't mean *he's* one of them.

She was down in the lobby at one minute to eight.
Christie did not play silly power-games to manipulate
the opposite sex, and she was pleased to see that Leo
had had the good manners to get there ahead of her.

Good manners were not to her an old-fashioned, outdated means of putting women in second place. Used
properly, they were simply an awareness of and a consideration for others. Of either sex. Had she been the
one to ask Leo to dinner she would have made sure she
was there ahead of him too.

She liked the way he smiled at her, openly taking in
her appearance and equally openly letting her know that
he found her attractive.

'The restaurant isn't very far away,' he told her. 'We
can walk or take a taxi.'

'Oh, walk, please,' Christie responded. 'It's so stuffy
in here that I'd welcome some fresh air.'

Although he was wearing a suit, it was more casually
tailored than the one in which he had arrived at the
airport. The cloth looked as though it was some kind of
silk mixture and not the kind that had been bought
cheaply in between flights to and from Hong Kong and
made up overnight, she recognised shrewdly. Which
meant either that he was independently wealthy or that
he had a generous expense account. Somehow she did
not think it was the latter.

He opened the main door for her, but allowed her to
walk freely and easily, choosing her own distance from
him, which had the effect of causing her to move a little

closer to him than she might normally have done. A subtle piece of clever manipulation or a genuine recognition of her equality?

'I don't know what the restaurant is going to be like,' he warned her as he indicated that they should turn left into a narrow street that led up towards the castle. 'It has been recommended to me.'

'You have friends in Edinburgh?' Christie asked him.

'Er—no.'

She tensed a little, sensing that he was uneasy, withholding something from her.

Damn, she had noticed that small betraying hesitation, Leo acknowledged, registering Christie's reflexive muscle tension and the quick assessing look she gave him.

He hated lying and he had never been any good at it. And to be a good liar one had to enjoy it, he admitted ruefully. To treat it as a mere pedestrian necessity rather than to indulge in it with flair and enjoyment might have been enough to have helped him get by, but whenever he was called upon to utter even the most basic of humdrum white lies he could almost feel himself flinching away from doing so.

Elle had laughed at him for it. Lying well was not just a skill, nor even a necessity, but one of life's greatest pleasures, she had told him, adding mockingly that she was surprised he was such a good lover when he lacked this most important loverly skill. It was probably because what he lacked in verbal deceptive flair he made up for with his sensitivity and awareness of people's emotions, she had decided.

Whether she was right about that or not, Leo knew one thing: Christie Jardine was not the kind of woman who would share Elle's views on the necessity of deceit.

'I...I heard about it from...from a business associate,' he told Christie now, grimly aware that his words, while technically true, still held that betraying note of tension.

A business associate. Did that mean another woman? Christie questioned inwardly, and then frowned quickly. What did it matter how he had learned about the restaurant? Or why her question had made him so uncomfortable? He was a stranger, someone she barely knew, she reminded herself as Leo touched her arm lightly and said, 'I think we turn left here.'

After all, she could hardly expect him to catalogue his life and the people in it for her, just because they were going out for dinner. She knew she would have been the first to object had he started cross-questioning her about her own life.

They were off the main thoroughfare now and in one of the maze of narrow streets—wynds, as they called them—which formed a maze of ginnels and alleys between the ancient tenement buildings. Once these tenements had been the city apartments of those wealthy high-born country Scots who would leave their estates to come to Edinburgh to enjoy the social season.

The wynd opened unexpectedly into a small courtyard, and Christie blinked in surprise and pleasure at the sight of the profusion of window-boxes, and pots full of flowers that filled the small grey space.

Someone had very cleverly elected to choose plants grey and silver in foliage with white, pale blue and the palest misty lavender-grey flowers, so that now at night with the dusk, the pale, ghostly blue-grey of a northern-lying land, the plants blended perfectly into their surroundings in a way that the hot, bright colours of the Mediterranean never could have done. Even the pots had been carefully chosen to enhance that effect, she observed as she moved closer to study the raised design on one of the lead containers.

Leo watched her as she moved forward to run her fingertip along the relief pattern. She had elegantly long fingers, but the nails were cut short and unpolished. She was totally absorbed in what she was doing, all her concentration focused on the pleasure the containers and their contents were giving her.

It was rare these days to see a child, never mind an adult, exhibit that kind of delight; natural; honest; unashamed of the emotion that others might see.

Her plait had swung forward on to her face and he discovered that he wanted to reach out and tuck it behind her ear so that he could watch her.

He saw her frown suddenly, a rueful look curling her mouth as she turned to him and said, 'They aren't lead at all, they're plastic.'

He could sense her disappointment. 'Lead would be prohibitively expensive and more at risk from thieves. The plastic is a very good facsimile.'

'Until you get too close to it,' she agreed.

'Like a good many things in life,' Leo suggested quietly.

Christie frowned. Had he guessed . . . known . . . that that was exactly what had been running through her mind, or had he simply voiced a belief that was his own? Either way, it disturbed her that their thoughts should have run so exactly parallel.

'At least the flowers are real.'

Leo looked at her as he held the restaurant door open for her. Reality in all things would be very important to this woman. Reality and truth.

The restaurant was busy without being overcrowded. The bar area was upstairs in an open gallery so that one could if one wished enjoy an aperitif while looking down on the dining area without being guilty of prying and, equally important, without making the diners below feel as though they were exhibits in a cage.

'Very clever,' Christie commented when they were seated at a table, waiting for their drinks, 'allowing

people to indulge in people-watching and to tempt their
appetites at the same time.'

'Mm... and hopefully to prevent them getting too
restless when they're kept waiting for a table.'

Christie gave him a shrewd look: intelligent and good-
looking, and, from what she had seen so far, without
that irritating male aggression that seemed to be a shared
vice of so many successful men.

Successful? She frowned. Now, why had she thought
that? Because he wore discreetly expensive clothes; because of his manner; the way he was so comfortably at
ease with himself and with his surroundings. The restaurant might not to the untutored eye appear luxurious,
and it certainly wasn't ostentatious, far from it; but
Christie had already discerned that the diners, local
people in the main, to judge from their soft accents,
were not those on their way up their chosen ladders in
life, but those who had reached the top and been there
long enough to feel relaxed and unimpressed by either
status or wealth.

This was a restaurant for people who knew what they
wanted out of life; who sought to please themselves and
were far removed from the necessity of pleasing others.
As Christie watched, a female diner shook her head over
the selection of vegetables she was being shown, her smile
rejecting the food without embarrassment or self-
consciousness, her manner towards the waiter as she
spoke to him very definitely that of someone who knew
beyond any kind of doubt that the restaurant would be
only too pleased to provide whatever it was she chose
to have; that there was no need for raised voices or aggressive demands; that she was there to be pleased and
pampered.

At another table a woman was sampling some fresh
raspberries, tasting a couple before opting to have them,
a tiny frown marring her immaculate made-up face as
she judged their flavour and texture.

'The restaurant specialises in providing fresh locally grown or produced food,' Leo told her. 'It isn't exclusively vegetarian but the menu doesn't carry very many rich red meat dishes. I'm not a vegetarian myself... but, I must admit, these days I seem to have lost the lust for very heavy meats.'

'As a doctor, I'm all too well aware of the dangers of too much fat consumption,' Christie told him. 'I'm a terrific fish fan, and Cathy and I both enjoy raw vegetables and fruit.'

'Cathy?'

Christie put down her glass, giving herself a few seconds to reply. It wasn't like her to introduce Cathy into her conversation like that; at least, not in this sort of situation. Cathy and her private life were things she preferred to keep private.

'My daughter,' she explained.

Her voice was terse enough for Leo to pick up on her reluctance to discuss the subject, but suddenly it had become very important to him to know if there was a man to go with the child. He gave her a quick look. She would not respond well to a direct question, he suspected; already she was on her guard, slightly tense, her body stiffening as she sat bolt-upright in her chair, her body language almost defying him to ask her anything more.

'You're lucky,' he told her quietly. 'I don't have any children, nor indeed a wife.'

'The two don't necessarily go hand in hand,' Christie pointed out drily.

Leo felt her tension relax a little. He had suspected she wouldn't be able to resist that kind of comment. 'No,' he agreed, and then added firmly, 'However, if I did have a child or children inside or outside marriage, whatever the status of my relationship with the mother, I would want to keep them within my life.'

For the first time Christie heard a certain steeliness in his voice and for some reason it made her sharply aware of the contrast between his attitude and that of Cathy's father.

Angrily she pointed out to him, 'You might not be given that choice. If your relationship with your child's mother broke down there would be no guarantee that you could continue to have a relationship with your child. Most courts still find in favour of a child's mother.'

'Yes. But *I* should like to think that, even if I and my child's mother could not continue with *our* relationship, both of us would be left with enough respect for one another and enough love for one child to come to some arrangement that would allow us both to remain in his or her life, even if we no longer remained there together.'

His idealism and the sincerity with which he spoke irritated Christie. He obviously had no idea of what life was really like. The break-up of a sexual and emotional relationship between two adults was a very painful thing, with neither of them inclined or even able to make sane, loving arrangements for sharing the child they had created together, but because she couldn't voice those thoughts without betraying her own emotions she said instead, 'What about the distance factor? Sometimes even with the best will in the world it's not always possible for a father to remain in contact with children who might live some distance away.'

With all the means of transport at his disposal it was extremely unlikely that there was anywhere in the world he could not be within twenty-four hours, Leo reflected, but he knew he could not say so. He had touched a nerve, quite obviously... Because her relationship with her child's father was not a good one? Why did that thought cause him such a sharp thrill of relief?

They had to break off their discussion to order their meal, and, once they had, Leo changed the subject by asking her about her work.

Her work was something about which Christie felt so passionate that her problem was not in talking about it but in trying to make sure she didn't totally monopolise conversations by doing so, but on this occasion she was also conscious of a tiny *frisson* of not exactly chagrin... not even really disappointment, but something that was most definitely not the relief she should have felt in having successfully indicated to Leo that Cathy and her private life were subjects she did not want to discuss.

What had she expected—that he would press her to answer his questions, ignoring her unspoken veto, as if she were a woman saying no when she meant yes?

Her muscles tensed reactively, her self-disgust that she might have been guilty of that kind of passive inability to make her own decisions as sharp as though she did indulge in the kind of fake shy sexual manipulation that meant she paid lip-service to the outdated notion that a woman could not be valued by a man in the sexual sense unless he had to coax or persuade her into acquiescing to his desire; as though a woman were some kind of passive vessel for sex, without the self-respect or pride to claim her rights to her own sexual needs; the right to say yes when she meant yes and to say no when she meant no without being judged on those responses.

Her voice, her manner had warned Leo to keep his conversation away from personal issues, so why now did she feel slighted almost because he had, as though in obeying her unspoken commands he was somehow indicating that he had no real interest in her?

She was still irritated by her own contrariness when their waiter came to escort them to their table.

As Leo walked behind her he observed the economical elegance of the way she moved; she had a natural physical grace, not the languid, calculated, sensual grace of Elle and her like. Christie's was more buoyant, more vital, her movements quick without being jerky or brittle. She would be an energetic lover, he suspected, one who might even deride him a little for his own slower-paced enjoyment of lingering over each caress and touch.

Leo liked foreplay, a fact that had openly amused Elle, who had told him once that the fates had given him a gift which potentially could make him irresistible to the whole of womankind.

'I thought it was stamina that women wanted in sex,' he had offered ruefully, conscious that Elle was already discreetly indicating that her recent orgasm, while enjoyable, had for her simply been a starter to the main meal.

'Almost any man can be made erect by a woman who has patience and skill,' Elle had shrugged. 'Teaching him that she desires more than the mechanical textbook manipulation of her body plus a brief period of penetration if she is to achieve the pleasure she has every right to expect is something else.

'The best that most women can hope for is that a man will have enough knowledge and self-control to suppress his own orgasm until she has had time to reach hers. To find a man who actually takes as much pleasure in helping her to reach that orgasm as he does in the relief of his own . . . a man who sometimes enjoys that journey so much that he is actually slower to reach that climax than she . . .' Elle had run a delicate fingertip down his body as she spoke, laughing softly under her breath as his quiescent body started to respond to her, conversation forgotten as she drew him down against her.

Christie could be an almost pragmatic, even aggressive lover, he suspected, demanding her right to be treated as an equal, the one who kissed, who controlled, who set the pace. While he had never had any desire to make a woman feel subservient or passive, Leo had also never been attracted to a woman who was sexual rather than sensual, and, on the face of it, Christie *was* that kind of woman, perhaps treating sex as an appetite to be appeased, as something separate from emotion, above all refusing to let go of her own self-control.

But he had seen the way she touched those flowers, the wondering, almost awed look of pleasure in her eyes, and he had known that, no matter how much she herself might seek to conceal it, she was as vulnerable to sensuality as he was himself.

CHAPTER FIFTEEN

MUCH as Christie enjoyed her meal, and she did enjoy it, it was her conversation with Leo she enjoyed most.

She was over halfway through her main course, expounding fiercely on her concern about the power of the huge modern drug companies, before she realised how much she was monopolising the conversation.

Wasn't it supposed to be the woman who stroked the man's ego by encouraging him to dominate the conversation, not the other way round? she wondered wryly as she apologised.

'You don't feel there is any place in modern medicine for the large drug companies, then; from a moral point of view, that is?' Leo questioned her.

His heart had sunk as he listened to her. While he shared many of her views, her passionate dislike of the large corporations and those who ran them had dismayed him.

'Not unless they are a lot more carefully monitored and controlled than they are now, and by an independent body,' Christie told him firmly. 'I'm not disputing the worth of some of the new drugs on the market, but, make no mistake about it, the drug companies are in the market for profit. Altruism does not generate profit and, given the fact that they have so much wealth, so much power, some of them are in a position to put pressure on not just the medical profession but in some cases on governments themselves to sanction drugs that might not have been thoroughly tested.'

'There are very strict laws,' Leo began mildly, but Christie shook her head.

'There *are* laws, but sometimes the effects of these drugs don't show up in clinical trials. Modern drugs are extremely powerful, capable of destroying whole nervous systems, of suppressing immune systems. In some cases doctors are encouraged to prescribe drugs that are potentially far too powerful...when something more gentle, more natural——'

'Nature creates drugs that are just as powerful as, if not more powerful than those created by man,' Leo pointed out.

Christie frowned at him.

'I'm not saying that you aren't right...that you don't have a valid point,' Leo added gently. 'But it would be foolish to deny that modern drugs have a very important role to play in health care and in the prevention and cure of certain diseases.

'The way I see it, since the aim is to help and protect the patient, there should be room for every kind of medicine to work in harmony.'

Christie gave him a cynical look. 'Just in the same way as it should be possible for people of every colour and creed to live in harmony?' she demanded pithily. 'Somehow it never works out like that, does it? The strong inevitably seem to end up oppressing the weak. I take it that your support of the drug companies isn't entirely detached?' she asked shrewdly. 'Do you work for one of them?'

'In a way, yes,' Leo agreed, relieved. Here was his opportunity to tell her the truth. And increasingly throughout the evening it had become more and more important to him that she *did* know the truth. Leo was well aware of the small subtle sexual signals he had been receiving from her; subtle enough to be ignored if he so chose and yet direct enough to indicate her own willingness for more intimacy with him.

'Well, I suppose a man ought to show some loyalty towards his employers,' Christie was commenting. 'Saul certainly believes so.'

'Saul?' Leo queried.

Christie felt a small spark of triumph as she recognised the male challenge in his voice. Did he think that Saul was her lover? 'My brother,' she told him calmly, watching his reaction with an unfamiliar female pleasure. 'We don't always see eye to eye on things, although he's always given me support when I needed it most.' She frowned a little, remembering her feeling that something in Saul's life, in his whole outlook, had changed; that something had disturbed and distressed him. His gulf between him and his children?

'So, although your opinions differ emotionally, you are close,' Leo suggested. 'I wish I could say the same about my relationship with *my* brother,' he told her. Now it was his turn to frown. What on earth had made him say that? His relationship with Wilhelm had no place here; and in fact it was something he never discussed with anyone. Because there had never been anyone close enough to him for him to be able to do so. But how could he think he was close to this woman? She didn't even know who he really was.

'Have you just the one brother?' Christie was asking him.

'Yes, and you...?'

He still hadn't told her who he was, and, as they progressed from the discovery that they both had elder brothers to the discovery that neither of them had parents living, Leo acknowledged that he had lost an important opportunity to be open and truthful with her. Lost it, or deliberately let it slip by, because he was still afraid of her reaction?

'You didn't get along too well with your father?' he asked Christie now, frowning as he picked up the note of hesitation in her voice when she mentioned him.

'Saul was always closer to him. I think in all fairness things might have been different had *I* been different. He was the kind of man who liked things, life, to be orderly and to conform. Had I been the kind of pretty, docile person he wanted me to be...' She gave a tiny shrug.

'He was afraid of your intelligence. Some men are like that often because it underlines their own inadequacies. I'm sorry,' he apologised quickly. 'I didn't mean to imply that your father...'

'I'm not offended,' Christie told him. 'In fact, in many ways he *did* feel inadequate. And because of that he pushed Saul...set him targets, goals that were what he wished he could have achieved himself.' She paused and looked at him, her eyes clear and calm. 'You may think it unfeminine, disloyal, even, of me to criticise him to you, but I believe in being honest. I hate people who pay lip-service to convention, saying one thing when they mean the complete opposite. I loved my father, but I didn't particularly like him and he certainly didn't like me.'

'Well, you are one up on me,' Leo told her. 'I neither liked nor loved mine.' He stopped abruptly. This was the first time he had ever said that to anyone. His dislike of his father had been something he had always kept to himself. Because he had never had anyone in his life with whom he could share those kind of feelings; because he had always been slightly afraid of them, guilty for having them even, while logic told him that he had every reason for feeling them and none whatsoever for loving the man who had always rejected and hurt him.

'It isn't easy, is it,' he said now, 'coming to terms with that feeling, that awareness that, no matter how much you try, you cannot be the person a parent wants you to be? At first you feel misery, guilt, pain...and that comes after the realisation that you have somehow disappointed.

'Then later comes that dull resignation and misery that you have somehow failed; that awareness that, whatever you do, there will never be for you the praise and acceptance there is for another, preferred sibling. And then, later still, if you are lucky, there comes the protection of anger because you are not accepted for what you are; and if you are even luckier an awareness that you have talents, gifts, skills that are uniquely yours and of value, even if they are not those admired by the rejecting parent.'

Christie was silent for so long that he thought for a moment that he had somehow alienated and offended her, and then as she ducked her head he saw the brief shimmer of tears in her eyes.

'It's such a dangerous thing, isn't it,' she told him huskily when she lifted her head, her emotions under control, 'meeting someone so very much on your own wavelength?'

'Dangerous?' Leo queried sombrely. 'Why do you say that? Isn't it what every human being craves—to be with another human being with whom they are emotionally in tune?'

'Not necessarily. Sometimes that kind of intimacy can be too powerful, too strong. It makes people feel too vulnerable. Like being with someone who can read every thought in your mind.'

'Too intrusive and possessive, you mean? I believe that it's a disease of our times, this fear people have of real intimacy, this desire to distance themselves, often using sex to do so, offering it as a false gift of intimacy.'

'It's normally women who express that view, not men,' Christie commented.

'Are you trying to suggest that because I'm a man I'm not allowed to put emotional intimacy higher on my list of priorities than sexual intimacy?' Leo asked her quietly. He had caught her off guard and her expression showed it.

'No, no, of course I'm not,' she denied, adding firmly, 'Any more than a woman should feel guilty about expressing her sexuality.'

They were virtually the last to leave the restaurant, but the staff made no attempt to rush them.

When they had walked back to the hotel Leo noticed that this time Christie walked much closer to him, the movements of her body harmonising with his. Or was he the one harmonising with her? he mused. He suspected she would have said so. Did it matter as long as they were in harmony? Again he suspected that Christie would think so.

He went with her up to the door of her room, and as she turned round, obviously about to invite him in, he leaned down and briefly kissed her.

Her mouth felt soft and warm beneath his, her body curving into his so that he could feel the soft firmness of her breasts against his chest.

He kissed her again, savouring the taste of her, his hand caressing her shoulder and then her throat, his fingers enjoying the sensual vitality of her hair as he slid them into it. So many different sensations, so many promised pleasures, and she was not, as he had half suspected, sexually aggressive after all. She was not passive either.

His brain managed to remain detached enough to note these facts while his senses absorbed the scent and taste of her, aware of the pliancy of her body, of its invitation and desire, of the fact that she was offering herself to him, inviting him to share her pleasure with a frank openness that caught at his heart because it was an invitation he could not accept, not without telling her who he was, and he knew she would not understand; that she would believe him guilty of deliberate deception; that that deception would sting her pride, would in her eyes reflect on her judgement. She had trusted him, told him things about herself he knew she had confided to few, if any, others, and she would consider that in keeping such information to himself he had trapped her into betraying herself to him under a false guise.

She would probably still have sex with him, but he didn't want to have sex; he wanted to make love.

Very slowly, very gently he released her, carefully distancing himself from her.

'I must go,' he told her quietly. 'I have some work I must do. I have enjoyed this evening more than I can say. I have some free time tomorrow morning. If you are free too perhaps we could see something of the city together.'

And somehow he would find an opportunity, make an opportunity if necessary, to tell her the truth. *Then* if she still wanted him they would be lovers. For one night? If that was all he wanted, why not go with her now? Why not spend *this* night with her?

As he saw the chagrin and the confusion chase one another through her eyes he forced himself to resist the temptation to kiss her again. Her mouth was still soft and moist from their last kiss, her nipples hard peaks against the silk of her dress. She had a small mole on the side of her neck and he badly wanted to bend his head and touch his mouth to it, but he fought back the impulse, waiting for her response.

What had gone wrong? Christie wondered. Why was he rejecting her? All through dinner she had been conscious of the intimacy, the rapport between them, conscious too of her own desire, her own arousal, sensually anticipating the moment when they would be alone together, but now he was distancing himself from her, telling her that the evening was over. Had she *really* made such an immense error of judgement? Had he not really wanted her at all? Had it been her own desire that had coloured and warmed the evening? But no...when he kissed her...when she kissed him back she had felt his response to her; had *known* that he wanted her.

She could hardly drag him into her room and rape him, she told herself, trying to regain something of her normal self-protecting cynicism.

Did he really want to see her tomorrow or was that simply a face-saving exercise—for both of them. It was hot in the corridor, too hot, but her body felt chilled—because it missed the warmth of his? It certainly ached with the disappointment of knowing that the evening was not after all going to end as she had imagined.

'I'm not sure whether I shall be free in the morning,' she responded cautiously. 'But certainly I should enjoy seeing something of the city if I am.' If he could play face-saving games then so could she. She allowed no hint to show of what she was feeling, of the sheer raw ache of sexual need that was tormenting her body, sharpened suddenly by the knowledge that it was a need that was not going to be satisfied, at least not in the way she had believed.

'If you *are* free, perhaps we could meet in the lobby, say, eleven?' Leo suggested.

'If I *am* free I shall be there,' Christie told him. She turned to open her bedroom door, the exhilaration of the evening draining from her, leaving her feeling all too conscious of the bitter after-taste of her disappointment.

She said goodnight to him as she let herself into her room, firmly closing the door behind her and then locking it. She had her pride, after all, she decided savagely as she threw her bag on to the bed. She was not going to beg him or any other man. If he got some kind of pleasure from letting her think that he had wanted her, from letting her believe that her desire was reciprocated, from subtly stage-managing the whole evening so that it had gone from phase to phase in the same climactic way their bodies might have later approached orgasm, well, then let him. She wasn't going to let it bother her and she certainly wasn't going to meet him tomorrow morning.

*   *   *

Nevertheless, at eleven o'clock the next day she was getting out of the lift and walking into the lobby, her body tensing with a sudden surge of excitement as she saw Leo standing waiting for her.

He hadn't seen her yet. Perhaps last night he *had* been too genuinely busy to be with her, and perhaps she *had* taken him a little off guard by signalling to him that she wanted him to stay with her.

She wondered how long his proposed tour of the city would take. Like her, he must want to attend this afternoon's lecture. It was, after all, the highlight of the entire weekend. A talk on the progress of modern drugs given by the head of Hessler Chemie.

She might be opposed to all that Hessler's and others like them stood for, she had been grimly disdainful of the product leaflet she had been showered with during the conference, the samples and sweeteners so freely handed out, but she *was* anxious to attend the lecture, since there was to be a question-and-answer session at the end of it, and she was interested to see how Hessler's would defend any criticisms if such criticism was allowed to be made. She had heard a rumour that Hessler Chemie were underwriting some of the costs of the conference.

Her stomach lurched as Leo turned round and saw her, his face breaking into a smile of such warmth and sweetness that all her doubts about seeing him again were banished.

She was within yards of him when a man rushed up to him, exclaiming urgently in German, 'Herr von Hessler; your brother is on the telephone. The call was put through to your suite at the other hotel. I am afraid he is not in too good a mood at the delay in reaching you.'

Herr *von Hessler*!

Christie's understanding of German was patchy, but just hearing his surname was more than enough to take in. She froze, unable to take her eyes off Leo's face. He was frowning, brushing aside the other man's anxiety, telling him firmly, 'I'm afraid my brother will have to wait. Tell him that I shall ring him back, will you, Jürgen? Christie,' he called out to her quickly, but she had already turned her back on him, shock and anger tensing her body. The crowd of people milling around the lobby made it impossible for her to escape as quickly as she had hoped. When she felt his hand on her arm, she demanded brittly,

'Please let go of me.'

He didn't make any pretence of not understanding. 'Christie, please listen, I can explain.'

'Why should you?' she asked him coldly. 'I can well understand that a man of your... importance... might feel it politic to conceal his identity.'

She was jostled by the crowd and had to turn half towards him, so she saw him wince, the skin round his mouth paling with tension as his jaw tensed. She had made no effort to conceal either her anger or her contempt. Why should she? He *had* deliberately deceived her.

'It wasn't like that,' he protested. 'I had intended to tell you.'

'But you decided not to bother.'

'We were getting on so well. We had formed such a rapport that I didn't want to spoil things.'

Christie laughed bitterly. 'What rapport?' she demanded acidly. 'How *could* there be any rapport between us when you were deceiving me? What was it? Did you think I might refuse to go to bed with you once I knew your real identity?'

His face suddenly burned with angry colour. 'You know better than that,' he told her sharply.

'Yes, I think I do,' Christie agreed, her own face white now. 'Was that why you backed off last night, Leo? A man in your position must have to be so careful. No carelessness, producing a child that might ultimately have some claim on the von Hessler millions. Is that it? Well, for your information——'

'Christie, stop it,' he commanded. 'That was *not* the reason at all, and you must know it. I didn't want us to be lovers until I had had a chance to tell you the truth. I *had* intended to do so this morning, only unfortunately Jürgen has forestalled me.'

'Unfortunately for you, but fortunately for me,' Christie told him. Her face felt hot and tight with anger, her whole body burning with it, and with the humiliation of being so easily deceived . . . like an unprotected child.

'I wanted to tell you last night,' he stressed.

'And last night *I* wanted to have sex with you,' Christie told him. 'Isn't it a good job that neither of us got what we wanted?'

'Christie, please——'

'No, Leo,' she told him, turning to face him, her eyes bright with anger and rejection. 'I hate deceit. I hate it more than anything else there is. And you did deceive me, even if only by omission. You let me expound freely and openly on my views and beliefs when all the time——'

'When all the time what?' he challenged. 'You would have edited and tailored them to suit my position with Hessler Chemie if you had known the truth?'

'Of course not,' Christie denied hotly.

'Then letting you speak genuinely and honestly can have done no harm, can it? I am a *man*, Christie, not a corporation; in fact, I——'

'I am not interested in what or who you are,' Christie cut him off. 'I am not interested in you in any way, Leo. Now, please let go of my arm. I loathe being manhandled.'

It was said with such contempt that he released her immediately, stepping back from her to give her the space her body language demanded.

'Think of it like this,' she told him fiercely as she moved away from him. 'If you had not been so careful last night, at least you would have had sex with me. As it was, all you did get was the bill for a very expensive meal.'

'I did not want to have *sex* with you,' Leo told her equally fiercely.

The look she gave him was corrosive and bitter.

'No, you didn't, did you?' she agreed as she turned her back and walked away from him, before he could tell her that what he had wanted, what he still wanted, was to *love* her!

CHAPTER SIXTEEN

AT FIRST when Giles woke up he couldn't even remember where he was. The angle of the light falling through the thin curtains fell harshly into his eyes, making him wince with pain. His mouth felt dry, sour, and the smell of the half-full tumbler of whisky beside his bed made his stomach churn with nausea.

Where the hell was he?

And then he remembered. He looked at the glass next to the bed and the bottle beside it, a thin film of colour darkening his skin.

What was happening to him? Was he really so weak, so lacking in self-control, so unable to focus himself on a goal and to reach it that he had to turn to drink to escape from his own sense of failure? No wonder Davina had refused to let him stay with her. He had never been a heavy drinker, not even really a social drinker, but just recently...

He remembered his row with Lucy, the things she had said to him. He groaned, leaning forward in bed. He had the most God-awful headache. It was probably just as well Davina had refused to let him stay last night. His mouth twisted bitterly. Even before he had demolished the better part of that bottle of whisky sitting on the bedside table, he had hardly been in a fit state to perform well as a lover.

Lucy had once told him that he was the most perfect lover she had ever had or had ever been able to imagine having. And he had told her truthfully that giving her pleasure, watching her face as he loved her, had been *his* pleasure. When she had started to turn away from him, to reject him, he had known that he had lost that ability to please her. The damage that knowledge had done to his sexual self-confidence had made him reluctant to touch her, afraid of disappointing, or, even worse, disgusting her.

Lucy... What had happened to the love they had once shared? As he now thirsted for the cool solace of Davina's calm orderliness, a part of him knew that he would never attain with her the heights he had reached with Lucy. Lucy, turbulent, temperamental, impossible to understand, impossible sometimes even to talk to, generating within him such a complexity of emotions that just thinking about them sometimes exhausted him.

A relationship with Lucy demanded one hundred and fifty per cent of a man and he simply didn't have that to give, especially not now, with Carey's and his job both so precarious.

Even before Gregory's death Lucy had been urging him to leave Carey's, to find a job that wasn't so demanding. He had agreed with her then, but after Gregory's death, when Davina had needed him so much...

Couldn't she see how selfish she was being? he had asked Lucy angrily one evening when she had barely let him get inside the door before launching an avalanche of bitter invective and complaints against him. He was the one who was being selfish, she had countered. More than selfish. She wasn't deceived; she *knew* it was Davina who was keeping him at Carey's, even if he refused to admit it.

He winced now, the brief denying movement of his body making his stomach heave. He pushed back the bedclothes and stood up slowly. His head swam with pain and nausea.

Half an hour later, showered and dressed, he studied his reflection in the mirror with grim distaste.

'Go to Davina and don't come back,' Lucy had told him, and in the heat of the moment he had done exactly what she had said. But of course he had to go back. He was an adult, not a child to run from his responsibilities.

If he and Lucy *were* to separate...divorce...there were arrangements that would have to be made. He winced again. Divorce. The word tasted bitter, its consonants harsh and jagged like the emotions it aroused within him.

Divorce. He hated everything that the word implied, but what alternative did he have?

An hour later Giles let himself into the house and stood for a moment in the hall. Empty silence greeted him and his heart started to race in panic and fear. The house was empty...Lucy had left. Gone. Why should that thought fill him with such despair?

He walked into the kitchen, unfamiliarly tidy, its surfaces and floor gleaming.

Lucy was the kind of woman who liked clutter, *things* around her; every room always seemed to have a jug of flowers somewhere in it, a collection of photographs; a display of china Lucy had collected from rummaging among the stalls of street markets and antique fairs.

In the kitchen, the billboard was normally covered in brightly penned notes, postcards, invitations, messages Lucy had written to herself. Once, a long, long time ago, or so it seemed now, she had written messages on it for him, sometimes huge scrawly ones, sometimes tiny hidden ones in the shape of a cut-out heart, sometimes more sexually explicit ones that employed a secret language of their own.

Today the billboard was empty.

Like the house. Like their lives together.

He went upstairs slowly and mechanically. He needed a change of clothes and another shower—the smell of the whisky was still on his skin, in his mouth, and he wanted to purge himself of it. As a divorce would purge him of the pain of their marriage?

The bedroom, like the kitchen, was immaculate and empty. In their adjoining bathroom the air carried a faint

trace of Lucy's perfume. Giles closed his eyes in denial
of a sudden image of Lucy's body, of the scent and feel
of it, its warmth and femininity; of the way she moved
when she was aroused; the way she touched and held
him; the sharp staccato cries she made as she approached her climax.

He had started to shake, his body cold with sweat,
beads of it formed on his skin as the desire to be violently sick overwhelmed him.

Fifteen minutes later, showered and dressed in clean
clothes, he closed the bedroom door behind him.

Wherever Lucy was, she hadn't left permanently. Her
clothes were still in their bedroom.

Perhaps she had gone to a friend.

He frowned, one foot on the top stair as he realised
that the door to the room that had once been her child's
nursery was half open. He went back and stood outside
it. He had come back from the hospital after Nicholas's
death and had systematically stripped the room of
everything, everything...even down to the wallpaper,
releasing the violence of his grief and pain in the
destruction of the room's pretty aqua and cream colour
scheme, in removing that border with its gambolling
animals, its message that a child's world was a secure,
happy one without clouds or pain.

His child's world had not been like that. His child's
world had been filled with pain and death.

He pushed the door open and went inside, and then
stopped abruptly. Lucy was curled up asleep in the
rocking-chair he had bought for the nursery and which
had escaped his destruction as it was away being re-
stored and cleaned.

Her face free of make-up, her curls tangled, she looked
more like a teenager than a woman, and he had to resist
the urge to push the heavy weight of her curls out of
her eyes; to straighten the arms and legs she had curled
around herself as she huddled asleep in a small cramped

ball. Her face was pale, the skin milk-white without its normal covering of make-up, her lashes thick and dark, matted together slightly, her mouth red and full.

In her hand she was clutching a piece of paper, and other pieces of paper littered the floor at her feet. Frowning, he bent down to pick one of them up. His heart raced as he realised that it was a piece of their marriage certificate.

Slowly he picked up every piece, carefully rearranging them on the chest below the window, carefully smoothing out the ones she had screwed up until, like doing a jigsaw, he had remade the whole.

He looked at her hand and gently removed the paper she was holding. It was their baby's death certificate.

He could feel the tears burning his own eyes. He ached to reach out to her, to hold her; to confess to her the burden of his own guilt and pain.

Why had they never talked about losing their son? He hadn't done so because he had been afraid of distressing her; because he had simply not known how to do so.

And she had behaved as though nothing had happened; as though there had never been a child...a life...a death.

Yesterday had been the anniversary of the day he died. An anniversary he and Lucy should have marked together. Instead they had both ignored it. And now it was too late. Or was it?

Quietly he walked out of the room and went downstairs, letting himself out of the house and getting into his car.

The garden centre was busy and it took him a long time to find a parking spot.

Of the two of them, Lucy was the gardener, but he knew exactly what he wanted.

Did he know exactly how large it would grow? the assistant asked him doubtfully. Giles felt the anger and grief welling up inside him.

'It's a large strong tree,' the youth persisted. 'A proper tree, not a pretty ornament for a suburban garden.'

'It's exactly what I want,' Giles informed him tersely. The tree would put down roots, it would grow and mature. It would live throughout his lifetime and well beyond it. It would thrive as their child had not been able to do. It would be steadfast and enduring . . . as he had failed to be for Lucy.

He couldn't get it in the car, of course. It would have to be delivered and planted. He paid for it, having given them their delivery instructions. And then he went back to the main part of the garden centre.

The girl inside the flower shop blinked a little as he gave his order. She had to help him carry the flowers out to his car.

'What do you suppose he means to do with them?' she asked her colleague. 'I mean, he bought enough to cover a whole room with them.'

'Or a whole body,' the other girl pointed out with a sigh. 'I have a fantasy about that, you know. Imagine making love on a bed covered in flowers, the scent of them on your skin as you crush them.'

'Some of them can leave awful stains on things,' her companion pointed out dubiously. 'I mean, those lily things. I ruined my black T-shirt with the pollen off them, and what if some of them were roses? Some of those thorns . . .'

Her companion sighed a little impatiently, only half listening as the other continued, 'Do you suppose that's why he bought them? He did have a bit of a wild look about him, didn't he?'

Giles had to hunt through several cupboards before he found enough jugs. An urgency, an anger, an emotion so powerful that it controlled him, rather than the other way around, directed him.

Quickly, roughly almost, he thrust handfuls of flowers into the jugs, oblivious to any discordance of colour or shape, a need driving him, obliterating everything else. Soon every downstairs room had its quota of jugs, deposited haphazardly on every conceivable surface.

As he worked there was only one image in his mind. That of his infant son. 'These are for you, Nicholas,' he whispered fiercely beneath his breath. 'For you; because you *did* exist . . . you did live . . . you *were* here, a part of us, and you always will be.' And, running through his heart in a silent refrain, were the words, Forgive me . . . forgive me.

He had tried to deny his son's existence, to deny him his right to remain a part of his life, but not any more.

'Giles . . . what are you doing?'

He turned round. Lucy was standing just inside the door. She had obviously heard him moving about and come down to see what was going on. She had evidently showered and dressed and there was no sign now of the vulnerability of the woman he had seen curled up asleep in the chair.

'These flowers . . .'

Was she remembering that once he had bought flowers for her . . . roses . . . a symbol of his love and joy? His heart ached with the weight of the burden of his thoughts.

'They're for Nicholas,' he told her quietly.

Lucy stared at him. 'It was yesterday,' she told him mechanically. All the colour had left her face. She seemed to be looking at them rather than him.

'Yes, I know,' he told her, but she scarcely seemed to have heard him.

'I knew. I knew he had gone,' she went on. She was speaking slowly, more to herself than to him, Giles recognised as he watched the emotions pass painfully across her face. 'I wanted to be with him, but they wouldn't let me. I wanted him to know I loved him . . . I wanted to hold him . . . I wanted him to have love. He shouldn't have died like that, alone . . .' Tears had filled her eyes and Giles felt the pain wrench at his guts as he listened

to her. 'It was my fault, all of it. I said I didn't want
him, but I did, and I let him die alone when he should
have been in my arms. When he should have been with
me. He should have had someone...'

'He did,' Giles told her thickly. 'He had me. *I* was
with him.'

Now for the first time, she focused on him.

'No!' she told him fiercely. 'Don't lie to me, Giles.
You left——'

'I went back,' he told her. 'I couldn't sleep...couldn't
get what you'd said out of my mind, so I went back.
He was looking at me when it happened. I think...I
think somehow he knew. All the knowledge of the world
seemed to be in his eyes as he looked at me. I felt so
helpless, so angry. He was my child and yet I couldn't
help him. I'd let him down and I'd let you down. If I'd
let you stay with him as you wanted...'

'No,' Lucy told him. 'We couldn't have kept him alive,
no one could.' She touched the petals of one of the
flowers. Her hand trembled violently. 'I thought you'd
forgotten,' she told him huskily. 'That you *wanted* to
forget him; to pretend he'd never been born. I thought
you wanted to push him out of your life, the way you
do me.'

'Lucy...'

She trembled violently as he took her in his arms; an
instinctive reaction to her pain, a physical denial of what
she had said, and once she was there he marvelled that
he could ever have forgotten just how it felt to hold her
like this.

'Why haven't we talked like this before?' he demanded helplessly.

'I thought you didn't want to...that you were angry
with me...that you blamed me for...'

'Blamed you? No! How could you ever think that?'

'I know I said I didn't want him. But I did love him,
Giles...I didn't want him to die. I never wanted that.'

'No... no, of course you didn't.' He was holding her, rocking her, aching with grief and pain as he listened to the words pouring from her.

Quite when grief and compassion turned to desire he never really knew; one moment he was holding her, stroking her, sharing with her the aching loss they were acknowledging together for the first time, the next, or so it seemed, her mouth was trembling beneath his in much the same way as her body had trembled in his arms.

The feel of her, the warmth of her body in his arms, the scent of her and his senses' familiarity with their sensuality hit him like a flash flood, one moment nothing, the next a sudden seizure of desire so acute, so powerful that it totally swamped everything else.

Somehow he must have undressed her, undressed them both, but he had no knowledge of having done so, only of the soft flesh of her breasts beneath his hands, the dark allure of her nipples, the sharp high sounds of pleasure she made as he suckled on them, using his tongue and then his teeth as he responded to the demand of the nails digging into his flesh and the movement of her body against him.

It was a fierce, frantic coming together, full of sharp sounds and almost violent movements, a physical expression of anger and pain, their bodies straining together.

It could have been a soulless physical exchange of greed, but oddly it was not. It was as though some tiny part of each of them managed to remain so deeply aware of the other that beneath the anger, the despair, the un-leavened physical ache there remained a recognition of each other's needs and pleasures, a faint echo of the loving harmony they had once shared.

As Lucy's orgasm jerked her body in fierce spasms against his own it brought his own release. Her body had never felt hotter, tighter, quicker, and he knew as his erection subsided that physically he still wanted her, his desire an itch still needing to be scratched.

He had never felt like that before; never known that raw ache of lust and need, and both it and the fierce surge of unfamiliar male triumph and power it had brought him left him feeling shaken and disturbed by this new vision of himself.

He looked down at Lucy. Her eyes were closed, her face wet with tears, her breathing shallow and erratic. Her skin had always marked easily and now he could see the faint beginnings of the bruises he had made in the heat of his need. The sight of her body naked, vulnerable, still caught in the after-shock of orgasm, touched a nerve within him.

'Lucy...'

Her eyes opened as he groaned her name and lowered his head to pillow it against her breasts, his arms holding her.

She hadn't meant anything like that to happen; it had been like a summer storm, all thunder and lightning, all quick, raw heat and atavistic passion. Now her body ached, inside and out; that unmistakable ache produced only by intense sex. She could smell the scent of the flowers Giles had bought. They made her head swim slightly, or was that because she had not had anything to eat? Not since yesterday morning...not since...

She felt Giles turn his head and start to nuzzle her breast. He had always been a considerate lover, a loving lover, never greedy and demanding. His mouth opened over her nipple, still tender and swollen so that his eager, fierce suckling caused her to cry out and protest.

'Not that...what, then?' he muttered thickly as he released her. 'What is it you want, then, Lucy? Is it this?'

As his hand moved between her legs she saw that he was erect again, wanting her as he hadn't wanted her in months, but his desire did nothing to melt the core of misery deep inside her; his physical intimacy could not breach the moat of loneliness that surrounded her.

This wasn't the Giles she knew, her lover...her husband...this was a different Giles, a Giles who might be able to make her body ache with shocked arousal with the skilled touch of fingers that rubbed so persuasively, so determinedly against her.

She tried to hold on to that thought, to remind herself that they were two people whose marriage was virtually over, but her love-starved body refused to listen.

This wasn't love. It was just sex, but her body refused to acknowledge the difference.

He was holding her now, stroking her, his tongue quickly parting the heavily swollen lips that protected her sex. She shuddered as she felt his mouth move on her, his tongue rubbing fiercely against her clitoris.

She cried out to him to stop and at the same time reached down to twist her fingers into his hair and hold him against her body, her breath panting from her lungs as her acutely sensitive flesh responded to the rhythmic roughness of his tongue. It was a caress, an intimacy to which she had always been vulnerably responsive, but never more so than now, her cries of denial harsh, guttural almost as his mouth opened on her, drawing her down into the inescapable darkness of her own pleasure.

Later, when it was over and he had exhausted both himself and her, he looked into her white, set face and asked hoarsely, 'What is it? What's wrong?'

'You used me,' she told him tautly. 'You *used* me as a substitute for Davina.'

Davina. He had completely forgotten about her, Giles realised guiltily. He had thought Lucy was going to accuse him of a lack of tenderness, a lack of consideration for her, and now his face flushed as he recognised exactly what he had done.

'No, Lucy, that isn't true,' he protested.

'You mean, now that you've had us both, you prefer me?' she demanded acidly. The Lucy who had cried in his arms for the loss of their son was gone, he recognised grimly.

'I haven't slept with Davina,' he told her angrily.

'So you *were* using me as a substitute.' She said it slowly, almost as though she was in pain, but as he reached out to touch her, to try to tell her that he had never even given Davina a thought, that his need, his desire, his urgency had been hers and hers alone, she pushed him off, temper burning bright patches of colour on her pale face as she reached for her clothes, holding them protectively against her.

'Well, now that you've had what you wanted, you'd better go, hadn't you?'

'Lucy...' He cursed as he stood up and tried to pull on his clothes. No man could reason effectively with a woman while he was stark naked and at the wrong side of a physically exhausting sexual encounter, he decided irritably. 'Lucy...listen...it wasn't——'

'What? Important?' She gave him a thin, curling non-smile. 'I wonder if Davina will share that opinion. Or aren't you going to bother telling her?'

Helpless and angry and all too well aware that his behaviour had been less than justifiable, and still shaken by his awareness of how quickly, how easily the woman he believed he loved had been forgotten, he felt powerless to make Lucy listen to any kind of reason and judged it wiser and safer simply to leave. Besides, he needed time to think. Time to understand himself what had happened and why.

As he pulled on his clothes he made one final stand. 'This is still my home, Lucy, and I intend to go on living here.'

'Refusing to let you share her house as well as her bed, is she?' Lucy glared at him.

He heard her slamming the bedroom door and stared round the room tiredly. He had never known she had felt such grief, such pain, such guilt at Nicholas's death. He had not known either that it would mean so much to her that he had been with him... The doctors had advised him not to raise the subject unless she did so first and yet, crying in his arms, she had told him how much she had wanted him to speak of their baby, how much she had wanted to talk about him and keep his memory alive.

It hurt him that he had never known any of these things. It hurt him and it made him feel guilty, just as remembering the way he had possessed her, needed her made him feel guilty as well.

Davina. He could never imagine *her* in that kind of sexual context. With Davina sex would be calm, restrained, conducted in the bedroom at night, discreetly, with control and tenderness. It would not invoke in him that hot, unbridled intensity he had experienced here with Lucy; it would not make him question himself or doubt his motives, his civilisation, his ability to be wholly in control of his sexuality.

Tiredly he shrugged on his jacket. How was he going to be able to face Davina after what he had done? How could he even face himself?

He walked into the hall and stood for a moment looking towards the stairs, unable to stop himself visualising Lucy as he had found her when he first walked in, curled up in that small foetal ball in the room that should have been their son's.

His thoughts, his emotions, his needs confused and bewildered him. Less than twenty-four hours ago he had told Davina that his marriage was over; that it could not be saved or resurrected. And yet he had still had sex with Lucy, had still desired her... wanted her, and had still felt joined to her as they shared their grief over their son.

Emotions caused by the final dying convulsions of his love, or... Or what? Was he going insane, turning into two different, separate men who loved two completely different and separate women?

His brain ached with the exhaustion of trying to think clearly. Last night he had gone to the motel knowing that he loved and wanted Davina.

Now...

Why hadn't he realised how Lucy felt about Nicholas's death? *Why* hadn't he seen... guessed? Why hadn't she felt able to tell him, to turn to him?

Had he really failed so badly, and, if he had, had he any right to ask another woman to risk that kind of failure?

He needed time, he decided tiredly. Time to get his thoughts, his emotions in order—but how could he have any time for himself with the full weight of the company's problems pressing down on him?

CHAPTER SEVENTEEN

SAUL and Cathy had picked Christie up from the airport. Saul had seen at once that something was wrong, but he waited until Cathy had gone to bed before saying anything.

'Want to talk about it?' he asked her, walking into the kitchen while she was making them both a cup of tea.

Her defences came up immediately, her back tensing as she went on with what she was doing, feigning ignorance as she asked him, 'Talk about what?'

'Whatever it is that's upsetting you so much,' Saul retorted. 'Come on, Christie, this is me,' he reminded her, taking hold of her and turning her round to face him. 'And you never were much good at hiding your feelings. Something happened in Edinburgh.'

'On the contrary,' she told him brittly. 'Nothing happened.'

Dammit, what was wrong with her? Aching like a teenager for a man who hadn't even touched her. A man who was all the things she most loathed in the male sex. Deceiving her.

'If you say so,' Saul agreed. He had been working on the file on Carey Chemicals, and Christie frowned as she walked past the table and saw it.

'Carey's?' she questioned him, her earlier suspicions confirmed. 'So I was right! But why on earth should Sir Alex want to acquire Carey's?' She sat down, handing him his mug of tea. 'I thought they were on the verge of going out of business.'

'He sees its acquisition as a way of getting a toehold in the drug market,' Saul told her carefully.

'And drugs are big business, highly profitable business,' Christie said bitterly.

Saul looked quickly at her. He knew how she felt about the large drug companies, but her bitterness had something new in it, something personal.

'Well, Alex won't get much from Carey's. Gregory has already picked it clean, by all accounts. By rights the whole place should be closed down anyway. As I said before, their safety record is appalling; I *know* they've been in breach of the health and safety laws; they've got people there handling drugs without any proper form of protection. And God knows what effects the stuff they're handling there might have on them, apart from the contact dermatitis.'

Saul frowned as he listened to her. Christie might be emotional and intense, but she was also a highly qualified professional and he knew she would not make those kind of judgements, accusations almost, without any foundation.

'You're sure about that?' he asked her. 'That Carey's *is* directly responsible?'

'Just about as sure as I can be without getting in to check on the actual stuff they're handling, which Gregory James took damned good care I was not allowed to do. He managed to fob off the inspector by giving the place a wholesale clean-up the day he did his inspection. How he knew when he was due to visit, I've no idea. Someone must have tipped him off, or been paid to tip him off. It's criminal, risking people's health, their lives perhaps *and* the lives of their children, and for what? For profit. It's worse than criminal. It's...it's grotesque.'

As she spoke, all the anger she had felt against Leo filled her; an anger intensified and fuelled by the bitter sharpness of her own awareness of how strong her disappointment and disillusionment had been. Knowing the truth, accepting it, had always been important to her and it hurt to know that she had actually almost wished it had not been revealed to her. Or that he had not held back from making love to her?

'Does Davina James know yet... that Alex wants to buy her out?'

'Not yet. I intend to approach her bankers tomorrow to arrange a preliminary discussion.'

'Surely she'll be only too glad to sell out? I've heard the company's in danger of going bankrupt.'

'Alex likes to drive a hard bargain,' Saul told her.

Christie gave him a quick look. There was something in his voice that suggested an unfamiliar distaste.

'At heart he's a gambler, and, like all gamblers, he likes to feel he's getting something for nothing.'

'You don't like him very much, do you?' Christie commented. 'That's strange. I've always thought you rather admired him.'

'Perhaps I did once. Before I realised I was looking at what I could too easily become. Then somehow it wasn't quite so easy to admire him any more. Tell me something, Christie,' he asked her, standing up to face her. 'What would you do if you were suddenly to discover that your way of life, that all this... that conventional medicine was all a sham and that instead of helping people, curing them, you might actually have been harming them? How would you feel? How would you react?'

Christie stared at him. 'I'd feel devastated,' she told him uncertainly. 'Angry... cheated. I'd feel as though everything I'd done... worked for... believed in had become totally meaningless... valueless.'

'Yes,' Saul agreed quietly. 'And how would you deal with that feeling?'

She looked helplessly at him. 'I don't know. I don't know how anyone could deal with it.'

'No. Neither do I.'

'Is that what's happened to you, Saul? Is that how you feel about your life... your work?'

'In a sense, yes. I don't know what's happened to me, Christie. I only know that the ambitions, the goals I took as mine aren't really mine any more, if they ever were.'

'No,' Christie agreed sombrely. 'They were Dad's.'

They looked at one another, Christie's eyes full of compassion, Saul's dark with pain.

'It isn't *his* fault,' he insisted.

Christie said nothing.

'I was always free to make my own choices.'

Still she said nothing.

'What is your choice now, Saul?' she asked him softly after a while.

'I don't know. All I do know is that this is my last job for Alex. In a sense I owe him Carey's. Payment for a debt I reneged on,' he told her confusingly. 'But once that debt *is* paid...'

'What will you do? Find another job in the City?'

'I don't know... I haven't thought that far ahead yet. I want to make time to spend with Josey and Tom. If it isn't too late. But first I have to get this acquisition out of the way.'

As he bent down to pick up the file he told her emotionlessly, 'I thought I had everything, and then one morning I woke up and I knew... I knew I had nothing. What is reality and what is an illusion, Christie? How do any of us ever know?'

'By our instincts,' she told him shakily. 'They tell us. The trouble is, we don't always listen to them.'

'Perhaps with good reason. Most of us are too afraid to listen to what they have to say.' As he kissed the top of her head he said quietly, 'Thanks, Christie.'

'What for?'

'For resisting the temptation to say "I told you so",' he told her sardonically, and then laughed at her expression. 'Hard work, was it?' he mocked. 'Well, I dare say I would have deserved it, but thanks for not saying it, all the same.'

'You're my brother. I love you.'

'And love tempers righteousness with compassion and makes indulgent allowances for weaknesses and flaws. That was my biggest mistake of all, Christie...in not understanding what is and what is not real love.'

His words stayed with her for a long time after she had gone to bed, moving her to tears and filling her with an aching loneliness for which she could not find a cause.

Saul too was awake.

Once he had believed his father loved him and that all his plans and ambitions for him had been motivated by that love. If accepting that this might not have been so was hard, then accepting that his father had been human and fallible, then gently and carefully removing him from the pedestal on which he had kept him for all of his life, then accepting his reduced stature, and going on loving him as the man he had been with ordinary flaws and weaknesses, was harder.

He tried not to think that his father must have known how he felt about him, must surely have recognised how vulnerable their relationship would one day make him. Had he not, then, loved him enough to remove that pedestal himself, to show himself to his son as he really was, and in doing so to give Saul himself permission to be human and fallible? And what about his own son...his own daughter? What about the love they had every right to expect to receive from him?

He moved restlessly in his bed, wishing the acquisition of Carey's were already behind him and that he was free to leave Alex with a clear conscience, the acquisition of Carey's payment for preventing him from acquiring Harper & Sons.

Free to turn to his children, to show them his love, to ask them to forgive his omissions, to begin a new way of life that was his and no one else's.

'Has Giles arrived yet?'

Giles winced as he heard Davina asking for him. Both

his mind and his body felt stupid, numb with the pressure of trying to process too much information, and as Davina walked into his office he felt guilty and uncomfortable.

Guilty for making love to his own wife?

Lucy had been up before him this morning. It had been a shock to go downstairs and find her in the kitchen, and even more of one to find that she had made his breakfast. He couldn't remember the last time he had actually seen her in the morning before going to work; what he did know was that he had been glad when she had finally taken to staying in bed until after he had gone, because that at least meant that he could start his day without one of the arguments that seemed to erupt the moment they were together.

This morning she had been very withdrawn. She looked as though she had been crying. For Nicholas?

When he had tried clumsily to thank her for his breakfast she had shrugged his thanks away, telling him curtly, 'I couldn't sleep. I don't suppose it's up to Davina's standards.' Her mouth had twisted, and he had tried to stop her, but she had ignored him, adding, 'Oh, it's all right, Giles. I know how you feel about her. What is it you want? A nice, quiet, civilised divorce? A neat tidying up of all the loose ends? That is what yesterday was all about, isn't it?' she had challenged him. 'Oh, don't worry,' she had told him. 'I'm not going to make things difficult for you. Not any more. Why should I?'

He had left the house half an hour later, wondering why instead of feeling relieved he had actually felt disturbed and distressed, his emotions still raw from the emotional outpouring of the previous day.

He felt angry and cheated, as though she was denying his need to share with her his grief over Nicholas, and he felt guilty because he had never known how deep and painful her own feelings had been.

And now here was Davina, smiling gently at him, reinforcing his guilt.

He avoided looking directly at her, shuffling some papers on his desk, frowning as he responded tersely to her greeting. Immediately aware of his tension, Davina paused for a moment. He looked pale and drawn. She could see the way his hand trembled a little as he moved his papers. For some reason her presence was making him feel defensive and edgy. Hardly the behaviour of an eager lover, she reflected wryly as she calmly made a couple of mundane comments about the weather, watching as his tension eased a little.

She had learned long ago, first with her father and then with Gregory, how to project an air of calm, safe unawareness of other people's darker moods, and she used that facility automatically now, appearing to Giles's unaware eyes to be supremely oblivious to either his guilt or his discomfort at being with her. She was nowhere near as sensitive to his moods as Lucy, he decided. Lucy would have known immediately that there was something wrong and would have questioned him until he revealed what it was to her.

Davina had not even made any reference to the weekend. She was talking about some problem with the drains in the ladies' lavatories, and he had to subdue a wild desire to take hold of her and tell her exactly how he had spent the previous afternoon. Anything to break through that stultifying placid calm.

Stultifying? Wasn't it her very calm placidness that had attracted him to her in the first place?

Irritably he promised that he would get someone in to sort out the problem, his irritation increased when Davina told him sunnily, 'Oh, it's all right. I've already organised a plumber.'

Giles frowned at her. If she had already solved the problem, then why was she bothering *him* with it? Why

was she bothering with it at all, when they had far more
important things to worry about?

He failed to see the wry glint of amusement in Davina's
eyes as she left, but it was an amusement spiked with
sharp self-knowledge.

Oh, Matt, *what* have you done to me? she asked herself
ruefully as she walked back to her own office. Am I
being impossibly idealistic, or just a little unfair? It isn't,
after all, Giles's fault that his worthiness isn't leavened
by a sharper sense of humour... or a sense of the
ridiculous.

What *did* she want in a man? she wondered as she sat
down. What were the qualities that were important to
her? Not ambition; not aggression; not the childish
demand of an outsized ego; not a man who would
demand that she step into the shadows so that he could
absorb more than his fair share of the sunlight. In fact,
it was easier to say what she *didn't* want rather than
what she did.

Certainly it wasn't anything to do with looks—she was
well beyond that stage of her life; kindness, then, compassion... yes, but with a certain amount of strength as
well. Her mouth twitched a little as she acknowledged
the deep-rooted feminine perversity of that. Sexual at-
traction *and* compatibility. Yes, she would want those.
Laughter, friendship, mutual respect and love. All of
those, but most of all she would want a man who was
strong enough, sure enough of himself and of her to
accept her as the woman she was; to accept that she
needed her independence and yet at the same time that
she would want to know he was there for her to lean on
if needed; to accept that, while it gave her pleasure to
be a home-maker, it was neither her duty nor her sole
responsibility to single-handedly run their home; to
accept that she had individual needs and desires that
might not tally with his, to give her support in times of
weakness and to share her joy in times of triumph; to

be her partner in every aspect of their shared lives; to be her lover in bed, accepting her sexuality as the rich vein of intimacy and pleasure that it was, and perhaps most important of all to love and respect her enough to let her fully and wholly into his life, its pain as well as its pleasure.

Was there such a man? She laughed at her own fantasy. Hardly likely, and if there was she would probably reject him as being too perfect . . . too ideal, not really human. But enough of dream men; she had other and far more important things to attend to.

Saul judged the timing of his telephone call to Davina's bank very carefully. It was a skill that over the years had become part of the arsenal of tactics responsible for his reputation as a man not merely capable of considerable shrewdness and machiavellian planning, but one also possessed of an almost mystical foresight. The City, like any other ancient institution, had its legends and folklore and was vulnerable to superstition, so that to its collective awe at Saul's carefully honed human skills it had added the aura of prophecy and the status of seer, and the effects of his reputation had become self-perpetuating.

A small Cheshire town could be a long way from the City of London, especially to someone who was not part of the underground of interlinking business networks, as Davina wasn't, and when her bank manager telephoned at half-past five, asking to speak to Giles, he was put through to her instead. When he informed her that he had been approached by someone representing a potential buyer for the company and that a meeting had been arranged to discuss the proposed purchase at the bank at nine in the morning, instead of sitting down to work out the best deal she could achieve for herself as the main shareholder, as Saul had intended she should do, what Davina did was to sit down and carefully start to prepare a list of the terms under which she would

want the business to be sold; terms which had nothing
to do with any financial benefits she might receive.

Saul, who had carefully timed his call to give her and
her advisers the minimum amount of time to prepare
themselves, suspected he knew what would happen at
the meeting. It would be put to him that Carey's was an
extremely valuable acquisition, which he would counter
with the fact that they were virtually on the edge of
bankruptcy. From there they would negotiate down until
they reached a figure that he judged would be satis-
factory to Alex. He doubted that after paying off the
bank and their other debtors Davina James would come
out of it with anything other than a handful of loose
change. She had, after all, nothing to bargain with.

Davina rang Giles at home to tell him what had happened—he had left work early for a dental appointment.
She hesitated for a second before dialling the number.

Lucy answered the phone, and Davina asked if she
could speak to Giles. She was glad that Lucy couldn't
see the guilty burn of colour staining her skin. Not that
she actually had anything to feel guilty about. She and
Giles had not been lovers and she had never actively encouraged him to leave Lucy.

But she had not actively deterred him either, had she?
It had been unnerving speaking to Lucy while she remained silent, and Giles was so long in coming to the
phone that she began to wonder if in fact Lucy had gone
to find him.

'Davina.' He sounded edgy and nervous. The guilty
husband, thrown off balance by his lover's phone call
to his home?

But she was *not* Giles's lover, Davina reminded herself
firmly as she told him what had happened.

'A prospective purchaser... Who?' Giles demanded
sharply. He was cursing under his breath. Why the hell
had this had to happen when he wasn't there?

'I don't know,' Davina told him. 'Apparently whoever it is is not prepared to reveal their identity as yet. A meeting's been arranged for the morning, Giles; that's why I'm ringing you. Nine at the bank.'

'Nine.' Giles swore audibly this time. 'That doesn't give us any time at all to prepare anything. You can bet whoever it is knows to a pound just what Carey's position is. They'll want to get the company at a knock-down price.'

'I don't care how little they're prepared to pay just as long as they're prepared to maintain the workforce and improve working conditions,' Davina told him sharply.

Giles sighed. 'Look, Davina. That isn't the way things work. You've got to convince these people that we're in a hell of a lot better financial shape than we actually are, otherwise...they'll be like sharks after bloody meat.'

'I doubt we'll have much chance of that if they've already talked to Philip Taylor,' Davina pointed out quietly.

'Taylor has no right to reveal our financial position to anyone else. It's his duty to——'

'It's his duty to protect the bank's interests, Giles,' Davina interrupted him quietly. 'I suspect that the very fact that these people, whoever they are, have gone through the bank rather than approach us direct suggests that they are well aware of our financial position. I've told you before, I'm not interested in getting *any* kind of personal profit from Carey's. What *is* important to me is securing the future of our employees.'

'No purchaser would ever take on board that kind of commitment,' Giles warned her grimly.

'That depends how much they want the business, doesn't it?' Davina countered quietly.

'*What* business?' Giles started to ask her, but Davina had already hung up.

Lucy came into the room as he cursed under his breath. 'Lovers' quarrel?' she asked him, acid-sweetly.

'There might be a buyer for Carey's,' Giles told her, ignoring the gibe. He was standing in the sitting-room; the flowers he had crammed into the jugs yesterday had been carefully rearranged, and he noticed something else as well.

On the small table, right where it could be seen every time anyone walked in or out of the room, was a photograph of Nicholas.

Lucy saw him looking at it.

'I went out this morning and bought the frame,' she told him stiffly, turning away from him, her body tense and guarded as though she half expected him to object, he recognised.

He walked over to the table and picked up the photograph, examining it silently.

Nicholas. Their son. Such a tiny baby; so obviously frail that it tore his heart just to look at him, and yet he *wanted* to look at him; he wanted to *remember*; to *feel*...

'I hadn't realised,' he began rawly. 'He looked so much like you.' But when he turned round he realised he was speaking to an empty room and that Lucy had gone.

Gently he replaced the silver frame.

It wasn't difficult for Davina to prepare an outline of the terms on which she was prepared to sell the business. What was going to be difficult, she suspected, was convincing Giles and Philip Taylor that she meant to stand by them.

How much power did the bank have to force her to sell? she wondered, chewing on her bottom lip. She was the major shareholder, but if the bank were to demand immediate repayment of their loans...

She reached for a piece of paper, scribbling down some figures. She had the house, and the money in Gregory's bank accounts. Not quite enough, but almost. Certainly enough to hold the bank at bay if they did decide to pressure her.

She had no illusions about the view Philip Taylor would take. He would advocate selling. She couldn't blame him really. He was under pressure from his head office to remove their debt from his books.

And Giles? Giles would want her to sell as well. And if she did it could well be an opportunity for Giles and Lucy to move away and make a fresh start together. If they did, how would she feel? She had valued Giles as a friend, and he had been a *good* friend, but she suspected that that friendship had been compromised by other emotions. Now it was impossible for them to go back to the relationship they had once had, and she suspected it was equally impossible for them to go on and become lovers. She wasn't sure if that knowledge caused her relief or disappointment, and neither, she suspected, was Giles.

It was gone one o'clock when she went to bed, her mind alert and keyed up in preparation for the conflict she sensed was to come.

Power dressing; suits and shirts tailored to be as close as possible facsimiles of men's clothes—wasn't *that* what the modern businesswoman was supposed to wear? Davina reflected wryly. Well, there was nothing like that in her wardrobe. Her clothes were more inclined to be plain and useful rather than designed to make a statement about her role in life.

She frowned as she started to reach into her wardrobe for the neat skirt and jacket she had been about to put on, and instead reached deeper into the cupboard until she found the zippered suit bag for which she was looking.

Some months before Gregory's death she had gone shopping to Chester with Lucy. Heaven alone knew why, because she wasn't normally given to extravagant impulse, nor to allowing herself to be coaxed and chivvied into illogical decisions.

Perhaps it had been something to do with the fact that it had been a bright sunny day, or perhaps it had been because of the faintly contemptuous, understanding look the saleswoman had given her, as though she was all too aware of how unlikely a customer Davina was for the cream designer suit with its ridiculous gold embroidery forming the four-inch letters that ran round the tiny waist of the jacket, spelling out the words 'Waist of Money'.

Well, it certainly had been that, because she had never worn it, and she had known even as she was making the fatal statement that she wanted to buy it that she never would, and what was worse and even more humiliating had been that she was sure the saleswoman had known it as well. After all, what did a woman with *her* lifestyle want with a suit that said quite plainly that it was designed for someone outgoing and confident, someone who couldn't care less what the rest of the world thought of her?

Now, if Lucy had been the one buying the suit... But Lucy had bought a dress instead, bright red with shoestring straps, which ought to have looked dreadful with her hair but which didn't.

As she unzipped the wrapper Davina acknowledged that the suit wasn't merely unsuitable for a business meeting, but that, given the nature of the meeting, it was virtually an act of aggression.

Well, why not? She had sensed from Philip Taylor's voice the faint condescension that warned her that her views, her requirements for the sale of Carey's were not likely to be treated seriously, so why not play the role they had designated for her to its hilt? Let them see that she intended to be taken very seriously indeed and that she did not need to conform to their male idea of what a businesswoman should be to make them do so.

Carey's was *her* company, its employees *her* responsibility, and she was not going to abdicate that responsibility as her father and her husband had done.

She removed the suit from its protective wrapper and held it against her.

Inappropriate. Ridiculous...yes. But it was her choice and to hell with what anyone else expected. As she put it on she thought that somewhere she could hear the echo of Matt's approving laughter.

She reached the bank at five to nine. Giles was already there, and as she parked her car he got out of his and came across to her. She saw the way his jaw dropped a little as he saw her suit, but she ignored his quick frown, giving him a serene and apparently unaware smile.

Philip Taylor's secretary, who eyed Davina's suit with awe and appreciation as well as disbelief, announced that Mr Taylor was waiting for them.

When they were shown into his office Philip Taylor was alone. He gave Davina a brief look and then a second startled, unnerved one as he took in the appearance.

'Mr Jardine isn't here yet, so I thought we could run through one or two points first.'

'Yes. Who exactly are the proposed purchasers?' Giles asked before Davina could speak.

'Why do they want Carey's?' Davina asked more quietly but very firmly.

'Those are both questions I think I'll leave to Jardine himself to answer. I must say, it's a real stroke of good fortune that this has happened. I thought we were going to have real problems in finding any kind of buyer——'

'I hope you haven't told him that,' Davina interrupted dulcetly.

He flushed a little and fiddled with the papers on his desk. 'The company's problems are no secret,' he said quickly. 'And naturally Jardine has done his homework. I think you'll find, though, that the terms are...reasonable...given the circumstances.'

'Let's hope that he finds my terms as...favourable as you seem to find his,' Davina murmured sweetly.

'*Your* terms?' Philip Taylor gave her an uncertain look. 'My dear Davina, I'm not sure that you understand the position,' he began.

'Of course I understand it, Philip,' Davina corrected him. '*You* want your loans repaid. This Mr Jardine wants Carey's... and *I* want guaranteed security for my employees.'

'Jardine will never agree to that,' Giles protested.

Davina gave him a thoughtful look. 'That depends, doesn't it?'

'On what?' Giles asked her.

'On how important it is to him to acquire Carey's.'

There was a small silence, and then Philip Taylor said uncomfortably, 'Davina, I really think it would be better if you let Giles and me handle the negotiations. I know that *technically* you are the main shareholder... I know you mean well, my dear, but when it comes to business——'

Ignoring his patronising "my dear", Davina smiled pleasantly. 'Oh, but I couldn't do that, Philip. I think I've let others shoulder my responsibilities for me for too long. No, as you say, I am the main shareholder and——'

She broke off as the secretary reappeared to announce that Mr Jardine had arrived.

'Show him in, please, Sylvia—oh, and bring us some coffee as well, will you?'

Davina was not seated facing the door, and without turning round, which she did not intend to do, she knew she would have no opportunity to assess or study Saul Jardine until he was close enough to her for him to be equally able to judge her reactions.

As Philip Taylor pushed back his chair and extended his hand, saying warmly, 'Saul,' she too stood up, her face composed and calm; another trick she had learned while living with her father.

He had drawn level with her now and she was at liberty to look directly at him.

In the shock of recognising him there was an unguarded split-second when her feelings showed on her face. She registered the brief mockery in his eyes as he glanced at her and her stomach churned with anger.

Why hadn't she guessed...realised...put two and two together?

Philip was introducing her. Instead of shaking hands she inclined her head and stepped back from him. She had herself back under control now, her brief study of him assessing and measuring.

He was obviously a man who liked playing games, who enjoyed deceit and intrigue. She could guess how much pleasure his quick-thinking lie that he was a walker must have given him the night she had surprised him outside the office.

What had he really been doing there? Taking a chance on the site's being unprotected, on being able to make an unauthorised inspection of the place? If so, he had been taking a risk. For all he had known, the premises could have been protected by guard dogs or alarmed. Was he, then, a man who liked taking risks, who enjoyed a challenge?

'Davina has been running the company since her husband's death,' Philip Taylor was explaining.

'Mrs James and I have already met. I called to see her the other day, hoping we might have an informal discussion, but she was—er—otherwise occupied...'

Giles, who had also recognised him, had gone a dark guilty red. Davina held on to her own temper...just.

'You should have made your purpose known, Mr Jardine. I would have been pleased to discuss your proposals with you. Oh, I'm sorry, they're not *your* proposals, are they?' she added sweetly. 'Philip did explain to me that you were acting on behalf of someone else.'

'Yes, that's correct.' His voice was more steely now, and the look he gave her was sharply clinical.

Davina refused to be quelled. 'And that someone else would be—er—a business associate...or your employer?' She watched as his mouth thinned.

'My employer, as it happens,' he told her tersely.

'And are we allowed to know the *identity* of this employer?' Davina pressed gently. She could see both Giles and Philip frowning, and for a moment she thought Saul Jardine intended to refuse her request.

'There's no reason why you shouldn't know, although you'll understand that Sir Alex Davidson wishes his interest in Carey's to be treated as confidential.'

'In case his interest inspires a similar interest in others?' Davina suggested shrewdly.

Saul looked at her. She was shrewder than he had expected, different as well. He wondered what had prompted her to wear such an unsuitable outfit. It was the kind of thing a sophisticated, a very sophisticated and clever woman might wear for lunch with her lover; the kind of woman with the self-confidence and the sexuality to perhaps choose to wear it over a body that was otherwise naked, *and* to find some subtle way of allowing her lover to know it.

Davina James simply wasn't that kind of woman. Or was she? He frowned as he gave her another quick look, deriding himself for even momentarily doubting his own judgement as he saw the pale shadow of the bra she was wearing beneath the fine fabric.

'Where Sir Alex leads, others *do* sometimes tend to follow,' he agreed suavely. 'However, I'm afraid, not always with his skill at avoiding hidden pitfalls.' He gave her a brief smile, the kind of smile that Davina recognised was designed to dismiss her comments as mere *badinage*, and his response to them chivalrous male indulgence.

'Let's be frank with one another, shall we? Your company is on the verge of bankruptcy, and, while my *employer* ...' he smiled again as he stressed the word, as though to indicate that he had not been offended by her pointed remark, but Davina knew otherwise ' ... would like to acquire the business, he has, naturally, to take market forces into account.'

'If you're trying to warn me that your employer expects to get Carey's for next to nothing, you aren't telling me anything I haven't been able to work out for myself, Mr Jardine,' Davina told him crisply.

She stood up, ignoring the tension she could see in both Philip's and Giles's faces.

'Let me be frank with you. I am not interested in gaining any financial benefit for myself from the sale of the company. Naturally there are the outstanding loans to be taken into account, but I am sure I don't need to go into these with you. Philip will have supplied you with all the details if you needed them.'

She gave the bank manager a brief look, recognising his irritation and confusion.

'What is much more important to me is what your employer intends to do with Carey's.'

'To do?' Saul questioned, his eyebrows lifting slightly as though he found her question a puzzling one.

'Yes,' Davina asserted. 'For what purpose does your employer want Carey's?'

'I'm afraid Sir Alex does not always confide wholly in me,' he told her smoothly. 'As you yourself remarked earlier, *I* am merely an employee.'

'I see.'

The look she gave him was unpleasantly assessing. He had, he realised with a sudden shaft of sharp perception, walked on to treacherous ground. Or been skilfully coerced on to it? The thought made his eyes narrow on her face, but Davina remained calm.

'Well, then, it seems that the wisest course for me is to discuss with you the terms on which I am prepared to sell Carey's, so that you can transmit them to Sir Alex.

'I have prepared a schedule. I think the best thing would be for you to study it and then perhaps we could arrange a further meeting. Preferably after you have consulted your employer.' As she finished speaking she extracted some neatly typed papers from the small case on the desk in front of her, and handed them to him.

'Davina...what...?' It was the lover who spoke to her...first.

'It's all right, Giles,' Davina smiled firmly. 'There's no point in wasting Mr Jardine's time, is there?' She handed him a copy of the schedule she had given to Saul and then gave one to Philip Taylor.

'When was this prepared?' Giles asked her in a dazed voice.

'Last night,' Davina told him gently. 'My father believed that every dutiful daughter should learn to type, Mr Jardine,' she told Saul quietly. 'Perhaps he was right.'

Was she actually telling him that she was well aware of why she had not been informed of this morning's early appointment until so very late in the afternoon, or was he simply imagining things?

'Davina...you never said anything about wanting to prepare a schedule of sale terms,' Philip Taylor was saying uncomfortably.

Davina turned to smile gently at him.

'Didn't I, Philip?'

CHAPTER EIGHTEEN

LUCY was upstairs when the men arrived with the tree, half the contents of her wardrobes strewn around the room, evidence of the furious burst of temper that had driven her.

Now it was exhausted. Like Giles's patience with her; his love for her? Her eyes blurred with tears. Why should she care about Giles, about what he felt—or, rather, about what he no longer felt for her? She could soon find another man. Her expression grew bitter. She had said no to enough of them during the years she and Giles had been married.

Giles had always been slightly naïve in that regard, never seeming to realise that the colleagues he introduced her to with such pride were, under the social smiles and compliments, assessing their chances of getting her into bed. She had been proud of her fidelity to Giles, to their marriage, and of the way she had denied herself the pleasure of allowing them to coax and flatter her. She had taken it as a mark of her maturity, an indication of the depth of her love for Giles; a symbol of its purity and rightness.

If either one of them had been going to be unfaithful to their marriage she had never expected it would be Giles. And with Davina James, of all people. Davina, whose *own* husband had made no secret of the fact that he despised his wife; who had flirted with Lucy and told her how much he would enjoy taking her to bed; how much they would both enjoy it.

Refusing Gregory James had been easy. She moved restlessly around the room, ignoring the clothes she had pulled out of the wardrobes in her furious despair.

She had come up here in a white-hot heat of temper after Giles had gone to work. Caution, control, moving slowly and carefully—these things were not for her, and now the months of indecision, of waiting for things to reach some sort of crisis point and the release of the inevitable explosion that would follow, had finally got the better of her.

Why should she wait around any longer for Giles to make up his mind which one of them he really wanted? Her mouth curled scornfully. Did he really think that Davina would give him the same kind of sexual stimulation and satisfaction that she did? Hadn't he already proved to both of them that secretly he knew she couldn't, by making love to *her*?

And yet when she looked in her mirror Lucy saw that, despite the scornful, triumphant curve of her mouth, her eyes were haunted with misery and self-doubt. What if other things, which Davina *could* give him, were more important, more necessary to him?

The fear that had always been there within her shocked through her, taking her over to the window. The sight of the two men digging a hole in the middle of Giles's immaculate lawn briefly drove Davina out of her thoughts.

She hurried downstairs and opened the kitchen door. The appreciative looks the two men gave her barely touched her. That lawn was Giles's pride and joy, and somewhere deep inside her the fear lurked, sharp and jagged as treacherous rocks hidden by a deceptive tide, that it might just be that Giles had already detached himself from her so much that he would no longer care about the desecration of his lawn.

Yes, they were sure they had got the right house, the two men assured her when she questioned them.

'It's all right, Lucy. *I* ordered the tree.'

The unexpected sound of Giles's voice from behind her caused her to tense and turn round quickly.

'Giles... What are you doing home?' A sharp tiny thrill of fear spiked through her, intensified by the white, tense expression on Giles's face. He had come home to tell her he had made up his mind and that he was leaving her. The protective veils she had wrapped around herself were suddenly ripped aside. She couldn't move, couldn't speak, couldn't do anything other than stare at him with stricken eyes.

'Let's go inside,' she heard him saying.

He reached out and touched her arm, but she wrenched away from him, unable to bear the thought of being touched by him, knowing that where once there had been love and need and desire there was now only a distant kind of pity and distaste.

Despite the sun pouring in through the windows, the kitchen felt cold. Lucy hugged her arms around herself as she watched the way Giles looked round the room.

What was he doing? she wondered painfully as she tried to visualise the room through his eyes. Was he comparing its untidiness, the breakfast things still on the table, this morning's mail still unopened, the untidy clutter of her possessions spread on every surface, with the immaculate, almost antiseptic neatness of Davina's kitchen?

The tidiness of Davina's house had always faintly repelled Lucy. She had taken her some flowers once and had watched while Davina touched the petals, something close to pain in her eyes as she thanked her for them. When she had gone back the following day there had been no sign of the flowers. Flushing, Davina had explained that Gregory did not approve of them unless they were in a classic arrangement for a dinner party.

Was that really the kind of home, the kind of life that Giles wanted, where everything was restrained, controlled...stifled?

She watched remotely now as he paced the kitchen; already the anaesthetising effect of dread and fear were beginning to take effect, distancing her from the pain she knew was to come.

'I can't believe what's happened this morning,' she heard Giles saying angrily. 'And Davina, of all people. I know she can't fully understand the ramifications of the situation, but to interfere like that...to virtually sabotage the only chance we're likely to get of selling Carey's... To even think she could get away with making those kind of demands...and without consulting me...without consulting anyone.'

Lucy stared at him. His face was flushed with temper...anger. An anger that wasn't directed at her, but at Davina. While she was still trying to take this in he stopped pacing and turned towards her.

'I still can't take it in. That Davina could have behaved like that. She was...she was like a different person,' he told her, and his voice betrayed not only his confusion and shock, but also his anger and disapproval. 'And attending the meeting dressed like that when she must have known.'

'Dressed like what?' Lucy questioned him. Her fear was receding now and something else was taking its place, a new realisation, a determination, an awareness that she was not yet fully prepared to put a name to, but that she knew now was there. Even so, his comment had aroused her curiosity enough for her to question it.

'Some pale-coloured thing...a suit...' Giles told her vaguely. 'It was totally inappropriate for a business meeting. It had words round the waist...in gold.' His disapproval and the confusion and shock he had experienced with it were more obvious now. Lucy knew exactly what Davina must have been wearing and for a second she allowed herself to remember that beneath her apparent reserve and the image of the rather dull and very dutiful wife she projected there was another Davina.

One who had a mischievous sense of humour, one whose kindness came from the experience of her own pain; one who could gently poke fun at herself rather than use her wit to hurt others... one who had promised to be one of the few genuine female friends she, Lucy, had ever had.

One who had stolen Lucy's husband. Only it wasn't *that* Davina Giles had wanted; it was the other Davina... the respectable, worthy and dull woman who never seemed to have an opinion or thought of her own; the woman who had been the perfect wife, quietly ignoring her husband's infidelities... quietly ignoring everything in life that was unpleasant or uncomfortable, the one who had thrown away a friend's gift of flowers rather than risk the ire of the man to whom she was married. *That* was the Davina Giles had wanted.

For the first time in her life Lucy controlled her emotions—the emotions that urged her to turn on Giles and spill out her anger and pain that he should dare to turn away from her to someone else—and instead listened to the calmer promptings of her brain, promptings that told her that here if she wanted it was an opportunity for her to turn events in her own favour.

She had never been a strategist, a planner, considering such methods too calculating, too lacking in real emotion, preferring instead to be carried by the impulse of the moment, and the more intense the impulse, the more creditable and important the emotion that lay behind it, but now, a little to her own surprise, she heard herself saying almost soothingly, 'It sounds most unlike Davina... perhaps it's the stress of having to take over the business. Look, why don't you sit down, Giles, and I'll make us both a cup of coffee?'

She saw the surprise in his eyes; the way he blinked and looked almost uncertainly at her before obeying her.

'I'm sure once she's had time to think things over Davina will realise that she ought to have consulted you first,' she added as she made the coffee.

'I still can't believe what she's done,' Giles complained. 'This...this...this thing she's produced... She must be insane if she really thinks anyone would accept these kind of terms. I applaud her loyalty to the workforce and naturally want the best for them, but she *can't* actually expect anyone to agree to keep on the entire workforce for a minimum period of three years.

'No one would ever agree to anything like that. Of course people are going to lose their jobs. That's a fact of life...and as for including in the terms a commitment on the part of the purchasing company to provide a workplace crèche with qualified staff...as well as guaranteeing a minimum wage with a proper salary scale...

'I can't believe she's actually done this...prejudicing everything. She's going to make herself...Carey's...all of us an utter laughing-stock. God, I bet Jardine can't wait to spread it all round the City. And of course *I'll* be the one held responsible. Who the hell is going to hire me when it gets round that I let her jeopardise what jobs *could* be saved for a foolhardy scheme?'

'Here's your coffee,' Lucy soothed him.

He stopped speaking and looked up at her, frowning a little, staring at her so that she suddenly remembered her earlier tears and what a mess she must look. Her appearance, normally so vitally important to her, her defence, her protection against the world, had been forgotten in her emotional surge of panic at seeing Giles's precious lawn destroyed—or, rather, in fearing that Giles himself no longer cared about his lawn...or her.

'Giles, the lawn...that tree,' she asked him. 'What...?'

'Yes, I'm sorry. I should have told you,' he apologised. He was, she saw, looking uncomfortable, his face flushing slightly, his shoulders hunching so that he was

looking away from her when he told her gruffly, 'I
bought it for Nicholas. It's a proper tree...and I
thought...'

Lucy stood completely still. She saw him turn round
to look at her and there wasn't time for her to hide what
she was feeling.

Immediately Giles stood up, his hand resting awkwardly on her shoulder, as though he wasn't sure whether
he should touch her or not. 'I'm sorry,' he told her. 'I
should have said something...asked you first. It was an
impulse...I just thought...a tree...well, it's something that goes on forever, isn't it? It will always be there,
even when we're not. I didn't mean to hurt you,
Lucy...to cause you pain.'

He could feel the rigidity of her body beneath his hand,
her shoulder bones so sharply defined that there seemed
to be barely any flesh covering them at all. She had
always been slender; now she was almost thin.
Unexpectedly a wave of protective tender love filled him.

'Look, I'll tell them to take it away,' he began huskily.
'I should never——'

'No...no. Leave it. You...you did the right thing,'
Lucy told him.

He could see that she was fighting not to cry. Lucy,
who had always given way to tears as easily and as naturally as a child. And for some reason seeing her fighting
them back now hurt him unbearably. He wanted to hold
her, to protect her, to tell her that everything was all
right, that he would make everything all right, but how
could he, when he was the cause of so much of her pain?

'I just...I just wanted to do something...to show
him that he wasn't forgotten,' he told her unsteadily,
groping for the words to make her understand what had
motivated him and aching with the knowledge that once
such words, such care would not have been necessary,
because she would have known.

'Oh, Giles.'

The emotion in her voice made him look at her. There was no anger there, no familiar warning of the kind of temperamental outburst he had been expecting, and when he looked at her he saw that although her eyes were bright with tears they were free of acrimony and rejection.

'Sometimes I feel that I'm the only person who can remember that he ever lived. As though no one else wants to remember.' The pain in her voice caught at his heart, tearing it like sharp thorns. 'No one ever says his name... talks about him.'

He could hear in her voice all that she was feeling, including her own shock that she should actually be telling him what she felt, and again he was filled with a sense of having let her down; of having failed to recognise and meet her most basic need.

How had it happened that he had been so blind to what she was feeling? Why had he relied on others to tell him what to say, how to behave? Why hadn't they been able to share their grief and guilt over the death of their child? They had shared in his conception; why hadn't they been able to share in his loss?

'It wasn't true that I didn't want him,' Lucy told him huskily. 'I was afraid, that was all... afraid.'

'I know,' Giles told her, and as he said it he knew that it was the truth. He raised his head and looked through the kitchen window.

The men had gone. The tree stood close to its supporting stake as though it was a little afraid... uncertain of its new environment; of its role. It was young and vulnerable and in need of support to help it grow and develop its own strength, just as everything and everyone vulnerable needed support.

'What is it?' Lucy asked him as he took hold of her hand and drew her towards the back door, following him nevertheless.

She frowned a little uncertainly as he guided her over to the tree, her frown deepening as he reached out and

touched it almost as though he was stroking it. Its bark
was thin and tender and hadn't hardened into a protective barrier as yet. She touched it herself, tentatively,
not really sure why she was doing so. It felt warm, like
living flesh; disconcerted, she stared at Giles.

'It needs our love,' he told her soberly. 'To help it
grow, to protect and support it.'

'Yes,' she agreed shakily. Her eyes stung with tears
of pain and loss, but now unexpectedly there was something else as well.

Knowledge . . . hope . . . awareness . . . love? She wasn't
sure. But what she did know suddenly was that she wasn't
going to make it easy for Davina to take Giles away from
her, not any more, and with that knowledge came a
sudden surge of energy and purposefulness.

Tiredly Davina stripped off her suit. After the elation
of having gained the upper hand, of having taken control
of the meeting and used to her own advantage the el-
ement of surprise she had deliberately contrived had
come a draining exhaustion.

As she pulled on her top and jeans she wondered how
long it would take Giles to get over his chagrin and shock.
After the meeting he had followed her over to her car,
barely able to control what he was feeling.

'Davina, what the *hell* do you think you're doing?'
he had demanded bitterly.

As she had turned to smile calmly at him she had seen
that his face was flushed with temper and disbelief. He
had looked more like a furious little boy than an adult
man, and irritatingly she had found herself contrasting
his reaction, his demeanour, to that of Saul Jardine.

That *he* had been equally if not more annoyed and
outraged by what had happened she had had no doubt,
but he had concealed it, controlled it, and was no doubt
even now using every one of the formidable weapons of
intelligence and instinct he possessed to find some way

of outmanoeuvring her. When he did, would she be strong enough to match him?

Giles had still been waiting for her to respond to his angry demand.

'I rather thought I was about to drive home, Giles,' she had told him pleasantly.

He had made a dismissive, baffled gesture and had said impatiently, 'No, I didn't mean now...I meant in the bank. That schedule.' He had stopped speaking, struggling to find the right words. 'You just don't *do* things like that. We aren't in a position to make those kinds of demands. Hell, Davina, you ought to be down on your knees thanking God that someone wants to buy you out at all.'

'Who says so? Saul Jardine?' she had asked him. It had been plain from the look he had given her that Giles had thought she had taken leave of her senses. 'What do you think of Jardine, Giles?' she had asked, changing tack, knowing it was unfair to vent her feelings on poor Giles.

'He's obviously a skilled negotiator,' Giles had told her shortly. 'And he's come in to get Carey's as quietly and for as little as he can. It won't do any good trying to antagonise him, Davina. That type doesn't play those kinds of games——'

'Mm. Would you say he held a fairly high position in his organisation?' Davina had seen the way Giles reacted to her cutting across the lecture he had been about to deliver, but she wasn't in the mood to be tactful and indulgent.

'According to Philip, he's Sir Alex's second-in-command,' Giles told her stiffly.

'A rather important position?' she had questioned.

'A *very* important position,' Giles had corrected her.

'Odd, then, surely, that he should come here to negotiate such a comparatively minor acquisition?'

'Odd...what do you mean?'

Wryly she had tried to explain. 'I mean, Giles, that I should like to know exactly why this Sir Alex wants to acquire Carey's, and if the acquisition isn't somehow important to him, then why send someone like Saul Jardine to negotiate it for him?'

'Because that's his job,' Giles had told her huffily.

Davina had laughed then. 'Is it?' she had asked him, but she wasn't laughing now, she acknowledged soberly as she looked out into the garden.

As she had discovered a long, long time ago, pulling out weeds was an extremely therapeutic task and one that was extremely good for getting rid of unwanted tension.

The sky had become overcast and was threatening rain but she didn't let that put her off. Grimly she kneeled down at the end of one long bed and started working.

There was nothing else she could do for Carey's now other than to wait, to wait and hope that, whatever the reason this Sir Alex wanted Carey's, it was important enough to him to accept her terms.

And if it wasn't?

She frowned as she searched beneath the surface of the soil for the tap-root of a spreading piece of buttercup.

If it wasn't, no doubt Giles and Philip Taylor would enjoy underlining to her how foolishly she had behaved.

Saul had glanced briefly through the document Davina had handed him during the meeting, but now he had time to assess and study it thoroughly he was torn between amazement and disbelief that she could actually imagine, with the state the company was in, that any buyer would be prepared to accept such terms.

He noticed absently how well the document was typed, and without the advantage of a self-correcting word processor; the wording was concise and exact, the grammar elegantly correct and the punctuation displaying an unexpected flair for the dramatic. Didn't she realise that no one used that kind of punctuation any more, or had she known but still chosen to do so? He frowned a little.

She worried him, irritated him, challenged him in some extraordinary way. Every time he thought he had her correctly assessed she did something to show him that he was wrong.

Take that ridiculous suit, for instance. It couldn't possibly be that she hadn't known how inappropriate it was. So why had she worn it...defiance...bravado...an odd sense of humour? Certainly not out of ignorance or carelessness—the document she had given him proved that.

She must know surely that neither Alex nor anyone else would accept those kind of terms: guarantee employment for three years for the entire workforce, plus a complete overhaul of their working conditions and practices, the same practices which had led his sister to tell him privately that she thought Carey's was guilty of negligence . . . those same practices instituted by her own husband; crèche facilities; job sharing. Alex would have laughed in her face.

There was one thing he wouldn't laugh at, though, and that was being told that there would be a delay in getting hold of Carey's.

Alex was not and never had been a patient man. What he wanted he wanted and expected to get now, and he wasn't inclined to be indulgent towards those who opposed him in any way.

Of course, she must know that she had no real chance of getting any of her terms accepted. All Alex had to do was simply wait.

It wouldn't be long before the bank, already showing signs of panic, reacted to Carey's problems by forcing Davina James either into bankruptcy or a break-up sale, and when that moment came Alex would be able to get the company for as low a price as he chose to offer. And, knowing Alex as he did, Saul knew that he would not be inclined to be generous. Far from it. He hated being thwarted by anyone, and most especially by a woman. He would enjoy humiliating Davina James, forcing her to acknowledge his supremacy.

Saul wondered why that knowledge irritated him so much, stirring him to anger against himself for not out-manoeuvring Davina James in the first place, and against her for being stupid enough to think she could ever force someone like Alex to even listen to her outrageous terms.

It wasn't up to *him* to make her see sense, he decided. If she didn't have the sense to see what was going to happen...

He frowned, reminding himself that he had to get this deal completed quickly, that Alex was not going to accept her ridiculous demands, and that meant getting Davina James to accept.

When he rang Carey's he was told that Davina wasn't there. He hesitated, drumming his fingers on Christie's kitchen table while he debated what to do.

Surprise was always a good advantage to have, he told himself, as Davina herself had proved this morning. If he rang her at home she might refuse to see him. She might refuse anyway, especially if she was with her lover. Not that there had been anything lover-like between them this morning.

Davina was too far away from the front of the house to hear the sound of Saul's car.

When his knock on the front door didn't bring any response Saul acted on instinct and walked around to the back of the house.

Davina was kneeling with her back to him at the other end of the garden. She neither heard nor saw his approach, so that his cool, 'You've missed a piece of chickweed here,' made her body jerk reflexively in fierce shock.

Anger made her eyes darker, her face and bare arms burned hotly with the force of it, but she had no self-consciousness about her appearance, or the fact that a recent shower had left her hair curling damply against her skin, Saul observed wryly as she stood up challengingly, her stance almost touchingly at odds with her appearance.

For a moment she could almost have been a young girl, the exposed curve of her shoulder oddly vulnerable. But she wasn't a girl, she was a woman, and an extremely irritating one as well.

'I knew Carey's wasn't exactly busy,' he drawled, carefully watching her, 'but——'

'What are you doing here, Mr Jardine?' Davina interrupted him coolly. 'I thought you said it would take some time to obtain your employer's reactions to my proposals and terms of sale.'

'I lied,' Saul told her calmly.

Just for a moment he allowed himself to enjoy the faint flicker of reaction that crossed her face.

'I already know what Alex's reaction will be,' he continued. 'He'll wonder why your advisers haven't had you certified,' he told her pleasantly. 'Look, what is it that you really want?' he asked her. 'You must know as well as I do that no one would accept these terms. I appreciate that this is a new world for you and that you're enjoying playing in it——'

'I am not *playing*, Mr Jardine,' Davina told him fiercely. 'I leave that to you and your kind.'

Her eyes flashed her contempt, and to his own surprise Saul actually felt himself reacting to it. Just in time he controlled his instinctive reaction to that contempt.

'What I want is contained in the terms I've written down for you.'

'Security for your employees. Nothing for yourself.' Now it was his turn to let *his* contempt, *his* disbelief show. 'Come off it. *No one* is that altruistic!'

'I don't consider it as altruism, Mr Jardine,' Davina told him grimly. 'I call it conscience.'

Saul stared at her.

'What's wrong? Haven't you ever heard of it before?' she asked him bitterly. 'First my father and then my husband took advantage of the people who work for Carey's. Maybe while they were alive I couldn't have done anything about it. But I could have tried and I didn't. I accepted my father's and then my husband's ruling that what went on at Carey's had nothing to do with me. Now it has everything to do with me, and if I can't right past wrongs, then at least I can ensure that they aren't continued. I have realised that people are more important than possessions; than wealth, or ambition. People matter, all of them, and if you deny them the right to that importance then you take away from them one of their most basic human rights; you demean and devalue them, and in doing so you demean and devalue yourself as well.'

Saul continued to stare at her. The last thing that he had expected was that she would reveal herself so openly to him. He had anticipated subterfuge; deceit; feigned reluctance to admit what she really wanted behind the smokescreen of implausible and outrageous demands she had thrown up around herself. What he had not anticipated was that she would actually genuinely want those terms; them and nothing else.

Did she *really* honestly believe there was any chance of getting Alex or anyone else to agree to even one of the things she was demanding?

'Alex will never agree to your terms,' he told her bluntly.

Davina flinched as she heard the conviction in his voice. 'Then I shall have to find someone else who will, won't I?' she challenged him defiantly.

'There *isn't* anyone else,' Saul told her. 'Don't you think we already know that?'

'If Carey's is of value to your Sir Alex then it will also be of value to someone else. Or do you think I'm naïve enough to believe that the Davidson Corporation is so mighty and unassailable that it doesn't have any rivals or competitors?'

'You still don't understand, do you?' Saul told her angrily. 'Alex ultimately *will* have Carey's; there's *nothing* you can do to stop that. All you can do is to negotiate with him now and——'

'But I thought that was exactly what I was trying to do,' Davina interrupted him quietly.

Saul felt helpless in the face of her seeming inability to understand her own vulnerability; helpless and angry... resentful almost of her clear-eyed honesty and sincerity. It irked him, irritated him, made him want to tell her exactly what Alex would do to her precious company, and at the same time somehow made him want to protect her from that knowledge. It made him feel almost as much envy as he did irritation; envy and a heavy awareness of how long, if ever, it had been since *he* had been motivated by that kind of selflessness.

It did no good telling himself that the wheels of commerce were oiled by deceit and intrigue and that someone like Davina James would be destroyed in such a world within days, if not hours. Just looking at her increased the weight of the burden he was already carrying to an almost intolerable level.

'It won't work,' he told her harshly.

She tilted her head and looked at him. 'Because you won't let it,' she challenged.

'As you've already pointed out, I don't have that kind of power. But if you don't believe me... ask your lover.'

'Giles is not my lover.'

The swift denial shocked them both. Davina looked away from him, her face flushing.

'Nothing you can say to me will make me change my mind about my terms of sale,' she told him quickly.

'If that's true then you're a fool,' Saul told her.

It was just as well she had no idea what Alex intended to do with Carey's. If she had she would never sell, but then soon she would not have any option...any choice...others would force the decision on her, Saul reminded himself grimly.

'I'll put your terms to Alex, of course, but I can tell you now that he won't agree.'

As he started to turn away he paused.

'By the way,' he told her, 'I see that you've recently cancelled several of your employers' liability policies. That leaves Carey's rather exposed, doesn't it, should any of your employees decide to sue you for, say...unsafe working practices?'

Davina watched him suspiciously. How had he learned about that? The premiums on those policies had become so high that Giles had insisted they would have to cancel them. She had been uneasy about having to do so, but both Giles and Philip had told her she had little option.

It worried her that so many of the women who worked for Carey's seemed to develop contact dermatitis, although Giles had assured her that no link had been found between their work and the skin disease.

Saul was starting to walk away from her now, but then he stopped and turned his head.

'One last thing.' He was smiling slightly now and a *frisson* of nervous tension ran down her spine, lifting the tiny hairs at her nape. 'That suit... A word of advice: the next time you wear it...'

Davina stared at him, refusing to give in to the swift tug of atavistic tension that gripped her.

'...wear it the way that it was designed to be worn— *without* a bra.'

His glance dropped quite deliberately to her breasts and rested there a second, and then he was turning away, leaving her shaking with fury and resentment and bitterly aware that she was too angry to risk giving vent to what she was feeling.

That last comment had been deliberately contentious, deliberately demeaning almost, *and* he had known it.

She heard the slam of his car door and then the engine firing.

'Alex will never agree to your terms,' he had told her, and she had known that he believed it.

Suddenly her body ached with tiredness. She felt alone and very, very afraid. *Was* she doing more harm than good? *Should* she have been less aggressive...more passive? Was she wrong to trust her instinct that something was being withheld from her; that the acquisition of Carey's was in some way far more important to Sir Alex than she was being allowed to see?

She ached for someone to talk to; someone to confide in; someone to lift her burdens from her shoulders? she questioned herself wryly. Was she really so weak, so afraid that she was ready to give up at the first confrontation? What had happened to this morning's elation...this morning's determination?

So Saul Jardine was a very powerful and subtly manipulative man. So what? He *was* only a man. He had to have some vulnerabilities, didn't he?

CHAPTER NINETEEN

LEO'S original plan following the end of the conference had been to drive straight from Edinburgh to Cheshire and once there to discreetly make contact with Davina Carey, or Davina James as she now was, but meeting Christie had thrown him so far off balance that instead of taking the direct motorway route south he opted to travel at a more leisurely pace through the countryside.

He needed time, he recognised, not only to prepare himself for what might lie ahead when he met Davina James, but also, just as importantly, if very much more personally, to adjust to the unexpected, almost unwanted in some ways, shock of Christie's impact on him.

Had he once as a young man daydreamed with idealistic fervour and ignorance of falling instantly and devastatingly in love with someone, of turning his head and seeing her and knowing immediately and incontrovertibly that she was The One? If so, it had obviously not occurred to him that she might not share his ideals, his emotions, and it had certainly not occurred to him that she might be the independent, firm-minded kind of woman who had relegated that kind of emotional immaturity very much to a past part of her life and who now placed his sex in predetermined and sharply divided sections of her life and kept them there: this man a friend, this one a colleague...this one a lover and this one an enemy.

Christie had touched some nerve within him he had thought long and mercifully anaesthetised, or even dead. Meeting her had proved to him that it was very much alive. He had found her physically attractive, almost instantly, overpoweringly so in a way that was discon-

certingly unfamiliar to him, but he had witnessed the
effects of 'conference fever' on his colleagues far too
often for him initially to be anything other than startled
and rather wryly amused that he himself had finally and
unexpectedly succumbed to it.

But then he had found himself thinking almost compulsively about her, wanting to see her; to be with her.
And then he had taken her out to dinner.

Long, long before the meal was over he had known
the truth: that here was the woman he had ached for,
dreamed of and wanted so desperately in the empty
painful years of his young manhood, his lover, partner,
companion, the other half that alone could make him
totally whole.

He had mocked himself even while the thoughts, the
knowledge filled him, and he had known as he'd listened
to her just how hard it was going to be to persuade her
to allow him into her life in the way he wanted to be
there; and not just because of who he was.

No matter what his role in life, she would have tried
to corral him into one role. She might have allowed him
to be her friend, but then would never have permitted
him to be her lover; he could have been her lover, but
then not her friend...

She was afraid, he saw, afraid in the way that those
who had been hurt when they were too young and too
giving, too loving to withstand that hurt, always were.
He had recognised that fear, that hurt within her because in so many ways it had mirrored his own.

He had managed to obtain a tape of her speech, and
all the way down from Edinburgh he had played it compulsively on the car's cassette machine so that now he
knew every nuance, every small inflexion of her voice.
And when she spoke it was almost as though his senses
could conjure up her whole image there in the car with
him.

So this was love—this raw agony of pain and help-
lessness; this knowledge of being totally powerless, totally
out of control, while yet seeming to be the very opposite; this awareness that the whole of his life's course
had been changed, this suppressed anger against himself
and foolishly, childishly against her, because things could
not have been different.

Things, or her? *Would* he have been drawn so powerfully to her had she been different—less passionate, less
fiercely protective of what mattered to her? Would he
really want her tamed and subjected to the same con-
straints that tied him to Hessler Chemie; to all the demands it made upon him, all the ways it frustrated him
and denied him the right to live his own life?

Even now, here in this car, he could not escape from
it. Already there had been phone calls from Hamburg,
urgent messages that he return as quickly as possible because his brother was stirring up so much trouble, pro-
voking so many quarrels and so much unease.

There had even apparently been rumours in the Press
about the internal rivalry within the corporation, hinting
that a power struggle might be about to develop between
the two brothers; hinting that Leo might have used some
secret means to pressurise their father into giving him
control of the corporation instead of his brother, and
Leo suspected that these 'rumours' had originally been
leaked to the Press by Wilhelm.

As he battled against his irritation with his brother he
reminded himself of how important the corporation had
always been to Wilhelm; he had based his whole life
around it and nothing mattered more to him, as Anna,
his wife, was constantly complaining.

Leo knew she had a valid complaint and that the power
and prestige of being the heir apparent to their father
had always dominated Wilhelm's life.

Now that prize had been snatched away from him,
and by his despised and disliked younger sibling. Oh,

yes, Leo could well understand what motivated Wilhelm in this constant guerrilla warfare he was waging against him.

His circuitous route south took him through the Yorkshire Dales. He stopped there for lunch and to get some fresh air. The landscape had an aura of timelessness and steadfastness about it that must have touched many men's souls, Leo reflected as he studied the expanse of sky above the bare, rolling hills.

Here time even more than nature somehow dwarfed mankind. How many countless centuries had gone into the making of these smooth hills, this powerful landscape? It ought to have put his own problems into perspective, but all it did do was sharpen the tensions within him.

It seemed an extra taunting dagger-thrust of fate that Davina James should live so close to Christie, but Leo knew that he would not make any attempt to see her again.

The business that was taking him to Cheshire must not be clouded by any other issues, especially not selfishly personal emotional ones. Besides, he could just imagine how Christie would react to the knowledge that he suspected his father might have founded Hessler Chemie on chemical research bought at the cost of the kind of cruel and sadistic practices used in Hitler's medical experiments. And that only took into account the possibility that his father had somehow merely obtained the information at the end of the war.

The other possibility, that his father might actually have been actively involved at a more personal level, caused Leo the same kind of gut reaction he had experienced as a child when he knew that his father was about to hit him: a churning mixture of panic, fear, pain and self-disgust. And it wasn't any easier to bear now than it had been then.

He got back into the car and started the engine. He had made his own booking for the hotel in Cheshire, telling his assistant simply that he was going to spend a few days with an old friend.

His slow, cautious research into the past—cautious because it had to be if he wasn't to arouse other people's curiosity, and slow because there was no one he could trust to do it other than himself—had done nothing to alleviate his suspicions. Alan Carey was dead and could not answer his questions. He had left behind a daughter. Would he have confided to her the truth about the past, told her how he had come by the knowledge on which his business had been founded? Not if he had been anything like his own father, Leo admitted.

Davina James had recently been widowed. Leo frowned, remembering what his careful enquiries had revealed about her husband and his infidelities, and then his frown deepened.

Before Alan Carey's death there had been a fire at the company's premises which had virtually gutted his office. No one seemed to know how the fire had originally started; the company had not even made a full claim against their insurers for recompense. It had been shortly after this event that Alan Carey had allowed his son-in-law to take virtual control of the financial running of the business. Because he recognised that he himself was beginning to grow older, or because his son-in-law had put pressure on him to do so?

That fire. *Had* it been an accident, an older man's momentary carelessness, or had it been something more? The blackmailer, blackmailed?

Why was it that evil seemed to have this way of re-producing and perpetuating itself?

Leo frowned, suddenly aware that he had reduced speed slightly as though subconsciously he was reluctant to reach his destination.

He had a momentary aching mental image of Christie. No need to ask himself how she would react to what he suspected his father had done.

Christie Jardine. Why the *hell* did he have to have met her?

Less than a hundred miles away Christie was thinking very much the same thing about him. The physical ache tormenting her was something she could control, subdue; the emotional pain she was suffering—that was something different, and, because it was and always had been her greatest fear and dread, her anger and resentment against Leo was all the more intense. After her childhood and then Cathy's birth she had promised herself that she would never be vulnerable through her emotions again; that she would make sure she avoided the kinds of relationships that would lead to her being hurt, and she had stuck to that decision. Until now...

As she fought frantically against her emotions she told herself that what she was experiencing, or what she thought she was experiencing, simply *couldn't* exist; that it was impossible to meet a man and, over the course of one meal with him, a handful of hours spent in his company, somehow allow him to become the entire focus of your life. But it *had* happened, and her fear and panic fuelled the anger that drove her.

Every time her thoughts veered treacherously in his direction she reminded herself of the way he had deceived her, and of the kind of man...of human being this made him.

She also reminded herself of how different their lives were, of how far apart their goals and aims. He could not be the head of a corporation like Hessler's without having absorbed and approved the kind of fallacious moral decisions that gave such organisations their life-blood; his outlook on life completely opposed hers. He represented everything she most detested. They were on opposite sides of a line which for her had been drawn

very clearly and sharply for almost all of her adult life.
She simply could not allow herself to cross that line, not
out of desire, need and wanting; not even out of love!
If she did she knew that ultimately she would choke on
the poison-laden atmosphere she was polluting with her
own betrayal of everything she believed in.

Not that Leo had asked her to cross that line; nor, in
fact, shown any indication of wanting to ask her. But if
all he had wanted from her had been impersonal sex,
then why had he rejected her, walked away from her?

Only she knew how much that had surprised and hurt
her, how she had raged against him and the tormenting
ache of her own need alone in her bedroom.

Tomorrow was her birthday, her thirty-fifth. Saul was
taking her and Cathy out to dinner at the Grosvenor
Hotel in Chester.

Cathy was almost giddy with excitement at the thought
of being treated almost as a grown-up. All *she* wanted
to do was to hide herself away somewhere and to block
out everything and everyone, but most especially of all
Leo von Hessler. The last thing *she* wanted to do was to
go out for a meal that might all too painfully remind
her of another night out, another meal...and a man
who had left her at her bedroom door with her body
aching for him and a pain in her heart which had begun
as innocently as a tiny thorn prick but which was now
poisoning the whole of her life.

She didn't *want* to feel like this about him; and at the
back of her mind lay the knowledge that it wasn't just
because her emotional and physical response to him
contravened the rules she had laid down for herself for
the way she wanted to run her life that made her so
afraid.

No, her fear went deeper than that, was more deep-
rooted, and sprang from that small seed of misery and
self-loathing which had been sown by her father's rejection of her in favour of Saul.

A long time ago, deep within her psyche, the connection had been made between loving a man and not having that love returned, being rejected by him, and it was that fear that fuelled her anger against Leo now; that and the knowledge that he had deceived her, deliberately and calculatedly.

And yet that knowledge, which *should* have made it so much easier for her to cut herself free of all that he had made her feel, somehow only added to the intensity of her emotions.

If he hadn't wanted to have sex with her then why bother deceiving her? It wasn't logical; it wasn't how she knew the male mind worked and it wasn't in line with the character her anger and pain had built for him to superimpose over the ache of her memories of the evening they had spent together. Face it, she derided herself as she listened to Cathy's chatter about her day, it was about as effective as trying to stop a heart attack with a placebo.

Davina was in the kitchen when the phone rang. Despite the fact that it was gone six o'clock, a fierce thrill of sensation ran through her as she had an instant mental image of Saul Jardine.

She had had to endure both the bank manager and Giles lecturing her about the folly of what she had done. Dealing with Giles had been harder than dealing with Philip Taylor, even though Philip had been the more irate and more acerbic of the two.

In Giles's eyes she had seen the beginnings of an awareness that she was not perhaps, after all, worthy of the pedestal on which he had placed her. She had hurt him, she acknowledged as she listened to him, if only by default.

Yesterday after Saul Jardine had gone Giles had rung her, his voice stiff and distant as he explained to her that he was staying at home for a few days.

This week had seen the anniversary of their baby's death, he had informed her, and he had felt that he owed it both to Lucy and the baby they had created together to be with her.

'She's been very upset,' he had told her, and Davina had caught the note of guilt in his voice, of self-justification almost. Giles needed to be leant on, she recognised. It made him feel strong and able, and *she* had leaned on him since Gregory's death.

She had smiled a little wryly to herself, wondering if Saul Jardine had ever felt the need to have someone dependent on him, already knowing the answer. He was simply not that kind of man.

She didn't ask herself *how* she knew so much about him on so short an acquaintanceship, much less why she should be thinking about him in the first place. And now, as the sharp command of the telephone sliced through the silence and her stomach lurched with tension, she was equally wary of asking herself questions she knew she wouldn't want to answer.

She picked up the receiver, forcing herself to smile, hoping that by doing so she might displace some of her tension.

'May I speak with Davina James, please?'

The voice at the other end of the line, while male, was unfamiliar, the English so perfect and accentless that she knew immediately it was not the speaker's first language.

'Speaking,' she announced, waiting uncertainly, trying to ignore the abrupt cessation of the adrenalin surge that had brought her to the phone.

Leo had rehearsed what he would say to Davina many times, and the words, the brief explanation that he believed their fathers had been friends during the war rolled easily enough from his lips, but much less easily from his heart.

Even without seeing her, he could sense Davina's surprise and uncertainty; and knew that it was good manners rather than conviction that led to her offering him the invitation he had blatantly fished for.

If she was startled by the way he responded so immediately and decisively to her hesitant agreement to his request that she agree to see him she managed to hide it.

He was relieved when she confirmed that she was free that evening. The less time he had to spend in Cheshire, the better; not so much because he was afraid that he might run into Christie—that, after all, was hardly likely. No, what he feared was that he might ignore all the arguments he had had with himself, all the logic which warned him that things were better, safer left as they were, even the knowledge that if his own control slipped to the point where he was in danger of using her physical desire for him to get closer to her he could easily endanger her and not just himself, and be drawn, lemming-like, into a storm of emotion that could engulf Christie as well as himself.

The last thing he wanted to do was hurt her, and yet incontravertibly he knew that, for her, to love him would be ultimately to be hurt because she could never adapt her life, her beliefs to accommodate the way he had to live his life.

It was bad enough for him, suffering the suppression of his own deeply held convictions, in the knowledge that he had to do so if he was to remain at the head of Hessler Chemie, and that to abdicate that responsibility in favour of his brother was to accept that the corporation with its great power could quite easily become corrupt, even to the point where people, their health, their lives were far less important than the profits the corporation generated; and even more important to Wilhelm than money was power. It was not his fault. He was addicted to it, had been force-fed that addiction all his growing life by their father. By *his* father, Leo corrected himself mentally.

No, to become a part of his world would ultimately
destroy Christie. And yet wouldn't living without her
destroy *him*?

He smiled grimly to himself as he thanked Davina for
agreeing to see him and replaced the receiver.

Frowning slightly, Davina wandered slowly back into
the kitchen. Leo von Hessler. She had recognised the
name, of course, but it was news to her that her father
had ever even known, never mind been friendly with his.

Davina had known her father well, or, rather, she had
thought she had. He had not been the kind of man who
would have kept quiet about such a prestigious
friendship. Never, as far as she could remember, had
anyone with that name written to or contacted her father,
and her father had never contacted him. Neither had he
ever visited Germany since the end of the war.

Davina's frown deepened as she recognised that she
ought perhaps to have questioned Leo von Hessler's assumption that they had known one another a little more
closely. But there had been something about his calm
certainty, about the quiet way he had stated their
friendship as an established fact, that had lulled her into
accepting that it must be so.

No, with hindsight she sensed something odd, something unknown and somehow slightly disturbing about
the phone call.

And yet why should she feel like that? Leo von Hessler
himself had sounded calm, pleasant and somehow reassuring, so why did she have this odd shiver of tension,
of unease?

She glanced at her watch. He would be here within
an hour. She wondered if she ought to offer him something to eat—and, if so, what?—wryly acknowledging
that this concern could quite easily be a way of dis-
placing the tension she felt and of pushing it to one side
so that she wouldn't *have* to deal with it.

It irritated her a little that the habit of self-evasion, which she had developed as a means of protecting herself, was still something she hadn't entirely escaped from even now when it was no longer necessary.

'Lie to the world if you have to,' Matt had once counselled her, 'but never lie to yourself—about anything.'

And now she was lying to herself, and not just about her unease over Leo von Hessler's imminent visit either.

He arrived on time, as Davina had expected. She watched him drive up from an upstairs window, noting the controlled way he parked the car.

Physically he wasn't what she had expected; more relaxed, less . . . less Teutonic than she had imagined from his voice, and startlingly good-looking, much more so, for instance, than Saul Jardine, whose hard bone-structure, while rendering him powerfully and very intensely male, did not possess the almost film-star good looks of this man.

Davina blinked a little as she watched him walk towards the front door. He moved easily and elegantly, but there was a slight air of tension about him, a hesitation almost before he rang the bell.

Quickly she hurried downstairs, her own tension increasing.

He was sensitive as well as good-looking, she decided ten minutes later, having welcomed him in and observed the way he kept a non-threatening distance from her, touching her only briefly and accidentally when he handed her the flowers he had bought for her. Freshly cut locally grown cottage-type blooms, Davina noticed approvingly, and not the too perfect, almost unreal hot-house ones she detested so much. Perhaps because they reminded her of Gregory and the early days of their marriage.

'Please come in,' Davina invited, leading the way to the sitting-room after she had placed the flowers in water in the kitchen. 'I wasn't sure whether or not you would have eaten.'

'Yes, earlier. Your afternoon tea . . . I had not realised it would be so filling.'

'The Grosvenor prides itself on its food,' Davina told him. She was conscious of the fact that they were both making small talk, both hesitant and wary, both on guard almost.

'You mentioned a friendship between your father and mine,' she encouraged him, taking the plunge and then discovering that she was holding her breath, her heartbeat just a little too fast and shallow.

'Yes.' Leo looked gravely at her. 'You knew nothing of such a friendship, I take it.'

'No,' Davina admitted. 'I knew, of course, that my father was in Germany at the end of the war . . .'

'Yes. He was with the first of the British forces there, I believe.' He mentioned the name of her father's regiment and where they had been stationed, and Davina looked at him uncertainly.

'You seem to know more about his war service than I do,' she admitted. 'My father wasn't . . . that is, he and I . . . He was a rather reserved man,' she told him hesitantly, groping for the right words to tell him just how little she knew about her father's past without betraying her real feelings towards him and their relationship.

'Something else our fathers seemed to have in common. Mine also was . . . reserved,' Leo told her quietly.

Something *else* they had in common? Davina watched him carefully. She could almost feel the tension increasing, and she wasn't sure which of them was generating it, or were both of them doing so, and if so why?

'Something else?' she questioned.

'They both founded drug companies,' Leo told her sombrely.

Davina frowned. 'My father *didn't* actually found Carey's. It was my grandfather, his father, who did that.

He was the one who accidentally discovered the formula for the heart drug.'

'When...when did he "accidentally" discover this formula?'

The sharpness of Leo's question took Davina slightly off guard. 'I'm not sure exactly,' she admitted. 'Some time before the war, I suppose, because my father was at university at the time. He opted out and volunteered...joined the army,' she explained, 'and then when he returned...'

'He did what?' Leo pressed her. 'Did he go back to university, take his degree?'

'No, he didn't,' Davina frowned and told him defensively. 'But neither did many others in the same position. I think there was a general feeling among them that they had experienced too much to go back.'

'But you don't *know* why your father did not complete his degree?' Leo persisted.

Davina shook her head. 'No, it was something we never discussed.' She moved restlessly in her chair. 'My father was...he was a very private man. He never talked much about himself...about his past.'

'But he *did* tell you that the drug formula was originally discovered by his father.'

'No. Not exactly,' Davina admitted. 'It was my mother who told me.' She frowned and then as she caught sight of Leo's expression her stomach lurched. 'What is it? What's wrong?' she demanded anxiously.

Helplessly Leo watched her. She obviously knew as little as he had done himself. Less, and suddenly he desperately wanted to protect her from the truth, but as he watched her he knew that he couldn't. That he had already said too much.

Inwardly he cursed himself for being so obsessed with his own need to find the truth. It was too late now to retract. Davina was waiting anxiously for him to give her an answer, and if he refused to give her one... No, he could not do that.

'I don't suppose you have a copy of the... of your grandfather's original notes anywhere, do you?' he asked her tonelessly.

'No. No, I don't... There was a fire in my father's office some years ago. Everything in it was destroyed.' It had been shortly after that that Gregory had announced that he was taking financial control of the company, she remembered.

She had never been sure just how Gregory had managed to wrest that agreement from her father. Certainly it had led to a great deal of enmity between them; a challenging hostility which Gregory seemed to enjoy and which her father had endured with a bitter resentment.

She had always assumed that it had had something to do with the fact that Carey's had not produced any new drugs, but then under Gregory's control, as she now knew, even less money had been invested in research than during her father's rule.

She got up abruptly and walked over to the window.

'Something's wrong, isn't it?' she challenged Leo as she turned round to face him. 'Our fathers were never friends.'

'Not friends, no... but I very much fear that they might have been accomplices,' Leo told her heavily.

As he watched her he found himself wishing that things might have been different. It would become a personal burden for her, this small, slight woman who watched him with such anxious, wary eyes. If his assumptions, his suspicions were right she would feel as he did; as, it seemed, neither of their fathers had been able to feel.

'It's a long and complicated story, full of gaps and uncertainties,' he told her quietly.

Davina had always been a good listener and she listened now, uneasy at first, and then dazed with disbelief as Leo gently told her what he had discovered, or, rather, as he corrected himself, what he believed he had discovered.

'So what are you telling me,' Davina interrupted him at one point, 'that my father... our fathers used medical research which had been developed by... by... by experimentation on human beings in places like Auschwitz?'

'*Your* father was probably only guilty of *using* it. I wish mine...'

When Davina saw his face, her own shock and sickening sense of horror was pushed to one side by her instinctive compassion.

'It's *not* your fault. Not your guilt,' she told him fiercely. '*You* are not responsible.'

'For my father, no, but for Hessler Chemie, yes... I am. There have always been rumours about my father... rumours which surfaced briefly over the years and were quickly suppressed. He had always claimed that he was out of Germany for most of the war. And that much is true, he was, but there are those who say that he did not leave Germany because, as he claims, he could not fight for Hitler and yet neither could he fight against his countrymen—but because he was a highly paid spy; someone high up enough in the confidence of others to know exactly what was going on in those death camps; someone even who knew this medical research existed... someone who was perhaps discovered by your father removing this particular research from some secret place.'

Davina went white. 'Are you saying... do you mean...?' Her throat was raw with horror, her voice a thin whisper of protest.

'I have no proof to say whether or not your father blackmailed mine into giving him one of those chemical equations. I do not have enough knowledge of your father to make that kind of accusation. All I *can* say is that I believe that the formula on which Carey Chemicals' major—only, in fact—drug is based bears far too close a resemblance to the one I found in my father's possessions for it merely to be coincidence.'

He had seen the way Davina's body had jerked in response to his use of the word 'blackmail' and now he looked at her and apologised sincerely. 'I'm sorry. Believe me ... I didn't come here to distress you. I know what you must feel and, besides, I could be wrong.'

Davina shook her head. 'No,' she told him painfully. 'I don't think you are.' She didn't know *how* she knew that his suspicions were correct, but it was as though listening to him had turned the key in a locked door within her own subconscious so that she was illuminatingly aware of just how capable her father could have been of that kind of act. 'I think you are probably right.' She shivered a little, trying not to think about the source of the money that now lay in Gregory's bank accounts, her bank accounts, the same money which had provided for the clothes on her back and the food in her mouth.

'Try not to think about it,' Leo advised her, correctly reading her thoughts.

'I can't help it. Those people...the ones in...in those camps. They...their families...*they* are the ones who should have benefited from the success of these drugs.' Her gorge rose at the images forming in her brain. 'I can't bear to think about it,' she told Leo rawly. 'How...?'

'I don't know,' Leo told her. 'I'm still trying to come to terms with it myself. Your father was merely guilty of blackmail, of perhaps simply taking the option of not reporting my father in return for the research, while mine... Did he simply come across the medical reports, discover them by accident, or was he looking for them, aware of their existence? Had he...?'

'The heart drug was the only one that Carey's ever produced successfully,' Davina murmured. 'But Hessler's ...'

'Who knows how my father came by the original workings for all the other drugs he claimed came from our laboratories, apart from the original tranquilliser?' Leo interrupted her painfully. 'Maybe they were genuinely produced there. I hope to God they were.'

'I can't bear to think of what they did,' Davina whispered.

'No,' Leo agreed. 'When I first knew, I wanted to destroy Hessler Chemie, to take it and physically scatter every particle of it into the dust, to scream my father's guilt from the roof-tops, so great was the burden of my own pain; but how *can* I do that? How can I put at risk the livelihoods of so many thousands of innocent people, people who have no knowledge of what the corporation they are working for was founded on?

'If I were to reveal the truth to the world to appease my own guilt it wouldn't be my father who would suffer, or so I tell myself.' He looked broodingly at Davina. 'Am I a moral coward as well as the son of a sadist and murderer?'

Davina winced at the tone of his voice but shook her head. 'No,' she told him huskily. 'But I know how you feel. Carey's ... the thought of ever having to go there again makes me feel physically sick ... like this house... like everything bought with my father's money, and yet if I desert Carey's now...' She paused and looked at him. 'I expect you know that we're on the verge of bankruptcy. You seem to know so much else.'

Leo nodded, and suddenly Davina wanted to ask his advice. He was a stranger, and yet in many ways he had come, through what he had told her, closer to her than if they had been born twin souls.

'I have been approached by someone who wants to buy the company. The bank wants me to sell, but I can't do that until I have categoric assurances that everyone's jobs will be safe and that their working conditions will be improved. Saul Jardine——'

'Jardine?' Leo questioned abruptly.

'Yes.' Davina hesitated uncertainly. 'Do you...do you know him?'

'No,' Leo told her.

'He...he works for Sir Alex Davidson,' Davina continued.

Leo frowned. He knew of Alex Davidson, an entrepreneur who was more pirate than anything else, a man with a good nose for a weak or unprotected business, but what could he possibly want with Carey's?

Leo was not surprised by Davina's admission that Carey's was on the verge of bankruptcy. What had surprised him was that someone, anyone should want to buy her out.

'We'll never really know, will we,' Davina asked him tiredly, 'about our fathers, I mean?'

'No,' Leo agreed sombrely.

'We were never close...we never really got on. I always knew he didn't love me, and *I* didn't particularly like him,' Davina admitted. 'But I never actually hated him before. How could he...?'

Leo didn't try to comfort her; he knew there was nothing he could say that would offer comfort.

'Thank God he's dead,' Davina said passionately at last. 'If he weren't...'

'I know,' Leo agreed.

'What will you do now?' Davina asked him.

He shook his head. 'There is nothing I can do; for the sake of the corporation, I cannot expose my father's past. I'm sorry you have been involved. I should not perhaps have burdened you with such knowledge.'

'No,' Davina told him fiercely, and as she said it she knew it was true. 'I'm glad in a way that I *do* know. It makes it easier somehow, knowing that perhaps, after all, I was not at fault for not loving him.'

'I understand,' Leo said grimly, and, looking at him, Davina had the feeling that he did.

'It can never be wholly confirmed, you know,' he told her gently. 'At best it is only surmise. I have been discreet,' he added. 'My enquiries will not put you at any kind of risk, although I am not sure now if my motives in seeking you out were quite as I had believed. I had told myself it was simply that I had to have confirmation of my suspicions of my father's guilt, but now I wonder if I wasn't also looking for someone to share with me the horror that goes with them.'

Davina touched his arm lightly. There was a bond between them now that could never be severed; it would be deeper and more binding than any bond of love or blood . . . as deep perhaps as the bond of guilt and deceit that had linked their fathers?

'I could still be wrong,' Leo persisted. 'There is no real proof.'

Davina shook her head. 'My father *was* the proof,' she told him quietly. 'And you are not wrong. What will you do now?' she asked him.

'Go back to Hamburg and pray that our fathers' crimes remain buried with them,' he told her grimly. 'And you?'

She shook her head. 'I don't know. First I must find a buyer . . . the right buyer for Carey's.' Only when she had done that would she be free to walk away from the burden of her father's guilt . . . his blood money.

She shuddered a little, knowing that she would never be entirely free of its taint, but she could not go back and alter the past.

The future was a different matter.

After his death Matt's solicitors had approached her, discreetly and very carefully, to advise her that he had left her a small legacy. In the letter they had given her he had written,

If you have not already found it, then let this be your passport to your own freedom. It is a gift of love,

Davina... the love I should have shared with you, but was afraid to admit.

She had never touched the money, investing it instead. It wasn't a large sum, but it was enough—more than enough for her to live on while she trained for some kind of occupation...enough to enable her to rent a small house or flat for long enough for her to start to make her own way financially.

It seemed almost prophetic that Matt, who had already given her so much, should also have given her this.

'I'm so sorry,' Leo began, but Davina shook her head. 'No...I'm glad you told me and...and...I'll go through my father's papers just to check. You're staying at the Grosvenor... How long for?'

'I'm leaving tomorrow, but I'll give you my number in Hamburg, and not just in case you do find something. I want us to keep in touch, Davina.'

'Yes,' she agreed shakily. 'So do I.'

He stood up and held out his hand to her to shake hers and then abruptly changed his mind, taking hold of her and hugging her. It was not a sexual embrace in any way, but it was one that was full of warmth and compassion.

'Don't feel you must share their guilt,' he told her.

'Don't you?' she asked him quietly.

As he released her Davina gave him a wan smile. 'If I discover anything I'll let you know,' she promised him as they said their goodbyes.

Half of her already suspected that she wouldn't. Surely her father would not have made that kind of mistake? But then, in keeping the equations in their original form, Leo's father had. Greed was a strange and powerful force and a very destructive one.

CHAPTER TWENTY

THE evening was not turning out to be a success. Of the three of them, only Cathy seemed to be enjoying herself, Christie acknowledged, thankful when the meal had finally come to an end and they were free to leave. Saul had been abstracted all evening and she herself had not been in the mood to enjoy herself.

She was walking ahead of Saul as they left the restaurant and moved into the reception area, but Saul was right behind her so that when she froze at the sight of the man standing with his back to her as he spoke to the receptionist, and whispered rawly, 'Leo,' Saul heard her as he almost walked into her.

'What is it?' he began urgently, but Christie wasn't listening. She could hear Leo speaking to the receptionist, asking her to make sure that if there was a telephone call for him from a Mrs Davina James he was paged.

Now it was Saul's turn to tense and watch as Leo turned away from the reception desk.

He saw Christie the moment he turned round.

'For God's sake, let's get out of here,' Christie implored Saul rawly as Leo automatically started to walk towards them, turning quickly on her heel and almost running over to the exit.

'Mum, what is it? What's wrong?' Cathy was anxiously asking as she and Saul caught up with her outside.

'It's nothing,'' Christie lied abruptly, and then, seeing Cathy's face, tried to soften her own tension a little by adding, 'I was just feeling slightly queasy, but I'm all right now that I'm outside.'

Leo, here in Chester, but obviously not because of her. What did he want with Davina James? She frowned, remembering Saul's own interest in Carey's.

Saul, after one look at her face, made no attempt to engage her in conversation on the drive home, and Cathy, obviously still sensing her tension, went to bed quietly, the expression in her eyes quickening Christie's heart with guilt and pain.

No matter what her own emotions were and no matter how much the unexpected sight of Leo had shocked her, she had no right to put her own feelings before those of her child.

As she pushed Cathy's soft hair off her face and bent to kiss her her eyes burned sharply with tears.

'I love you, Mum,' Cathy whispered as she hugged her. Wordlessly Christie hugged her in return. Although she was far too young truly to understand or recognise what she was experiencing, her daughter was now past the age when she could be deceived by a small white lie, Christie recognised as she heard in Cathy's words the knowledge that she knew quite well that it was more than a fictitious bout of nausea which had prompted Christie's hurried exit from the hotel.

When she went back downstairs and found Saul waiting for her in the kitchen she wasn't sure whether she wanted him there or not.

'Want to talk about it?' he offered.

'There isn't much point,' she told him tiredly. 'There isn't really anything to talk about.'

The look he gave her made her muscles tense defensively.

'All right . . . all right . . . I met him in Edinburgh; we shared a taxi to the hotel. We went out together for dinner.'

'And?' Saul prompted. He had never seen Christie like this before. Normally her passion was wholly re-served for her daughter, her beliefs and her work. He had seen how after Cathy's birth she had distanced herself emotionally from his sex, separating emotion from desire, and then as she matured controlling even that aspect of her personality, so that he suspected the discreet physical liaisons she had once shared with like-minded men were now no longer an indulgence she permitted herself.

Once when he had queried this she had told him shortly that she had Cathy to consider, and she wasn't going to be the kind of mother who paraded a string of male 'friends' in front of her impressionable child. 'Besides,' she had added wryly, 'I'm a doctor. How can I take on the responsibility for warning my patients about the dangers of unprotected sex with a variety of partners if I can't observe those safeguards myself?'

Now, as he watched and waited, he wondered if perhaps Leo von Hessler had been an exception to that personal rule. The man was certainly physically attractive enough, even he could recognise that, and she was perhaps now suffering the after-effects of that self-indulgence.

'And nothing,' Christie told him fiercely. He could see, from the way she was tensing her body, the anger and emotions she was trying to control. 'Nothing happened,' she continued. 'Nothing. All evening I'd thought...'

She was pacing the kitchen now, almost unaware of his presence as the words burst from her, small staccato volleys of anger and pain as her control finally snapped.

'I wanted him, Saul, and I thought he wanted me.' She swung round abruptly, the expression on her face making Saul wince, taking him back to their shared childhood. The despair and confusion he could see in her eyes now were just adult versions of the emotions he had seen there so often in the past. His throat ached with compassion and the same old helpless feeling of wanting to comfort her but somehow being unable to either do or say anything to show her how much he cared.

'I made it as clear to him as day that I...' She swallowed and then asked him rawly, 'Is it like this for a man when a woman rejects him, or...?'

'Sometimes,' Saul told her. 'It depends on the woman and how much he wants her, how much of himself he's revealed to her.'

'He let me tell him so much about myself,' Christie continued bitterly. 'I was actually beginning to think...' She stopped, her skin suddenly flushing, and Saul ached inside for her obvious vulnerability.

She had offered von Hessler her body and been rejected, but both of them knew that there was more to it than that... much more. How much more she had revealed in those few betraying words and the look in her eyes.

'I'm too old to be feeling like this,' she said helplessly. 'God knows, I don't want to.'

'To what?' Saul probed gently. 'To love him?'

'*Love* him?' Christie gave him a bitter, tight smile. 'How can I possibly love him? He represents everything I most detest, Saul; he even lied to me about who he actually was. I *can't* love him. I don't even think I believe that such an emotion exists... not between adults... and especially not when sex is involved. Oh, we call it love, but in reality...'

Saul watched her gravely. He had heard her propound this theory before, but this time the passion and the belief were missing from her angry words.

'Chris, come back down to earth,' he told her gently. He went up to her and took hold of her, surprising them both. They had never been particularly physically affectionate with one another, although they were close in their way. It was almost, Christie recognised, as though in the past something had kept them physically apart. Something, or someone? she wondered, remembering how much their father had always disliked anyone going too physically close to him, sending out signals that both of them had picked up on and reacted to in their different ways.

Now as Saul held her, awkwardly at first and then more easily, she experienced an intense surge of emotion, of being close to him, of the bond of blood and flesh that linked them. It carried her past the barriers of her own self-protection and defensiveness.

'Oh, Saul, I'm so afraid,' she told him. 'I don't *want* to feel like this. The whole thing's so... so ridiculous and impossible. I don't even know him. He's all the things I most detest.'

'He's still a man, Christie,' Saul told her quietly. 'And he must feel something for you to have come here... looking for you.'

Immediately Christie stiffened, pulling herself away from him. 'He hasn't come here for *me*, Saul. He's come here to see Davina James. I heard him telling the receptionist that he was expecting a call from her.' Her mouth twisted in a bitter smile. 'Perhaps, like Alex, he wants to buy her out of Carey's.'

Now it was Saul's turn to tense, his brain suddenly as clinically cold as a programmed computer as he slotted the facts into place.

Someone as important as Leo von Hessler didn't suddenly appear out of the blue to impulsively make an offer for a company like Carey's. Just to make a slot wide enough in his diary to fit in a trip to Cheshire would take weeks of careful planning. Nor would he just arrive without having first ascertained that the person he wanted to see was at least receptive to his offer. Which meant...

Which meant that all along Davina James had known... *must* have known of his interest. Had known and had deliberately kept that knowledge to herself... had deliberately lied to him... amused herself with him ... played with him by producing that ridiculous set of conditions for sale, knowing all the time that she had another potential buyer, and a far richer and more powerful buyer than Alex, in the background.

No need to ask himself what was in her mind. He already knew: she was going to play them off against each other, skilfully manipulating them both until she got the deal she wanted...a deal that would have nothing whatsoever to do with obtaining security for Carey's employees.

How could he have been stupid enough to be taken in by her? She was the novice, he the expert, and yet he had *actually* believed that she was concerned for her employees, so much so, in fact... He took a deep breath as he felt the anger grip him, sharp and savage.

He had believed her, and not just believed her but actually envied her her honesty, her compassion, the moral high ground which she had seemed to occupy so effortlessly and so genuinely. She had made him bitterly and painfully aware of what he saw as his own failure to match those achievements, his own sacrificing of his beliefs, his own betrayal of self, and not even for his own gain but for that of others.

He had believed her and been dazzled, blinded by that belief, and now, confronted with the truth, he succumbed to the savage whiplash reaction of that self-betrayal.

'Saul, what is it?' Christie demanded as she saw his expression change.

'I'm going to see Davina James,' he told her grimly.

She stared at him in disbelief. 'What? You *can't*... It's almost ten o'clock at night. Saul, for heaven's sake...whatever it is, it can surely wait until tomorrow. You——'

'*This* can't wait,' he told her.

All the way to Davina's he could feel the anger inside him mounting, pulsing against the thin veil of his self-control. He was vaguely aware that he was over-reacting, but his fury pushed him on, overwhelming caution and restraint.

As he misjudged a sharp bend and the car lurched, protesting under the additional pressure on the brakes, he realised he was driving too fast and too carelessly. His knuckles whitened with the strain of imposing some physical control on what he was doing. He had what he knew to be a dangerous, almost insane impulse simply to press his foot down on the accelerator and to give way to the need to let the tension inside him burst past its barriers.

There were lights on downstairs when he reached the house and he experienced a momentary stab of disappointment. He would have liked to wake her from sleep, to have the advantage of surprise, he acknowledged bitterly.

What was she doing? Smugly waiting for him to come back to her to tell her that Alex wasn't going to accept any one of her terms?

Would she laugh at him, armed by her own duplicity, when he told her about von Hessler's offer, or would she continue to play the role she had so expertly cast for herself?

Would those extraordinary eyes of hers reflect a false concern and warmth when she told him that someone else was also interested in acquiring the company, the same false compassion and warmth they had reflected when she had told him why she had set such unexpected and unrealistic conditions?

She had taken him in so easily, so cleverly, so completely.

He got out of the car and walked quickly towards the door.

Davina was in the room where she had stored all her father's papers when she heard the irate banging on her front door.

After Leo had gone she had come up here to this small, empty box-room and had meticulously gone through everything, but, as she had expected, she had found nothing.

Except several blank pages in the photograph album she remembered her mother carefully compiling; an album which had contained photographs taken from before and during the war, and nowhere could she find any mention of her father's service in Germany, even though she *knew* he had been there.

Only her father could have destroyed those photographs, those records, and the weight of knowing just why he might have done so bowed her shoulders, and slowed down her movements so that initially she was slow to react to Saul's insistent pounding on her front door.

The sensitive nerves that would normally have alerted her and warned her were blocked by the knowledge she had gained. How could any possible threat or alarm which lay outside her doors match that which lay within them, within her heart, her soul, her blood? She shuddered as she stood up slowly. Even that was tainted, diseased, by what her father had been.

How could he have borne to use that research, knowing how it had been gained?

She could not allow herself the false comfort of pretending that he might not have known. Her father had been many things, but he had never been a fool. She wondered bitterly just how much of von Hessler's past he *had* actually known. A man would have to be very desperate indeed to part with something as potentially valuable as that research. She doubted, for instance that her father had merely caught Heinrich von Hessler out in some small petty crime.

According to Leo, *his* father had covered his tracks well. There was no proof that he had ever been anything other than what he had claimed to be, merely rumour, and, from what Leo had told her about his father, he had obviously been the kind of man well used to bluffing his way out of a treacherous situation.

So she suspected her father, in order to blackmail him successfully, must have known what he actually was...might have learnt von Hessler's name from the dying camp prisoner pictured in the newspaper article Leo had mentioned.

Which had come first: von Hessler's offer of the research in return for her father's silence, or her father's decision to blackmail him?

As she went downstairs her gorge rose. One thing was obvious to her, and that was that once her father had accepted that information he was as bound to silence and secrecy as von Hessler himself.

Had he ever once thought, when he was reaping the financial benefits of marketing that drug, just how it had been discovered, just what pain and suffering had been inflicted on those poor souls who had been used for 'medical experimentation'?

Her stomach rolled at the thought; at the knowledge that she too, even if innocently, had benefited from that torture. Even to think about it made her experience a desire to rip her clothes from her back, to tear at the skin that covered her own bones, a wild, primitive need to destroy everything that her father had tainted.

No wonder Carey's labs had always been so ill equipped, their technicians so apparently carelessly recruited. That hadn't been carelessness at all. Her father must have deliberately chosen not to employ anyone who might accidentally stumble on the truth, or to question too deeply the provenance of the original research.

Leo's father had taken the opposite road, of course, using the research to build a vast pharmaceutical empire. But then, as Leo had grimly pointed out to her, he had no way of knowing if the details of that particular drug had actually been the *only* research his father had had access to.

Davina shuddered as she went downstairs.

Leo had been right to say that they were now linked by one of life's most powerful bonds. He should not have told her, should not have burdened her, he had said unhappily, but she had shaken her head. In a strange way she was glad that she did actually know. It freed her from the last of her bonds of guilt and pain that in not loving her father she had been at fault, and it made it far easier for her to follow the dictates of her own heart and to walk away without looking back. It had also solved the problem that had been taxing her ever since she had discovered just how much money she personally had been left; money which originally had come from the company, even if it was his unorthodox use of it which had caused it to multiply so greatly.

She herself wanted nothing to do with it, could not bear the thought of its contaminating her life any longer. But she was having to fight hard to assure herself that the money as such was inanimate and free of the burden carried by those who had generated it and that in donating it to various charities she would not be condemning the recipients to share in her own burden of dread and guilt.

And as for Carey's... One half of her wanted the entire business destroyed, its very buildings razed to the ground and the earth itself decontaminated; the other knew that she could not sacrifice the livelihoods of those who worked there simply to appease her own conscience. All she could hope for was that Alex Davidson wanted Carey's enough to meet her terms; and that, she knew, was a very forlorn hope indeed.

The lights were already on in the hall. She opened the door automatically without having formed any thoughts as to who might be outside, staring in confusion at Saul

Jardine as he thrust his way into the hall and slammed the door behind him.

That he was angry she recognised immediately, but she had no awareness that she was the cause of his anger until he said savagely, 'You lied to me, didn't you? Didn't you? All that rubbish about wanting to protect your employees . . . all those high-minded principles; those fake claims about not wanting anything for yourself—they were just so many lies; just a clever technique for pushing up your price. You don't give a *damn* about the people you've got working for you, you never have. You were just using them, and me, to get what you wanted. You knew all along that Alex would never agree, didn't you . . . *didn't* you?'

Davina stepped back from him in alarm. Her heart had started to beat frantically fast; she could hardly equate this furious, passionately intense man with the same cool, controlled opponent of Philip Taylor's office, nor the man to whom she had hesitantly and stupidly confided her passionate belief that it was her duty to protect those who worked for Carey's, to put their needs above her own, and yet strangely she was not actually physically afraid of him. She had gone through too much for that, she suspected, her body and her brain's ability to respond to any more pain blessedly numbed.

'Well, don't think you're going to get any more out of von Hessler than you would out of Alex; they both want Carey's for the same reason; and you know *exactly* what that is, don't you? You've got to know.'

He seemed almost to be speaking more to himself than to her, Davina recognised as her heartbeat steadied slightly.

Saul had no idea how von Hessler had found out about the proposed government grant. No doubt in much the same way as Alex, and she had to know or have guessed something as well, to be playing them off so skilfully against one another.

Once he might have admired such astuteness, but that had been before... before he had confronted the truth about himself and what he really wanted from life.

Somewhere at the root of the anger that possessed him lay vulnerability and the pain from which it had grown; the knowledge not just that he had been deceived by her, but that the virtues he had thought he had seen within her, virtues which he had admired and envied as well as resented, could simply not exist; but he didn't want to acknowledge that vulnerability's existence, preferring to give vent to his anger instead, to take refuge in it almost.

'Von Hessler, Alex—you don't care *which* of them rips Carey's apart and throws it to the dogs, do you, just so long as the fat from the deal ends up with you?

'You must have known all along about this meeting with von Hessler. He must want Carey's very badly to negotiate the deal himself, or is it simply that he wants the whole thing kept safely secret until after the new legislation comes in?

'What were you going to do? Wait until I came back with Alex's rejection of your terms before putting the pressure on?'

He took an aggressive step towards her.

'Well, for your information, I have a little pressure to apply of my own. As far as this legislation is concerned, it's essential that Carey's changes ownership as a going concern.'

He wasn't sure if that was the truth, but he was willing to take a gamble that she didn't know either. He could see from the look on her face that he had shocked her. That knowledge gave him a savage sense of satisfaction, helping to dispel some of the rawness of what he was actually feeling.

'You know as well as I do how close Carey's is not just to bankruptcy but to actually being closed down. Your accident and health record, for instance. All those cases of contact dermatitis.'

He saw the way she blenched and told himself she had deserved that threat, reminding himself that she was an expert manipulator and well practised in the art of deceit.

'Alex intends to have Carey's, and it's my job to make sure that he does. And as for this...this rubbish you palmed off on me...' He waved a roll of paper in front of her and Davina realised numbly that it must be the terms she had prepared so carefully and protectively. Her stomach lurched sickly as she tried to gather her thoughts together.

She watched in silence as Saul tore the papers in half and then in half again and let them fall to the floor.

'Just as well I discovered the truth in time, isn't it...before I made a most complete fool of myself with Alex? How you must have been laughing at me. Now we can really get down to business.' He gave her a thin, biting smile. 'Alex wants Carey's and I intend to see that he gets it, no matter what I have to do to achieve that...and if you don't believe me...'

Davina found her voice at last.

'Oh, I believe you,' she told him shakily. She was angry herself now; angry not just with him but with herself; with her life, with her vulnerability and her guilt, and most of all with her father and the legacy he had left her. 'But you're wrong, you know. Leo von Hessler *didn't* come here to make me an offer for Carey's.' Her voice was shaking, she recognised, and so was her body. She took a deep breath, locking her muscles and willing herself not to lose her self control.

'Don't lie to me, dammit.' He was over-reacting, Saul knew, but he couldn't stop himself, couldn't stop the venom, the anger pouring out of him, couldn't suppress the intensity of his disillusionment and bitterness.

'I am *not* lying,' Davina told him stubbornly. 'If you must know...not that it's any business of yours, Leo and I...'

She stopped, turning her head away, avoiding looking at him, and, as he watched her, for one half-second of time Saul thought she was actually going to try to tell him that she and the German were lovers, but then she looked back at him, her eyes defiant, filled with a mixture of pain and shock, which he knew could not possibly be genuine, but which looked so real that it increased his rage to almost demoniac proportions.

'Our fathers knew one another. We...they...they met during the war.'

He watched as she shuddered, derision twisting his mouth; even she couldn't get that patent falsehood out without physically reacting to it.

'Like hell they did,' he told her flatly.

His contempt hit Davina like a blow. Impulsively she tried to push past him, intending to open the front door and demand that he leave, but, to her shock and his, he caught hold of her, forcing her back against the wall.

Such was the speed of his action that Davina closed her eyes instinctively, tensing as she waited, almost expecting to feel his hands imprisoning her head and forcing it back against the plaster. She was shaking inside with fury; too angry herself to be conscious of any fear; too shocked by the unexpectedness and speed of what was happening to react with caution as she lashed out at him with a small bunched fist in a blow that made no impact at all against the solid muscularity of his imprisoning arm, but which helped relieve a little of her own impotent rage.

To Saul, though, the effect of her touch was immediate and shockingly unexpected, dragging him through the fierce heat of his own rage into a stunningly abrupt awareness of her as a woman; a woman whose flesh felt absurdly silken against his hands, whose bones were almost childishly fragile and fine, whose eyes had dilated with an intense mixture of shock and fury, whose breasts rose and fell with the angry tension of her breathing, whose body-scent was released by the heat that anger had generated, and it was that awareness which provided the dangerous spark for the already volatile cocktail of tinder-dry emotions and sensations churning through him.

The result was inevitable, a surge of physically driven hunger he had forgotten it was possible to experience and which took him so off guard that Davina was aware of its existence before he recognised it himself.

She sensed the change in him instinctively. Between one heartbeat and the next she felt rather than logically knew what was happening and reacted to it, so that her reaction simply added to what was already there.

Her body stiffened as his shifted balance, as he leaned forward, his heat engulfing her, overpowering her, dizzying her senses and her resistance. It was a mixture of anger and excitement that made her tremble so weakly, and not fear; and it was that same anger, coupled with a furious resistance to what he was doing, that held her immobile as he lowered his head towards her, and the grip of his fingers against her flesh changed so subtly that its meaning was perceived only by their senses and not by their brains.

'You lied to me,' he told her, and he could feel the pain bursting in him like raw salt in a wound.

'No,' Davina told him equally furiously, but she made the denial against his mouth, and her response to its silencing punishing pressure was as violent as his.

Later she would wonder a little at her own ability to match his sensual aggression. It was not an expression of physical desire she had learned from Matt, and yet somehow it *had* answered a need within herself, a dark vein of rage and reaction which had led her to claw furiously at his flesh, enjoying the sensation of his wincing, even somehow enjoying the fierce assault of his mouth and the opportunity it gave her to be equally aggressive back, using her teeth to savage his bottom lip, her fingers locking in his hair in a parody of a lover's embrace as she tugged furiously at it.

It was the sensation of her breasts pressed flat against his chest, the realisation of how he might be hurting their softness, that and the knowledge that he was so intensely aroused that he could quite easily have made love to her there and then, without any thought in his mind other than that he *had* to subdue her, to teach her... to punish her for the way she had deceived him, that finally brought Saul to his senses with a sickening jolt of self-loathing which had him releasing her and stepping back from her with one disgusted movement.

Her mouth looked sore and swollen. He could taste the blood on his own and thought at first that it was hers.

She was breathing quickly and shallowly—*both* of them were, he recognised. His own body was wet with sweat, his arms and legs weak with stress and shock. For a second his vision blurred slightly and he had to look away from the bright defiance in her eyes.

There was an ache in his throat and an even more painful one in his heart. No matter *how* much she had deceived him—his mind would not allow him to use the word 'hurt'—there was no excuse for what he had done.

He felt like someone who had been in the grip of an intense bout of fever, shaken, weak, vulnerable and somehow afraid.

He turned towards the door while Davina watched him. Silently he opened it and walked slowly towards his car. He moved like someone in the first stages of recovering from some form of paralysis or a debilitating illness, Davina recognised. Her own body was shaking violently but her mind felt oddly clear, cleansed almost.

She had needed that anger, that release... that safety valve, she acknowledged. As he got into the car and she closed the door and then locked it she tried not to admit that she had needed something else as well. That she had needed that physical contact with him. That a part of her still did ... she shivered tensely.

Violent aggressive sex had never held any appeal for her, quite the reverse, and yet just for a second a part of her had almost been willing him to take hold of her and to expose her body to the angry possession of his hands and mouth; a need so elemental and strong that she would have actually welcomed the fierce thrust of his body within hers.

And he had wanted *her*. She had almost seen the images burning in his mind, had actually known the exact second when he had nearly reached for her and lifted her against his own body.

She shivered again.

Once Matt had made love to her like that. Not with anger or violence, but teasing her a little, knowing how much she wanted him and rejoicing in it, teaching her not to be ashamed of the strength of her own desire, showing her that the urgency of immediate penetration was not merely a masculine prerogative and that there was a distinctly pleasurable and, for her then, faintly shocking eroticism that her sexuality should hold that kind of power. Later Matt had made love to her again slowly and tenderly, satisfying her senses as well as her body.

What kind of lover would Saul Jardine be after that anger had left him? Dark images suddenly flooded her mind: his head against her breast as he stroked her skin and then kissed the swollen erect points of her nipples. His head against her belly, his face and breath hot, his mouth open as his tongue circled her navel and his hand sought her sex.

Frantically she pushed the images aside, her face overheating with anger and confusion. He was her enemy, not her lover, and it was the dangerous implosion of her own emotions that was responsible for

what she was now feeling, and not the man who had
touched her.

Two miles down the road Saul brought his car to an
abrupt halt and stumbled out. The night air felt cold
against his skin. He was trembling violently, he recognised, and in no fit state to drive, a danger to others as
well as to himself. His stomach was churning nauseously
with self-loathing and shock. No matter *what* Davina
James had done, it was no excuse for his behaving the
way he had. He had *never* been a violent man, and not
even a sexually aggressive one; the urge to physically
dominate a woman had always been something that was
alien and distasteful to him, and yet just now...for a
second of time...

He swayed slightly and leaned against the body of the
car. When he touched his forehead it was drenched in
sweat, his heart was pounding as though he had been
running hard, his pulse jumping unevenly, his muscles
leaden and exhausted, but beneath all that he could still
feel the echo of that hot, savage surge of physical desire.

It *wasn't* just that she had fooled him...deceived
him...not even that her duplicity had destroyed something within him, some small frail thread of hope that
there were, after all, people to whom other things mattered far more than personal material gain and ad-
vancement. There was also the knowledge that now it
was going to be that much harder, take that much longer
to complete this self-imposed final duty to Alex.

His job, Alex's threats: these were things he could walk
away from; he was a single man and could if need be
live simply enough—his flat, his investments would realise enough to see both Josey and Tom through their
education—so even if Alex managed to get every door,
every job barred to him he would still survive. In that
sense there was nothing to stop him from simply walking
away now, from telling Alex that he had had enough.
So why couldn't he do so? Was he, after all, still walking

in his father's shadow, still feeling that he must match some alien yardstick, fulfil some unwanted and unsatisfying code that wasn't even his?

With or without him, Alex would fight now to get Carey's. He hated any kind of opposition and knowing that Hessler Chemie was also after Carey's would only increase Alex's determination to buy them out. But once he had done so he would exact his revenge for having been made to fight. Alex was not a man who had ever been generous in victory. So why not simply walk away and leave Davina James to the fate she deserved, the fate she had invited? Was it because her deceit had been so convincing that, against his will and regardless of the fact that it was not his concern, he was aware of the truth of what she had said to him: that Carey's wasn't just a company, it was *people*, people who needed jobs, the income, the purpose that working for the company gave them?

Why should he care? All over the country there were hundreds, thousands of companies like Carey's disappearing every year, thousands of people in the same situation Davina James had claimed so passionately she was going to resist. Why should he care now...*suffer* now, when he never had done so before?

His whole body, his emotions, his very soul felt as though they had been left raw and bleeding and vulnerable to the pain of that unfamiliar exposure.

He could feel the emotions building up inside him: anger, panic, fear; the sense of being alone and lost in a world that was unfamiliar and without any signposts for him to follow. The guiding light that had been his father's ambitions for him had gone and there was, he recognised bleakly, nothing he had to put in its place.

He got back in his car and switched on the engine. He had no stomach left for the battle which lay ahead, a battle he knew Alex would expect that he win on his behalf.

As he drove towards Christie's he acknowledged the irony of the fact that it had taken one small female human being to give him the two polar extremes between which his life was now stretched.

First there had been his anger, his resentment, his awareness that in putting the needs of others so clearly above her own she was underlining for him the discontent and alienation he was experiencing with his own life, and the way he had used it; and then, while he was still trying to come to terms with that and with his own awe and envy of her values, she had shown him that all he had begun to believe in and hope for was not only a sham but a deliberately contrived deceit, and as for that lie that her father and von Hessler's had been *friends* . . . she had looked as shocked by it as he had felt, so much so that he had thought for a second that she might actually rescind her claim, but she had not even had the honesty to do that.

She should not have said anything to Saul Jardine about her father and Leo's knowing one another, Davina acknowledged. That had been a stupid, dangerous thing to do, but his allegation that she was deliberately playing Leo off against him had shocked her so much that she had instinctively tried to defend herself.

It was just as well that he had not believed her. She gnawed on her bottom lip. Ought she to warn Leo? It was too late to ring him now, but she could telephone him first thing in the morning.

CHAPTER TWENTY-ONE

LEO frowned as he listened to Davina's anxious voice, relating what had happened the previous evening.

His frown deepened when she told him how, in a moment of unguarded anger, she had defended herself from Saul's accusations by telling him that their fathers had been friends and that Leo's visit had been a personal one.

'He didn't believe me,' she added. 'I'm sorry, Leo, I shouldn't have said anything.'

'It doesn't matter,' he assured her.

'I haven't been able to find anything in Dad's papers either, but I'm sure you're right and that they did know one another; that for some reason my father was able to blackmail yours into giving him that information.' She shivered a little. 'I'm glad he's dead,' she told Leo. 'I don't think now that I could bring myself to live with him; speak to him even. I'm glad now that he never loved me and that I never loved him.'

'Yes, I know how you feel,' Leo agreed sombrely, and Davina knew that he did.

Christie lifted her head tiredly from her paperwork when the phone rang. She hadn't slept well and it showed: there were dark circles beneath her eyes, the skin was drawn tight against her cheekbones and jaw, and when she had looked in the mirror the face looking back at her had been unfamiliarly strained and tense.

Cathy had already gone to school—another mother had picked her up earlier—and Christie wasn't due in her surgery until after lunch.

This was no way to spend her precious time off, she warned herself as she got up to answer the phone.

She had no hope that it might be Leo. Why should he want to get in touch with her, after all? To explain why he had lied to her? He had had his chance to do that in Edinburgh, and besides, what difference would knowing the reasons make? They would not alter the facts.

And the facts were that Leo von Hessler inhabited a different world from hers, a world she could never inhabit without being sickened and stifled by its—to her—contaminated values, even if he should ask her to share it with him.

And just as she knew she could not give up the way she wanted to live, the things she believed in, she knew that neither could he. No matter how in tune, how close she had felt they were during those few hours they had shared together, she must not forget that for him that closeness had simply been a fiction.

He lived by other values than hers, other needs, and if seeing him so unexpectedly at the Grosvenor had stirred up aches and desires, emotionally based as well as physical, well, then, it was up to her to remind herself of reality.

Even if he *had* loved her, wanted her, they could not be together. It wasn't so much his actual wealth that separated them as the way it had been earned, the fact that he was obviously content and, for all she knew, proud to be at the head of his vast empire.

She picked up the receiver and said the number, and then after listening to the voice at the other end she handed the receiver over to Saul.

'It's for you,' she told him.

She had been reading a book last night when Saul returned from seeing Davina James, or, rather, she had been pretending to do so. In reality she had been too anxious about the anger Saul had displayed before he had left to concentrate on anything other than worrying about what he might be doing. She had *never* seen her brother react like that before, no matter what the provocation.

He had seemed calmer when he returned, but it hadn't been a peaceful calm, rather a drained, empty one. She hadn't tried to question him, sensing that he needed some time to distance himself from what had happened.

She had already guessed that acquiring Carey's must be important to Alex for him to have sent Saul to negotiate the deal. As far as she could see, there was no reason why either Alex or Leo should be so anxious to acquire such a run-down company, and she frowned a little as she walked out of the kitchen, leaving Saul to speak in privacy.

She had become settled in this small rural part of the world, and initially when Saul had told her that Alex wanted to acquire Carey's she had only thought that at last there might be a chance for those who worked for the company to obtain more security and better working conditions, but now, as she thought about the size and power of an organisation like Hessler's, she wondered uneasily how its potential involvement would affect their lives.

More jobs, better jobs, better working conditions— that was one side of it, the best side; the other...

And that was something else Leo had not told her. He had known she lived here, she had mentioned it to him, but he had said nothing about Carey's, nothing about visiting Davina James, when he must have already planned that visit.

Saul's only comment when he had returned last night had been a bitter, 'She tried to tell me that von Hessler's visit was purely social; that their fathers were old friends.'

'Well, maybe they were,' she had tried to reason. 'After all, they *were* both involved in the same industry.'

'And at completely opposite ends of it,' Saul had derided.

'Saul ... I'm glad I've managed to catch you in. Got everything tied up there now, have you?'

Saul wasn't deceived by Alex's genial tone. 'Not yet,' he told him crisply.

'I see. Now, I hope things aren't going to be difficult. You know how important speed and secrecy are with this one, Saul.'

Now the geniality had been overlaid by a terser, slightly hectoring tone. Saul ignored it. He had long, long ago ceased to be afraid of Alex; Alex was a bully and like all bullies he enjoyed his power if you let him. 'It seems that someone else is also interested in acquiring Carey's,' Saul told him.

'Someone else? That's impossible. Unless you've been criminally careless. I hope you haven't done anything foolish, Saul. It doesn't pay to try to be too clever, you know. I hope I don't have to remind you that I can destroy you as easily as I made you. Without the Davidson Corporation——'

'Without the Davidson Corporation I'd survive somehow,' Saul told him tersely. 'But it isn't me who's been careless, Alex. I should look a little closer to home, if I were you...or rather a little closer to the friend whose indiscreet whispers led you to want Carey's in the first place. Hessler Chemie are after Carey's,' he told him.

'Hessler Chemie?' He could hear Alex's shock. 'The pharmaceutical people? But that's impossible.'

'Leo von Hessler himself has been down here to see Davina James,' Saul told him grimly.

There was a small pause, and Saul had the satisfaction of knowing that he had caught Alex off guard.

'It doesn't make sense,' Alex snapped eventually. 'What possible use would Carey's be to Hessler's?'

'Much the same as it would be to you, I imagine,' Saul told him drily.

There was another pause.

'But this legislation will only benefit UK companies,' Alex told him angrily.

'Perhaps Hessler's intend to establish a separate UK offshoot.'

'Why haven't you been in touch with me about this before now?'

'I only found out about it last night,' Saul told him.

'Well, *I* want Carey's, Saul, and I can't risk stirring up other people's curiosity or to waste time looking for another suitable company, not at this stage. I want Carey's, and I want you to get it for me.'

'Well, it should be easy enough, provided you're prepared to meet Davina James's price.'

'Which is?' Alex demanded.

'I don't know yet. Obviously she intends to play us off against Hessler's.'

'No,' Alex told him, as Saul had known he would. 'Carey's has no market value . . . that's the whole beauty of acquiring it, and if some damned woman thinks she's going to get the better of me . . . There must be another way. Something we can use. Find it, Saul,' he told him, 'and find it fast. No more time-wasting games.'

'And if I can't find a way?' Saul asked him quietly.

There was another silence, longer this time than any of the others.

'I'm surprised you need to ask,' Alex told him acidly. 'And it won't just be your job you'll lose, Saul. The City doesn't like failures . . . losers. They make it very, very nervous.'

'Problems?' Christie asked him lightly when she came back into the kitchen and found him standing staring out into the garden.

'You could say that.'

'Saul, what exactly *does* Alex want with Carey's?' she asked him quietly. 'I thought at first that someone else taking over the company would be a good thing for everyone who works there, but...'

'Well, let's put it this way,' Saul told her, his mouth twisting, 'Alex's attitude towards Carey Chemicals' workers won't vary very much from Davina James's. As far as both of them are concerned, people are an expendable commodity, especially when personal financial gain is involved.'

'But I thought Davina *was* concerned about Carey Chemicals' employees.'

'There's only one thing Davina James cares about, and it isn't Carey's or the people who work there.'

Christie heard the bitterness in his voice, and she heard something else as well. Did Saul realise just what he was betraying to her? she wondered as she caught that angry undertone of disillusionment and pain.

'Alex wasn't too pleased to be told that Hessler's are also interested in Carey's. The last thing he wants to get involved in is some kind of Dutch auction for the business, especially one presided over by a woman.'

'So what do you intend to do?' Christie asked him, ignoring his reference to Alex's chauvinism.

'I haven't been given much choice. Alex wants me to find out some way to put some pressure on Davina James so that she sells out to him quickly and cheaply.' He saw his sister's expression and his own face hardened. 'Don't waste your sympathy on her, Chris.'

'But she seemed so genuinely anxious to protect her employees.'

'Didn't she just!' He paused and then said slowly, 'Tell me again, Chris...about the safety infringements and those cases of dermatitis.'

Christie looked horrified. 'Saul, you can't use that. It's privileged information I would never have told you if I'd thought——'

She paused as the sound of the telephone ringing interrupted her.

*   *   *

Leo frowned as he replaced the telephone receiver after Davina's call. It was obvious that Saul Jardine's visit had upset her. He had observed yesterday how careful she was to exert control over betraying her private emotions, and, even though she had been shocked and distressed by his disclosures, she had not reacted to them with the passionate intensity Saul Jardine had obviously aroused in her.

Leo could think of no obvious reason why Alex Davidson should want to acquire Carey's, nor why Christie's brother should assume that Hessler Chemie was a rival.

Leo had liked Davina. He had recognised almost immediately the virtues in her and the strength. In other circumstances, if he had not first met Christie Jardine... He smiled a little grimly to himself. It would have been easy to form a close relationship with Davina; she was that kind of woman; there was something spiritually refreshing about her, something that a man could draw strength and hope from, and their shared knowledge of their father's blood-guilt would have formed a strong bond between them... still would form that bond.

He had heard in her voice as they talked her concern for the future of Carey's, her sense of responsibility towards its employees, and that too was awareness, a responsibility he knew, if on a much larger scale. Both of them in their different ways bore the burden of rectifying their fathers' omissions.

Sins of the fathers? He steepled his fingers together and frowned. Experience and caution warned him not to get involved. There was already risk enough in the fact that someone else had made a connection between them, even if it was the wrong one. Much better, safer simply to let matters lie as they were...to let Saul Jardine believe that Hessler Chemie *was* interested in acquiring Carey's than to risk anyone making any other kind of connection.

'I told him that our fathers were friends,' Davina had said. 'But he didn't believe me.' And he had heard in her voice more than anger or resentment.

Davina was not his concern; not his responsibility. He had problems enough with the family he already had, and this sense he had that he and Davina were now linked at one of the deepest human levels there could be was one he should not encourage or dwell upon.

There was a telephone directory in his room. He looked at it for a moment and then picked it up, his long lean fingers flicking through its pages until he found what he was looking for.

Jardine. Dr Christie. He wrote down the number and then picked up the receiver.

'Christie.' She had recognised his voice long before he said quietly, 'This is Leo von Hessler; please do not hang up.'

Her heart was pounding heavily, her body reacting as though it had been under some kind of intense physical strain so that she heard, saw and felt everything at a thick, blanketing distance, as though they were events taking place in a dream in which she was only an onlooker.

'Christie, I should like to speak with your brother if he is there, but first... There is something I should like to say to you before my flight leaves for Hamburg. And I should like to say it in person.'

He had never intended this; his own vulnerability had told him that it would be safer, simpler, *wiser* simply to go, and then last night he had seen her face, had felt her anger and pain. If nothing else, at least he could take those from her. He had recognised from her eyes that she had misunderstood his motives in leaving her at her bedroom door, that she had seen them as a rejection.

'I can't really see that there is any point,' Christie started to tell him acidly.

'Perhaps not, but I should appreciate the opportunity to see you nevertheless.'

His calm determination confused her. It wasn't what she had expected. Or wanted?

She held the receiver away from her ear, and said shortly to Saul, 'It's Leo von Hessler. He wants to speak with you.'

It was a good fifteen minutes before Saul replaced the receiver. He was frowning, his face blank of all emotion.

'What is it...what did he want?' Christie asked him.

'He wanted to tell me that Hessler Chemie has no interest in acquiring Carey's, and that in fact Davina James was speaking the truth when she said that their fathers knew each other.'

'And you believe him?'

'Yes,' Saul told her tersely.

'But you *didn't* believe Davina.'

'No,' he agreed, and now his expression had changed, his reactions not quite quick enough for him to conceal what he was feeling for her.

Christie looked away from him, swallowing down her own pity.

'Oh, I told him you'd meet him at the Grosvenor.' He glanced at his watch. 'You've got just under an hour. Would you like me to drive you?' Now it was his turn to read her thoughts. 'That *is* what you want, isn't it...to see him?' For a moment Saul thought she was going to lie and deny it; her eyes were wild with the same feral intensity he remembered from her childhood, and his heart ached for her.

'Whatever he has to say, it can't make any difference,' Christie told him doggedly.

Saul said nothing. He would have to go and see Davina, of course. Apologise...explain. Explain? Explain what? And *how*?

Well, even if he couldn't explain, he still had to apologise. He stood up, removing his suit jacket from the back of the chair.

He was halfway towards the door when the phone rang again.

Christie answered it. He heard the quickening concern in her voice, the sharp anxiety as she said firmly, 'Now, calm down and...' He was opening the door when she covered the mouthpiece of the receiver and called out quickly to him, 'Saul, it's Karen. There's some problem with Josephine. I think you'd better speak to her.'

It took him close on five minutes to decipher what Karen was saying. She was half hysterical, blaming him, accusing him, complaining that she had not even known where to get in touch with him; that he cared nothing for his children; that he had abdicated his responsibility towards them.

'She *is* your daughter, Saul,' she told him.

'Yes,' he agreed calmly. 'She is.'

'What is it?' Christie asked him anxiously when he eventually hung up.

'Josey's been suspended from school for possessing drugs. According to Karen, they've been having problems with her for several months. My fault, apparently, because she's my child. Karen seems more concerned with what her neighbours and boss are going to think than in helping Josey.'

'What are you going to do?' Christie asked him gently.

Saul shrugged. 'What the hell *can* I do? Josey has always made it plain enough what she thinks of me. Now, according to Karen, she's shut herself in her room and is refusing to see or speak to anyone.'

'Go and see her, Saul,' Christie suggested. She saw the indecision in his eyes and pressed, 'She needs you.'

'I can't,' Saul told her. 'I have to see Davina James, and I have to get this deal tied up. If I don't... There's no point in my going anyway, Chris. What the hell can

I do to help her? If she won't talk to her mother... You'd better leave if you're going to get to Chester in time to see von Hessler,' he told her, changing the subject.

He saw the uncertainty in her eyes and shook his head. 'You can't do anything for Josey by staying here.'

'No,' Christie agreed heavily. 'I don't suppose I can.'

Ten minutes later, having watched her drive off, Saul closed the front door. It was all right Christie's saying 'go', but his relationship with Josey was not like hers with Cathy. She *knew* that. The last person Josey would want now was him. Her contempt for him had never been something she'd bothered to hide, her duty visits grimly hostile spaces of time she treated as something unpleasant that had to be endured, like him.

And even if she *had* wanted him, how the hell could he go?

He closed his eyes, and suddenly he could hear the echo of the emotion in Davina's voice when she had told him, 'People are more important than possessions; than wealth, or ambition. People matter, all of them, and if you deny them the right to that importance then you take away from them one of their most basic human rights, you demean and devalue them, and in doing so you demean and devalue yourself as well.'

Behind his shuttered eyelids dark images formed: Josephine as a baby, a toddler, a child. Josey, the last time he had seen her, almost on the brink of womanhood, her eyes blazing contempt and resentment, her face set with rejection, her body willing him not to come near her; to touch her.

How long had it been since he had last touched her, held her, shown her how much he loved and valued her?

But she didn't *want* his love; she never had; even as a small child she had turned from him fiercely, denying him the right to claim his fatherhood.

'You're not my father,' she had spat at him once. 'I don't *have* a father and I don't want one.'

But she *was* his child.

Without intending to, and certainly without wanting to, he found he was asking himself how Davina would react in the same circumstances. Why did he even need to ask the question?

There was a notepad on the table. He sat down and wrote quickly on it, folding the piece of paper before reaching for a fresh sheet and writing on that as well.

He found an envelope on Christie's desk, and put the folded note in it, sealing it. He then placed it with the second note in the middle of the kitchen table where Christie couldn't miss it.

There was no point at all to what he was doing, he told himself as he climbed into his car; no point. It would probably lose him his job and destroy his career, and it meant he was breaking all the rules he had ever set for himself about seeing a task through to its completion; about grimly keeping to whatever path he had set for himself.

And it certainly wouldn't help Josephine, who would probably refuse to see him, which would mean he would have to get straight back in his car and drive all the way back to Cheshire.

But he still headed for the motorway, grimly trying to ignore the thudding message of his tyres on the tarmac, which seemed to sound out a flat, hard chant of 'It's your fault... your fault... your fault...'

Christie was not a nervous woman, nor one given to awkward self-consciousness, but her self-confidence had not been easily won, and as she walked into the Grosvenor she was suddenly reminded of an occasion as a child when her mother had taken her shopping and then on to meet her father as he left work.

She remembered how excited she had been; how thrilled and proud. They had waited outside the building for him. She had wanted to go in, but her mother had told her that her daddy didn't like being interrupted at his work.

Christie had known that this wasn't true. Saul often spent Saturday morning at the office with their father; a treat which had never been permitted her. But this unfairness was forgotten when her father had finally emerged from the building. Christie had broken free of her mother's hold and run up to him.

'Christie, for goodness' sake, why do you have to be such a hoyden? Jean, can't you do something about this wretched child's hair, and why are her socks dirty?' As she listened to him, all Christie's excitement had faded. In its place had come guilt and misery; the knowledge that in so many ways she displeased her father and was not the child he wanted. Now for no reason at all she remembered those feelings and what it had been like to know that she was not wanted ... not loved.

It was dark inside the hotel foyer after the sunlight outside, and she shivered, suddenly afraid and uncertain, turning instinctively back towards the exit.

'Christie.' His voice, the light detaining touch of his hand on her arm, her sensitive awareness of the height and breadth of him, the subtle dismayingly familiar personal scent of him, held her rigid.

She turned round, unaware of how clearly her eyes betrayed her contradictory emotions.

What he saw in them made Leo catch his breath. She really was the most extraordinary woman. Her eyes now held pride and anger, the knowledge of maturity and self-awareness, and yet with them was the innocence and pain of a child.

'I'm glad you came.'

Something in his voice soothed her, broke the imprisoning spell of the past.

'I didn't want to,' she told him, 'but Saul thought I should.'

Leo looked gravely at her. 'And you, of course, always do as your brother suggests.'

Christie had the grace to laugh. The sound of her laughter, spontaneous, rich and warm, gave Leo hope.

'We can't talk here,' he told her. 'The hotel management has been kind enough to lend us a small spare conference-room. I thought you'd prefer to talk there.'

Rather than in his room? He was extraordinarily sensitive and tactful, she had to give him that, Christie acknowledged.

'How did you manage that?' she taunted him. 'Or do I need to ask?'

'I merely explained that I needed privacy for a short space of time to talk with someone,' Leo told her, unruffled by her cynicism. He acknowledged it, though, adding gently, 'Contrary to what you seem to think, Christie, I do not wield the power of the von Hessler name round me like a war mace. I never have. Personally I find that good manners, consideration and honesty are much more effective.'

'Honesty?' Christie challenged, her expression suddenly hardening.

As though he sensed that she was about to change her mind and walk away from him, Leo took hold of her. He had a surprisingly firm grip, she recognised as he guided her along a small corridor and stopped outside a polished wooden door.

'You can let go of me now, Leo,' she told him as he opened the door with his free hand. 'This isn't Germany circa 1940-odd, and you aren't the SS.'

It was a childish taunt, but its effect on him was immediate and intense. His face went white as he released her, his eyes suddenly blank and unfocused as though he couldn't bear to look at her.

Against her will she wished she had been less abrasive, but as always her stubborn pride refused to allow her to say so.

'You wanted to talk to me,' she said palliatively instead. 'To explain. Although why you should think it necessary I can't pretend to understand.' She was back on the defensive, her chin tilting as she refused to admit what they both already knew; trying to reduce what had happened between them to something of no importance.

Instead of reacting to her challenge, as her father might have done, to her surprise, Leo laughed. 'You are very British, Christie, aren't you?'

Caught off guard, Christie stared at him suspiciously. 'What does that mean?'

Leo's smile deepened. 'Wasn't it a British admiral who raised his telescope to his blind eye and claimed, "I do not see the signal"?'

To her consternation, Christie knew that she was blushing. Blushing. Something she hadn't done since she had left her teens behind. Just for a second she was tempted to try to bluff her way out, driven by stubbornness and pride, and then she reminded herself that she was supposed to be mature enough now to have conquered or at least controlled those betraying petty vices.

'I simply meant that I could see no point in resurrecting something which, with hindsight, both of us know wouldn't...' She stopped abruptly, biting her lip. Now she had said...betrayed far more than she had intended, and she cursed her stupidity and her vulnerability silently.

'I didn't lie to you deliberately, Christie,' Leo told her quietly.

If he was aware of her self-betrayal either he was too tactful to show it or, more probably, he didn't want to get involved in that kind of emotional issue, she decided.

'I *had* decided to tell you the truth about who I was.'

'It wasn't not telling me your *name*,' Christie retorted. 'You let me confide in you...tell you things...air

views you must have *known* I would not have shared
with you had I realised who you were.'

She couldn't bring herself to say how much he *had*
hurt her by letting her believe he shared those views, or
at least some of them, that he was sympathetic to what
she felt, when he couldn't possibly be. Not with the position he held in Hessler's.

'Yes,' he agreed quietly. 'But I am a *man*, Christie...an
individual. I might share my name with the corporation,
but I am *not* that corporation.'

'But you work for it, you stand at its head; you are
not *forced* to do that, Leo. You must have *chosen* that
role at some stage in your life. Just as you must have
known when we were talking that I would never...' She
stopped, unable to go on. 'There isn't any point to this,'
she told him flatly. 'I don't even know what I'm doing
here. After all, what really happened? We had dinner
together. I wanted to have sex with you.' She gave a small
shrug, forcing herself to meet his eyes. 'I made a mistake,
drew the wrong conclusions, and, although at the time
it was an embarrassing as well as frustrating mistake,
it's hardly the end of the world.'

'I wanted you,' Leo told her quietly. 'I wanted you
then and I want you now. Would you like me to prove
it?'

Just for an instant she had a brief mental image of
them; of him taking hold of her, kissing her, touching
her, lifting her against his body, while he groaned with
need. She could almost feel his arousal; taste his kiss.
Her own body ached sharply, her skin hot.

Just in time she managed to snatch herself back to
reality.

'No, I would *not*,' she told him fiercely. 'That *isn't*
why I came here, Leo, to have sex with you.'

'Good,' he told her unequivocally. 'Because it isn't
sex I want from you, Christie. It never has been.' He
saw her face and his mouth curled. 'Surely you knew

that—otherwise what has this been about? You may be
wrong about my motivation for being with the corporation, but you *are* right about my inability to leave it,
and you, I think, are not a woman who would count the
rest of the world well lost for love.'

For a moment she was almost too shocked to speak.
Even though she had known how *she* felt about *him*, a
declaration of love from him was the last thing she had
expected. She had fought against her feelings, denied
and stifled them, and now suddenly he was making her
feel as though she was almost guilty of murder, of destroying something rare and precious.

Valiantly she tried to fight back.

'Would *you*?' she challenged him. 'Would you give
up everything to be with me, to live a life you knew was
alien to you, a life that went against all your beliefs, a
life that would suffocate and destroy you? Is that what
you expect *me* to do, Leo?'

'No,' he told her quietly. 'And it was because of that
that I left you at your bedroom door, Christie. Because
I knew that if once I touched you... held you... loved
you I would have moved heaven and earth to keep you
with me, done anything——'

'Except give up Hessler's,' Christie interrupted him
quickly. She dared not let him say any more; already her
heart was beating far too fast, her body, her soul aching
with a fierce need to reach out and claim what he was
offering her, to beg him, plead with him to take the responsibility for the decision away from her, to compel
her physically, with the drug of his body, if necessary,
to say that she would stay with him.

It was like standing on a bridge over swirling water,
wanting to lean forward and simply let oneself fall, the
lure of self-destruction so inviting, so strong that it was
almost irresistible. Almost. It only took one step to move
back from the danger, and in the end Leo himself helped

her make it by saying quietly, 'Except that . . . I am not free to make that decision, Christie,' he told her.

She tried to smile, knowing that her eyes were brilliant with the tears she could not allow herself to shed. 'You mean you will *not* allow yourself to be free to make it,' she told him, and then she opened the door.

As she walked through it she stopped.

'There isn't anything else we can say to one another, is there, Leo, other than that I wish you had *had* sex with me that night, and that it had been the worst sex I had ever had in my life?' She saw his face and smiled bitterly. 'You say you *love* me, but you couldn't even do that for me, could you?'

It was unkind and unfair, but her own pain was so great that she had to have some means of releasing it. And she was crying so much as she drove home that she had to pull into a lay-by.

While she was there a plane flew noisily overhead. It couldn't, of course, be Leo's flight, but nevertheless she watched it until it had disappeared.

CHAPTER TWENTY-TWO

'MAY I come in?'

Davina frowned as she recognised her visitor. Christie Jardine. She looked, Davina recognised, as though she had been crying, and recently. Her heart gave a frantic jolt. Saul—had something happened to him? She shuddered, recognising the self-betrayal of her own thoughts.

Unable to speak, she nodded as she opened the front door wider.

'Saul asked me to call,' Christie told her. 'He's been called away on...on some urgent family business. He left you a note.'

Mentally deriding herself for her stupidity, Davina took the note. It was habit and the good manners instilled in her as a child that prompted her to offer Christie a cup of tea. She was surprised when Christie accepted, automatically leading the way into the small sitting-room and inviting Christie to sit down.

In the kitchen she made the tea quickly, Saul's note still unread. What did it contain? More threats? Her hand shook a little. Her mouth was still slightly bruised and sensitive. To be kissed by him now would be like making love after a night spent sharing every lover's intimacy; pleasurable almost to the point of over-sensitivity. Her body shuddered as she cut herself off from her thoughts.

Christie saw that her face was slightly flushed when she came in with the tea but said nothing.

'I hope it isn't anything too serious that has called your brother away,' Davina said politely as she poured Christie's tea. It was an automatic remark, the kind she had trained herself to make in the days when she had had to play the role of her father's hostess and then

415

Gregory's and, as when one enquired to another's health, it required merely a standard meaningless response.

Only Christie didn't make that response; instead she said, 'Unfortunately, it *is* serious. Saul's daughter, Josey, has been suspended from school, allegedly for possessing drugs.'

Christie paused, annoyed with herself. What on earth was she doing, telling Davina James that? It certainly hadn't been her intention when she had first read Saul's hastily written note asking her to call and deliver the letter he had left for Davina, but there was something about the other woman that was so instantly genuinely sympathetic and compassionate that Christie had somehow found her own anxiety for both her brother and her niece spilling over into the kind of emotional unburdening she was more used to hearing rather than giving.

And, contrary to what she might have supposed, Davina did not look shocked, withdrawing herself both mentally and actually physically, as Christie had seen so many people do when confronted by something that made them feel uncomfortable or uneasy; as though somehow merely to have received such a confidence might in some way endanger or contaminate them.

Christie knew enough about people to accept that this was an instinctive and subconscious reaction, and one which was generally quickly retracted, but it still surprised her a little that someone like Davina had not actually made it.

And now Davina was waiting quietly, allowing her to decide for herself whether or not to continue. And somehow, although she had not intended to do so, *because* Davina was not pressing her she heard herself adding, 'Josey has told her mother that the drugs weren't hers; that another girl had asked her to look after them because she was afraid she was about to be found out. Of course, Josey refuses to say who this girl is. Saul's ex-wife is the kind of person who places great store on

'I'm sure he won't have done that,' she said quietly. 'After all, you haven't forgotten *him*, have you?'

Forgotten him. If only she could have, Christie wished savagely after Davina had gone.

Only last night she had woken in her sleep and had actually been reaching out for him before she came fully awake and realised what she was doing.

How had it happened that she had this subconscious, intense awareness within her body, burned into her flesh and her bones almost, of how it would feel had they been lovers, this aching sense of loss and malaise for an intimacy they had never actually shared? It was as though they had physically been lovers; as though in her sleep, when her subconscious mind was anaesthetised, her senses ached and longed for what they had once known and what was now denied to them.

And she knew whom they blamed for that denial... whom they punished. It wasn't *her* fault that she had never even once physically assuaged that ache for him. She had been willing enough for them to be lovers. He was the one who——

'What is it? What's wrong?' Cathy asked her anxiously now.

Angry with herself for allowing her own emotions to be so visible to Cathy, Christie forced herself to smile. 'Nothing,' she fibbed. 'Nothing's wrong. I was just thinking about your uncle Saul and wondering how they're getting on.'

'Tom wrote on his card that Provence is ace,' Cathy informed her. 'He said that the house is mega and that they've got real peaches growing on trees in the garden.'

Christie had to laugh. 'Real peaches—mm. Well, shall we go and see if the birds have left us any real raspberries for our tea?'

Dwelling on what might have been did no good. There was no future for Leo and herself. There couldn't be. And, if she thought this was pain and self-denial now, then how much more would she be suffering if she had actually allowed any real kind of intimacy to develop between them? She could not sacrifice her values and her beliefs to be with him any more than he could sacrifice Hessler Chemie to be with her.

At least the wounds, the pain she was suffering now were clean and would eventually heal; those they would inflict on one another if they came together, only to have to part because they could not reconcile their different lives, would never heal; they would become infected and gangrenous with the bitterness and corruption of all that they would do to one another... in the name of love.

So Saul was in Provence with his children. Why did she feel so dismayed, so deserted, almost, by that knowledge? Davina asked herself. Why should she feel such a surge of emotion; such an intense mingling of anger and resentment, as though he had no right to go without first telling her? After all, what was she to him... or he to her? Nothing. Nothing at all.

Leo tensed as he heard the phone ring. He had just lived through three of the most exhausting, draining and demanding days of his whole life, and now he needed time to recoup, to replenish himself, to revitalise himself before he moved on.

There had been protests, of course, shock, anger, and, amazingly in the circumstances, it had been Wilhelm who had protested the most vociferously when he made his announcement. Wilhelm, who was now, on the face of it at least, to get what he had always wanted and to step into Leo's shoes.

His talks with the government had been the most difficult and intense; there were so many loose ends to be tied up, so many safeguards to be made, so much legal paperwork to be got through, but now at least it was done. This afternoon he had put his signature to the documents that would transfer control of Hessler Chemie to a managing board of directors who would be monitored and advised by a specially appointed board, containing representatives from each of the major political parties, from the judiciary, from the church and from the academic world, and this august body would oversee the future moral and financial progress and development of Hessler's.

On their shoulders would now fall the heavy weight of monitoring the corporation and of advising on the decisions that would govern its future.

Wilhelm would be the corporation's figurehead, the chairman, but a figurehead was all that he would be— Leo had seen to that: he would have no real power, no real control.

And at the back of Leo's mind lay the knowledge that, should he ever need to do so, should Wilhelm try to break through the restraints he had placed around him, he could always use the final, the ultimate deterrent and reveal to Wilhelm the truth about his birth.

Not that that could ever be anything other than a last resort. Wilhelm was not a compassionate man; there was no softer, gentler side to his nature, but Leo still feared what it could do to him to learn that Heinrich had not been his father, and it was because of this that he had not used that knowledge against him, acknowledging as he did so that, had their positions been reversed, Wilhelm would not have had the slightest qualm about using it against him, would have relished doing so, in fact.

But then, he was not Wilhelm. Thank God.

Like the fabled Gnomes of Zurich, the newly appointed advisory board would work behind the scenes to control the corporation, to control Wilhelm; and they would also make sure that neither of them transgressed life's moral laws; that they did not use their power in ways that worked against rather than for humankind.

The chancellor had refused to believe him at first, had thought that what he was suggesting was merely a joke, but eventually Leo had managed to convince him. Being the majority shareholder of such a powerful company did possess some advantages, Leo had discovered, and for the first and last time in his life he had used the power that conferred on him to force through his plans.

There had been objections, of course. What he was proposing was unheard-of... And to announce that he himself would henceforward receive no profits from the corporation, that his shareholding would be held in trust for the benefit of others...

He didn't need any more money, he had said quietly.

There was to be no official announcement in the Press until the end of the month, by which time all the small investors in the corporation would have been reassured that their money was not at risk, but by then he...

He reached for the receiver. It would probably be Wilhelm... again.

To hear Davina's voice instead of his brother's startled him. She sounded uncertain and hesitant, and once he had recovered he was quick to reassure her that she had not rung at a bad time and that he *was* pleased to hear from her.

'In fact, your call is extremely fortuitous. *I* was intending to ring you.'

What he had actually been intending to do was to fly over to Cheshire, and he had on his notepad a reminder to call the airport and book himself a seat on the first convenient flight.

There were things he needed to talk over with Davina. Things that affected them both, and besides...

Besides what? Besides... Christie was in Cheshire. Christie... He fought down the fierce surge of urgency and need that invaded his body at the thought of her and tried to concentrate instead on what Davina was saying.

He picked up on the word 'loan' and the tension in her voice, and interrupted her quickly. 'Davina... I *am* still prepared to give you a loan, but before we discuss it I have a proposition I'd like to put to you. I'll outline it briefly to you now, and if you're interested I could fly over to England so that we can discuss it in more detail.'

Two hours later, when she finally replaced her receiver, Davina could still hardly believe what had happened. She stared at the wall and blinked slowly, trying to steady her racing heartbeat.

What Leo had suggested was so revolutionary and unexpected that at first she had thought she must have misheard him.

He wanted to use Carey's as the vehicle through which the two of them together would establish a new company, but, unlike Hessler Chemie and unlike Carey's, the drugs this one produced would not have a chemical base but would be based instead on properly researched natural remedies.

'Where we can we will develop the means to produce synthetic copies of these natural drugs; especially where the life-forms that give rise to them are in danger of extinction will we do so, but we will always follow where nature leads rather than seeking to "improve" on her work by producing drugs which are more powerful and consequently more dangerous than hers.

'We will not be an organisation devoted to the making of obscenely huge profits; that will not be our goal. Our goal will be to aid humanity, to provide what relief we can for its pains and ills.

'It won't be easy,' he had warned her when Davina expressed enthusiasm and delight at his suggestions. 'We shall initially face antagonism from the general public as well as the established drug industry; it is in the nature of human beings to fear change and to treat it with suspicion and derision, but with perseverance it can be done.'

It was only after she had calmed down a little that it actually occurred to Davina to wonder why Leo had chosen to site his new venture here in Cheshire. She frowned a little. That was something she could ask him when she saw him.

Sleepily, she yawned. She wasn't sure what the bank was going to think of Carey's transformation. It had startled her how closely Leo's plans had followed the guidelines Saul had outlined in his note to her. Saul...

What was he doing now? Enjoying the balmy heat of a Provence evening, breathing in the scented dusty air? Was he alone, or...?

She gave a tiny shiver. She hadn't experienced this kind of intensity, of longing, of needing to know what another person, the other person, was thinking, feeling, doing, ever before, not even with Matt.

'You should have seen the fish I caught this afternoon. It was this big,' Tom boasted noisily to Josey.

'So where is it now?' Josey demanded derisively.

'Dad made me throw it back...'

Saul saw the brief assessing look Josey gave him. He and Tom had spent the afternoon together fishing before joining another British holidaying family for an impromptu barbecue supper.

Josey had declined to join them. She had some studying to do, she said. Evidence of it now lay scattered over the kitchen table together with the remnants of the meal she had made for herself. Saul hadn't argued with her or tried to persuade her to change her mind.

She was still very wary with him, he recognised, still in many ways testing him, and who could blame her? He had yet to prove himself to her as a father, to earn her respect and her trust. And her love?

He was beginning to recognise that, while Tom possessed a solid, untemperamental, easygoing nature, Josey was very much his child. Very much.

She was also a teenager, a girl on the brink of womanhood, touchily self-conscious and vulnerable one moment, and fiercely self-defensive the next. Like him, she had a deep-rooted need to be able to retreat into herself occasionally, and Saul had been aware of the quick, sharp look of surprise she had given him earlier when he had accepted her decision not to accompany them without trying to persuade her to change her mind.

'Get much done?' he asked her now, watching as she flipped her hair back off her face, awed by the way the womanliness within her was developing and terrified at the same time because of it. She was growing up so fast. He had lost so much time already. He went cold with horror at the thought of how easily he could have left it too late. As it was...

'Mm...a fair bit. I thought I might have a break tomorrow and go into Aix. There's a train...'

'The Baileys have invited Tom to spend the day with them tomorrow,' Saul told her. 'They're off to the coast. Why don't I drive you into Aix, and then perhaps later we could meet up somewhere for lunch?' He watched her out of the corner of his eye, preparing himself for her rejection, tensing against it as she gave a small, apparently dismissive shrug.

'If you like.'

Saul released his pent-up breath. The casual pose did not quite mask the brief flush of pleasure that stained her skin, the emergent woman momentarily eclipsed by the child.

It would be a long time before she accepted him fully, before she tucked her arm through his with the same easy, loving confidence he had seen the teenage Susan Bailey display towards her father, rubbing her head against his shoulder, laughing up at him as she coaxed some small favour out of him.

But at least it was there, the tentative beginnings of the relationship, the trust, the love he believed they would one day share.

Oh, she would make him pay for the past, make him earn their future, test him and go on testing him until she was sure, until she felt safe, but that was his fault, not hers.

Inwardly he thanked God and fate that he had been given this second chance with her, with both of them. God, fate, and Davina.

Davina... When he'd left England he had told himself that he was not going to think about her, not going to allow himself to become full of self-pity and yearning, but the ache, the need, the love he felt for her was always there; would always be there, he recognised.

'Dad ... I'm hungry...'

'Don't you ever think about anything but your stomach?' he heard Josey responding to Tom's complaint with sisterly disgust.

Hunger. One of man's most basic instincts, Saul reflected as he dutifully headed for the fridge. In *all* its many forms.

Tiredly Leo stretched his muscles, trying to ease their tension. Davina had welcomed his proposals with an enthusiasm that had made him reflect again how closely attuned they were in their outlook and values, how in a way, like two orphans, they turned instinctively and needfully to one another for support and reaffirmation of all that they believed in, clinging together as they tried to blot out the dark shadows.

'By the way,' she had told him apparently casually, 'I saw Christie Jardine the other day. She mentioned meeting you at a conference. She asked if I'd heard anything from you recently.'

She didn't say any more, but it was enough. More than enough to ease the doubting ache that had been tormenting his heart, making him ask himself if, after all, all that he was doing would mean nothing to her...if it was, after all, *him* she had been rejecting and not, as she had told him, his role within Hessler Chemie.

And if she *did* reject him, would he have any regrets about the decision he had taken?

He smiled to himself. No. He had known the moment he had realised that Anna was right and that there was always a way, that he could no longer go on playing a role which had been so onerous to him.

Duty was one thing; self-sacrifice was another, especially when there was no need for that sacrifice.

He flew into Manchester at lunchtime the next day, and drove straight to Christie's.

She had woken up with the beginnings of a migraine and had gone straight back to bed.

The sound of someone ringing her doorbell brought her abruptly out of her drugged sleep. Blessedly her head felt clear, although her body was lethargic and heavy.

It had been a hot, sultry morning, and she had been feeling too ill to do more than remove her clothes and slide into bed. Now she quickly pulled on a loose T-shirt and hurried down to answer the door. Being a doctor meant that she was always aware that the unexpected impatient summons could herald more than merely an unwanted caller.

As she opened the door she pushed the heavy weight of her hair back off her face, blinking in the brightness of the sunlight, so dazzled by it that at first all she could see was Leo's outline and the golden halo of his hair.

And then she felt the warmth of his touch on her skin, heard the familiar softness of his voice, drowned in the physical and emotional responses of her senses to him as he pushed her gently inside and then took her in his arms, his back against the door as he pushed it closed.

In her imagination she had pictured them as lovers, savoured all the intimacies of their relationship, all its nuances and passions many times, and yet strangely she had never actually imagined the innocence of them sharing a kiss.

And yet now that they *were* doing that, she recognised with a sharp leap of her heart that she had been foolish in not doing so. Because if she had done she might have been better guarded, better protected against the actuality of Leo's kiss.

It was slow, thorough, gentle, demanding, tentative and knowing, giving and taking, and she was drowning helplessly in the sharply sweet pleasure of it, clinging to him like a teenager to her first real love as she pressed herself against him, so that they were locked closely together, body to body, mouth to mouth, and she could feel the suddenly urgent change in his heartbeat as his body reacted to hers.

And then she did something she would never in a hundred lifetimes have imagined herself doing. She panicked and reacted to his arousal like a virgin with her first real experience of a man's sexuality, breaking the kiss and pushing frantically against his chest, her face and body hot with tension as she demanded huskily, 'Leo. No...please...I don't...'

She wouldn't have blamed him if he'd shown either disbelief or irritation. She was sure she would have done in the same circumstances, but instead he released her immediately, watching her with concerned eyes, gently tucking her hair behind her ear and touching her hot face with cool fingers.

'It's all right,' he told her gently. 'Christie, it's all right.'

She had to turn her back on him so that he wouldn't see her emotion; her weakness.

'No, it isn't,' she told him savagely. 'How can it *ever* be all right for us, Leo? You know it can't. You know——'

'I know that I love you,' he interrupted her. 'And I know that I believe you love me.'

Christie swung round. 'Of course I love you, damn you,' she raged at him. Her body was aching tautly now for all that she had denied it and all that Leo's touch had promised it. She was having to fight herself as well as him, she recognised as she battled to save herself the added anguish and humiliation of begging him to take her to bed, of telling him she wanted to ignore...to forget everything but the need to at least once experience the intimacy of sharing her body, her desire, her need...her love with him. 'But what the hell does *that* mean? I love you, Leo...but I can't live with you. You *know* that. We both know that.'

'I thought it was Hessler Chemie you couldn't live with.'

The words were quiet, casual almost, but he was watching her intently, his body held stiffly, as though he was half expecting to have to ward off a mortal blow.

'You...Hessler's...what's the difference? You're one and the same thing,' she retorted bitterly, angry with him and with herself because his tension and her awareness of it weakened her, made her ache to touch him, to hold him...made her want to weep for having made him so vulnerable.

'No, we aren't,' Leo corrected her. 'Not any more.'

It took several seconds for what he had said to actually sink in. When it did, her face lost all its colour, her body swaying slightly.

'You don't mean that,' she whispered drily. 'You can't. It isn't possible. You *are* Hessler Chemie.'

'I was,' he corrected. 'I'm not any more.' He watched her gravely and then told her, 'There isn't time for any more pretence between us, Christie. I love you. I want us to be together. Hessler Chemie is no longer a part of my life. If you want me...'

'Of course I want you.'

She was laughing and crying at the same time, unable to deal with her own emotions, her own shock.

'But what are you going to do?' she protested as he took hold of her. She heard him laugh.

'What I am going to do is what I should have done in Edinburgh. I'm going to take you to bed and make love to you—unless, of course, you've got any better ideas.'

'I didn't mean that. I meant...'

Leo knew what she meant, but there would be time enough later to tell her about his plans. Right now...

He kissed her as he picked her up, and Christie, who had never considered herself the kind of tiny, fragile woman who would ever be idiotic enough to enjoy that kind of male drama, was astonished by the fierce *frisson* of pleasure that went through her.

Leo was a sensual lover, more so than, perhaps, she was herself, Christie recognised as her body relaxed into post-coital torpor.

His self-control had surprised her as well; a tiny satisfied feminine smile curled her mouth. But she had very quickly shown him that she was more than able to demolish that control. He had protested at first at the warm touch of her mouth against his body, as she had caressed him intimately, but then he had allowed her to have her way, groaning softly under his breath as she alternately stroked him with her tongue and whispered to him that she had ached to know him like this, to know his scent and taste, to know the shape and texture of his flesh.

He had had his revenge, though, if it could be called revenge. She smiled ruefully to herself, remembering how in the end her own self-control had broken and she had begged him, pleaded with him to let her feel his mouth against her body. Her breasts still ached a little now from that loving, were still vaguely tender.

'I'm never going to let you go now. You know that, don't you?' Leo murmured against her ear.

She had thought he was asleep, and she gently punched him, warning him, 'I'm not someone who can be owned, Leo. I'm an individual.' But inwardly she knew she *was* committed to him now and that she would never want him to let her go.

It humbled her a little to know what he had done. In his shoes, would she have been able to make that decision ... to put her love for him first?

'Where's Cathy?'

Christie smiled. 'She has tennis practice today. She won't be home until six ... Of course, if you've had enough ...'

Leo laughed. 'Never,' he told her. 'Never, never, never...'

There were things to be discussed, of course, arrangements to be made, following Leo's and Davina's future plans for Carey's.

When Davina approached Giles to tell him what was happening her manner was so businesslike and matter-of-fact that Giles knew immediately that whatever might once have been on the verge of happening between them was now very firmly in the past.

'I'd like to stay on,' he told Lucy when he explained to her what was happening. 'It will all be quite different, of course. Nothing like the old Carey's, and there's no guarantee that it will be successful, although von Hessler seems to know what he's talking about.'

'If it's what you want then I'm quite happy to stay,' Lucy told him, and then added quietly, 'besides, we could hardly leave Nicholas's tree, could we?'

'I can take charge of the research and development side of things,' Leo told Davina one evening as they discussed the finer points of how the new company would be run. 'You say you're happy to take over staff personnel from Giles, and he will handle the day-to-day running of the place. But we need someone else, someone who can have an over-view of the whole thing, someone well enough versed in the business world to sell our ideals to it, to make it treat us seriously.

'We need someone who can bridge the gap between the establishment and industry, someone whose word carries weight in both worlds. I can't do it,' he frowned. 'I'm a biochemist, not a negotiator, and, besides, the fact that I've left Hessler Chemie is bound to cause an adverse reaction in certain circles, initially at least. No...what we need...'

'I think I know what we need,' Davina told him quietly. 'And I know where to find him.'

Davina wrote to Saul that night, explaining what was happening.

'There is a place here for you, if you want it,' she told him, and wondered as she wrote the words if when he read them he would also read what she had *not* said and know that it was not just a job that waited for him.

She waited for a week, her heart in her mouth every morning when the post arrived, every time the phone rang, but there was no response from him.

She knew from Christie that he was back from Provence and making arrangements for Josey to transfer to another school. She had only spoken briefly to him by telephone, Christie told her casually when Davina had enquired about him. Christie was too wrapped up in Leo and what was happening between them to be aware of anyone else's emotions, Davina recognised thankfully. A warm relationship was beginning to develop between the two women.

She was not going to marry Leo, Christie had told Davina positively. Relationships changed when lovers married, expectations, even feelings were somehow altered. She was an individual, a woman, a person with her own needs and goals, which she could not, *would* not subordinate to those which would be involved in being Leo's wife. She marvelled at the sacrifices he had made to be with her, admired all that he was doing, was interested in it and excited by it, but she still had her own life to lead, her own career path to follow.

'But you *do* love him?' Davina had asked her.

'Yes, I love him,' Christie agreed. 'Too much, I sometimes think,' she added ruefully. 'And Cathy adores him.'

'Yes,' Davina acknowledged, laughing. But when she was on her own she didn't feel much like laughing.

There had been no response from Saul, and she simply didn't have the courage, the forcefulness she suspected Christie would have exhibited. She could not take things any further by phoning him, or even writing to him a second time.

She had made her offer. He must know that it had not only been the job that was waiting here for him; that she too... She bit her lip and told herself stoically that it was perhaps, after all, all for the best, but her rebellious heart refused to accept it.

All the way from London Saul had been rehearsing what he intended to say—that he didn't need her job, didn't want her charity or her pity—but when Davina opened the door to him and he saw the look on her face he reacted instinctively and emotionally rather than logically, and simply opened his arms to her.

The few seconds for which she hesitated seemed like the longest space of time he had ever known. He wondered if he had been wrong after all, if he had misinterpreted the message in her eyes, and then she smiled at him. Not her normal controlled, grave smile, but one that wobbled slightly and revealed a vulnerability that made him ache as she took one step towards him and then another, while he waited, hardly daring to breathe until she was close enough for him to lock his arms around her and hold her, rocking her gently against him as they kissed and then kissed again.

'I still can't believe this is really happening,' Davina told him shakily some time later.

They were in her sitting-room, her body tucked snugly into his as they sat together on the settee.

Saul slid his hand against her throat, breathing in the warm scent of her skin and hair. 'Do you wish it weren't?' he asked, watching her.

'No,' she told him positively. 'Do you?'

'No.' He paused, and then said quietly, 'I've never done anything like this before.' He saw the quick startled glance she gave him and grinned. 'No, not *this*,' he corrected, kissing her briefly. 'I meant I've never allowed myself to act like this before...never even allowed myself to *think* of acting like this...spontaneously, naturally, following my own needs...my own path.'

They had been talking for hours, exchanging information with one another. Davina knew about his childhood, his father, and he knew about hers. She touched him gently now, love and compassion mingling in her eyes.

'I want you,' he told her softly. 'I want you so much, but if you'd prefer to take things more slowly... to wait... to——'

'No,' Davina told him swiftly, cutting through his hesitant speech. 'No... I... I want to celebrate what we have, Saul. I *want* us to... to take each other on trust. To have faith that——'

'That we aren't wrong in allowing our emotions, our instincts, our feelings to govern us. Both of us have had to repress those feelings and instincts for too long, haven't we? It's time to give up those lingering shadows from the past and look to the future.' He touched her gently. 'I'm so afraid of disappointing you. I'm only human, Davina. If you find I'm not the man you want... if it doesn't work out... then what?'

His own humility hurt her more than she could bear. 'Then at least we shall have had this,' she told him fiercely, lifting her head and placing her hand against his jaw as she kissed him.

He wasn't sure what he had expected. He knew he desired her, and how much. Her letter had shown him that she was prepared to acknowledge that she desired him, but her kiss took his breath away. It was so sweet with promise and trust, so open in its ardour, so giving and generous in its warmth that it was seconds before he could do anything other than simply passively wonder at everything she was giving him.

He had had no idea that there could be a woman like this one, strong enough to cast aside her own defences and to come to him without their protection, soft enough to tremble when he touched her; sure enough of herself, of her sensuality to want him to share its potency with her and so honest in her admission of her needs and fears that she made him ache to wrap her in tenderness and love.

Love.

'We hardly know one another yet.' He said the words against her mouth.

'Not yet, but we will.' It was a statement and not a question.

'Oh, yes,' he agreed huskily. 'We will.'

Her lovemaking was a revelation and a joy, her sensuality a deep, deep pool in which he could totally submerge himself, totally lose himself and yet still feel safe.

She watched him gravely as he studied her naked body and then studied his with equal gravity plus an open appreciation he had not expected.

'Nice,' she told him with a smile that was almost a grin, and then she leaned forward and kissed him, first at the base of this throat and then along his breast-bone; then the flat plane of his belly.

'Davina,' he protested as he hauled her away.

'I want you,' she told him quietly.

'I want you as well.'

'Show me. Show me so that I can show you how much you can please me, and how much I want to please you.'

No, there had never been a woman like her before and he knew there never would be again. She was unique, special, rare, precious. He told her so in between kisses and caresses while she laughed a little and then fell sharply silent as her body responded to his touch.

She had no artifice, no coy mock-shyness, no hesitation about showing him what she liked and how much his touch pleased her.

'Here . . . kiss me here, Saul,' she whispered to him, pulling him down against her breast and then shuddering as he did so.

'Like this?' he asked her thickly as he caressed her nipple gently. 'Or like this?' He stroked her with his tongue, his touch a little more rough so that she shivered in a paroxysm of frantic pleasure.

He recognised with a sense of wonder that he had never actually know what it was to make love before. To have sex, yes... but to make love, no, and this *was* making love, and it was Davina who showed him how, who touched and held him, who kissed and caressed him, who was woman enough and who loved him enough to ask him openly and lovingly what it was that pleased him best, and who told him what it was that would most please her.

She was seductive, uninhibited, tender, giving, sensual, openly showing him her desire and her need in a way he had never envisaged.

And when the time finally came she abandoned her self-control and gave herself so easily and so completely to him that the feel of her body, the sound of her small cries of pleasure made his throat ache with emotion.

'I love you,' he told her emotionally as he kissed her mouth and then the damp place between her breasts. 'I love you. I love you. I love you.'

Davina smiled as she held him. She had him now. He was hers. As she held him close silently she thanked Matt for all he had given her that had made it possible for her to find the courage to leave the shadows behind, to love Saul and to show him that she loved him.

'Thank you,' she whispered. Saul looked curiously at her and hugged her, and she didn't tell him that her thanks were not just for him—not even for the fate which had brought them together, but also for the man who had made it possible for her to recognise what fate was offering her, and to have the certainty to reach out and take hold of it.

EPILOGUE

'I SEE the establishment has turned out in full force and accepted our invitations, despite all the bullying tactics of the past couple of years and their determined political lobbying to put us out of business.'

Davina laughed as she looked up at her husband. 'Well, you always prophesied that ultimately they'd *have* to accept us,' she reminded him. 'Although I must admit, Saul, there *have* been one or two occasions when I seriously doubted that you were right.'

'Only one or two?' Saul teased her.

The large marquee erected next to the company's car park was filled not only with their business colleagues and rivals, but also with Carey's staff and their families as well.

It had been a mutual decision to invite every one of Carey Chemicals' employees to join in these celebrations to mark not only the company's first two years in business under its new management, and the success it had achieved, but also to thank all those who had been involved in making that success.

It certainly hadn't been easy. In the early days the financial Press had mocked them for their naïveté, prophesying that the newly formed company would never survive; that it was impossible for any company to build a successful business on the kind of ethics that the new owners and directors of Carey's were propounding.

Saul had been openly derided and mocked by their competitors, and no one knew more than Davina how hard he had had to work to establish the company's reputation, to get people to actually listen to their plans, and to try their products; but gradually they were building up a sound reputation, and the months Leo had spent in South America studying the natural drug products used by the natives, and the samples he had brought back with him, had formed a strong base for the company's products.

The public, it seemed, had short memories. Where once the Press had reviled and mocked them, now they praised and fêted them; they were in the vanguard of a new wave of business, a new code of working practices, a new kind of business morals that did not place profits above people.

Profit and power growth was not what they planned for Carey's, nor what they wanted, all of them were agreed on that.

They had been lucky in that they had inadvertently caught the tide as it changed and had been carried forward on the crest of its wave, but, as Saul and Leo had both pointed out, luck was one thing, having something solid to underpin and reinforce that luck was another; and that kind of base only came from hard work, from research, from being able to say confidently and truthfully that the products they produced were exactly what they purported to be.

Carey's did not claim to produce any miracle cures, any instant remedies: each new product was being painstakingly researched and developed.

It had been Lucy who had suggested that while the more serious side of the business was being developed, while they were undergoing the inevitable lengthy wait involved in the testing of the drugs they hoped to patent and market, they develop as a sideline a range of naturally based cosmetic products.

Leo, the chemist, and Saul as well had been uncertain at first, but Davina had been convinced that Lucy's almost casual suggestion was a good one, and she had been right.

Now both Lucy and Giles were also on the board. Davina smiled as she leaned against Saul. They had been married for just over a year, and during the time they had been together their relationship had strengthened and deepened so that now there were no secrets they could not share, no hidden, shadowed areas of their lives.

'Josey looks as though she's enjoying herself,' she commented to him.

Saul had been hesitant at first when Josey had asked to come and live with them. She was in her final year at school and planning to go on to university, but unsure as yet about her final career plans.

There was no rush, Davina had wisely counselled her, suggesting that, should she wish to do so, it might be worthwhile her considering taking a year's sabbatical in order to travel and taste a little of what life had to offer before making any final decision about her future.

'I can't expect you to have her here, living with us,' Saul had protested six months ago when Josey had first broached the subject of living with them. 'I know the two of you get on well, but...'

He hadn't needed to say any more. Davina had gently placed her fingers against his lips, silencing him.

'She *loves* you, Saul, and yes, occasionally she's inclined to be a bit possessive about you, but that's only natural, and I promise you I do understand. I'm not going to say there won't be times when I don't feel irritated and even jealous...but she's almost an adult and yet still so much a child. She *needs* this time with you. Personally I doubt she will stay long. I suspect that just knowing that you want her will be enough.

'She'll move in, stay a few months until she's got her self-confidence, and then the next thing we'll know is that she'll be talking about moving out again, wanting her independence, wanting all the things that all teenagers want when they suddenly discover the intoxication of being adult, or of thinking they're adult; but what is important is that we give her that confidence, that knowledge that she *is* wanted and welcomed, not just in our homes but in our lives and in your heart. She does need that.'

And so Saul had given in.

It hadn't been easy, Davina admitted; there had been times when she had had to grit her teeth, times when she and Saul had been interrupted at a less than appropriate moment by Josey's unthinking arrival in their bedroom; times when Davina ached to have her house and her husband to herself, when she told herself angrily that if she wanted to moan and cry when Saul made love to her she should be able to do so without having to worry about his teenage daughter overhearing them, but these had been fleeting, minor irritations when set against the way this time with her father had rounded off Josey's raw, sore edges; the way her self-confidence had blossomed; the way the bitterness and sharpness had softened to be replaced by a sunny warmth that came from knowing she was loved and wanted.

Of course, there had been arguments, quarrels, slammed doors and threats to leave; but three weeks ago on her birthday when Davina had handed Josey the pretty antique gold bluebird with the seed-pearl locked in its beak, promising her that she would do her best to find an appropriate chain for it for Christmas, the spontaneous warmth of the hug Josey had given her had more than made up for it all.

Saul had given his daughter his own present and Davina had read the message of awareness and thanks in Josey's eyes as she looked at her. In that message she had seen the birth of the woman Josey would one day become, and she had felt all the joy of any adult who felt that she had had a hand in nourishing that maturity.

She had never tried to become a second mother to Josey, nor to establish herself in any particular role in her life, and she had her reward now in the way that Josey not just accepted her, but genuinely felt affection and warmth for her.

Tom was another matter. He was a less sensitive, less emotional child than Josey, and he and Davina had got on well right from the start. He would be spending most of his summer holiday with them. They were taking him to Provence; she and Saul had now bought a small property there.

Her mouth curled in warm reminiscent pleasure. They had managed a brief visit there four months ago. It had been warm enough then and private enough for them to make love outside in the neglected garden, the sun heating and then later soothing their naked bodies.

They had discussed having a child of their own, and perhaps they would, but for now Davina was content, more than content, she acknowledged, with what they had.

'Stop looking at me like that,' Saul warned her, 'otherwise I'll have to take you home and...' He broke off, groaning. 'Oh, no, here comes Alex.'

Davina laughed. 'He probably wants to make you an offer you can't refuse.'

Both of them had been astonished and then amused at the way Saul's old boss was trying to coax Saul away from Carey's and back to him.

'It's the old story of the one who got away,' Saul had told her, but Davina knew better. However, it was too late now for Sir Alex to realise what he had thrown away when he'd dismissed Saul.

On the other side of the marquee, Lucy gently removed the small sticky fingers clinging to her hand without overbalancing their young owner.

When Davina had first approached her tentatively to ask if she would be interested in helping her to set up crèche facilities for Carey's she had been wary and uncertain, not really sure what had been behind Davina's offer.

She had been pregnant at the time and full of anxieties and fears for her child, resentful in a way of Davina's calm assumption that she would want to interest herself in anything other than its safety, but the idea *had* taken root. She had seen the enthusiasm with which Giles was approaching his work after Carey Chemicals' transformation, and a part of her did want to be involved in that world.

Now she reflected that allowing Davina to gently persuade her to involve herself in this side of the company's welfare programme had been one of the best things she had ever done, probably *the* best after marrying Giles and having little Jemma.

Her almost eighteen-month-old daughter was sitting on the other side of the enclosed nursery space, playing with another child. Physically she looked nothing like Nicholas; from the moment she had been born, full term and exactly on time, she had been a vigorous, healthy child. Giles adored her. So much so that Lucy occasionally felt it necessary to warn him against spoiling her.

As she straightened up her hand rested on the small bulge of her stomach for a second.

With Jemma she had wanted a girl, not another boy...not another Nicholas. As though there ever *could* have been another Nicholas; no child was ever a pattern card of another. With this baby she had no preference as to sex at all.

'Feeling OK?'

She smiled as Giles came up to her. 'Fine,' she assured him, leaning against him. 'It all seems to be going well.'

'There's still a lot of curiosity about Carey's, about what we're doing. Saul has handled that side of things well.'

His admiration for the other man was sincere. Giles had matured over the last two years and so had she, Lucy recognised; their relationship was far more stable now, far more secure, based less on sexual intensity and more on their shared love for Jemma and their delight in her second pregnancy.

She smiled again. She had, without being aware of it herself, turned into the kind of woman she had once sworn she would never be, and what was more she was delighted to have done so.

To outsiders their lives might not seem exciting, but excitement was something she no longer wanted or needed.

'I don't want you overtiring yourself,' Giles told her gently.

She laughed. 'Stop fussing,' she warned him, but her eyes told him how much she enjoyed his concern.

It seemed impossible now to believe she had ever worried that she might lose him to Davina...Davina, who had so unexpectedly married Saul Jardine.

'Do you think Christie and Leo will ever marry?' she asked Giles curiously, her thoughts transferring to the other couple who made up the new main board of directors of Carey's.

'They might...if they decide to have children,' Giles responded, patently more interested in Lucy than anyone else.

'All right, I already know you don't approve of all this razzmatazz,' Leo told Christie teasingly.

'I never said that.'

It amused him that she still responded so quickly and so vehemently to his deliberate baiting. Everything she felt or did she felt and did with passionate intensity.

Sometimes he suspected that the sexual side of their relationship was perhaps more important to her than it was to him. Because it was her main way of being able to show what she felt?

Some—*most* of her barriers had come down during the time they had been together, but there were still guarded private areas in which he was not allowed to trespass; nor did he try to do so.

Sometimes she told him in exasperation that he was too good to be true; too perfect; that he made her feel guilty because of her own shortcomings and his tolerance of them.

'I love you as you are,' was his answer. 'Just as I hope you love me as I am.'

'You know I do,' she had told him, and he knew she meant it. She *did* love him, but she still insisted on retaining her independence.

Leo understood her need for that independence. As he had told her smilingly once when she had asked him if it hurt him that she would not commit herself to marriage, a piece of paper could not guarantee her continued love, and it was that he wanted. And he already knew that her insistence on her independence had nothing to do with any desire on her part to keep open her sexual and emotional options to find another man.

'Why don't you two get married?' Cathy had asked them recently.

'Because we don't need to,' Leo had told her.

'But what if you had children?' she had persisted, and reading the look in Christie's eyes had reinforced Leo's awareness of what Christie had told him about her feelings of guilt for having denied Cathy a 'real' father.

Not that that would ever be an issue with them. He had already told Christie calmly and without any drama that he did not want a child of his own, and why. She had at first been shocked to learn about his father's past, but her love for Leo remained unshaken.

'He or she might *not* be like your father,' she had told him.

'I know,' he had agreed, 'and I know as well that it's an illogical fear, but that fear is just as much a part of me, Christie, as *your* need for independence, *your* fear of rejection are of you.'

'Come on,' Christie urged him, taking hold of his arm. 'Time to go and make your speech.' She was laughing at him but there was pride and love in her eyes as well.

As he walked towards the small podium Leo noticed the small group collected together in a huddle several yards away: Cathy, Christie's child, Saul's daughter

Josey, her cousin, his own two nephews, Fritz and
Martin.

He had kept his promise to Anna and in doing so had
perhaps set in motion something that might have much
broader implications and benefits in the future.

His nephews, Wilhelm's sons, would no doubt one
day join their father at Hessler Chemie. When they did
it would be no bad thing if they carried with them an
awareness of all that *they* were trying to achieve here at
Carey's.

Change was not always effected dramatically and
overnight. Sometimes it evolved slowly and gently, from
one generation to the next and on to the one beyond
that. It could be a golden chain of hope and promise,
linking those generations together in love and understanding, or it could be a leaden means of im-
prisonment, binding them in mutual resentment and
distrust.

He had broken the tarnished chain that linked him to
his father and was now forging a new one of his own.
Only infinity and the future knew whether *his* had the
purity to endure, whether out of all the pain and darkness
of the past it would shine like a beacon to light the way
to that future.

He stepped up on to the podium and faced his
audience.

'Today,' he told them, 'we are here to celebrate and
to welcome the future.'

The future... As Alex Davidson listened to him he
grunted derisively. He had been in two minds as to
whether he should come here today, accepting the olive
branch Saul had extended to him.

He had fought hard and not always cleanly, wanting,
needing to punish Saul for his disobedience, his dis-
loyalty, but in the end he had been obliged to acknowledge defeat.

And in victory Saul had been far more generous than
he would have been in the same circumstances. But then,

that was the difference between them, and that was why Saul had won, he acknowledged wryly. It was Saul himself who had told him gently that times had changed; that people had more knowledge, more awareness, more scruples ... more ideals.

'You mean they've turned soft,' Alex had derided, but he had known in his heart that Saul was right. 'The old order changeth...'

Well, he had fought against it, had fought hard, but he had not won. Saul and the rest of them had established their company, and successfully.

And somewhere within him, edging out his anger and malice, there was a reluctant feeling of pride in what Saul had done, a reluctant admiration for all that he had achieved.

'Shall we call a truce?' Saul had asked him.

Even then half of him had been inclined to argue, but that pretty wife of Saul's had caught his eye and smiled at him, and somehow without meaning to he had heard himself saying, 'Yes.'

He still thought Saul was wrong, of course. Always would do. All this namby-pamby stuff about natural products ... it was just a fad, that was all.

Still, it had surprised him to recognise so many influential people here, so many hard-headed money men, and, after all, Saul couldn't have forgotten everything he had taught him. He mustn't let anyone forget that he had been one of the first to spot Saul's potential. Craftily he started to plot and plan, suddenly feeling much more cheerful.

The future. Lucy touched her stomach and gently shushed Jemma as she moved closer to Giles's side.

The future—Josey, Tom, they were the future, Davina acknowledged, but so was she and so was Saul. They *still* had their parts to play, their love to enjoy. She smiled warmly up at him as Saul reached for her hand, lacing his fingers with hers.

'I wonder what Alex is up to,' he murmured in her ear, 'he's grinning like a Cheshire cat. Want some good news?' he added. 'Josey has just informed me that she's going out this evening—all evening.'

'Shush,' Davina told him, but her eyes were bright with laughter—and anticipation.

The future—sometimes it frustrated her that there was still so much she wanted to do, so much she felt she ought to have done, Christie admitted; she even felt guilty at times when she was with Leo because he was so important to her. More important than she sometimes wanted to admit to herself. But *he* knew it. He loved her too much to say so—to gloat. But he still knew.

She loved him with such a passionate intensity that it terrified her at times, and yet if she could have changed things, redirected the path of her life so that she had never met him, she knew she would not have done so.

Across the space that divided them she smiled at Leo and saw him smile back at her.

He was her future... perhaps tonight she might tell him so. Her smile warmed and deepened, reflecting not just love, but the beginnings of tranquillity and acceptance as well.

Relive the romance...
Harlequin is proud to bring you

A new collection of three complete novels every
month. By the most requested authors, featuring
the most requested themes.

Be sure to look for the next BY REQUEST volume
available in August.

How can you create a future if you've
forgotten the past?

Three people who are strangers even to
themselves are determined to create a future,
haunted by echoes of the past.
A future with love in view.

Three complete novels in one special collection:

HOME AT LAST by Barbara Kaye
UNTIL SPRING by Pamela Browning
BEYOND THE DREAM by Nancy Martin

Available in August wherever Harlequin and
Silhouette books are sold.   HRE01R